Praise for Running on Broken Bones

"A page turner if I ever have read one!" – M.T., Goodreads

***

"For enthusiasts of the suspense and action genres looking for a story that excels in both pacing and depth, *Running on Broken Bones* is a compelling selection. This second book in Pepper's celebrated series not only meets but surpasses the high expectations set by its predecessor, firmly establishing itself as a notable work in its field. Whether you are a seasoned reader of thrillers or new to the genre, this book promises an adventure that will keep you hooked until the last word."
– Literary Titan (5-Star Review, Gold Medal Winner)

***

"I'm not looking for a slow fix. I needed something, if not permanent, then drastic. Like the ice pick lobotomy, but hopefully with better side effects." Thriller audiences shouldn't be looking for a slow fix to Tanto's problems either, and will find the simmering cauldron of adversity and challenge comes packed with unexpected twists and turns that keep the protagonist and his readers on their toes." – Diane Donovan, Senior Reviewer, Midwest Book Review

Running on Broken Bones

A Tanto Thriller

W. A. Pepper

HUSTLE VALLEY PRESS

Hustle Valley Press, LLC

Print and eBook cover design by Damonza

Formatted by W.A. Pepper.

Published by Taddy Pepper (Publisher) at Hustle Valley Press, LLC.

Author photo by Hadonica Murphy.

Danger's photo permission provided by his people.

ISBN 978-1-958011-05-8 (Ebook)

ISBN 978-1-958011-06-5 (Paperback)

ISBN 978-1-958011-07-2 (Hardcover)

Previously in the Tanto Thriller Series

Author's Note: Thank you for reading this book! This is the second full-length novel in the Tanto Thriller series. Before this one came the novella DoGoodR and then the full-length novel You Will Know Vengeance (YWKV). In order to fully understand this adventure, it will be beneficial to start with DoGoodr, then read YWKV. However, for those of you who have already read those two, the next page starts a brief summary of some (though not all) of the important events that occurred previously. Again, if you haven't read those other books, it is best to start your reading with DoGoodR, then YWKV, and then come back to Running on Broken Bones to get the full Tanto experience. Happy Reading! W.A.

***

A Brief Summary for *DoGoodR* (Warning: Contains Spoilers)

(If you haven't read *DoGoodR* yet, you can download the ebook for free at http://tanto-dogoodr.wapepperwrites.com.)

When the US Government throws the book at a teenager, codenamed DoGoodR, for hacking NASA, Bushido Code-following hacker Tanto risks everything to keep the kid from getting life imprisonment.

A woman, claiming to be the sister of the imprisoned teen, hires Tanto, along with the firecracker hacker Mane-Eac. Their mission: to hold hostage the US Attorney General's servers. And, while they barely succeed in besting the *sister*, the undercover Agent Michelle and her team from the unstoppable Mercator Agency, this good deed puts a target on their backs the size of Texas.

A Brief Summary for *YWKV* (Warning: Contains Spoilers)

Eight years have passed since the Mercator Agency threw Tanto in a clandestine prison known as Hackers' Haven. He and all the other hackvicts (hacking convicts) are forced to capture others online under the guise of national security. Besides this, the warden forced Tanto to design Gakunodo, an AI-level software that captures unsuspecting people on the web. Even though the government has stripped away his human rights, Tanto makes a family in his prison with Samoan AldenSong, Cajun PoBones, and his aging mentor, Lance-A-Little. He even takes a new prisoner, Quidlee, under his wing, and tries to keep the kid from going crazy. However, when sadistic Warden Cyfib brings in Barca, Tanto's old nemesis, everything goes to hell. Somehow Barca avoids all punishment and operates above the rules...even when he kills Quidlee. In order to appease this monster, Tanto must either kill him, or help the two of them escape. Only after the duo breaks out does Tanto allow a third-party their much-earned vengeance on Barca. Now, free from his prison for the first time in almost a decade, Tanto finds himself on the run as things go from bad to worse.

Professionally: This book is dedicated to Beau Willimon and Vince Gilligan. Their abilities to create anti-heroic worlds and characters have helped me create my own. Thank you for letting me stand on your shoulders.

Personally: To our fans that were patient when this book got delayed due to personal tragedy. Thank you for standing by us.

Disclaimer and Trigger Warning

Some advance readers were concerned about certain elements in this book, while others were not. To handle any potential concerns, this trigger warning is here to point out that certain elements exist, but not to assess (or guarantee) the impact they will have on the individual reader.

While this thriller is a work of fiction, it contains many of the dark things that, unfortunately, exist in our world: physical, emotional, and mental violence, discrimination, sexual assault, suicide, intolerance, drug abuse, and neglect. Further, the sentence above is not an all-inclusive list of the potential triggers in this book.

This book is not a call to action to hurt people, pets, or even yourself, whether that hurt is physical, mental, emotional, or spiritual.

This book is about overcoming those horrible obstacles, about diligence and resilience in your life, and about how evil will never triumph over good.

Finally, please don't cause yourself or anyone else harm. Love people and love yourself.

Taddy and W. A. Pepper

For assistance, there is a glossary containing technical terms used in this book at the end for your convenience.

Table of Contents

Pages were numbered according to the Paperback Print Edition of this book and may vary from various e-readers and formats.

Chapter One

Brisk Dip in the Pool

SOON

While most Americans spend their Sunday mornings watching sports or listening to robed men tell magic resurrection stories, I schedule my day around an eighty-five-year-old prostitute who ensures I don't swallow my tongue. Sure, anyone can do this, but I am loyal to a fault. Plus, this bag of bones won't ask questions unless you pay her to, like I do.

At noon I check into the kind of hourly motel known for serving adultery with a side of bedbugs. "Rusty" knocks at 12:30. I swing open the door and am greeted with that yellow yet dependable Jack-o-Lantern grin. She travels in a cloud of nicotine, ticking me off and burning my sensitive nostrils. Alas, I'm too polite to even write "please stop smoking menthols before my session, lady," so I tolerate her Pig Pen impersonation.

She greets me the way all in her profession welcome clients: with an open hand. I insert two bills featuring a man smart enough to avoid the presidency. She shoves them portrait-first into her lacy and ragged bra. Ole Benny Franklin probably would've loved motorboating Rusty.

My pants drop to the floor. I slip on a man's diaper. Its smooth, lacy feel comforts my junk and inner thigh. This brand can also take the damage. Truthfully, I have browned my pants during "therapy" with Rusty before.

Diapers cost less than thrift shop jeans.

I stretch out on top of a paramedic's backboard on the bed. Rusty knows the routine: strap my head, chest, right arm, left arm, waist, right leg, and left leg firmly to the board, and then shove a pillow under my ass and one between my legs.

She whips out my laptop and more safety tools from my red-leather suitcase. From my position on the board, I am too nervous to complain when Rusty sanitizes the Shock Doctor Adult Pro Strapless Mouthguard, known for handling internal impact absorption, by breathing on it and then rubbing it on her torn jeggings before shoving it in my mouth.

Great. If therapy doesn't kill me, gingivitis will.

As I stare at the watermark in the stucco ceiling that looks like a whale, I hear the laptop chime. Rusty is now running the Interrogator: a USB connectable lie detector. She straps a sensor just under my hard nipples, then on my lower abdomen, and finally puts finger sleeves on my left hand's ring and index fingers to record the chaos.

Rusty knows not to ask questions until I signal her. The meds have left my system, so it's time.

I nod.

Rusty asks, "Are we in a motel room?"

At first, my mind hears the sentence almost like I've caught half a conversation from a TV in another room. I breathe deep and open my mouth. Nothing comes. Any answer would have sufficed. Any sound or grunt would have marked a vast improvement over the last test. Then it comes. The mouth guard rumbles as my body shakes like an earthquake. Tears roll out of my eyes and the front of the diaper shifts from white to yellow as I convulse through the small seizure.

She squeezes my hand once, lets go, and asks again.

"Are we in a motel room?"

This time, the seizures pop like short bass beats. The mouth guard flies across the room as if Mike Tyson has just punched it from my face. Good ole Rusty snatches it up and shoves it back in, past my chattering teeth, saving my tongue.

Not like I need it.

Even through the pain, I hear the rumble of my body against the paramedic board. An internal current pumps through my body for a full minute until only slight tremors remain.

Rusty wipes my brow and says, "All right, sweetie, lighten up. I can't have my favorite non-penetrator dying on me. Just rest."

Rest. I crack a smile—just a twitch short of madness. I don't remember a time in my life when *rest* was a viable option.

After ten minutes, we try again. Again, we fail. No, I fail. As I *rest*, I hear the madman, my former warden, Cyfib's internal voice plaguing my consciousness. He tells me I am a *dog*, and *old dogs get put down.* Even though he is not here, he is the voice of my continued failures.

And, of course, I see the other monster in the shadows, glaring at me in my peripheral. He's not only a giant but also my biggest sin.

What the hell did Cyfib do to me in Hackers' Haven to cause this?

How do I fix myself when I can't even communicate?

And how do I stop him from doing this to anyone ever again?

Who'd have thought that the hellacious torture I experienced until a few months ago would've seemed like a brisk dip in the pool?

Chapter Two

Even More Dangerous

NOW

Stupid, stupid, stupid, I think. *In a city where no one knows I'm alive, how did I get a tail?*

When someone is following you, the last thing you attempt is the movie montage run: a fast-paced sprint across a city. You know those movies, the ones where the hero and the villain dart down crowded streets, through impromptu pop-up markets with food vendors and, for some reason, loose chickens. It always culminates in a race on rooftops as the hero jumps from ledge to ledge.

In real life, when you get a tail, you get into a crowd and stand perfectly still. You let the crowd flow around you. Chances are your stalker will either bolt or pretend to do something. Standing still gives you time to think. It disrupts your predator's plan. It gives you a forced clarity because you discover your options. In Bushido, using a calming technique to gain awareness of your situation is called the Zanshin, or remaining mind. Once you do this, the odds are that you will find an opening, either to charge the person and cause a scene, or duck into a hiding spot when they aren't looking.

Unfortunately, it is broad freaking daylight on a Tuesday in 2011 in Memphis, Tennessee. There is no crowd. The main hiding spot I can see from my steady-paced walk is an alley which, as I shuffle past it, is a dead end. The only other person on the street is the elderly white lady that I just spoke with and, unless she secretly knows Kung Fu, she's less of an ally than a liability. Maybe she has a Glock in her purse. This is the South, so there is a fifty-fifty chance granny is packing heat. Even lifting her purse to check is not worth the risk because I might wind up getting her killed in the process, and I've already maxed my death tab out.

Damnation. I thought I was doing so well hiding.

Of course, I couldn't run away if I wanted to. My damaged knee and ankle from the prison escape only allow me a pace slightly faster than a three-toed sloth. I am nowhere near healed. That's why, for the past four weeks, I've bounced around the country via buses. You know what they say, heal when you can, but never stop moving your ass.

I'm sure someone says that.

My first instinct after escaping from Hackers' Haven was to get here to Memphis, Tennessee, and protect Penny like I swore to her dead brother I would.

Poor Quidlee. He's on my death tab.

However, I now have a tail. I'm running semi-blind. In my right hand is a shiny, silver coffee mug. I don't have it with me to drink hot bean soup. The reflection shows that my stalker is twenty feet behind me. His pace matches mine. He's not trying to overtake me.

Not yet, at least.

In my left hand is a landline phone number for Penny Lee, Quidlee's sister. I found her address in a phone book, of all places. Of course, I used a three-dollar gas station map to find the actual location because I didn't want to search the Web. Little motions draw major attention. Once I got to Penny's row house, the pile of letters in her mailbox and the dead and dying flowers in her yard showed me she has not been here in quite some time.

Too late. Again.

I squint at the reflection as I keep moving. I cannot make out his face, but it looks as if my new *friend* is wearing goggles. Not the kind you go swimming in. The kind you expect to see someone wearing during Steampunk cosplay: a mirrored covering from eyebrows to nose.

A car horn blares as I get nicked by the bumper of a car.

"Watch where you're going, asshole!"

I nod and step back on the curb. As I do, the black hoodie disappears from the reflection on my mug. I turn around.

Where the hell is he?

My gut tells me now is the time to dart into a store, any store, and sneak out the employees' entrance or fire exit. Then the part of my brain that often gets me in trouble calls dibs on my next bad move.

As I tiptoe over to the dead-end alley, my already-pounding heart feels like a base beat in my chest. I have no weapon nor martial arts training. All I have is a metal mug that my sweaty hand is about to drop, a backpack full of computer hardware, and maybe the element of surprise. That, and two dollars will get me a hot cup of coffee, which would be more of a formidable weapon than my current arsenal.

My throat goes dry as I pin my back against the brick wall. My house-party-level heartbeat in my ears isn't helping me listen for my tail. With the alley to my left, I hold my breath and dive into it, screaming.

Except for an overflowing dumpster and a few startled rats, the alley is empty.

He could be in the dumpster.

Without thinking, I kick the metal receptacle and immediately regret my decision as a million little stabs overpower the pain receptors in my ankle. Because of course, I kicked with the leg that had been impaled with a nail during my escape from Hackers' Haven. *Genius.* The resulting battle cry is a cross between a huff and a child seeing a mouse.

At the top of the dumpster pile is a broken broomstick. Grabbing it, I stab into the bags and debris.

No one screams out.

It is then that I spot the slightly ajar manhole cover.

This Goggleman has literally gone underground.

What really stinks is that this confirms I am not paranoid. All I've done is let my stalker know I am onto him. And now that he knows that, he is even more dangerous.

Chapter Three

This Isn't Mine

Even though I am fairly certain that the Goggleman is long gone, I dart in and out of several stores. The hardest part about hiding is staying hidden. The moment I let my guard down, he'll probably pounce.

If that is his intention.

I dart into a greeting card store and, ignoring the teenage clerk asking me if I need any help, find myself in the Sympathy Card section. The bell above the door rings but it's only a small African-American man in a brown pork pie hat leaving the store. No one enters.

For cover, I pick up a handful of random cards. I don't read the words as I occasionally flip through them and use my peripheral vision to watch for anyone entering the store.

For two minutes, no one does.

A cool sense of calm covers my shoulders. After I let out a breath I didn't realize I was holding, my vision focuses on the words of the latest card.

Sorrow is not a season you get through. It is part of the waves that surround you as you swim. Some waves are gentle and even relaxing.

Others will topple you and drag you under if you are not ready. Just know that all waves level out at some point. Keep swimming.

I cannot tell you how long I read and reread those words on the periwinkle blue card with frilly lace. *How can you get through sorrow when so much of it is your own damned fault?* By the time I notice drops of blood from my nose had dripped on the card, spots flash before my eyes. I consciously swallow the pool-ball-sized lump in my throat.

You can grieve about what you've done when you are dead, I lie to myself, then wipe blood from my nose on the sleeve of my brown jacket. *Think about this later, Tanto.* There is no telling how many pieces I will shatter into if I let down my shield or even allow myself a slight peep behind my psyche's curtain.

I shove the card back into a random spot in the shelving. Then card next to it featuring a wooden door with a brass knocker on it and the words *Opportunity Knocks* reminds me of what I am doing here.

***

Twenty-three minutes ago, I must've walked up to the red door with a brass knocker four times and held my hand over it. I never had the courage to knock.

"Can I help you?" came a female voice from behind me. My lack of planning meant that Penny's first impression of me would be my stress-induced bald spot. However, when I turned around, I realized that unless Penny had repeatedly bathed in Wite-Out while smoking two packs of cigarettes a day, this elderly, paper-skinned white lady in front of me wasn't Penny.

"Uh, uh, uh, um, sorry ma'am," The words crawled out of me at an idiotic pace, probably because I'm expecting Penny to reject me and my mission from the moment we meet. "I was trying to locate P-P-Penny."

"Me too." Her hands immediately went to her hips, signaling that this conversation wasn't going to get better. "She borrowed my cast-iron skillet last week and still hasn't returned it."

"When was the last time you saw her?" I asked, my blood turning to molasses.

"Three, maybe five days ago."

There was a chance that Penny was fine. There was also a chance that the gang that Quidlee screwed over, the Memphibians, shifted from roughing Penny up to finishing the job. And, of course, there was a chance that the warden Cyfib somehow figured out I was still alive and retaliated with finality.

Still, I had to keep moving forward to get any information I could because she needed protection. If she didn't, then I had no hope of salvation.

I pulled out her photo from my wallet, the one I stole from Quidlee the day I met him, and asked, "Does she still look like this?"

The lady adjusted her glasses and nodded. "Hair's a little longer and she's put on a little weight. Having kids will do that, but yes, that is her...why do you ask?"

I wanted to tell her I was a friend of Penny's brother. Or ask if anyone else had asked about Penny. That might endanger this lady's life even more than what I was doing right now.

I opened my mouth to offer something noncommittal, but nothing came out.

"She's a criminal," the woman babbled on, not seeming to notice my lack of response, "that's what she is. Always hacking into my WiFi, even though my grandson put a passcode on it."

Quidlee once told me he hacked an ATM just to switch out the money with Monopoly money. If Penny was half as mischievous and arrogant as Quid, I might find her on the Dark Web.

"Thank you for your time, m-m-ma'am, and-"

Before I said anything else, my body shook and I accidentally lunged forward, my hands instinctively moving to catch myself. And catch myself, I did: right on top of the lady's breasts.

With a slap away with one hand and a purse smack to my face with another, the lady yelled, shot around me, and ran down the street yelling help. I hightailed it out of there before police arrived.

***

Now, minutes later and back in reality at the card store, I remember why I'd lunged forward: when I turned around, I'd spotted my stalker, the Goggleman. He turned at the end of the street after shooting past me. It wasn't until I was able to assess the situation and watch the Goggleman that I'd realized he was, indeed, following me.

But why did he bump into me? If he wanted to hurt me, he had every opportunity...

It is at this point that my hands drop into my jacket pockets. There, in my right one, is a folded white piece of paper.

This isn't mine.

Chapter Four

Never Easy

Before opening the note, I survey the card store. Except for the guy working the counter whose Elvis pompadour haircut and joyful eyes make him a dead-ringer for Jon Cryer's Duckie from *Pretty in Pink,* the store is empty. I'm not concerned with him seeing me: he keeps smiling at the ground, clearly doing something on his phone from behind the counter. I lean close to the card rack and open the piece of paper.

On the outside of the paper is some sticky gunk. I use the bloodied sympathy card to scrape it off. Inside, there is a vertical list of numbers. I've dealt with enough encryption situations to know that what I am looking at is more than a series of numbered pairs: it is a code.

The problem is, I have a code, but not the cypher.

To even start, I need a computer.

Against the far wall, I spot a computer below a printed-out banner that reads *Design Your Own Greeting Cards Here.* I scoot over to it, press the *Enter* key, and watch the blank screen light up to show *Greeting Card Maker 7.8.*

I hit some quick keys to exit the program, but they are locked. It looks like I'll have to access this through the BIOS.

I turn my head to the lone employee and clear my throat. He never looks up.

"Um, th-th-the screen is f-f-frozen," I ask with a stutter.

A stutter? That's new.

"Huh?" the pimply-faced kid rolls up his head from staring at his crotch.

"Should I r-r-reboot?"

Those words hit his brain on a five-second delay. "Oh, yeah, right on." And he turns back to his phone.

Perfect. A soft reboot and a few magic moves on my end and, boom, I should have access to the Internet.

Emphasis on *should.* Apparently, I need a dial-up connection to access the Web, and there's not a phone line in sight.

It is never easy.

Darting out of the store, Goggleman is nowhere to be seen. I do, however, spot a coffee shop.

That's my ticket, I think, as a passive numbness runs from my fingers to my shoulders.

Chapter Five

Poking the Rest of My Brain

The store window has a rough outline of poorly scraped-away words I trace my fingers on: Internet Cafe. This warms my soul. Internet cafes were big in the '90s and 2000s. Then they went the way of the dodo when everyone got their own laptops and smartphones. However, there's a slim chance they still have a public desktop computer.

This is a waste of time, says a little voice in my head. *I should get back to saving Penny.*

The store's bell dings when I open it. I see several teens manspread in leather chairs, sipping lattes and playing on their smartphones. After one does something, the others laugh. I guess they're thumb people doing that new fad called *texting*. I don't see how that's fun.

Then again, my Tamagotchi also starved to death.

College students on laptops fill the four tables. Most look normal, but the guy with the Unibomber beard and whose laptop is covered in tinfoil catches my eye. Well, mostly tinfoil. There's a sticker on it that reads "A Taste of DejuVu" on it that does a shitty job of covering up the paranoia.

At least I'm not the weirdest guy here.

Then, I see it: a corner desk with a boxy monitor, a relic from easier, less software-tracking days.

I point to the barista in the yellow apron and then to the computer. She tells me to knock myself out.if I can get it working.

Six minutes later, I'm online.

Before accessing the Web, I backdoor into the computer's privacy settings. The old Gateway is secure as far as publicly available computing goes. Of course, there is no Virtual Private Network integration built on it, but the system's tracking is low because it is a nearly obsolete clunker.

Desperate hackers can't be choosers.

After opening the Web Browser in Private Mode and then going to DuckDuckGo, my favorite non-tracking search engine, I type in those mystery numbers.

Nothing.

Ain't nothing good easy, I guess.

As I run the number through several online code crackers, the keyboard beneath my fingers feels equally right and foreign to me. I haven't clickety-clacked in nineteen, maybe twenty days.

The last time I went online was to transfer funds that I had hidden away so deep on the Web I'd buried them next to Jimmy Hoffa. KronosPay, a Russian-led cryptocurrency, started a digital revolution. Correction: cryptos came from black hat hackers who would hijack the company's accounts and, for payment, they would convert the ransom money into crypto. I'm sure crypto will become legit at one point. Hell, while they incarcerated me, Steve Jobs and Apple turned music piracy into a legit enterprise. They call it iTunes.

KronosPay is like Paypal, in that you can accept and transfer money over the Internet for a fee. It has no features except for deposit and withdrawal. I'm not sure who runs Paypal, but there are probably fewer warrants out on their employees. Not to mention KronosPay's technical support component probably comes in the form of a glob of C4 affixed to your automobile.

Generally, KronosPay takes 50 percent, like any good charity. In exchange, they filter money to hackers and other fine criminals in cash mailed to the various extorted businesses, expanding their enterprise into their very own criminal version of FedEx. ConEx, if you will.

Before I went off to camp, aka Hackers' Haven, I'd developed my own way of laundering money through cryptocurrency. If I looked hard enough, I could find where I stored the software in The Deeps. Until such time, though, as much as I hate working with these bastards, even Bushi worked with criminals to reach a greater goal. And that's where I got the ten thousand dollars I needed to survive on the run.

I almost don't want to touch it. Having lived most of the last decade running on captures or *kills* as currency, the whole idea of it turns my stomach.

"Princess..."

A shudder passes through my body at the sound. I look around, but no one is near me. I shake it off and continue my fruitless efforts.

After twenty wasted minutes, I give up. Whatever these numbers mean will have to wait because I have bigger fish to fry right now.

Yet, something in the back of my mind refuses to stop poking this bear.

Who is after me?

Chapter Six

Like Me

When you are *on the run*, the best way to stay hidden is to stay off the Internet. There is not a second-best way. All use of the World Superhighway exposes you to cookies, viruses, and, most importantly, tracking. Tracking of preferences, keystrokes, and definitely location.

With that in mind, I skim the perimeter of information that I need on the Goggleman, using the peripherals to search for any clues. It takes longer but tracks less. I search for Hackers' Haven by checking newspapers, online blogs, and other items out of Houston, Texas for disruptions, such as car accidents, like the one I used to fake my death. Yes, there is a chance that someone in the Double-H, specifically warden Cyfib, has an algorithm gathering information on anyone who searches these terms.

Let's hope I'm stealthy enough to stay under their radar.

From several sources, I find my "death" online: *Unidentified body found in burning automobile.* The police report ruled it a *carjacking gone wrong* and implied that the thief, that is the corpse that looked enough like me to pass when burned to a crisp, died in the accident.

After several careful searches, I find nothing on "escaped convict" in the Houston area.

Someone covered this up, like the way you throw a rug over a stain on a wood floor and never mention it again.

In my right ear comes the sound of Barca's body catching bullet after bullet.

Pock.

Pock.

Pock.

The blasts of Mr. Longfellow's .22 pistol putting holes into Barca's body should have satisfied my desire for vengeance against that monster.

Instead the shots are now part of the soundtrack to my life. Like the song *Tequila,* this soundtrack only has a one-word sound that goes along with it.

Agency.

Barca's last plea for mercy was his excuse for destroying so many lives.

Agency.

But which Agency?

I type something but stop mid-sentence and delete the words. Whichever *Agency* Barca was with is bound to know he is missing from Hackers' Haven, even if there is nothing about it in the news.

I can't risk looking Barca up now. That's a mistake for another time. As I reach into my pocket and pull out the number I have for Penny, I spot a landline phone next to the computer.

I can't say how, but an idea hits me: I should check the Woot website that my recently paroled mentor Lance-a-Little set up for me. I still remember the forum, so I go there.

There's a new link listed under the *Everything But Woot* section. I see the numbers from the note in the corner of the subforums.

Was it Lance that approached me? Surely not. The guy was taller and built like a truck. Lance is that lean muscle that swimmers have.

A spasm hits my hand.

Just nerves. I click on the link.

Six, no, ten different screens flicker before a web portal opens. I'm no dummy; it's a trace.

Disconnect. Get out of here.

I hold the power button to the old Gateway as a squawk blasts from the dusty internal sound card. The noise reminds me of the Hackers' Haven alarm that would hit us hackvicts so hard that some of us would throw up.

The computer stays on.

Shit.

"That sucks, man."

I smell Barca's stench, stale Corn Nuts and rotting flesh. Before I know it, I've pinned myself against the wall, looking for the beast. I look left just as his hovering stature covers me like an eclipse.

But Barca is not there.

What the hell is going on?

As I panic and turn back to the machine, I notice that the icon in the bottom right of the monitor that says I'm online shifts from *connected* to *disconnected.*

I sit back down and, before I can rejoice that the computer is offline or check to see if I've actually shit myself, a hand wraps around the monitor's corners. My shoulder sends lightning up my spine. I jump back, for an instant, and I bump into a giant behind me. Heat and hatred cover my shoulders. I turn my head upward and spot Barca's maniacal grin and dead eyes as they tower over me.

"What's so funny?"

Barca jerks his face toward me, daring me to flinch. It works, because I fall to the floor. I scurry around looking everywhere, ceiling and floor included, for the monster.

He's-not-here-he's-not-here-he's-not-here.

Then an arm with long gray hair hovers in front of my face. I scream before it clamps over my mouth.

"Dude, shut the hell up. I just saved your life, man." The voice isn't Barca's. It's the guy with the handlebar mustache with the government conspiracy tinfoiled laptop. "You're gonna get caught if you keep doing dumb shit."

I shake the nastiness from my head and try to focus.

Barca's not here. He's dead. What the hell is happening to me?

My heartbeat goes from rapid fire to single burst. The sun reflecting off a passing car hits my eyes, and a migraine stabs them shut.

"No, man, don't let them get to you." Mustache Man pops something under my nose. My blood sugar plummets, and I close my eyes. Then a red-hot poker hits my brain. Smelling salts: man's way of bringing the dead back to life.

I scream, and he drags me by the hand to the back of the store.

"Sorry, everyone, my son's not feeling well."

He shoves me into a bathroom the size of a La-Z-Boy recliner and shuts the door behind us.

"Who the h-h-hell are you?" I ask.

"No, no questions."

I try to scoot past, but the man about forty years my senior shoves me back like I am a fluffy pillow.

"Spread your arms."

"Oh, f-f-f-for c-c-crying out loud."

"Do it."

I've done this scanning for bugs on potential clients too many times. I know that I'm clean. However, when Mustache Man gets to my leg where I used to have my Hackers' Haven disciplinary chip, he stops.

Even though the device doesn't beep. Before I can stop him, he yanks up my pants' leg and touches where my chip was before I electrocuted myself and cut it out.

"So, you're a true-to-life escapee, huh?"

I yank down my leg and realize that this isn't some nutjob.

He's a hacker like me.

W. A. Pepper

Chapter Seven

They Got You

Time stands still as neither of us speak. Of course, he's an old-school hippie hacker. That's why he looked at the door and back entrance when the bell rang. Only a true criminal or ex-military checks all the exits when a new variable enters the equation. Then there's the way he set up his laptop. If memory serves me, it is in the corner with his back to the wall. Not plugged into an outlet, so he can just grab it and bolt.

The tinfoil is a little much, though.

As his flash drive earrings dance about, he waits for me to speak.

"I don't know who you think I am or w-w-what you think is happening, but I am leaving."

I grab the doorknob.

Mr. Mustache braces the door.

"Oh, you're exactly who I've been looking for."

A cold sweat covers me like I just stepped out into winter rain.

He's here to drag me back to Hackers' Haven. He could even be a sleeper agent with the Mercator Agency. This guy might even work with

Agent Michelle and her team, the ones who ruined my life during the DoGoodR case.

Before I do anything else, I remember the Bushido Code demands breathing and patience. My captor has my body trapped, not my mind.

There's a tattoo on the inside of my captor's arm: a character with a long nose peering over a wall. I know my history; he was one of the first hackers during World War II.

I take a chance and point at it.

"Kilroy, is it?"

Mr. Mustache covers it, then says, "Sure, Kilroy will work. Call me that. And what do I call you?"

"T. will work."

T? Seriously Tanto? Why not just give him your full name while you're at it?

"Okay, T." Kilroy studies me for a few seconds before patting me on the back. "Let's leave before someone thinks we're banging in here."

"I'm not going anywhere with you."

"Well, I'm going to get my laptop and get out of here because if you haven't set off a government tracking alarm, you came damn close. That's why I pulled the cables. You hit a VOIP gatekeeper, man." Even though I know about Voice Over Internet Protocol, because I've been in prison, not on the moon, I stare at him like he's speaking Klingon. *Something in my head is off, and it is killing me.*

"Damn, you don't know anything, do you?" I let Kilroy get his insult in as he tugs on his beard and sighs. "That *ta-tunk* sound it made is like a freaking Internet doorbell. Now, if you know the password, you might be okay. That's only if it's not a required voice. See, VOIPs are new yet tricky, dude. They can't quite key everything to a voice imprint yet, so it works more like a vocal keyboard than anything else."

What he says is correct. And yet, how much can I trust someone that is clearly two berries short of a fruitcake?

I'm just waiting for this dude to quote the band R.E.M. by calling me Kenneth and asking about the frequency.

As he reaches for the doorknob, it is my turn to stop him from opening.

"Hold up. How do you know about my l-l-leg implant?"

Kilroy leans against the bathroom wall and scratches his arms. It's not an addiction scratch like poor, dead Quidlee's. It's in one spot.

That has a scar.

"I know a lot, okay? I know about the missing hackers, the abductions, the torture..." He trails off, his blue eyes focusing on a memory I could probably relate to. "If I could ever get my hands on Prisoner Zero. No. Nevermind. There are things at play, man, things on the outside that are dangerous, like you wouldn't believe if I told you—."

"Hey!" A pounding on the door jerks our focus. "Y'all okay?"

"Uh, yeah, my son's okay. He just has mad diarrhea."

As the barista walks away, she mumbles, "Geez, okay, damn..."

I give Kilroy props. If you're going to make up an excuse to get someone away from a door, mad diarrhea *is golden.*

Kilroy scratches again. He is wearing multiple cloth bracelets. He catches me staring and yanks one off.

"I'm getting out of here." He hands me the bracelet. "There's a HAM radio frequency written on the inside of the bracelet. Contact me and...um...you okay?"

Then, like an old monitor, my brain flickers. I stumble; someone has replaced my knees with silly putty. I try to talk, but nothing comes out of my mouth. Kilroy stops and stares at me. I cannot blame him because I must look like I feel: a fish helplessly opening its mouth out of water, begging for life.

As his hands grab my arms and shake me, everything gets worse. Kilroy clearly is attempting to speak to me, but all I hear is a coffee grinder running in the background or static. Maybe both.

"T., you...paroled, didn't you?"

No, I wasn't paroled. I escaped. Did Hackers' Haven put some kind of failsafe in me? Some words fade in and out, while the others sound like they come from the bottom of a well.

Then the words stop, not on Kilroy's end, but mine. He speaks; all I hear is a playing record scratch.

Nails on a chalkboard tear me apart. Like a spike to the brain, it hits me: I cannot interpret words. Sure, that happens sometimes when I get a migraine, which often occurs when you spend fifteen hours a day glaring at a screen.

This is different. I get migraines that tear at my brain, but they never shut the world out. Now, somehow, the words disappear into the ether.

Even though the sound is gone, my blurry vision works enough that I can still read Kilroy's over-enunciating lips.

They. Got. You.

I open my mouth again. All that escapes is a puff of air.

My body screams *Get Out.*

I slam my shoulder into the bathroom door and run into the cafe. I am two steps into my sprint when I notice my knees buckling. A loud series of grunts tumble out of my throat.

Don't...pass...out...

As my hand grabs the front door's handle, a shock, much like the disciplinary ones in Hackers' Haven, shoots up my leg. I collapse on the ground.

Through tremors, I spot Kilroy grabbing his computer and dashing out the door.

As my body locks up, a warm, wet sensation covers my face. I am foaming at the mouth as uncontrollable shaking sets in.

Stuck. My body is shutting down and I am stuck.

As the fluorescent overhead lights flicker in and out of my vision, customers circle around me. One face leaning over me looks more familiar than I would ever care to admit.

"That sucks, man," says Barca as he loudly sucks on a lollipop. "I was just joking around."

He's not here, he can't be, but now I realize that I am in a waking coma, forced into a sort of conscious isolation, like a turtle stuck in his shell.

As everything fades from light to dark, Kilroy's words ring in my ear.

They got you...they got you...they got you.

Chapter Eight

The E.N.D.

The next part phases in and out like fuzzy memories the morning after a night of hard drinking: flashes. Medical personnel strapping me to a board with rough, locking strips. Jarring ambulance doors shutting to a loud screech. A siren filling my ears in whoops and whines. The smell of antiseptic and the pain of needles stabbing flesh. Snippets of conversations with words like "responsive only to pain stimuli," "noncommunicative," "blood pressure elevated," "probable seizure," and "suction ready."

Barca sits on my chest with a smile and the weight of an elephant. Lightning flashes through my body as a clamp grabs my heart and squeezes. More words fade in and out. *Crashing. Paddles. Clear. Steady.*

Air sneaks into my lungs and a word unlike the others sinks in.

Epilepsy.

Epilepsy. The lights in the cafe did not cause this vegetative state. The sound did. Only I can't communicate that.

Was it Kilroy? Or was it something on that website? Is this what Lance warned me about? Did the Double-H have some sort of fail-safe installed in me?

I wouldn't put it past the bastard Cyfib to hide some kind of cryptic seizure-causing subliminal code that shut down my body.

Hours, maybe days, pass. An invisible spike through my frontal lobe throbs. Every time I try to speak, my pulse skyrockets and I shake like a car going a hundred miles an hour on a gravel road. The beep of machines reminds me of the numbing drugs in my system. That and the tight restraints on my arms keep me from yanking the tube invading my windpipe.

I am a dead man with a heartbeat.

My vision and recollection of the events of hospitalization strobe like the lights of the ambulance that deposited me in the ER. Several times nurses ask me my name. Even if I could speak, I wouldn't tell them. My real name equals real jail time. The black ink on my hands means they fingerprinted me while I slept. That's not good. Most hospitals don't fingerprint people. Of course, without a set of fingerprints in the system, I am not identifiable.

For now.

As I try to speak, my throat feels like I just swallowed a handful of nails. My right arm is strapped to the hospital bed's immovable frame. On the arm is an identification tag with the name from the first fake ID. I guess they just grabbed what was at the top of the stack in my wallet. Any cursory check on that name should pass the basics: a birthplace and a social security number. The problem is the name associated with that Driver's License, "Vice, Eric," a kid who never drove a car. He ran away from home at sixteen and, like most runaways, disappeared. While the missing kid doesn't have a searchable obituary, if someone dug deep enough, they'd find out that I'm not him.

Being strapped to the bed means I can't write either. One nurse, the one with the extremely curly hair like the girl in that TV show *Blossom,* sneaks a white Bic pen in my hand and a notepad underneath it. I attempt to write a single word, but it comes out as an angry scribble.

The drugs they pump into me through the IV bag dry my mouth, yet tears roll down my cheeks. For all their attempts to communicate, nothing succeeds. Ultimately, they roll me, a very unfunny Mr. Bean, from an ICU room to feed, bathe, and walk me in a different wing of this hospital: the Epilepsy and Neurological Disorder wing.

As I stare at the stucco ceiling tiles, the same damn tiles that Quidlee and I crawled through when planning his escape from Hackers' Haven, I chuckle. Well, only on the inside.

I bet the nurses and doctors refer to this department under its acronym: The E.N.D.

Chapter Nine

Hope

When the staff in my new wing speak, it resembles something sub-human, as if I am watching a foreign movie spoken in a language as far away from English as Earth is from Pluto. Everyone in my eyeline moves their mouths like fish. I am sure they say words that are encouraging or inquisitive, but all I hear is everything else: footsteps, music (even with the lyrics), gurneys squeaking past, alarms from various timers and medical machines, and all that staticky jazz.

Yet every single time I try to read lips, if I focus on their subtle movements and run the list of possible words mouthed my way, my body seizes up. It always starts the same: my tongue clicks my teeth before it slams into the back of my throat. An invisible hook yanks my sternum skyward as my back attempts to snap. My toes curl. My fingers shoot out like a wizard casting a spell. Finally, some poor medical person jams a needle into my side, and the edges of my vision get fuzzy. The world turns gray just before the dark blanket of unconsciousness covers my head.

I don't know if it's day two or two hundred. From what I can tell, the doctors are letting anyone with a First Aid Merit Badge from the

Boy Scouts try to communicate with me because someone on the staff apparently thought that playing rap music with a strong bass beat and gyrating in front of me would provoke a response. I've endured physical, mental, and spiritual torture from the best in the business, but nothing could have prepared me for *The Thong Song*.

As if I had a say, the nurses took it further. They untied me and one attempted to snatch me up by my arms and get me on my feet during the song. I can't tell them I understand what they are trying to do and probably can physically *shake what my mama gave me*, but dancing is not my thing.

I recall the wisdom of Bushido Warrior Kato Kiyomasa: "A samurai who practices dancing should be ordered to commit hara-kiri."

As those two female nurses *clubbed* around me, clearly enjoying this up-tempo song more than I ever could, my mind flashes to a memory of someone who loves dancing.

AldenSong. *Shit.*

The thought takes my mind back to earlier, though not necessarily better, days.

Like the time PoBones bet AldenSong that our Hackers' Haven resident Samoan couldn't shove fifty Cheetos in his mouth. Not only did Aldy win that Snickers bar bet, he probably set the Guinness World Record for that...if convicts could compete.

Or the time he comforted Trub_E after the death of the dwarf's father. AldenSong just sat with him in a room as Trub_E cried. I think he sat there for ten hours. Never talking, just existing, where he was needed.

He is the only reason I am alive today.

Aldy is the one who got the gear together for my escape from Hackers' Haven.

He is the one who found the courier willing to transport a corpse and fake papers across state lines. Mr. Longfellow was the only man willing to risk everything for vengeance and assist in my successful *death*.

AldenSong is also the person who stopped me from ending my life when Quidlee died.

How did I repay him?

By abandoning him. If the meds I am on would allow me to shudder, just remembering this failure would make me shake like a tree in a hurricane.

My best friend and the kindest man I have ever known is getting tortured. Because of me.

Hours turn into days. I'm on day four, I think. I am just thankful that the hospital hasn't reported me to the authorities. I know my fake ID carries little-to-no history in the world's databases. Neither do my altered fingerprints. Sooner rather than later, someone will put two and two together and find they add up to "criminal."

Luckily for me, there is Dr. Line.

My eyes are shut when someone in a baseball cap with a smiling bird on it slides a piece of paper into my left hand. Instantly, I think, *are they going to try to get me to write again? Why?*

By the time I opened my eyes, my visitor is gone. Something is in my hand. At first glance, I think it is a blank piece of paper. Upon further inspection, there is a one-page document with the title *Newsletter* written across the top.

Headline – Patient Eric Vice Exhibits Signs of Limited Vocal Cognition

Memphis, TN – Three days ago at a small local coffee shop near Downtown, an unidentified man experienced a seizure and has been unresponsive to any level of communication yet maintains consciousness.

Local staff and physicians at WestGroup Med's Hospital have attempted various techniques, from normal conversations to written communication to speaking in rhymes to singing songs to attempts at startling Mr. Vice, all unsuccessfully. Drs. Oldman and Foldstein, Chiefs of Neurology and Otolaryngology, respectively, tasked Associate Dr. Line with sourcing unconventional means to communicate with Mr. Vice. Currently, Dr. Line is attempting to bypass first-person communications and present findings through the omnipresent communication tool known as media.

The press at WestGroup Med's Gazette welcome complaints, compliments, and letters from readers, as well as articles from around town. To have your article reviewed by the editor, please write on the back of this newsletter and return to any attending staff.

I wait for the shakes.

I brace for my tongue to try to touch my stomach via my throat.

My eyes clench for the self-created electroshock therapy.

But the seizures remain dormant. Tears well up in my eyes. So far, my brain has fled anything remotely like a conversation like a cat from water. And that's included first- or second-person writing.

For the first time in close to a week, I can attempt something new. Maybe I can communicate, or at least I can try to.

I see a light at the end of the tunnel, but remain wary that it might just be a train headed my way.

Go...slow...

Then I again think of AldenSong, and the words that saved my life.

Be still.

I can do this, but I must crawl before I can run. I glance at my other hand. Not only did someone sneak a pen into it, but whoever did that also untied my strap.

I lean up and my hands tremble as I flip over the *newsletter.* The backside is blank.

I don't know if taking a beat is the same as praying. Aldy is more of the religious type. I'm a man of science, or at least I think I am. Science is all about taking risks.

Hiding like a turtle in a shell is no way to live.

My even writing a word in this fashion could send me into cardiac arrest. Being brave and dumb do not have to be synonymous, so I figure it is best to follow my dance partner's lead and write my response as a story.

I bite my already dry tongue, bracing it, and write the words *Headline – Patient Scared.*

The shakes do not come.

I have hope.

Chapter Ten

Stain on a Leather Chair

Headline – Patient Scared

Memphis, TN – Patient Eric Vice successfully received communication from his medical team today. Mr. Vice, while unable to respond without fear of additional body trauma, could pass on a full account of this victory to our reporter. More to follow in the next issue.

PoBones, Hackers' Haven resident Cajun rascal, used to say that hope is like air: it costs nothing but without it you die. I think he stole this concept from *The Shawshank Redemption*, but who am I to judge?

I'm concerned that whatever is wrong with me is here to stay. It may even be unfixable, and there's nothing quick about a disease no one knows how to freaking fix. My father's muteness, his slip into silent madness, took years. I still remember the recliner in the living room, *The Captain's Chair* we called it, even though he never made it past the rank of Second Lieutenant. It was a dark leather chair, the color of wet dirt. Not mud, but the color that a light sprinkling of summer rain adds to the dry summer ground. It wasn't the type of leather you find in a jacket or purse. There was a smoothness to it I remember running my hand along or putting my sweaty head on when I returned from playing outside. The texture would cool my brow, but I would get in trouble for touching it.

I would love to say that the last time I saw the chair was when the garbage men hauled it off after dad blew his brains out while sitting in it, but nope. Instead, my mother just had it reupholstered on the cheap with some gaudy leopard print. Even after my father's suicide, I never sat in that chair. I'd sit on the floor. On days when the power company wasn't taking pity on us and turned off our power, something in the chair would swell in the summer heat. When the temperature reached eighty-five, I swear I could make out a dark stain in the shape of Idaho just where the top of the chair curved.

Oddly enough, on the night I found my mother OD'd, and I left that hellhole, she was sitting in that exact chair, a bottle of rotgut liquor in one hand and a spilled pill bottle in the other.

Back in the hospital, a pain like a bouncing, broken shard of glass in my head takes hold. Sure, the anti-convulsants are doing their job, but no drug is without its myriad of side effects. Plus, I haven't had a decent growler in days. My stomach protrudes like a drunkard's in a black-and-white comic strip.

The next day, I stop taking my phenytoin pills. My brain needs a reprieve. Maybe I can get my sense of what is going on. Around that time, a nurse smelling like a hint of Dove Soap under a plethora of Camel lights takes me to a room with the word *Library* on it. To be fair, you can consider any room with more than one book a library. That made this room with three computers, six recliners, two desks, and four bookcases the Library of Congress to some people.

After Miss Smokes-a-Lot rolls me in front of a TV with some talk show on and locks my wheelchair, she's already fishing out a pack of cigs from her front pocket. As my eyes roll her way, she extends the pack to me and says something, probably asking if I want one.

I hate smoking, but I'd puff away if it warmed up my vocal cords so I could speak. The nurse takes my staring as a *no* and disappears to spark one up.

The room reminds me of my junior high detention room, with its cracked ceiling tiles and cobwebbed corners. Except we didn't have a TV in the Dehaw, the slang word for Detention Hall. We had an old Compaq computer with dial-up Internet and a lazy math teacher running out the clock until retirement—Mr. Farrow, who we called Mr. Ferret because he was one jittery sucker. Looking back, it was probably a meth addiction. You don't drug test teachers in a poor county where no one wants to teach, because then you wouldn't have a single adult in the building.

It was also in Dehaw that I first hacked the school's excuse for a database. Mr. Ferret had finished taking roll and disappeared in short order, probably to snort or burn something into his lungs. There was something in the corner under a pile of books. I was the littlest guy in the room, but that crew of fellow hooligans, many of whom were twice my size, were some of the best teammates I'd had up to that point. With Fat Morty—a six-foot-nine, one-hundred-and-sixty-pound bean pole of a white guy—and Tiny Rick—a five-foot-nothing, two-hundred-pound black guy—watching the door, I hacked into the system and changed all of our grades. Once a semester, all ten of us would just so happen to get in trouble around the same time again. Lather. Rinse. Repeat.

I guess that prepared me for a life of working with others hacking, even though I prefer to work alone. That's my pride messing with me,

I guess. They said something about that in *Pulp Fiction*, but only Ving Rhames can say those words with gravitas.

Now I have no Fat Morty or Tiny Rick. Nobody is watching my back.

Outstanding.

However, someone just left me alone with computer access.

It was time to either fix something or crash. Anything else would be a stain on a leather chair.

Chapter Eleven

Dust

Hacking a computer is much like picking a lock: easier when you have the right tools and the right training. Unfortunately, my toolbox of password crackers and rootkit God-mode code collections are in a hidden partition on a folder in The Deeps that this abacus of a computer might crash trying to reach.

Okay, if I just reboot and force my way into the operating system folder, since there's a good chance that the operating system is lacking updates, no, wait...

The drug-induced fog that covers my brain in a thin film halts my thought process.

I'm over-thinking this.

That is a problem with using newer technology: it makes you believe that the older tech works the same way.

Then it hits me: *everyone like me who is a patient is on medicine a lot like mine, which makes us docile and apathetic, which means...*

I grab the computer's keyboard and flip it upside down. There, on the bottom of the plain gray surface, is my answer:

Administrative username:_*Library1*

Administrative password: *Library2*

This computer is more vulnerable to a break-in than a liquor store with the keys left in the front door.

I can customize it anyway I want.

Should I partition the hard drive and create a virtual HD to keep all of my work on?

If there is enough hard drive space, should I mount encryption that shreds all my work if someone discovers it?

If this computer is so vulnerable, what other viruses are on here, and who has access to the root?

I shake the bottleneck of overlapping thoughts from my head.

For someone who can't think straight, I'm over-thinking in crossing-patterns. First things first...

For the next few minutes, I scan medical databases for details about my disease. I do not bother with hiding my tracks beyond the basics of using Mozilla on Admin Mode for my browser, DuckDuckGo for non-tracking search, and clearing the computer's cookies and cache before the use and setting them to zero.

You know, rookie stuff.

After scouring close to fifteen different websites, I have no answers, but am less body-stressed but more mentally sore. I don't know what my disease is. Brain disease. Throat disease. Lung disease even. These giant and medically splintered sections of the body are home to dozens of different disciplines.

Of course, this does not rule out the likely culprit: Hackers' Haven.

What failsafe did they install in me?

Just that thought is mind-blowing. It's easier to think of my illness as a sport. In a sport, one team wins and another loses. I just have to figure out which sport I am playing.

As someone who knows virtually nothing about all things bouncy-bouncy, I'm pretty screwed here.

Bouncy-bouncy. The memory of Barca comes to mind when I think of a bouncing ball.

I may not understand God, but I do thank the Sky Daddy out there that the world is rid of that monster.

Time passes. My thoughts fade in and out. *Dammit.* The drugs, even though I stopped taking them, are still in my system. It will take days to flush them out.

At least I can communicate with the doctor now. Third-person dissociative disorder is what I'll call this disease. For now. I am sure there is a medical name, but that's for the fellas and fellettes in white coats to decide.

I wonder if that one newsletter interaction broke the dam in my brain.

It is possible. Many a breakthrough succeeds with a Eureka! moment, and from there, the patient is immediately better. There is a chance, though minuscule, that the newsletter idea reconnected the synapses in my brain.

There is only one way to know.

A nurse enters the room, sees me, and waves. His hand's movement is a more obligatory *hello* than *can I do anything for you type* wave.

Now's my chance.

I lean my head back. He smirks and strolls over. From this angle, I spot a booger the size of a piece of rice in his right nostril.

Okay, all I have to do is talk to him in third person. I'll say something about the booger. That's all.

I take a breath. My heart pounds faster, the fear of the body shock imminent.

"A man would like another to know there is something in his nose."

My mouth opens, but my tongue refuses to move.

A man would like another to know there is something in his nose.

"Ah-ah-ah--"

A man would like another to know there is something in his nose.

A tremor starts in my right arm. I snatch it and pin my arm down like Dr. Strangelove.

Slow down...Be still...

"Good to see you, too." While that came out of the nurse's mouth, his eyes say *boredom.*

"Ahhhhh..." creeps out, the first word uttered from my throat in about a month, at the speed of a sloth emerging from a half-day's sleep. Just as slowly, a ripple starts in my right big toe. I ignore it until it shoots up my ankle, zig-zagging around my calf, and jarring my knee like a doctor just whacked it with a tiny hammer. My mind says to stop, but my gut always gets the final vote. I continue my trip down this rickety train track.

"Ah-ah-ah!"

The nurse pats me on the back, then turns toward the door.

By the time he exits, a spasm erupts in my liver. It sends a grappling claw into my chest that pulls me to the floor. I shake like someone just plugged me into a wall socket. My top and bottom teeth go to war with each other, each row trying to smash the other.

I remember that there aren't any staff around.

No one can save you now.

As I lose control of my motor skills and bodily functions and prepare to find out what the afterlife is like while surrounded by outdated magazines and cobwebs, I snag a dusty TV Guide. Through convulsions, I shove it into my mouth and save myself from making a meal of my tongue. The next thing I know, four staff members appear out of thin air and jam a needle into my side.

As tears flow and alarms sound, I focus my rage.
Curse you, Cyfib, and whoever else did this to me.

Chapter Twelve

Fading to Black

After a day in the ICU, they wheel my back-to-square-one ass to my room and start again. Luckily, through newsletters in our fake publication, the docs help assemble a sliver of an idea of what type of barrel of monkey crap my brain morphed into. One nurse even commented that they should get me a laptop to make this easier. Her idea got poo-poo'd by her boss who said they didn't have an extra one lying around.

The problem with having a slight idea of how to help means that some people use a small solution in way too big of a quantity. Hence, the staff overwhelms me with newsletters. My brain, while receptive, moves at a snail's pace. Like a rusted gate's hinges that just got its first coat of WD-40, it will take lots of opening and closing for the squeaks to silence, or, in my case, respond.

For the next week, they pass on bits of information and, from what I glean, my brain's Mute button is more than a doozy of a disease and rarer than a leprechaun riding a unicorn on the White House lawn.

I call it the Mute button because, technically, they cannot name it. I mean, even Lou Gehrig's disease ultimately was named, well,

Lou Gehrig's disease, but mine is so fresh that it still has that just-out-of-the-dryer smell, apparently.

Further, because a spell of seizures brings the risk of brain damage, especially to the short-term memory, the docs assemble what Dr. Line called *The Gazette Summary*, an ever-growing newsletter that walks my muddled head through the daily problems. I think they did the same thing in a Drew Barrymore movie with the guy from Billy Madison, but maybe my memory is fuzzy.

Every morning, a member of the staff hands me the updated printout and I read a version of the following:

Memphis, TN – The reporter wants to point out that, despite popular opinion, epilepsy is not restricted to ocular or visual stimuli. In the last decade, research discovered a newer type of epilepsy called Autosomal Dominant Partial Epilepsy with Auditory Features, or ADPEAF. The possible culprit for this disease is a protein found in the lateral temporal lobe. This part of the brain is associated with processing sensory input and deriving meaning from visuals, language, sounds, and emotions.

Part of me wonders if such a protein is injectable. That would explain why Lance-a-Little told me to stay in Hackers' Haven because, once out, my missing Dr. Fel's weekly medical checkups no longer kept this protein in check in my body.

To understand where it is in a human body, if you were to compare your brain to a map of the United States, imagine that your eyes are the Pacific Ocean, and the back of your head is the Atlantic Ocean. The lateral temporal lobe would be the southern part of the United States.

So, the Bible Belt is giving me seizures. I require an exorcist, not a surgeon.

I continue my reading:

This newer, rare disease ADPEAF was first diagnosed in the 1990s, so there is a growing yet limited pool of information. Most patients reported having seizures or seizure-like eruptions before the age of ten, having a couple a year, and then they fade away in the mid-thirties or forties. They start like an ear migraine, coming from a buzzing or ringing, and build from there. There is a possibility the disease runs in families and the complexity of these seizures could run from partial (limited to certain areas of the brain) to tonic-clonic, leaving the brain and attacking the muscles and impairing consciousness.

I put the summary down and stare at the ceiling tiles. *What if it wasn't Hackers' Haven? Maybe this was my mother's genetics. Not only did she screw up her own life, but she fastened her demons to my back.*

I stop that train of thought. Hypothesizing will get me nowhere without more information.

Initial research points to this problem potentially originating from mutations in the leucine-rich, glioma inactivated one gene, but findings are premature. Since each family's case is unique, universal treatment is non-existent for this type of medical focus.

Some veterans, particularly of the Vietnam War, heard their deceased friends calling for medics or help and screaming, yet the parts of the brain associated with flashbacks did not illuminate. The voices wanted them to kill themselves and join them.

Some creatives and artists have reported this same problem over the years, and many have been mislabeled with schizophrenia, multiple personality disorder, or other diagnoses. The author Virginia Woolf wrote the voices went from subtle to a constant nagging, that she would never escape them until she took her own life. Poet and artist William Blake chatted daily with his long dead brother. Beach Boy Brian Wilson's head was filled with more than pet sounds, including human voices of doubt and hate.

Loss of normal sleeping and eating patterns might occur, as will an increase in depression and suicidal thoughts.

Blah, blah, blah.

No amount of buzz words could keep The Book of Me from getting bleaker. So far, the docs' Best-Case Scenarios involve more poking and prodding. The Worst-Case one ends with me giving myself a 9mm of lead poisoning. Sure, Dr. Line continues to point out that this might be a manageable situation and may not necessarily require surgery. He tries to boost my spirits by informing me that there is only a very slight chance that the disorder arose from cancer, because only around 4 percent of people who suffer from epilepsy have a brain tumor.

So, what is killing me is killing me differently.

Out-freaking-standing.

These jokers can't fix me; they just can’t say it. I can't trust anyone anymore. They're hammers, and everything—including me—is a nail. The brain is a computer. Sometimes my job is to fix computers. I p-own them. I can do this. Then I can have some sort of life outside of these sterile white walls.

Unfortunately, I'm not allowed to be on my own for even one shift. The neurologists have a field day with me. I now know what a puppy swarmed by sugar-filled children at a playground feels like. Today I was in the MRI fast-pass lane to get microwaved more than a hot pocket. When I'm not getting blood drawn or mind-zapped, they pelt me with questions on a screen for me to attempt to communicate.

Above me, written like our newsletter communications, a paragraph flashes above the viewing slot above my head.

Memphis, TN – This reporter states the following descriptions and tests his interviewee's reactions through an MRI machine to record a series of mixed reviews. Previous experiments were calculated through eye contact responsiveness, such as the subject blinking once to respond to an answer with a "no," and the subject blinking twice for "yes." Further reporting will continue next issue.

A void screen flashes before my eyes before the next line and every subsequent line pops up.

When people speak to an individual, the individual hears a motor like a dishwasher go off, like clicks and whirs, before getting louder.

No.

When people speak to an individual, the individual hears a noise like a small firecracker in the distance, getting louder until he/she loses consciousness.

No. This is getting nowhere.

When people speak to an individual, the individual hears bells ringing.

Again, no. What in the world do they want from me?

When people speak to an individual, the individual hears a muffled speaking and then suddenly cannot hear anything from the speaker. It is like changing altitude, having an individual's ears pop, and then nothing.

No, wait, yes. Yes, that's it.

I blink, but my second blink does not occur before the next slide appears.

Wait...

When people speak to an individual, the individual hears a roar of a helicopter.

No, dammit, go back to the last one.

When people speak to an individual, the individual hears a buzzing like bees.

Go back! Go back to the popping thing!

I shake and kick the sides of my tube.

Go back!

When people speak to an individual, the individual hears a popping and then feels a tremor.

Hold on. I stop my shaking and deliberately blink twice.

When people speak to an individual, the individual feels like he/she just finished swimming and there is water in his/her ears, muffling the sound.

Did they read my previous blinkage? Hello? Anyone! I try to speak, but nothing, not even a croak of air escaping, emerges from my throat.

When people speak to an individual, the individual hears a jingle or song from the radio.

Get me out of here!

I thrash my legs. A dinging error alarm sounds like an ajar car door. I keep kicking.

The lid pops open. A white male orderly the size of a truck leans down. I headbutt him and get up.

I need a doctor, not a wrestler. As I hit the floor, I not only hear the words from his throat but also understand them.

"You bwoke my noze..."

Then the word, "Sor-sor-" almost makes it past my lips before my upper body shakes like a gallon of ice water just hit my spine.

Fight...through...it...

I try again to speak out about which lines matter, but my body twists into a pretzel. I lock up.

The last thing I remember is someone jamming a needle into my butt and the world fading to black.

Chapter Thirteen

Right Some of the Time

The next morning's newsletter analysis on the MRI basically shows that when I read a false statement that is written from a third-person perspective, my brain remains in neutral, not lighting up the readout like a pinball machine when you achieve a Multi-Ball Power-Up. However, when I read accurate statements about my condition written in the same manner, the areas of the brain associated with auditory description decisions or tasks light up. That means I understand what happens to an individual and associate it with myself, but not directly. The filtering process somehow links short-term interactions with long-term memory and causes me to get the shaky-shakys.

A picture is in the center of our newsletter for the first time. It is of the MRI of two brains or, more specifically, my brain at two different times. The first image, the one on the left, shows a brain's shape with no highlighted areas. The second image is that of "an individual's brain" with some red flashes. In the actual article, Dr. Line divides the brain, my brain, into clock-like segments where, when certain statements draw a positive reaction or hit home and I want to respond to them, the two o'clock and the ten o'clock flash red.

Fan-freaking-tastic. My messed-up brain not only can tell the truth but also knows the proper places to hold a steering wheel.

Further details in the report include some of the worst words in medicine, like *chronic* and *incurable.*

My every instinct is to crumple up the newsletter. I go one step further and rip it lengthwise. Then I overlap the two pieces and tear again.

And again.

And again.

And again, until the stacked paper scraps won't rip in my hands. I ball them up as tight as I can and throw them at the wall, hoping they will explode into a million pieces upon impact. Instead, it merely hits with an unsatisfying fwap and drops to the floor.

Bullshit. It is all bullshit.

As I stare at the ball on the floor, I clasp my hands together and notice I cannot even feel my fingertips touch.

The disease may have moved to the part of my brain that allows for physical sensations.

I get out of bed and walk around barefoot. Even though I should feel a cold floor, my numb toes do not tingle. I could almost laugh. The lack of feeling reminds me of a non-Bushido movie that, apparently, I am now living: *Darkman.*

The horror movie stars Liam Neeson and Frances McDormand and was written by the horror-master-turned-Spider-Man-director Sam Raimi. In this film, Neeson's character, Peyton Westlake, is a scientist that gets burned alive in his lab by bad guys, including the always-the-villain Larry Drake. Luckily, or unluckily, depending on your viewpoint, a chemical that Westlake was developing or whatever causes him to feel no pain. Fortunately, Westlake also developed a synthetic skin that temporarily allows him to look normal. Now, as a hero that can handle any type of pain, he exacts his revenge on those that wronged him.

But he cannot feel anything for the rest of his life. Not the wind on his face, nor the touch of another's skin on his.

Nothing.

Was he dying? I am not sure, although one sequel is called *Die Darkman Die.*

Am I dying?

Of course, the drugs could cause my numbness, but in depths of despair, you really don't take time to think logically. Instead, I ponder my mortality while roaming the halls, hoping that an increase in circulation will give me some feeling.

The Bushido Code believes that only in death are we truly complete. However, The Code also believes it is dishonorable to leave any weapons in your arsenal and die before you've done all that you can.

If I am dying, or at least entering the final chapter of my relatively brief life, I will not go out without a fight.

Maybe I'm just paranoid.

Then again, even paranoid people are right sometimes.

As I follow this train of thought, I walk around the corner of the hall and run smack into the Goggleman.

Chapter Fourteen

They Know

There are many commandments in The Bushido Code about running away from battle. For example, take Asakura Norikage, a warrior who became a priest and still fought until almost the age of eighty. He believed that even accepting slander against you is cowardice, and thus should require a duel. Fleeing from battle demands that a warrior commit seppuku and that they give him no honor at his funeral. Even surrendering is cowardice.

There is a major difference between fleeing and regrouping. However, as the Goggleman's hands wrap around my shoulders, I'm not sure which option I'm set on once I break free.

Before, when he trailed me outside of Penny's apartment and snuck the coded note into my pocket, all I could make out were the goggles: gray oversized ones with mirrored lenses straight out of *Mad Max*. Now, from under the hood, I see his dark, unkempt hair that curls just under his filthy, mangy beard. His shoes are old generic tennis shoes with holes and rips along them. His black pants contain the same level of disheveledness. The smell of piss and sour, rancid sweat comes from his body.

He's talking to me, actually yelling, but all I hear is static. My brain and fear receptors are working overtime as the basic instincts of *fight* or *flight* now deal with a new variable: filter.

I see stars, not from my attacker's hands putting pressure on me. He's not strangling; he's shaking me. My slippers have no traction, so I slide them off and use my bare feet to feel around the cold tile. The roughness of brick hits where my heel meets my Achilles tendon.

I'm near a wall.

Using this chance, I jump up and kick off the wall, propelling the Goggleman backwards. The Goggleman releases his grip on me, trying to catch himself. He smacks into the floor, and I land on top of him.

Who is this guy?

I grab his goggles with both hands, but the Goggleman wraps his hands around mine and holds the goggles firm.

Why doesn't he show me who he is?

Two orderlies yank me off him. The Goggleman reaches into his pocket, grabs at my hands, yells something, and gets pulled away. I plummet to the floor and my brain rattles as my hands grip into tight little balls.

A shiver runs up my body; I know this shock is only beginning.

With all my strength, I roll my right arm up to my face and place my radius in-between my teeth right before my jaw locks. The pain of biting my flesh and drawing blood is nothing to losing my tongue if the biting gets worse. That taste of wet copper hits my mouth. A nurse, I think Nurse Johnson, pins me to the ground and tries to remove my bloody arm from my face.

The static in my ears shifts to a high-pitched ringing. My eyes pulse. Tears stream down my face. The salt burns my bleeding arm.

As other hospital staff hold me down, a jabbing pain enters my side.

Whether or not I like it, the tranquilizer will kick in soon.

As the world gets hazy and my jaw relaxes, I notice something in my hand. Something only my assailant, the Goggleman, could've put in there:

An empty pill bottle.

Only one group of people knows that this totally useless thing is my good luck charm. Something I always kept on me in prison, so I would remember where I came from and what I'd never return to.

The Goggleman is connected to Hackers' Haven.

The only thing scarier than this knowledge is the text written on the empty pill bottle:

They know you are here.

Chapter Fifteen

427-B

A day passes like a fart in the wind before I can string two thoughts together without my brain ripping them to shreds. No newsletters arrive and there are no pills for me to avoid taking. Now my medication is injected in my ass. My guess is that someone drew my blood, or at least used a syringe to soak up what I spilled on the floor during my seizure and took it to the lab. There, they found out I am not taking my meds. Maybe this is punishment. I notice I now have a new wristband on: Code Three: Non-communicative, 427-B.

Maybe this is punishment. Also, I don't think a newsletter apology on my end will either explain this situation I've caused or convey any type of appropriate apology.

Mostly because I am not sorry.

I am too focused on trying to figure out how someone from Hackers' Haven found me.

*How? Did someone here at the hospital upload something from my genetic code, from my blood, to a database to identify me?*_While a longshot, that might make sense; Dr. Fel's weekly "checkups" with the prisoners often included blood draws outside of the MRI's. My markers and DNA probably are on some server somewhere and, if there's a server with that on it, someone in the Double-H has access to it.

I have to get out of here.

However, it is at this moment, I remember something actually useful my mother once said.

She was taking a nap while we were supposed to be getting ready to have dinner. At the time, I assumed she'd just mixed alcohol and anti-depressants, but maybe she was really just tired. When she awoke an hour later, I told her we were late, and she needed to hurry. She told me that she wouldn't be in a hurry. When I asked her why she wasn't hurrying, she smiled.

"You can only be late once."

For me, I can only get caught leaving this hospital once. If someone knows I am here, they already know how to get to me. They have the upper hand. They can come get me as I walk the halls, as I sleep, whenever. Whether it is the Feds, Cyfib, or this mysterious Goggleman, anything I do quickly plays into their hands.

Maybe the Goggleman wants me to react rashly. That could be why he put the pill bottle in my hand. If I bolt out the hospital's front door, who's to say he's not there with a net just waiting to catch me?

I feel like the Roadrunner in those Wile E. Coyote cartoons about to enter a tunnel and there is the damn ACME anvil just waiting to drop on my head the second I emerge.

It will take a while to make my own tunnel.

Once back in my room, I open the top drawer in the end table to the right of my bed and pull out the newsletters. I scan them, then frustration grits my teeth and I toss them around the room.

Be still.

I take a moment, close my eyes, and breathe. A firm belief in the Bushido Code is that one should decide within seven breaths. A decision is one step. That decision may have a million steps to reach the ultimate goal: a successful escape.

As my eyes drop, I breathe deep. The sounds of the world drift away like a train whistle fading in the background. My mind relaxes. My shoulders loosen. I focus on the breath.

A different answer, or at least the possibility of one, awakens me from my trance so quickly that I cough and gasp, trying to breathe.

That number on my wrist, "427-B." I've not only seen it before; I've lived it.

Unless my brain is complete mush, which is likely, that is the code for a prisoner transfer order.

That means the authorities know I'm here.

Which means Feds.

Which means the Mercator Agency.

I have to escape now.

Chapter Sixteen

I Know Computers

My current shitty plan of action to get my medical files before I escape didn't actually originate from me. I have those dancing and singing nurses to thank for it. Who would've thought that I would also need to thank a patient with an aversion to wearing clothes?

I dart up from my bed and sprint barefoot into the hall, my gown flying open, showing all the staff my "tasties." That's what PoBones calls private parts. I do not know why he calls them that and, frankly, I cannot imagine any answer would be a pleasant one.

The column I lean against obscures me just enough from the view of the nurse working behind the desk that I want—no, *need*—to get to. The library's computer doesn't have access to a medical database. Sure, I could access some Wiki's or WebMD, but I need a deep dive, not a diagnosis for a cough. That means access on something only medical staff use.

I'm lucky it is the nurse with the straight golden hair that uses one of those teeth whitening mouth guards I keep seeing ads for. If I remember correctly, you use it for thirty minutes, then brush your teeth for three or four, and then use some special mouthwash as a chaser or something. Why this information is stuck in my head, yet I can't form a freaking sentence boggles my mind, but luckily someone's vanity will help me. Hopefully.

After a few minutes, a timer goes off on the nurse's watch. She stops it, gathers her purse, and heads to the bathroom.

Now's my chance.

I plop down, bare-assed, at the nurse's station. The monitor hasn't even had time to enter automatic lock mode.

Go.

There's no time to worry about tracking software. Besides, after a quick glance at the right corner of the screen, the only thing always running on this system is Solitaire for some reason.

"So, I told him, I told him, if he keeps living with his mama-"

Shit. I planned on one nurse, not the whole damn staff. I dart under the desk. It sounds like the nurse that reminds me of the mom in the TV show *Family Matters* chatting with the doctor that looks like the white version of that show's star, Steve Urkel.

"Nurse Johnson, I really need to get-"

"Hmm hmm...Oh, I told him, if he keeps having his mama as his landlord, he better be looking for another hot piece for his girl."

I push as far back as possible. The doc's bright white New Balance shoes protrude into my space. One peak under and I'm caught.

"Good for you, good for you, so I'm late for-"

"As TLC said, 'don't want no scrubs.' Shoot, the only scrubs I deal with are the ones I'm wearing. Ha! You feel me, Doc?"

"Yes, yes, consider yourself *felt,* no, wait, that came out wrong..."

If I get caught by someone whose catch phrase is *Did I do that?* I deserve to get put in a padded room and the key tossed away.

"Hey, Doc, ain't you late for rounds?"

The air let out from the doctor's sigh could fill the Goodyear Blimp.

"Yes...thank you for reminding me, Nurse Johnson. Good day."

"Hmm hmm...without me, you'd lose your head."

"I'm sure I would..."

As the shoes disappear down the hallway, I wrap my hands on the sides of the desk and pull myself to my feet.

With only a minute or two left, I have two options: consider this attempt burned, or find a way to stall. That's when my eyes spot the most beautiful of distractions: a man who'd rather show you his tasties than talk to you.

Now all I need is a handful of pixie dust.

Chapter Seventeen

Life's Bill

If you build things out of bricks, you're a bricklayer.

For most of my life, I've hacked. I've hacked computers, infrastructure, and even people. That makes me a hacker. This makes sense.

However, during my time in Hackers' Haven, I morphed into something more. As broken as I currently am, there was a time when I helped others, and willingly took on the weight of an invisible cloak of the Bushido Code's Chu, or Duty, on my already heavy shoulders. It gave me purpose.

More than a hacker, I became a hacktivist.

My upcoming hack of this database requires a distraction that is at least in the gray area of ethics and may encroach on inhumane.

I snatch a pen and notepad and quickly jot down a newsletter article as fast as possible.

I just hope he doesn't disappear before I'm done.

Thankfully, when I finish my impromptu journalism, the old man in the robe is still leaning against the wall with a devilish smirk on his face.

He has a real name, but most just call him Nude Ned. He calls me Silent Boob.

As I sneak towards my target, I take a breath and fall back on my Bushido code. Focus. Meditate. Act. I know not to close my eyes because the side effects of the medical cocktail in my system are more than just agitation and depression. They include poor balance and fainting, so walking with my eyes closed isn't advised.

"Hey...Silent Boob...what's...?"

A tremor starts in my right foot of all places. *Dammit, I didn't come here to get a freaking seizure.* Quickly, I shove the note into Nude Ned's left hand and something else into his right. I cover my ears with my hands and dart back to the desk.

I don't know how many meds he is on today, but it won't take a genius to know if he accepts my offer. Nude Ned scans the note, and his mischievous eyes dance.

I'll take it as a yes.

Nude Ned uses the scissors I found in a desk drawer and then put into his hand to cut the plastic restraint that holds his robe on. With a battle cry worthy of *Braveheart,* Nude Ned takes off running down the hall and collides with the nurse returning from her teeth whitening.

She screams.

He screams.

Then he rushes down the hall as every nurse within earshot chases him.

I swear I've seen that man's genitals more times this past week than I've seen my own.

In the confusion, I dart over to my dropped handwritten newsletter and pick it up. I already know what it reads:

Memphis, Tennessee -- In other news, a patient at St. Patricia's was found streaking down the hallway and ran smack into a nurse returning from the bathroom. When asked why the patient acted out, he responded, "Some dude that won't speak offered me his phenytoin pills for the week, and it was an offer I couldn't refuse." More as the story develops.

I pocket the paper and shoot over to the computer and dive into the root directory. First up: I add an administrator account to the system that sounds authentic enough: *Admin-2*. Then I log in through that.

The in-house database doesn't link directly to any other company's database. It astounds me that companies operate without linking their systems.

Then, disconcertingly, my brain goes blank; the damn medical cobwebs smother my thoughts. If I attempt to fight them, they will tighten further, like a Chinese finger trap for my brain. So, I accept them. They are slowing me, but all I can do is move at their pace.

Instead of speed, I focus on deliberation. Then I find my file. However, instead of finding the download button, I do something stupid.

I open it.

There, at the top, just under the name "Vice, Eric," are the words I've dreaded to read: "untreatable without further medical history."

Then next to that, is a date three days from today, with the code "427-B."

There's that damn transfer order, officially.

I blink the bullshit away and look for a way to download the file. In the screen's corner, I spot it: the icon of an old-school 3.5in floppy disk.

Bingo.

In the first drawer I open, I find four multi-colored flash drives. I take the one with the image of an angry bear and *Memphis Grizzlies* on it.

I did not know that this city had a problem with bear attacks.

I copy my file to the flash drive, log off, and duck out right as the teeth-whitening nurse rounds the corner with Nude Ned strapped to a gurney.

With a smile as big as the moon, I know that whatever meds I owe him don't compare to the ones currently coursing through his veins.

Nude Ned is just another debt on my life's bill.

Chapter Eighteen

Locked in

Go time.

I wait one hour and then stumble outside of my room right as the night work shift changes. There, I faceplant into the floor tile so hard something in my nose pops. For once, I plan my fall. Two male nurses lift me up, so I teeter into the largest one who smells of sandalwood and peppermint, and snag the Radio Frequency Identification card from his pocket.

After palming the card, I shake them off and give them a thumbs-up to signal I am *okay*. When they turn away from me, I dash to the empty shift manager's desk. If my calculations are correct, nine minutes are all I've got.

Thankfully, nine minutes to a hacker is like leaving Pooh Bear alone with a honeypot.

I log in using my fake administrative ID and password.

The biggest problem exists in the hospital's open network. Yes, they have a generic firewall, but it has the same protection that a piece of two-ply toilet paper has against a 9mm bullet. Further, if someone realizes what I am doing and slows or shuts down the Internet connection, I'm double-trapped.

Tanto, it's not the time to burn bright. Burn fast.

If I make even one mistake, they'll lock in and know my exact location. Perfection is key.

I open a zipped file I downloaded a few hours ago when I was at the nurse's station. It's a poor man's hacking toolbox called K-Zuse, named for the first computer hacker Konrad Zuse. The kit contains a few webscript worms called Gummiez to gobble up data, a basic systems analysis and trace blocker called Flakk because it slows down the trace with false targets, and a password breaker named P-Doney. I don't get the name for the last one, but none of these tools would hold up against anything with real security measures.

That's the thing: people that need actual security have real initiatives. Everyone I'm hacking only has limited budgets, and most of those are the bare minimum for information technology.

Can I hack with just these basics?

Now is not the time to doubt myself though, so I open the password-cracking executable file for P-Doney. My fingers fly across the keyboard, but the speed of the screen slams a mental spike between my eyes. I retch into the garbage can next to me.

There's no time for a migraine. Push through.

Boom. I'm through the city grid of stop lights. The overly complicated system frustrates me, but I do find the cameras in my region. I pull up four. I don't see the Goggleman, but that doesn't mean anything. Besides him, all areas look clear...except...

In the corner of camera four is a side view of a black car with tinted windows. I zoom in on the tint, but still cannot see in. After enhancing it, I notice a reflection of yellow on the curb.

Yellow is a Tow-Away Zone.

Someone has authority to park there since that car isn't a tow truck. This removes the back exit option.

That leaves the front damn door.

Curses.

The computer dings. It's too early for this to happen. I open Flakk. Someone just started drawing bandwidth away from here.

I'm made.

Ding. That second ding meant they sent a trace, but someone might think I am just a curious Internet worm. I hit the decoy command and send out four thousand different IP address options. This will only slow down the hunt.

How is someone this advanced tracking me? *Keep moving.*

I access the cameras in the hospital and hit the kill command.

They stay on.

Shit.

A different ding, one an octave lower, blasts from the computer. My mouse icon jerks right as someone is running a root kit on my system and trying to override my computer and control my input. Luckily, the computer is so old that it actually slows their hack. I use the Gummiez command to assault the hospital's network.

These worms will cause no damage, but every computer with an anti-virus system will alarm and do what it does, protect the system, further slowing the outside force messing with my computer.

It will also slow every other option I had planned.

With nothing left to do but hope, I hit the All-Open commands for the RFID doors. If they close before I get there, I have the RFID badge I stole.

Nothing happens.

I hit it again.

This time an error noise sounds from my CPU.

I'm locked in.

Then a helicopter roars above me.

Chapter Nineteen

Deep Into Cover

How the hell did they get a chopper here in under four minutes?

There's no time to dwell on that. I grab the bag of my belongings and pull the fire alarm. This will open all doors.

In theory.

As I dart towards the front, a hand slips under my arm. I jerk back to meet Dr. Line's gaze.

I stammer to say something, but nothing comes out. The disappointment in his eyes scorches my confidence like an ant under a magnifying glass. As he pops his neck side to side, my mind already hears his upcoming call for security, sealing my inevitable return to captivity, whether here or in Hackers' Haven. What comes out of his mouth isn't what I expect at all.

"If only the escaped patient had thought to take his doctor's handwritten notes with him, along with his possessions which seemed to include a large amount of cash, then maybe, just maybe, he wouldn't have had a seizure a couple of days down the road."

That's when he pulls a bag with my possessions from behind his back. Dr. Line pushes it and a notepad into my chest before I can think. Then he grabs a business card from his shirt pocket and slides it into my pocket.

"Goodbye, Mr. Vice. Be good and catch a ballgame sometime," he says before he strolls out in front of me, blocking the view from people outside.

I never get the chance to thank him. Armed S.W.A.T. descends upon the building and I am forced to slip into the bushes.

The helicopter above sweeps the area I need to reach: a wooded park with plenty of cover.

There's one last Gummiez worm left in the system to do its magic. It should be hitting any minute now...

The streetlights, which run on the same computer network as the cameras installed on them, all flash at their maximum intensity, forcing a series of bulb explosions. That catches the attention of the helicopter's spotlight operator.

By the time the spotlight returns to the wooded perimeter, I am already one click deep into cover.

Chapter Twenty

Rusty

Even as I gain distance from the hospital, slipping between trees, hiding in the shadows, sirens get louder. Either the city, the Feds, or someone else, just went apeshit.

For the next week, I sleep with one eye open. Every sound, real or imaginary, turns me into a paranoid cat, jumping at nothing. I hide in the shadows at night, and in the crowds during the day as I move.

During this time, I read Dr. Line's personal notes enough times that it tattoos on my brain: *Patient Vice's reaction to phenytoin seems to even out any tremors and appears to allow yes or no level of questions. Recommended dosage is unsure. Customizing this prescription, as well as the addition of others, will be required for an unknown period to minimize the side effects. Without family medical history, treatment could hurt patient more than helping in the long run.*

Sadly, I cannot find any medicine that can produce the effects that Dr. Line's recommended scripts do. No one is selling phenytoin on the streets. Plus, the random shit I'm taking is causing my hair to fall out in clumps. Maybe that's stress. Maybe it's both.

I also keep reading the card that Dr. Line put in my pocket.

I have epilepsy. At times, I cannot speak. Please be patient with me.

Patience is the last thing I have.

I stay at flea bag motels and attempt conversations with myself in the mirror. Even on the highest of meds, all I get out is a whimper.

I even purchase this generic lie detector that is supposed to help analyze brainwaves. If my brain shows more blue markings than red, I'm improving. So far, I'm as red as Communist China. Further, using this machine is a two-person job.

That's when, while I sit alone at a Huddle House, a scantily clad lady old and smelly enough to be my long-dead grandmother cozies up next to me in the booth.

"Are you looking for a good time?"

I nod, though it comes out in a tremor.

Luckily, the lady wearing a torn, gray Ramones tee that shows her pink bra and enough lines on her face to double as a road map for Atlanta takes my quirky answer as *yes*.

That's how I meet my trusty side-kick prostitute, Rusty.

Chapter Twenty-One

Buying a Ticket

For two days, this chain-smoking female Gargamel plays nurse to my Dr. Mute. Like a live-action version of Operation—except I was not only the surgeon but also the patient. And, as opposed to getting shocks from the game's dime-store battery, my body powered its own electric chair.

That brings us to today.

Damn. How has it only been three months since I escaped?

Rusty strolls over to the stained yet flowery wallpapered bathroom where I am taking a breather, and lights up a menthol cigarette. She dangles the butt of the death stick over the sink's rim, rubbing the bags under her eyes.

"Do we continue?" she asks in a gravelly voice, looking at her watch.

I attempt a "yes" through the mouth guard that is hanging together by two strips of rubber. This is the fifth one I've gnawed through already. When only air comes out, I nod instead.

Rusty rests her cig on the rim of the sink so the ash dangles on the edge. She removes my guard and pushes two anti-convulsants into my throat to dry swallow, just in case any tremors return. The seizures were minor, barely even TIAs, but once you open the seizure door, it never fully shuts.

I hate doing this on the meds because there's something in them that dulls my mind, making it feel like a dated operating system. Even at top functionality, it will not work like a non-broken one.

I know this is a poor analogy, but as I said, my brain don't work quite right.

Before I get back on the board for another round of shocks, I chuck my diaper in a garbage bag, take a whore's bath in the sink, dry off, and slip on a fresh one. When I enter the bedroom, Rusty is on her second cancer stick and scrolling through my laptop. I know she's not prying; she's too dedicated to her clients to do that.

"Your heart rate slowed before spiking...that's different."

I can see the spikes and valleys of the chart. I need them leveling, not jumping like a heart rate during a horror movie.

Dammit. That's not progress.

I point to one of the tabs at the bottom of the screen. Rusty clicks through and puts the historical data on the screen.

Curses.

Comparing the four sessions on meds with the four ones off of them, I do better on the medication. Less shaky and vulnerable. However, it is not working like it should because I am taking generic junk. I need consistent phenytoin dosage levels. Plus, there is a huge difference between generic medication and brand name, and not just the price. Generic medication can shift in each pill as much as 10 percent above or below the brand level of dosage. That means that I could get as much as a 20 percent shift in medical punch in a twenty-four-hour span. Too little, I stay a mute. Too much, I'll eventually shut down my liver. Also, this flux skews our data the same way downing a shot of whiskey before blowing in a Breathalyzer would.

Maybe tomorrow will be different.

Yeah, and maybe you can win the lottery without buying a ticket.

Chapter Twenty-Two

Abandoned

NOW

As I look over the printout of my recent failure, I hang my head. Nothing works. Nothing has gone right since the damn day I escaped Hackers' Haven.

My brain throbs, the pain, both physical and mental, beating down my body. I go *old school* and communicate to Rusty through a poorly written newsletter I need her to leave.

I load all of my gear into a red suitcase straight out of a '70s movie, complete with fake leather and a beaded handle. Rusty reads my letter in silence, though her eyebrows dance along each word.

I carry my suitcase towards the door, my black laptop case tucked under my other arm. Lost in my own little world, planning and scheming, I don't notice her blocking the door until I literally bump into her.

I thought my note was self-explanatory.

"I've read too many a note like this." She crumples the paper in one hand while the other holds a smoky cig. "It is not what the note says, but what it don't."

Before I can move, Rusty pelts me in the face with the ball. It doesn't hurt, but it gets her point across.

"Just because you're considering ending things, don't mean you have to exit alone."

Exit? Oh God, she misread the whole meaning.

Then again, I can't blame her. If someone sick gives you a note that he or she is going away and may not come back, it is a forgone conclusion that suicide is on the table.

I shake *no.* Her eyes stay flat, staring me down, demanding clarification. I drop the laptop case on the bed, unzip it, and pop up a screen to write something out. However, as I touch the keyboard, two leathery hands cover mine.

As her gray hair dangles near my nose, I stay still. For once, I no longer smell her, that odor that oozes from her pores: the stench of years of hard living and chain smoking and a fast-food diet. Instead, behind her unwavering green eyes, away from the always bloodshot white area, Rusty shares a layer of painful kindness. One that comes from making hard, permanent choices when they matter.

"All I'm saying is, if it, this..." Rusty circles my head in cigarette smoke the way a priest swings incense around. "Whatever this is, when, not if, it gets worse than you can handle, let me know."

She's no Mary Poppins, that's for sure. Still, she has helped make the medicine and treatment go down better. So, if I'm ever taking a spoonful of arsenic, I know I can count on her to be there for my final minutes.

Rusty puts her hand on my shoulder and does something she's never done before: she hugs me. She hugs me so hard, her shoulders pop. Like AldenSong's hugs do.

Did.

Truthfully, Rusty and I rarely even make eye contact, which I'm sure is common in her profession. As she releases me and heads out, Rusty tilts her head back and rasps.

"I never hug my Johns—only my friends."

And, like that, the only ally I have shuts the door behind her.

While I doubt Rusty is a practicing Bushi, she certainly knows a thing or two about the compassion virtue, and to never overlook kindness, even from semi-strangers.

Who said that Christians were the only ones to draw knowledge and stories from prostitutes?

People credit Albert Einstein with saying insanity is doing the same thing over and over again and expecting a different result. That is why, as much as it pains me to do so, I must abandon my current failures of self-treatment and risk exposure to the outside world. I must do something incredibly dumb to hope to get incredibly lucky.

Two hours later, donning a prosthetic nose I bought from the backroom of a tattoo parlor I board a bus. The fake nose, while clearly fake up close, should be good enough to throw off any digital forensic software.

I think.

Truthfully, people really should stop making fun of bus travel. Sure, it is not the smoothest ride, and most riders look like stand-ins for a movie about homelessness. However, with little-to-no luggage, you can journey across the country in three days for just over a Franklin.

I'm not going that far. No. I'm just going back to where everything started: Houston, Texas, home of the Lyndon B. Johnson Space

Center, a place that encourages exploration and dreams, and Hackers' Haven, a prison that does the exact opposite.

Turns out, when everything you own is in two bags and you've got every piece of paper about your disease strewn across three seats and you keep closing your eyes and moaning because you can't damn well speak to yourself, you stick out. I know I might draw attention from passengers because they hop on and off, so I pack up and move every other stop to a different seat to keep the watchers at bay.

Then, after thirteen and a half hours, I arrive at the Interstate Station in Baytown, Texas. This area is several miles North of Hackers' Haven, but anywhere closer might draw watchful eyes.

Even on no sleep, I hoof it the six miles to my former home. I have no plan, no way in—or out—of the building. All I have is the vague idea that if I watch from the shadows, I can ambush Dr. Fel.

For hours, I walk. My stomach rumbles and my sides hurt. I haven't eaten in two days. Wait, maybe I ate some cashews...or was that three days ago? The drugs fog me, dry me, and constipate me. I'm more backed up than rush hour. The days don't blur, but the memories of them do, like my memory is faulty. Either way, something besides nourishment fuels me.

For now.

Three blocks from Hackers' Haven the second-guessing kicks in.

What if I get spotted spying? How long should I hide? What if Dr. Fel never enters the building?

Funny how that goes when you have no plan. Regardless, the doubts aren't enough to halt my march. I trudge forward to the street of my prison. Then I walk two streets over and crisscross through alleys until I stand in the exact spot where I got Barca killed.

It's funny that my mind phrases it that way. *Got Barca killed.* Not *ended a monster*, or *helped a man get vengeance*, but *got Barca killed.*

Part of me regrets the part I had in taking a human life. And, even though I know the shooting of Barca was justified, I hope I never stop listening to the part of my soul that believes we can all be saved.

I shake the self-pity from my mind. The alley looks the same but is different. I remember this overflowing dumpster, just not the rats that skeeter around my feet. The bricks on the walls are a different color. The red is now white. Not to mention there is no trace of the burned-out car. No scorch marks on the ground. No glass shards or scraps of metal.

It is like it never happened.

I sneak down the alley to grab a view of the building, a peek at my horrible home from around a corner. What I spot there drags my feet out from the shadows.

I am no longer a human, just a piece of metal caught in a magnetic pull. I stumble across the middle of the street, straight through oncoming traffic. Two cars honk their horns and swerve around me. I do not even blink. They are nothing but buzzing gnats to me.

As I stand, mouth agape, staring at the place I'd hoped to find Dr. Fel—to find answers—my brain screams. My teeth clench and my fingernails dig into my palms.

All I find is an abandoned city park where Hackers' Haven apparently never was.

Chapter Twenty-Three

Gone Mad

Dear God, no!

If I could speak, a wail worthy of a horror movie would erupt from my throat. A flood of ice immediately follows the flood of fire that courses through my body.

Where my former home, the torment capital of Texas, Hackers' Haven, should be, sits nothing more than a park.

What is happening?

For the millionth time, I doubt myself. Ignoring my breathing techniques, Bushido Code teachings of patience, Rei or Respect, and even in my medical condition, I sprint into the *park.*

I stand between two buildings that should be there: an empty cobbler store named Wiley's Walkings and the generically named City Funeral Home and Cremation Services. However, while the former was already out of business, the funeral home was still functioning when Quidlee and I stepped out during our test escape.

Wait...hold on...I don't think I stepped out...maybe...

I rotate my body and walk backwards, easing into a memory. Less than a year ago, Quidlee and I stood here. I think! But how could I have done that in a place that never existed? My mind overlays the memory, possibly a false one, of the Rook dancing in the street, his taste of freedom, and my stomach knots up.

Maybe it's because I didn't step out. Or maybe it's because that little dance was the closest Quidlee ever got to freedom.

I shake the memory or lie from my brain and focus on the present. From this angle, there is no way to see if the crematorium is still in business or closed for good. All I can see is the white brick wall.

It wasn't white before...it was red...just like the bricks in the alley where Mr. Longfellow shot Barca. They were red before.

Right?

Everything is off. My ears pop like I've just submerged in the Liquid Ocular Display Interceptor System, or LODIS, from Hackers' Haven. My mouth dries and my chest aches as I sink deeper in doubt.

I inspect this children's playground. It's not that there is a public park—complete with two slides that bookmark three swings—where I used to get tortured, and where I would capture people online that's setting me off like this.

No, what floods my basement is that these metal amusement contraptions are covered. In rust.

I run my hand along the pole that holds up part of the first slide. My fingers feel a layer of thirsty metal and break the rust off into my hand. The grimy, flaky metal shreds in my fingers the way a broken sliver of a too-thin potato chip does.

As I lean in to examine the spot where I removed the rust scab, a slightly lighter rust layer exists. I pick at this mark as well and tear it away, getting deeper. Even there, rust exists on this inner epidermis.

No fake *rust spray* did this. This is from neglect, rainy springs, and harsh summers.

I'm no scientist, but this damage took more than a year to make.

Has this place always been here?

I plop down on the slide and roll up my pants to examine the spot where Hackers' Haven embedded that RFID chip in my leg. I want to see the scar that has to be there, so I move my leg hair around.

After three attempts, I find no scar.

Have I gone mad?

Chapter Twenty-Four

Crystal

There is no Hackers' Haven. There is no building, guard tower, or basement.

And nothing in between. It is gone. As in, it doesn't exist.

Did it ever?

I pull at my hair and shake. My body wants to tear itself apart.

How much have I made up?

I woke up in the hospital after my coffee shop episode. Why did I feel safe there? Wasn't it odd that I didn't try to escape earlier? Maybe I've always been in hospitals.

Was Hackers' Haven all in my head? Was it just another hospital stay?

A thought worse than madness hits me. Not that I have lost my mind. That train has already crashed into the station. No, what has hit me is worse.

Have I always been crazy?

While the term crazy is misused and overused, in my case madness makes sense. I mean, what are the odds that a teenage runaway with no formal education would grow up to become a computer hacker? And when I really think about it, it makes little sense that the United States of Freaking America has a prison that uses captured hackers like indentured servants.

My body abandons my muddled brain and moves me toward the corner of the park. There, my feral side takes over. I dig. First, in little swipes through the grass and dirt, but then onto heaving out clump after clump of earth. Primitive grunts crawl out of my throat. Deep huffs start in my throat and slip between my gritted teeth.

I furiously, frantically dig, not knowing why, until I find something that kicks me further into denial.

The dirty plastic soda drink bottle is not what gets under my skin. It is the faded white label that has one word in red and another in blue.

I remember this drink, but not from anytime recent. I remember it from my childhood.

When I first had it, I was twelve years old. It tasted like the main company's drink, sweet and fizzy, but looked nothing like it. The clearness of the drink was supposed to make it stand out.

A few months later, I was stopping by the local Pic-A-Bit to grab some original Lay's chips for my mom, when I asked the clerk behind the counter where all the Crystal Pepsi went. He said they stopped making it all together.

That was seventeen years ago.

As I roll the Crystal Pepsi bottle around my hands and examine it for any signs that this is a newer product, my stomach lurches.

Hackers' Haven didn't exist.

Chapter Twenty-Five

Bell

I wind up straddling the left swing of the child's playset. The right swing's broken seat dangles a hair above the ground, no longer useful. The irony of the situation is not lost on me, as my broken mind uselessly rocks on its own rusted chain.

I'm sure this is an uncomfortable way to sit, but neither my body nor my mind cares. Everything in my body has rebooted into Safe Mode: I function, just not well.

I'd read where people presented with an unfixable situation often mentally trail off. My Bushido Code training rarely allows me such a luxury as running away.

Training? What training? Did I make that up as well?

The hot wind coming from the water a few hundred yards away stirs some dirt into the air. My chest heaves as I cough and wipe my eyes. Then, in the distance, I hear a single church bell chime marking the new hour. The sound draws me back to a time a few years after Crystal Pepsi left my life.

Chapter Twenty-Six

Fighting Dirty

Years Ago

A few months had passed since the last time I saw my mother: one dead hand holding cheap, shitty liquor, and the other holding an empty pill bottle. I was living in the alleys of New Orleans. I'd taken to doing odd jobs, outside of some illegal stuff such as ATM hacking.

I'd also taken to petty crime, which ultimately turned into big crime. Mrs. Lin found me after I stabbed a man. The five-foot Japanese lady with Coke-bottle-sized lenses in her glasses took me in, dusted the dirt off of me, and put me to work. Despite being old enough to have babysat Moses, she was as solid as granite. Hell, there were times my sixteen-year-old ass couldn't lift a fifty-pound bag of rice. Mrs. Lin threw it over her back like it was full of cotton balls.

I was ten days into living in her basement and working as a janitor for the building she owned just past the French Quarter, the tourist trap of New Orleans, when trouble began. She lived in an area called Treme, which was apparently an area of glorious music and pride for the city. For me, it was my job and home, so I had some pride there, too.

Jedediah McIntosh, a mid-twenties yuppie with an ancient name, had used daddy's money to buy up all the property around Mrs. Lin's watch-repair-shop-slash-home. He was like Richie Rich, except instead of dressing like a spoiled rich kid, he dressed like a vagrant: worn-out shoes with their toes opened, and torn jeans with a bike chain as a belt.

He was one of those guys that thought poor was cool because he'd never actually been poor.

He also rode one of those touristy bicycles, the ones with only one gear and a bell on it. Every time he got close to our door, he rang that little bell.

Mrs. Lin and I were alone. Outnumbered against deep pockets. However, the one thing Jedediah McIntosh and his family did not plan for was going toe-to-toe with people with nothing to lose. When you find yourself against an opponent like that, you'd better be ready for anything because they will bring a new definition to the phrase fighting dirty.

Chapter Twenty-Seven

I Did This

Staring at the barred-up entrance to the funeral parlor where the authorities at Hackers' Haven used to take new prisoners, my gut tells me that the key to my sanity lies in the beast's belly.

When the city comes across an abandoned building, they do two things: one, cut the water and utilities. And two, bar up the front door with wooden planks to scare off any homeless people looking for shelter.

So of course, the entrances are locked. My mind is low on oil, but still knows how to pick a lock.

The padlocked entrance, the one off to the basement, has a decent lock. One that, if I had my kit on me, might take five minutes to pick. With limited gear on me, I check the *Employees Only* entrance, a firmly shut, solid grey, metal door.

Then in the dirt, I spot my salvation: cigarette butts.

Smoke breaks are the ultimate resource for breaking into a building. Smokers often get locked out of their buildings. And as such, they often hide a key or a way to open the door.

I check for a fake rock, but all I find are real ones. However, next to a patch of dead grass, something out of the ordinary junk debris catches my attention.

A tiny crowbar.

I pick up the matte black instrument the size of my hand. On the prongs are layers of consistent scrapes. As I return to the door, I examine the frame to discover worn notches at the bottom of the door just below the handle.

I insert the small crowbar and step down on it, creating a fulcrum that lifts the door's weight enough for the lock to ease. Then, with my chewed-down fingernail, I move the lock to the side and unlock the door.

The creaking of the opening door, followed by the plume of heavy dust exiting the building, brings on a headache and coughing fit at the same time. Still, I shut the door behind me to hopefully blind any prying eyes. The room I stumble into has just a trace of daylight creeping in from a small window near the top left of the room.

My eyes adjust to grayness, revealing I am in the employee changing room. Several protective suits hang on hooks. I grab the yellow one and put it on. Then I put on a dust-covered gas mask from a shelf next to that to avoid breathing in toxic chemicals that got left to rot.

Luckily, there is a working silver flashlight next to a sign that reads *Caution: This workplace is full of flammable items. Please do not smoke inside.*

I wander to the top floor first. They smuggled us into Hackers' Haven through the basement, but my best chance of finding a set of working keys to any locked doors I encounter will come from the staff offices.

On the top floor, I open the door labeled *Office* and meet an unnerving sight. There is nothing beyond the wooden door but concrete. There is no furniture. There are no floor or wall outlets. There isn't even any overhead lighting.

Maybe this sight should shake me. It doesn't.

This is the proof that the funeral home was a front for Double H's nefarious activities. And far from unsettling me, it lights me up as if I just stood next to a hot stove.

The floor below the offices is as barren as the dusty office floor.

When I check the main floor and enter the room visible from the street, something shifts. Someone completely furnished half of the front room from a half rug to pictures hung on the wall. A green-and-white-striped couch between wooden end tables appears to be where those mourning the loss of a loved one would sit.

Directly across from it, but still visible to the passersby, are two plain wooden chairs. Those are where a funeral director and the director's assistant would sit, consoling the family, while also taking notes for the funeral. Finally, between the chairs and the couch, is a glass table complete with old copies of *Funerals Today*, a coloring book, some crayons, and a box of tissue.

That is 'tissue' singular. I yank out the tissue that flows over the top of the box, leaving the box empty.

On the other side of the room, completely hidden from the windows, is nothing but concrete. This must be what a movie set is like: only what the cameras film needs to exist.

I head to the basement. My heart and breathing accelerate like I just jumped out of a plane.

These are the rooms where they interrogated new prisoners and prepped them to enter Hackers' Haven. Stars from the memory flash before my eyes. I almost black out glancing at the cold steel table where men behind surgical masks poked and prodded me while I was under light sedation.

This is where they implanted the tracking chip in my leg. Only now do I realize I am rubbing the healed spot where I burned it out. There, under the hair, is a tiny scar.

How'd I miss it before?

I leave the small room and enter the only legitimate room in this funeral parlor: the crematorium. It comprises a series of sinks, machines with tubes, and a cold, metal table where the dead wait for the great, final burn.

A flash of a memory hits me: right before the guards shoved a black hood over my head, I glimpsed a tunnel that was next to the crematorium. I run my hands around the bricked-up entrance. Even this *new tunnel* has dust on it.

Something on the giant iron door of the crematorium catches my eye. It has a smudged look on a small window that probably allows the staff to look in at the body being reduced to ashes. I try to rub it away, to clear the window, and two things become apparent.

One, it is not a smudge; it is a handprint.

Two, it's *inside* the crematorium.

It takes all my strength to turn the wheel. Rust from the wheel yellows my gloved hands. The screech of dry metal against dry metal fills the room.

With a suction sound, the door opens. Inside, it's overflowing with ashes.

The average human body, after cremation, shrinks down to around seven pounds, roughly the size and weight of an old household iron.

This pile is easily a dozen irons in size.

There were as many as a dozen hackvicts in Hackers' Haven. A dozen ashy irons.

I run my fingers through the ashes, the proof of life.

Are these the remains of my fellow hackvicts?

PoBones. Foshi. X_Marks_Da_Hot.

AldenSong.

My head swims in a sea of glass, with every stroke cutting me deeper and deeper. I prop my lowered forehead against the cold steel table. This is the last item my friends existed on. A painful clarity hits me right between the eyes.

I did this.

Chapter Twenty-Eight

Hula

I don't know how long I slept there. I don't remember pulling myself up onto the steel table and closing my eyes.

Now, I find myself in a memory. I was on this table a decade ago.

Bright surgical lights blinded me. The pain of countless injections stabbed my sides. The needles' contents equally burned and froze my blood as toxins flooded my veins. I even attempted to scream, but the ball gag muffled my cries for help.

For relief.

For it all to end.

A car alarm in the distance awakens me to the puddle of drool formed in my gas mask.

A bass beat of stress bumps my eyes so hard my vision blurs. I sit up and wince as my lower back sends lightning up my spine from sleeping on the hard table.

All I did to stop Barca was for nothing. Cyfib killed them all any way. He put down the dogs because I was bad.

As the cloud of dread and failure soaks into my soul, I spot a water drain on the floor. It is just like the ones that Quidlee, AldenSong, and I used to pour mop water down in the latrine. However, there is one difference.

This one is not screwed down.

I grab the flashlight and lean over the drain. Inside, I spot something, but I cannot make out what it is.

The lid refuses to move, even when I take off my gloves and get my fingernails under the edge of the lid. It is going to take something way longer than my chewed-down nails to pry this off.

The tiny crowbar that helped me break in is too thick. I look for anything that can pry the drain's lid off at the first sink. I explore cabinet after cabinet, sink after sink, finding nothing.

Then it hits me: I can use the glass lens of the flashlight.

As I unscrew the top of the flashlight, its beam flickers and cuts off. In the complete darkness, I slowly remove the bulb of the flashlight and pocket it. *I still need to see to get out of this room.*

With my thumbnail, I pry the thin glass from its hold and then kneel on the ground. Using just my sense of feel, I move my hands along the grimy and dusty floor until they encounter the lid. I slide the glass along the ground until it catches under the lid.

Gently, I shimmy the glass under the lid. Every little push emits a slight cracking of the glass. I just hope it doesn't shatter until I get this thing open.

Finally, I get two fingers under this poorly made lever and lift the glass. The high-pitched scrape of metal against glass fills the room. As I lift, the drain's lid pops free.

I reach into the hole blindly and feel around. There is a sliminess to the walls of the pipe. I gag for a second as I think about what nastiness covers my hand and forearm.

My fingers connect with something small, about the size of my palm. Gently, I pull it from the pipe and hold it in the darkness.

It feels like an action figure, one of those kinds that is without poseable limbs. However, it does have a center that rotates.

Clumsily, I reassemble the flashlight in the dark, repeatedly missing the grooves of the cylinder that connect the batteries to the bulb.

Only when the light hits the gunky thing do I know exactly what I hold, something that affirms my sanity and gives me hope that I am on the right path.

A small hula girl figure with a bouncy bottom.

This was AldenSong's lucky charm.

Excited, I take off the rest of my suit. I wipe the gunk covering the figure onto my white shirt. Something is scratched into the bottom of the figure. The gunk fills those scratches in and allows me to read the one word Aldy was able to write whoever found this memento.

Moved.

Moved, I note, *not safe.*

Chapter Twenty-Nine

Took You Long Enough

With this vague answer about what happened to my fellow hackvicts, I explore the entire funeral home one more time before exiting the building. But I find nothing—no medical records or details about where they moved my friends.

Before I leave out the back door, I put the flashlight back on its shelf, lining it up in the dust spot from where I found it.

I keep my head down as I walk out into the sunlight, heading across the street, deep in thought.

I've been more than a little careless up to now, so when the hair on my neck stands up, I'm not surprised to find someone watching me.

He's leaning against the brick wall of the alley where Mr. Longfellow used his grandfather's .22 pistol to take Barca's life. The Goggleman.

Then his head turns away from the light like a vampire in the sun.

I haven't seen this particular man in over a year. He's grown a woolly beard since then. I should have recognized the confidence in his stance. His fingerless gloved hands slow clap for me, equal parts praise and sarcasm. His torn clothes sway in the wind. His smirk sends me back to my earliest screw-ups at Hackers' Haven.

My feet defy my mind, and I walk towards him, extending my hand as I approach. If he's gone through half of what I am currently facing, he knows I can't speak. He probably knows about the seizures because he has gone through them, too.

His right hand takes mine, then he cups it with his left.

"Took you long enough, Tanto," says Lance-a-Little, his voice shaky but kind. "Now let's get you acquainted with the rest of the team."

Chapter Thirty

We are Not Alone

With his hand on my back, Lance-a-Little walks me to a white van with tinted windows and the words *Willie's Welders: On-Call Repairs and Ironwork* painted in red on the side.

Inside the van are two other Gogglemen and one Gogglewoman working on laptops linked to four monitors that are affixed to the side wall. At the tinted back glass is a directional microphone on a stand, best used for eavesdropping. Even the ceiling has blue ethernet cables running along it.

There is enough surveillance equipment in this vehicle to make the FBI look like the Girl Scouts.

"Hold him."

Before I can react to Lance's command, the other Gogglemen pin me to the ground face-first. Instinctively, I struggle, but there is a foot in my back as well as hands pinning me. My nose gets shoved into some faded green carpet and I probably inhale a decade's worth of dirt and dust.

A handheld device beeps in my ear.

"Tanto, we're just taking precautions," Lance rubs his throat before he continues. "You'd do the same."

While Lance-a-Little is right, I would hope that I would have a gentler touch than this.

"Roll up his pants," one of them says.

"His chip is gone or broken," another adds, as the coldness of the device touches my leg. "As for anything else, he's clean."

Anything else?

Then, like I hadn't just gotten felt up, I'm put into a passenger seat.

"Well, now that that's done." Lance takes the seat across from me. "I probably should have led with this, but can you understand me?"

I nod.

"That's different," says the driver of the vehicle. "Most can't even handle hearing any spoken words when they are only six days out. You're a lot more than that out. Weird."

How does the driver know that?

"Can you talk?"

I shake my head.

Lance-a-Little strokes his gray and black beard while he chews on his cheek. "Well, we have a way to fix that. Sort of."

Lance bangs on the ceiling twice. The driver cranks the engine and eases onto the road and I take in my fellow passengers.

One is an African American woman I do not know with long dreadlocks and ripped arms. She stares at a laptop screen that shows a sort of radar or sonar tracking system.

Another Goggleman is an Asian man with purple hair in a mohawk so large it bends when the top of it hits the van's ceiling. I can't see his eyes and we have never met, but I know *of* him.

If I am right, he's a damn fine hacker. I mostly know him as the hacker that crashed the scrolling ticker at the New York Stock Exchange the day that a dozen business analysts announced cryptocurrency was *fake* and not worth investing in. I think his hack posted something that read *All Currency is Fake. Everything You are Doing Is Fake. Believe in the Fake.*

As someone who has money hidden in various cryptos around the world, I, too, *believe in the fake.*

From my seat in the back, the angle obscures the driver's full face. I can't tell who he is behind the balding, gray hair, but he must be a power player to be part of this team.

Lance-a-Little says, "Where are my manners? Everyone, this is Tanto. Tanto, this is--"

"Hold up," says the lady. "Tanto? As in *THE Tanto*?"

Apparently, my reputation as a talented hacker has preceded me.

She continues, "As in *THE Tanto* that escaped your facility and forced everyone underground, causing everything we've been working on to go tits-up?"

Apparently, my reputation as a talented asshole has preceded me.

"You interrupt too much, Wrecking-Ballz," says Lance.

Ah. I remember her. She crashed the live stream of Paris Fashion Week and replaced all the footage with photos of models that had died from anorexia, bulimia, and overdose. If memory serves, she'd actually installed backup batteries and hidden her Internet hotspot signal behind two news vans. It took the authorities sixteen hours to find the source.

"T., you probably know Alakazam_R."

I extend my hand. The guy never looks up from his laptop.

"I know Tanto," Alakazam_R says. "You're the white boy who's racially appropriated a Japanese term to use as your handle because you thought it was cool."

On the outside, I understand how it might look exactly like what Alakazam_R said, so I don't react. I will not defend myself. Not now. Even if I could speak and explain how my handle was given, not chosen, I might still come across as a whiny, white brat.

Lance-a-Little clears his throat, but not in an attention-getting way. In the painful way that sounds like nails in a blender.

"Our limo driver here is Dendro_Crusher. He's told me he's worked with you before."

Crap. Have we worked together? My brain is accurate about some things these days, but for others it is as accurate as a broken Magic 8 ball. However, I think the handle Dendro_Crusher is for a hacker that went AWOL from the military.

"Sup, T., it is good to finally catch up with you." He sounds almost sincere. "Also, just call me Dendro."

I double tap on the ceiling. It's the most I can do without shaking.

I take out a piece of paper and write out a newsletter, and hand it to Lance. He glances over it.

"No, the first contact we made with you was at the hospital, not on the Memphis street. Huh. That's weird."

Maybe I am misremembering things again. I can't be sure of my memories anymore.

We hit traffic, but keep to two-lane streets. It seems like a route that avoids traffic cameras, which only makes sense.

An alarm goes off on Lance's watch. "Pop 'em if you got 'em."

Like trained monkeys, all the Gogglemen reach into their pockets for plastic pill cases packed with capsules. Wrecking-Ballz puts two pills in her right hand and reaches for a sealed water bottle from the cupholder nearest her. I recognize the initials on the pills because they were a favorite *after dinner mint* for my mother's crippling addiction: RP 15.

That's fifteen milligrams of Oxycodone Hydrochloride. If memory serves me right, doctors prescribe a maximum of fifteen milligrams every four to six hours for extreme pain. And these Gogglemen are taking double that.

What is their pain?

Wrecking-Ballz chokes down her medicine and coughs twice.

“So, y’all are both from Twelve?” she asks.

Twelve? What's that mean?

"Yeah," answers Lance. "You're a Sixteen alumnus, right?"

"Yep," replies Wrecking-Ballz. "Ole Alakazam_R here is an OG at One."

What do these numbers mean?

My confusion must have shown because Lance pats me on the shoulder and types something into a laptop.

"What is that line they say in every movie about alien invasion?" asks Lance as all the monitors display one giant view of the USA's datagrid. Thousands upon thousands of blue and red lines connect the interconnected forty-eight states. I guess Alaska and Hawaii get their own maps.

"Take us to your leader," answers Alakazam_R.

"Naw, that's not what I'm shooting for," Lance-a-Little says as he punches a few more keystrokes. "Wrecking, would you please key in the overlay code for a shotgun ping?"

Shotgun ping? Why a shotgun ping?

That's when you target multiple servers at once. Historically, this type of action does very little good because all it does is show you several targets while gathering virtually no data.

"And...done," says Wrecking-Ballz as she stabs at her keyboard with her two index fingers. "Also, what you are looking for...is..."

Suddenly the map shifts, not in location but in color. More importantly, lack of. There are over forty blank spots the size of my fingertip.

"We are not alone," finishes Wrecking-Ballz.

Like staring at one of those 3-D hidden image posters, it takes a moment before it hits me. I start at the watershed in Houston near where we are. There, where Hackers' Haven, my home used to be, is a blank spot.

There is a peppering of these types of spots throughout the map.

My wide eyes meet Lance's goggles.

"Yep," he says. "What? You thought we were special?"

There are over forty Hackers' Havens operating on or near spots that are hidden from the public.

This is bigger than I ever thought.

Chapter Thirty-One

To Get Better

For the next two hours, the team sits in silence. Even if I could speak, I don't know what I would say. Just like I was worried about crashing Quidlee's brain with the details of his incarceration and subsequent use as a *tool* to catch other hackers when he entered Hackers' Haven, I know that these Gogglemen are letting me suck on that last thought morsel for a while.

We are not alone.

This statement about other Hackers' Havens existing throughout the country equally shakes my soul and confirms what I've always feared. In the Double-H, our team discussed why there were no ladies in our prison. A sexist comment would fly like they must've gotten off on a misdemeanor.

Now I understand they must have had their own prison or, more likely, prisons.

"As near as we can tell, all the prisoners are in a holding pattern." Lance paces and rubs his throat. "However, when you escaped, well, that caused a flux in traffic, both digital and physical, like we've never seen. For two months, we couldn't get a signal. Not one ping. Then, like the flip of a light switch, everything went back on. The voids are visible on the high-speed superhighway. It's like if your radio flickers for no reason when driving; that means a highway patrolmen just hit you with his radar gun."

Even if half of those dead zone spots are inactive, that means we have over twenty prisons like my Hackers' Haven operating. If each is occupied by only ten hackvicts, then two hundred are in captivity.

Two hundred under forced labor, captured people on the Internet because they wandered into our spiderweb traps.

Two hundred like Quidlee, scared and threatened to the point they would rather die than spend any more time destroying the lives of others.

We are not alone.

A full body shudder runs through me. Lance-a-Little catches my involuntary movement and puts his hand on my knee.

"Yeah, we all had those seizures," he says. "Just hold on a little while longer, T., then we can work on getting you...functional."

The way that Lance paused before saying the word *functional* shot an extra ounce of ice water into my veins. It sounds just like something warden Cyfib would say. After all, we were *tools*, and *tools* without functionality are discarded.

It occurs to me that there could be over twenty wardens like Cyfib out there making hackvicts' lives a living hell.

Outside my window, our van passes a series of pastures between densely forested areas. We are quite a way from Houston proper. The vehicle slows as we approach a large, rusted gate. Lance exits the vehicle, enters a code on the keypad next to the gate, and the gate screeches open.

As he hops back in, he points. "Down there is as close to a War Room you'll get outside of a Double-H."

I nod and let that sink in.

What war are you waging?

The car's tires crunch the long, gravel road we drive down. Large oak trees line the driveway for hundreds of yards. At the end of the drive is a mansion that I would expect to see in *Gone with the Wind* or something. A three-story behemoth with white columns thirty feet high greets us as the driver parks in front.

Someone from outside the vehicle slides open the van door. An ungloved hand greets me, and I take it to step out into the sun.

"Welcome to Churchill," says an African American guy with a smile that could light up a room. "My handle is Murrah-HeWrote."

I nod, wishing that I more clearly remembered his work. I think he's the hacker that tracked down Timothy McVeigh, the Oklahoma City Bomber, by cross-checking the bomber's exploding U-Haul's vehicle identification number with McVeigh's brother's credit card. Supposedly, Murrah-HeWrote lost someone in his family in the bombing. At least, that's what I'd heard on the dark web.

The van's team, complete with laptops under their arms, marches on the gravel through the giant white wooden double doors of the house. Once inside, the interior of the vast foyer is about as opposite of a classic movie as you could get.

Green rubber mats cover the floor, probably designed to take the pressure off the feet of people who work behind standing desks sprinkled between a dozen sitting cubicles. Each workstation features two monitors full of computer code. Three long monitors on each wall show the same code and a map of the United States. It is the same map that I saw in the van, with blank spots that were, or worse, *are* locations of hackvict prisons.

At the top of a long staircase is a stacked collection of computer servers, their blue ethernet cables dripping down the stairs toward the workstations like flowing water.

Finally, covering every window to the outside, are solar panels that pump fresh energy into all the attached computers.

The dim room is what gets me the most. Even the backlit monitors emit just enough light that I would need to squint to read what was on any screen.

It is about this time that sucking noises start throughout the room, like suction cups releasing from their holds. While I'd never taken any scuba diving lessons, there was a hackvict whose name escapes me at this moment, who told me about the pain of The Squeeze. Scuba divers call it that when the pressure of the dive gets to your mask. He told me that, once you surfaced, you could hear every diver's mask pop loose from its hold from across the boat.

That's when I notice all the van's Gogglemen have removed their goggles. Even in the low light, they squint like Lance did when he removed his mask. The closest one to me is Wrecking-Ballz. I try to look at her eyes, but she tilts her head away and her long, brown curls block my view.

It isn't until Lance puts both hands on my shoulders and meets my gaze do I understand: his irises are large, black dots that eclipse any whiteness surrounding his eyes.

"The first thing to go is your voice," he says as he walks me out of the room into a dining room. "It starts with stutters, then silence, and ends with fatal seizures."

The dining room has a yellow-and-blue floral wallpaper complete with various dark stains. A long oak dining table is in the middle of the room. On it is a silver briefcase.

"Some of us didn't make it past that point, but those of us who did have extreme sensitivity to daylight." He bends down and pops the latches on the briefcase. Lance opens it so that I cannot see its contents. He reaches in, grabs a silk bag the size of a book, and tosses it to me.

Unprepared for this, I juggle the bag between my hands until it settles in my right. I loosen the drawstring and withdraw a pair of black goggles. I run my finger along the scratches on the thick, tinted right lens.

"Yeah, we reuse everything here," says Lance as he clears his throat. "Those were...hell...I can't even remember whose those were anymo re..."

The rubber sides of the goggles feature more scratches.

Either a cat attacked him, or this guy tried to claw his mask off.

"The goggles have polycarbonate lenses in them. The kind welders use so they don't go blind. They're the simple part of the...transition." Lance-A-Little closes the lid and spins several times before he speaks again. "The pills cut down the pain you will go through, but there's something we must do first to get you...functional."

There's that word again.

Lance slides the closed briefcase down the table so that it stops right in front of me. I pop the latches and open the lid. Inside, I find a leather kit the size of a video game controller.

With bile filling my stomach, I unzip the zipper on the side of the kit. Then I flip open the kit to reveal two surgical instruments.

One is a small hammer, almost like a tack hammer or the one that Andy Dufresne used in *The Shawshank Redemption.*

The other is a long, steel needle with a round end.

I'd seen these tools in horror movies about doctors trying to rid patients of what they declared as *madness,* but I'd never thought they used these instruments in the modern world.

When I meet Lance's stare, that's when I see the darkened dot just above his right eye.

Chapter Thirty-Two

Ting

The room equally spins around me and sucks all the air from my lungs. Even though the medical instruments appear clean, the copper smell of blood fills my nostrils. Along the top of the icepick-looking part are various dents from prior use. I stumble backwards. My left hand catches the wall.

This is not how to fix me.

Lance tries to put his hand on me, but I swat it away. My Hackers' Haven mentor is not my friend.

"There's some bad code in our systems, probably put there by Dr. Fel or someone higher in the food chain. T., this is the only method we've discovered that forces your brain to reboot. Despite our collective work, no one has discovered a way to stop the progression of what they did to us. You don't know how bad it will get if you don't let us stop the virus that runs through your system. Dammit, just come here."

Lance-a-Little grabs my hand and drags me to an old-fashioned chalkboard with various code on it. He flips the wooden board on its axis to reveal the backside with a bunch of names in a column under the heading H.O.D.

"These are the Handles of the Dead." Then he holds the spike just under my nose. "I do not want to add your name to the list."

This is not the way.

I dash into the War Room. I go to each hacker's area, looking for a pen and paper. Somewhere, I've lost my set from the van. After I ransack the third occupied workstation while thoroughly pissing off its occupant, I find my only communication instruments and return to the dining room.

Lance keeps quiet as I scribble, scratch through, and rewrite my third person reporting newsletter. With sweaty, shaky hands, I pass my note to him.

Lance bites his lip with his front teeth as he reads. The only sound is the clickety-clacks from the War Room trailing in.

"Do you want me to lie to you?" asks Lance. Considering what I just asked of him, part of me desires the warm blanket of a bold lie.

I shake my head.

"They're not good, Tanto," he starts. "Immediately after the surgery, your brain will fight the change. Seizures will occur, much more severe than anything you've experienced. If you...make it through...you will still have to medicate to keep the migraines at bay. You will lose all sense of smell and taste. Your hearing will come-and-go for the first month, but then it will even out to a mild-to-moderate loss of hearing. The sensitivity to light will always be a problem. Anything above candlelight will hurt. And, of course, there will be the random fits of rage..."

The cure sounds worse than the disease.

I write another newsletter and hand it to Lance.

"Well...," he says, "if you don't do this, not only will you not be able to work with us here at Churchill, but it will cast a great bit of doubt on your role in this crusade."

Lance points to the War Room.

"You and me both know that they don't just let hackvicts escape from Hackers' Haven. Only one person has allegedly escaped, and that was before both of our times. I trust you and your intentions, but these people don't know you from Santa. If you don't do this, there is no way I can convince a team that the newest recruit is legit. You'll be viewed as nothing more than a potential spy, and it will hurt my credibility."

It never occurred to me he might not run this team of Gogglemen. In Hackers' Haven, Lance-a-Little had seniority. Out here, he has what, about a year of parole under his belt?

Just thinking of the term *parole* makes me ponder what he and the others went through once they were let out, but that question doesn't move us forward. Not right now, at least.

"Remember this, no matter what." Lance squeezes my shoulder in a kind, yet firm way. "Life is like a game of chance. It's poker, and the deck is as stacked as a swimsuit model."

This helps nothing.

A hacker that I don't know sticks his head into the dining room. "Lance, we've got a change of frequency."

Lance's swollen eyes widen. "Shit."

He shoots past me like I am invisible. Maybe I am, at least to this cause. Left alone, I pick up the hammer and icepick. I am sure they have other proper medical names, but that doesn't matter. All that matters is, to become a Goggleman, I must sacrifice.

I touch the tip of the icepick. It's razor sharpness pricks my index finger. A tiny drop trickles down onto the dining room table.

The hammer in my hand weighs less than a TV remote. Like a child that has to touch a stove to know that is it hot, I tap the icepick with the steel hammer.

Ting.

The sound echoes in the room as I throw up.

Lance re-enters the room and notices the vomit on the table. He puts his arm on my shoulder and pulls me away.

"Don't worry about that right now. We're in trouble."

Chapter Thirty-Three

Cannot Be Here

The hackvicts in the War Room buzz like bees after someone hits their home with a shovel. One monitor shows a giant map of the USA. At various locations, it flashes with blue square icons. If my unstable memory serves me right, those flashes are where the previous blank spots were.

Somehow, the hidden prisons are showing up on the map!

"We think the company that owns our prisons is doing a software update." Lance snatches a laser pointer from a table and highlights a map opposite of me that shows the data voids from earlier. "Tanto, you did enough inventory in the Double-H to recognize their name, Poseidon United Company."

He is right. There are a gazillion different tech companies out there, so I just figured that those servers in Hackers' Haven were just from the lowest bidder assembling the machines. I should've known that we had some of the best tech on the planet.

"Well, the short story is that, since the good ole government removed our human rights with Section 18 of US Code 2331 of the US Constitution, that meant that all of us imprisoned hackvicts were more than just tools. We were inventory. And inventory can be used. Depreciated. And even sold."

The floor beneath my feet shifts as if I am on a ship in a storm.

"So, a tech company technically owns us. Horrifying Constitutional implications aside, Poseidon has to report to a government agency and follow its guidelines. Unfortunately, the bastards they report to are the Mercator Agency."

The mental boat I'm on hits a rock. I tumble to the floor.

The Agency that imprisoned me.

As I curl into a ball, my mind flashes back to a hack gone badly over ten years ago. One of my favorite contract hackers, Mane-Eac, a tiny powerhouse with the spirit of a wild stallion and the hacking skills of a robot on speed, and I were almost incarcerated by this same agency. The hack placed a stadium-sized target on my back. All to free the young hacker DoGoodR.

I remember the rage and the passion that the agent in charge, my fake client Agent Michelle, had for destroying and capturing hackers. To know that this division is the one that controls all incarcerated hackvicts' fates equally answers some of my deep-rooted questions and also terrifies me to my core.

Before I know it, Lance-a-Little has me on my feet and dusts me off.

"T., are you okay?"

I nod, even though I am pretty damn far from *okay*.

"In the past few months, Poseidon United has not done a systems update. We assumed they were doing them by having someone travel from site-to-site with the files on them to upload. Kind of an Intranet-over-Internet thing. They never do this online, so someone on their end screwed up. We have to move fast if we're going to lock in on the unscrambled signals and discover how many active Hackers' Havens there are."

I shake my head and stumble to the closest empty workstation. The monitor is already lit up. The interface looks a lot like the HoneyBadger system we used in Hackers' Haven. I am not even sure what use I will be for this hack, either a Dam Breaker or Flooder or something else, but I need to clear my head.

I use my breathing technique to focus. Whatever they need me for, I will be ready. I've done this type of thing a million times.

As I shake out my fingers and dance them across the keyboard, readying for battle, Lance-a-Little's hand yanks the Microsoft natural-form keyboard out from under my hands.

"T., you cannot be here."

Chapter Thirty-Four

I'm Sorry, T.

You cannot be here. Those words punch me in the gut, grab my intestines, and squeeze. I reach for my pen and pad to counter a response, but Lance-a-Little knocks them on the ground.

"Tanto, right now, you cannot be trusted."

Lance must know how much that sentence destroys me, someone that has built his life around honor and duty. The Bushido Code, my damn code, is more than just about honor, duty, respect, integrity, courage, and compassion. It is a bond between warriors, especially between a warrior and his master. And now my master, the man who I have followed for almost a third of my life, has just thrown me into the streets.

"It is nothing personal," adds Dendro. "Only business."

This is as personal as it gets.

Lance leaves the War Room and heads into the dining room. He returns with the lobotomy and goggle kit closed and shoves them in my chest.

"The timing of this update and you showing up might be a coincidence, but we have to play it safe and remove any unknown variables before we attempt a trace."

Calling me an *unknown variable* does not sting as much as I would've thought. Maybe that's a byproduct of having been considered a part of a company's *inventory* for so long.

With a sweep of his hand, Lance orders the Gogglemen to get me on my feet. "Get him to the safehouse near Site 14."

"I'll take him," says Dendro, the van driver, as he does jazz-hands. "I mean, I still have my driving gloves on."

I try to speak, but my teeth and tongue go to war with each other. All that comes out is a high-pitched squeal.

"I'm sorry, T."

Those are the last words I hear from my mentor before I am tossed into the back of the white van and the sliding door slams shut.

Chapter Thirty-Five

Home

The van idles as the driver, Dendro, gets in. I am so far away in my own world that I don't even hear his door slam.

He asks, "You good, Tanto?"

I am far from *good.*

I am broken.

We're still parked, but I'm already lost in my thoughts. I do not even bother to buckle my seat belt or to check to see if the sliding door locks. There is no reason for me to dash back to the mansion and beg for my inclusion in the hack. Doing so might trigger more doubt than just sitting here. However, all the air from my balloon has burst out.

"That's right, you can't talk yet, my bad." Dendro shifts the van into drive. The vehicle lurches forward as the sound of gravel crunching under tires fills my head. "Buckle up, please."

One snap later, I'm secure in my seat. With the long driveway in front of us, I let my shoulders retract from my ears.

Useless. Untrustworthy. Unfriended. All the negative words one can use to describe a traitor, a coward, and a fool rush into my brain and stomp my gray matter like it just got caught stealing from the Mafia.

The Welcome-to-the-Gogglemen kit mocks me from the filthy floorboard. I take the leather kit in both hands, opening and sifting through it. The heavy goggles are there, on top of the icepick and small silver hammer.

Now there is a folded note in the box.

On one side are instructions on how to use the lobotomy tools. How to prep for the pain. How many hits it will take to hit the area of my brain that the Gogglemen think is backfiring. How deep the pick will go into my skull.

On the other side is a note from Lance-a-Little.

T., this is the only way.

In Bushido, there are many sayings about selfishness. You are required to make changes, not excuses. In my dense brain fog, I cannot remember who said that. In the same passage, it talks about being motivated, not manipulated. To listen to your inner voice, not the opinions of others.

My inner voice tells me this is not the way. It is currently so small and scared, all I hear is a faint whisper against the mighty roar of my self-doubt.

We make it to the end of the driveway, where the gravel turns to paved concrete, and the van stops. Maybe the driver forgot something. He shifts the car into reverse and turns us around to face the mansion in the distance.

Dendro puts the car in park.

"You're a hard man to find, Tanto," he says.

I respond with a double thump to the ceiling and he chuckles, reaching under his seat and pulling out a flip cellphone.

What is going on?

"All clear," Dendro says with the phone at his ear.

He rolls his seat back, kicks his head back, and puts his hands behind his head. I guess we're not going to the safehouse. Maybe Lance-a-Little wanted me off the property. Maybe they just wanted to put this fussy baby in a corner so that the grownups could work.

Dendro uses the hand crank to lower his window, then leans over to the front passenger side, and does the same.

"Hey, Tanto, can you please roll down those back windows?"

With a furrowed brow, I comply, though I can only reach the window closest to me. A roar of thunder on a clear day threatens in the distance.

"Thank ya, buddy." Dendro turns his neck with his left hand. A loud crack echoes. "Man, you were screwing with my timetable."

Timetable?

"Also, you're gonna want to save your hearing by keeping your mouth open."

What is happening?

There's a growing rumble, then a deep bass-like hum, in the van.

Earthquake?

But the vibrations do not come from below, but from above.

All the air sucks from our vehicle out the windows. Time stops. It is like when you drop a glass: the split second before it hits the ground, you're at the cross-section between fixed and broken, between the status quo and all hell breaking loose.

The sound of the mansion exploding reaches me before the visual.

In a fraction of a second, something tears from the sky and dives through the mansion's roof like it is made of tissue paper. A sideways halo of debris, full of brick, mortar, and lives, floods toward the van. The trees near the mansion snap and topple.

When the shockwave of destruction hits us, it still possesses enough force to crack the windshield and knock the vehicle backwards at an angle. A heat like a million hair dryers shoved into my face covers my body. My skin instantly feels like I've cooked in a desert's sun. My nostrils flood with the smell of burning, dust, dirt, and death.

The van turns and teeters on two wheels. We hover on the precipice of flipping. Then the van slams back down, facing away from the home of any hope I had of finding and saving my fellow hackvicts.

"Whoo! Yeah, son! That's how you make the big bucks!" I barely hear Dendro's voice over my ringing ears.

Disbelief fills my head. My mind refuses to accept what my eyes and ears witnessed.

Am I dreaming? Did I fall asleep?

Maybe the shock of Lance-a-Little's expulsion from his group sent me into a protective slumber.

Then the driver lets loose another yell and slams his fists into the dashboard.

"And now for the easy part!" Dendro cranks the engine and shifts into drive. He accelerates as if nothing happened at all. I glance behind, but all I can see is a cloud of dust where once stood a mansion. A home full of the only hope my fellow hackvicts had.

As we move down the road, Dendro answers a question I have not yet become brave enough to ask. Even myself.

"Let's get you home."

Chapter Thirty-Six

Kill Us Both

Home.

Home to many is a safe place. To me, safe is surviving this day.

"Cyfib's got a hefty bounty on you, Tanto." My captor lets out a whistle. "And now it's all mine."

Then it clicks. His build is bigger than other hackers, yet it is familiar. That is because Dendro is the one who tried to drug me back in Memphis. He's not a hacker; he's a mercenary.

Damn you Cyfib. Damn you to the hottest level of hell.

His abuse of absolute power in Hackers' Haven led his hellbent crusade to build a world-ending piece of software that I called Gakunodo. Its sole purpose: to capture the ignorant and force them into the same type of life that the Mercator Agency forced me to live. Now, this psychopath somehow just blew up and killed everyone that could help me free my friends.

And he did it just to get me.

"I'm just glad I didn't need to bring anyone else in." The monster scoffs before adding, "we've got enough of you code jockeys as it is."

I don't even have time to grieve for Lance, let alone the deaths of all of those. I claw at the seat belt in a desperate yet shortsighted plan to escape. I am locked in from the waist up with just enough slack to breathe. The release button on the seatbelt's clasp holds firm, despite several attempts to click free.

"Yeah, there was a capsule of quick drying gorilla glue that hid in the belt," Dendro chuckles as we make eye contact in the vehicle's center rearview mirror as he chews on a toothpick. "It'll take a decent solvent to get you loose."

I hyperventilate and tug at the side of the belt. Around the vehicle, I reach for anything. Keyboards. Computer mice. Anything to try to get free. None of it helps. I toss a kick toward the back of the driver's seat, but the chair is far enough away that all that occurs is I tap it with my toes.

"Calm down back there, or you're gonna make me use this." The driver holds up a nine-millimeter Glock pistol. Knowing Cyfib, he wants me back in his prison, but probably doesn't care if I'm down a few quarts of blood. I sift through my pockets but find nothing with which to cut my straps. Then, it comes to me. My only escape route.

The Goggleman kit.

The explosion pinned the leather pouch under the edge of the black floor mat. I extend my left hand, but it's outside my reach by at least a foot. I try again, willing my bones to grow and my muscles to lengthen. I even attempt to dislocate my shoulder to get to it, but all I get is a searing pain up my arm and into my neck.

Despite all my straining, the pouch remains out of my reach. At this point, I'm such a sweaty mess, it's a wonder that I don't just slip out of the seatbelt. Instead, all the straps around me just irritate my sweaty skin. Even the bracelet on my left wrist is annoying me.

Kilroy's bracelet.

"I'd ask if you want a water or something before we hit the road, but two things," Dendro garbles the words around that toothpick, and his drawl is strong enough for an episode of *The Beverly Hillbillies,* but still I understand him. "One, I don't really give a shit and, two, we're actually much closer to Poseidon's new headquarters than any of those goggled idiots ever understood."

I unclasp my bracelet and go to work. The old, leather band is worn in so many places that I am surprised it hasn't already broken off. I bring my left shoe up and loop the strap under the shoelace closest to my toe. The clasp that fastens the band around the wrist closes the circle of my poorly made hook. Willing my body to turn into the stop-animation super stretchy character Gumby, I extend my leg as far as I can toward the kit.

It lands right on top of the kit, but, the van hits a bump, sending the kit two more inches away from me.

"Damn Houston potholes." Dendro turns right. "Would it kill the county to fill them in once a while?"

In the distance, the greenish-blue color of water is barely noticeable.

It would make perfect sense that the next prison would be on or near water, since ours was in the watershed area outside of Houston. That way it was not officially part of the United States.

I stretch my leg out, but the case is simply too far away.

Change tactics, Tanto. You're stuck, not trapped.

I drastically shift my weight from side to side.

"Quit it," Dendro says, holding up his gun.

Since I can't reach the kit, I'm going to have to find another way.

On top of it all, now I'm either hyperventilating, or the seatbelt has cinched even tighter. I cannot catch a deep breath. We hit another bump in the road. This time, one of the computer mice on the other side of the van drops to the floor. It bounces under to my feet as if it was a scared, real mouse.

Using my feet as chopsticks, I snare the mouse between my shoes. I lift it toward my lap, but the van hits another pothole. It plummets to the floor and skids between me and the *Welcome to the Goggleman* kit.

"Geez, where do the tax dollars actually go?"

Sweat stings my eyes. Outside the vehicle, the water draws closer. We're approaching a bridge, but I don't know which direction we're going.

At this moment, I take a beat. I close my eyes and breathe deep, at least as deep as this torture-corset will allow.

The greatest of Bushido warriors often took time to meditate, even during battle. To center oneself, to clear one's mind, was as common as sharpening a katana or polishing armor.

Around my sixth breath, two away from completion of my focus, the van hits a bump. It is not the pothole kind, where your body jars toward whichever poor tire hit the jagged concrete. It is the elevating kind, the one where your head kicks back.

We're on a bridge.

As I finish my last two breaths, my plan forms.

It will either free me or kill us both.

Chapter Thirty-Seven

Plummet

The smell of fresh water hits my nostrils and stings my eyes.

The rolled down window...

I think about using the glass to cut my seatbelt. Extreme force is not enough to shatter the window. It will draw the complete attention of my captor; that includes his gun and its nine closest friends that like to put holes in things.

"You know why there are never any potholes on bridges?" asks Dendro as he spits the toothpick out his open window. "Different regulations. Bridges fall under the Corp of Engineers. Ever known someone who worked there? They run that outfit tight!"

A small white-and-brown street sign on the right reads *Scenic Overview.* That must mean that, in a few hundred feet, there is a section of that bridge that is either built up with a parking area or attached to something secure, like a built-up island or something.

I get one shot at this.

"Yeah, the Corp has some smarties."

I snatch the computer mouse from the floor with my feet and flip it into my lap.

"I was almost employed by them once."

With the corded mouse in my hand, I stretch it out in my lap.

Five feet of cord.

My foot barely reached the back of the driver's seat. If I hook the flat USB end through my shoelaces, there is a small chance the length will be enough.

And, by small, I mean rice-sized.

"Sure, the pay was great, but the hours, whew..."

Keep monologuing, Dendro, keep monologuing...

A hundred or so feet away, I spot the rounded area of the bridge. It is wide enough for about six cars to park. Luckily, there is only one car there.

Unluckily, the car's owners, a family of four, are taking what appears to be a family picture.

Gonna have to time this just right.

The driver leans towards me.

"Tanto, you good back there?"

Shit. He's blocking my angle.

With time running out, I frown, shake my head, and cover my mouth.

"Got it, yeah, I get motion sickness, too. They make wristbands for things like that. Let me check if I've got something for queasiness in here because I don't need you puking all over my backseat."

I slump down in my seat as he reaches into the passenger's glove compartment, only keeping his left thumb and index finger on the steering wheel.

Shifting as much as I can on my hip, I maximize my reach.

In two seconds, we will pass the only shot I have at escape.

Come on, come on...

With Dendro outstretched, I flip my leg and the mouse over his head. My hip pops in pain. I bite down on my lip and stifle a yell. The palm-sized mouse lassos around the steering wheel two times.

I spot the flash of a camera as I put all my weight into the leg and yank us left.

We crash into the family's car, knocking it and our van into a small railing. I swear the child with the pigtails holding the melting ice cream screams as her older brother mouths the word *cool* as I either continue my escape plan or plummet to my death.

Chapter Thirty-Eight

Save Us

People often say you see your life flash before your eyes right before a life-or-death situation. PoBones, the hackvict from New Orleans, once said that when he crashed a jet ski into a coral reef in the Gulf Coast, he saw everything from the time he tried Moonpies to when he tried moonshine.

My flash of life refuses to play because Dendro is screaming like a banshee in a blender.

The inertia of the impact from crashing into the rental car at 60 miles per hour spins our vehicle up onto the railing. Glass pelts my face as the harsh screech of metal upon metal fills my ears. All the electronics, including monitors, keyboards, and other input devices, slam into me as our vehicle teeters.

And tips over the edge.

I brace my feet against the van's ceiling as my brain gets tossed around my skull. My long-empty stomach fills with bile. Through the windshield, the spin of sky and water continues.

Sky.

Water.

Sky.

Bigger water.

Sky.

Impact.

The seatbelt does its job as we slam into the water. Dendro's screams muffle as the driver's side airbag hits him with the force of a shotgun blast. His head whips back, and the gray balloon is covered with blood, probably from his now-broken nose. A split second later, the passenger side airbag deploys, apparently delayed from the impact. The balloon blasts glass bits into my face. It also sends the driver's handgun into my chest.

I catch it with my pinky finger on the trigger guard. A coldness hits my legs. Water gushes in the open van windows.

As we sink, the nine-millimeter pistol balances on my outstretched right hand. Adrenaline coursing through my body, I ease the balanced gun close enough to catch it with my left hand as it falls.

As a smile crosses my lips, the smells of salt and gasoline assault my nostrils.

The impact has ruptured the fuel line.

And the engine is still running.

As if the rising waters weren't bad enough, we must worry about this sinking ship exploding.

Dendro's head rests on top of the spent airbag. He won't drown.

At least not yet.

With the gun in my hands, it occurs to me that I know enough about firearms to fill a matchbox. The main thing I know about them is they are like claymores: you point the explosive end toward the thing you want to destroy.

I take my right hand and hold the gun under the water. I'd read where some firearms will fire when submerged. I have zero idea if this is one of those kinds of guns.

I place the muzzle where the straps hold me down. I can't risk shooting something metal like the clasp that holds me hostage because the bullet could ricochet.

I pull the trigger.

Nothing happens.

I curse, but then the safety does what it is supposed to do. I find this little lever and push it down to reveal a red marking.

After a breath, I pull the trigger.

The gun's blast erupts like a cannon. A million church bells ring in my head. I scream but cannot hear it.

The van's dome light reflects off a sheen on top of the rising water.

The gasoline is getting closer.

I don't know if firing the gun will set off the fire, but I can't risk it once the gas overtakes me. I aim and fire into the belt again.

Unfortunately, my body must've braced for the sound, because my aim is off. A searing pain, followed an intense burn, shoots through my right love handle next to my stomach.

The water turns pink. *I just shot my damn self.*

The gasoline floats an inch from my now water-covered nose and mouth. Another blast could start a fire and kill us both.

With no other choice, I fire. One thunderous noise later, with no sign of a fiery explosion, the seatbelt is loose.

By this time though, Dendro is submerged. Do I risk saving a man who was going to sell me to someone I hate the most?

I already know that answer as I crawl toward the bastard.

Now I've got to save us both.

Chapter Thirty-Nine

I Hear It

Air equally nourishes and burns my lungs as we break the water's surface. Exhausted and bleeding, I swim with Dendro—an unconscious sack of rocks—the hundred feet to the shore. Once we plop down on the sand, the only sound louder than my pounding heartbeat is a barking dog somewhere. I crawl up to my knees and check on the mercenary.

I find a pulse, which is the most I can hope for.

A police siren sounds in the distance as the midday sun blinds me. I jam my hands into the driver's wet jean pockets and fight through the constricted denim for his phone, wallet, keys, a granola bar, and a soggy piece of paper.

I'll remove the phone's SIM card once I get a block from here.

Around the shore is an abandoned canoe. I drag Dendro's unconscious body near it, flip the vessel, and hide him under it.

Just as I finish, something licks my leg. I jump and discover a small dog. I'd say that it might've come from that rental car's family, but it has no collar.

Even though it looks at me with the biggest brown eyes I've ever seen, I *shoo* the purse with teeth away. It moves a few steps back, then barks at me. I grab Dendro's granola bar, unwrap it, and show it to the little bastard. As it licks its lips, I fling it into the water. The furball dives into the water after its snack.

Damn dogs. I love them, but they are some entitled creatures.

As my shoes squish on the sand, I spot something on the beach that shouldn't have survived the crash. Something that should not have floated up on the shore.

Yet it did.

The Goggleman kit rests where the water meets sand.

I do the dumbest thing I can think of: I pick the kit up.

Inside is the soaked note from Lance-a-Little. Now a series of numbers is visible behind, no, underneath the writing.

There's a code in here...

"Freeze," interrupts a voice from behind me with the worst word in a criminal's vocabulary.

Chapter Forty

Funk Monster

Of all the ways to get caught red-handed, soaking wet with an unconscious mercenary in close proximity wasn't one I'd predicted.

The officer looks twenty-five going on twelve. Between his peach-fuzz beard and the way he's holding his standard issue Glock, it's clear he's not far out of the Academy. If he were a veteran, he'd merely have his hand resting on his gunbelt.

Don't overreact, Tanto. They train them to evaluate a situation, so saying Freeze *does not mean I'm caught.*

"What are you doing down here in the water?"

My guess is I'm only a few seconds away from his radio reporting a 911 call about our crashed, now submerged, van.

I try to speak, but nothing happens.

I swear I still see acne forming on his baby-face as he reaches for his radio.

I can't write anything down since any paper I have is soaked. *Do I rush him?*

Then the brown-and-white dog catches sight of its food-provider and bites my leg. I push it away, then follow my gut and pick up the greedy little sucker.

"You know, sir, there's a leash law, and that's a seventy-five dollar fine for not having your dog on a leash," said the officer with kind green eyes.

I send a smile, a genuine one, not one that means p*ut it on my tab, buddy.* That's when I have an idea: I slowly reach into my drenched pants and pull out Dr. Line's epilepsy card. I've carried it long enough and there's never been a better time than right now to use it.

As I hand it to the officer, this little funk monster then has the audacity to lean forward and lick the officer's face. As the officer chuckles and reads the card, I put the grumbling Dirt Devil under my arm.

"You know, my mother had one of these Yorkshire Terriers. Different color, but a great breed. They *will* jump in the water first chance they get, as you can see."

The dog wiggles and barks, which is currently equal parts cute and annoying.

"Just make sure you keep it on a leash."

As if on cue, my furry diversion barks and licks her lips as the officer hands me back my card, tips his cap, and strolls away.

This dog is not my master. This dog is not my master. This dog is not my master.

I repeat this lie over and over. *But she saved me.*

I shift the hold I have on the sucker and get a faceful of dog tongue.

All right, Funk Monster, welcome to the revolution.

Chapter Forty-One

Quit Pointing Out Problems, Dog

For three days, I hide. In alleys. In dumpsters. In the dark places of the city that tourists and rich people forget exist. Once I get back to Memphis, I can get some of the ft from my final KronosPay withdrawal. Hopefully, it is still safe in that locker I rented.

Until then, Dendro's wallet actually had eighty bucks in it, which is a fortune if you know how to spend it right. After some browsing, I find a secondhand store without surveillance cameras and mildly refresh my wardrobe.

Funk Monster is a pretty decent companion, all things considered. It turns out she's semi-quiet, and her mere presence has a calming effect that I didn't know I needed.

To boot, I am one lucky duck because my misfiring during the escape only clipped my skin. I bled for a bit before I found a med student who needed the practice stitching up a patient. He took my sloppily written newsletter asking for assistance as a sign that I wasn't mentally capable of explaining to him how I got a rip in my side.

As I predicted, the driver's phone was a burner. As soon as it dried out after I got away from that beach, I removed the sim card. The call history only had texts to one number. And something already deleted all the actual texts, probably upon reading or something like that. I sure don't have the equipment to scramble a call or decode a text to give me a shot at discovering who is the person on the other end, but I don't dare text that number or call it from a payphone.

It doesn't immediately matter if the person on the receiving end of the call is Cyfib, or someone potentially more powerful.

All I know is that Dendro merely said two words, *all clear,* and they destroyed lives and any hope I had in under thirty seconds.

With power like that at someone's disposal, my next move must be covert.

I'm out of options, so I call in a probably expired marker. There is a 10 percent chance that Mane-Eac, a hacker that's been through some shit with me that would blow your mind, is using the same phone number as she was ten years ago. Hackers stay mobile and stay hidden. Mane-Eac is one of the smartest and least visible of our kind.

There's a chance calling her is a trap because, if someone is looking for me, they're watching anyone I was ever close to. And yet my dumb ass is still about to make some incriminating calls.

I find a convenience store with a payphone and no security cameras. I unscrew the black phone's bottom receiver, the end you speak into, and place two copper pennies in it. Then I screw it back on and call the number I memorized back before my incarceration.

The phone rings twice, then nothing. It is as if someone has picked up but hasn't spoken.

Someone is listening.

That is unlike Mane-Eac. She runs everything through an answering machine. Or at least she did.

I hang up and dial the other number I remember. Over the years, I've helped a reporter with various stories. We've only met once, but I can't risk his freedom along with mine.

I dial his number. He answers on the first ring.

"Dallas Robinette, if it's weird, I want it."

I forgot how much I hate his corny catchphrase. Dallas sounds like an old timey reporter, one from the 1950's. He speaks in a clipped Southern accent that is both funny and off-putting. The whole thing catches me off-guard because it is only now that I remember that I can't talk. I was so focused on surviving that I forgot my inability to speak.

"Hello?"

I try to say something, anything, but the shocks prevent me.

"Hey! I can hear you breathing, you creep."

In gasps of cries and chokes of laughter, I collapse into the payphone's glass booth. I scream and a long line of spit shoots from my mouth and connects to the phone's number pad.

I jam phone buttons with my finger. I jam them again and again. Over and over. My brain even remembers a bit of Morse Code, but the subconscious part of my disease won't let me key anything in. All I can do is hit button after button with my fingers. Tremors run up my arm. I slam my elbow into the numbers. When my arm goes numb, I toss my knee into the metal number pad.

"Don't call here again, sicko."

And, with that, Dallas hangs up.

Exhausted, I collapse into the bottom of the phone booth as the phone's dangling receiver swings in front of my face, its slowing pendulum taunting me.

Funk Monster studies me before climbing between the wall of the phone booth and my legs. I lean out of the booth onto the city concrete, defeated. With nowhere else to turn, the black Goggleman kit mocks me from its resting place next to the phonebooth. I close my eyes and clench my fists. Even without seeing the kit, I hear it mocking me.

I want to get to know you, the kit says in my mind in Cyfib's flat and inhuman voice. Only my sick brain would link the monster in my head with the master of my torment.

Quit pointing out problems, dog, I hear my old warden say, *unless you have a solution.*

And, Lord please help me, the only solution I have is about to puncture my brain.

Chapter Forty-Two

Menthol

I awaken to a broomstick in the gut.

"You cannot sleep here!"

A man pokes me. He is as wide as he is tall and with a beard so bushy that I half expect to see a family of birds living in it. Through sleep-crusted eyes and Funk Monster's protective bark, I barely notice his nametag, so he must be an employee of the convenience store.

I must've dozed off after my mental breakdown. As I slink out of the booth, every part of my body aches from the impromptu nap. I snatch up the Goggleman kit from the ground. Part of me hates that no one stole it while I slept. The other part of me has accepted that I am the only one that can use its contents.

I stumble onto the sidewalk, flip the clerk an apology wave, and head for the nearest Greyhound station.

Minutes pass, maybe an hour. I no longer care about time. Or being discrete. A small portion of my mind tells me to take the long way around to the station's ticket office to ensure I am not being followed.

A larger part of me tells that smaller part what it can go do to itself with a rented hammer as I enter the station's ticket booth.

I arrive in Memphis many hours later. The fog of frequent bus stops and passengers boarding and disembarking blur all together in a brain mush. When we reach Memphis, the driver taps me on the shoulder. Apparently, I'd written a newsletter to him on the back of a napkin that told him I was deaf and mute. It also said that Funk Monster is my service animal. Finally, the note says I require extra attention to ensure that I get dropped off at the right city.

That's me; the broken brain guy who can't even take care of himself. The burden.

Funk Monster and I find Rusty working her corner off of Brooks Road. Luckily, the bus station was only two miles from her *office*, so the walk was a breeze. She's leaning into the passenger window of an old Cadillac as I grab a seat on a public bench with an ad for one of the many city's lawyers that reads *Got wreck? We win.*

I guess advertising has gone back to the days of the telegraph and it's pay-by-the-word now.

I can't make out what Rusty and the client are saying. She's wearing her gray, torn Ramones t-shirt that shows her pink bra through one slash and classically torn jeans. By *classically*, I mean wear-and-tear made those rips, not children in a sweatshop. Rusty blows a bubble with her pink gum. The negotiation ends. They must've reached an agreement, because she grips the door's handle and opens it.

Depending on the individual, she might be gone a minute or an hour. I can wait. Even as the overhead sun cooks my skin, I no longer care. I'm running on borrowed time, anyway.

"Scram."

I first think Rusty's husky voice barked that order to me. Then I hear profanity from the car's driver as a car door slams and he speeds away.

I'd usually catch a whiff of Rusty's CHANEL N°5 and cigarettes aroma from across a room. She either snuck up on me, or my medicine's side effects have blocked my sinuses. Her hand tousles my hair before it moves down to my cheek and gives it a squeeze.

"You're a sight for..." Rusty coughs up a lung before finishing the cliché. "...Whore eyes."

I don't respond. She knows I can't, but I don't even raise my head. I don't shrug.

"New friend?" Rusty lowers her weathered hand and lets Funk Monster get a smell. Apparently, FM knows good people, because she gives Rusty a lick before my whore scratches my stray behind her ears.

"Let's get y'all something to eat."

Ever my trusty sidekick prostitute, Rusty. With her arm under mine, she angles me toward the closest diner.

Who'd've thought the wind beneath my wings would stink of menthol?

Chapter Forty-Three

Every Red Penny

We eat in silence in a divey diner with six people in it, including the staff. Two fluorescent lights in the ceiling strobe, begging for death, but trying to remain useful for just a bit longer.

Maybe I'm projecting.

I take two bites of grilled cheese on sourdough and leave my water untouched. Funk Monster, who the waitress thinks is my service animal, eats a hot dog, no bun. Rusty gets a salad the size of a car's tire. I'd say she was eating healthy, but in addition to the veggies, she added on bacon, pepperoni, ham, chicken, and strips of sirloin. All covered in three tiny cups of ranch dressing.

Then she ate my remaining sandwich.

Despite my protests, Rusty paid. She means well, but somehow it just adds to my emo feeling of burdensomeness.

We leave there and get our usual room at the *Brooks Bed'n Breakfast.* This isn't its real name, but this nickname serves several purposes. One, it has an hourly rate, mainly for people like Rusty and their clients. That's the *Bed'n.* Second, if you hear a knock on your door, it's the police, so you'd better *break fast* out the intentionally large and unlocked back window.

I sit on the bed as Rusty snatches the complimentary pen and pad from the nightstand and pushes them into my chest. Then I swat them onto the floor.

I'm so damn tired of trying.

Even from three feet away, Rusty's sigh covers me. Her breath adds to this room's odor of bleach and lube. Rusty snatches the pen and pad from the floor and puts them on the small black-and-white television on the faded red dresser. Then my trusty whore takes the leatherbound kit from my lap and unzips it. As she flips open the top, the lifting of the cover slows as her eyes widen. Rusty lets the kit flop open.

"Well, that's not that kinky..." Rusty says, seeing the goggles first. Then she moves them to the side to reveal the case's more monstrous occupants. For the first time, her hands shake as Rusty moves them toward the tools. "I thought I'd seen everything."

She comes within a hair's breadth of the icepick before her hand freezes as if there is an invisible pane of glass that exists between her and the mind eraser. She gently closes the case and joins me on the bed.

The rickety ceiling fan turns, catches every other second and clicks. A car alarm sounds in the parking lot outside before silencing. Two men and a woman argue over who-knows-what. Other than that, we sit in silence.

"I wasn't always a pro," Rusty begins. "Most of my coworkers don't start out in our current...occupation. Life was good to me, like great to me, for a portion of my days on this floating marble." She reaches for her lit cigarette and takes an extra-long drag, the ash reaching over an inch long. "Most people think that big choices define your life. Wrong. Life is full of little choices that, what's the damn word, hold on, accumulate. Some you can undo, even redo. Others, well, you can't. And most, them, yeah, you just wish you never even considered doing them in the damned first place."

The wall unit air conditioner cuts on full blast, sending warm air instead of cool into the room. A bead of sweat now runs down to the tip of my nose. I leave it there.

"This ain't a little choice." Rusty reaches over and taps the Goggle-man kit. "Now, I will not argue with you on this, but this, this choice here...is a permanent one."

I know. I've seen the damage that this will do. But, I'm the only one that can stop Cyfib.

There is no one else left.

Rusty takes another drag, catching the hunk of ash as it breaks off, and flicking it into the ashtray and rubbing her right temple.

"I told you that if you were considering ending things, you didn't have to exit alone. I still stand by that." Rusty's eyes run along the ceiling as she searches for her next words. "I just don't know if I can stand by...this."

Even if I could speak, the words would elude me. I've put Rusty in an equally impossible situation.

She avoids my gaze. You know you've crossed a line when a hooker that might vividly remember World War II refuses to look you in the eyes. I place my hand over Rusty's and give it a squeeze.

"Well, thank you, dear boy," she chuckles. "Also, touching costs you another twenty."

Even though my body interprets it as communication, I eek out the whisp of a laugh.

Worth every red penny.

Chapter Forty-Four

One Sound

Every red penny...Penny...

For a brief second, I remember I don't exist on this planet for me. I exist to help those that need help.

My mind flashes to AldenSong, praying. He taught my heathen ass a prayer or two, even though my communication and understanding with an all-powerful being isn't exactly sound. The one that sticks out right now is the Serenity Prayer by Reinhold Niebuhr, a theologian who believed that human life would always be persecuted by evil.

I think the prayer, that Alcoholics Anonymous use as a mantra, goes something like, 'Grant me the serenity to accept the things I cannot change, the courage to change the things I can, and the wisdom to know the difference.'

I cannot change that I have this disease, this infection, that is destroying my body. In that leather pouch, I possess the tools to possibly stop that evil from spreading throughout my body. Now is the time I ask for the courage to use those tools to fix myself.

Rusty, clearly unaware of my plan to go forward with this lobotomy, says, "What do you say I head out to the parking lot and find one of those traveling...entrepreneurs...that can sell me some of those pills that keep you from getting the shaky-shakes?"

She's out the door before I respond. I put the deadbolt lock on the door after she steps outside. Then I ready myself.

With newfound energy, I place the lobotomy kit on the bed and open it up. Then I examine my face in the bathroom mirror. No hospital or back-alley doctor will do this for me, no matter what money I scrounge up to pay them. Rusty sure won't. She might try to get me to change my mind.

I run hot water over the icepick for a good minute. Then I put Funk Monster in the bathroom and shut the door to the toilet and shower area. Through the door, my little sidekick scratches and whimpers. She's never done this before...

The instructions that Lance-a-Little put in the case are straightforward: the icepick needs to go in three inches to hit the frontal lobe. That's all.

Ok. It is just like hammering a nail.

I line up the icepick in my left hand with the tear ducts, the area between your eye and nose. The warm tip of the icepick equally burns and stabs. With my right hand, I hold the small, cold silver hammer.

Just like hammering a nail.

With trembling hands, the hammer lightly taps the end of the icepick. A *ting* echoes in the silent room. With virtually no force behind the tap, all that happens is that I feel the sensation of a small bee sting near my eye.

As tears flow down my cheek, I blink. I cannot do this.

'The courage to change the things I can.'

From outside the room, Rusty yells out.

"R.V.!"

Around this shady motel that stands for *Recreational Vernon*. He's a guy that sells *the cure for what ails ya* from his shiny red bicycle with a little bell attached to it. Whenever he rings it, that means the police are nearby. Luckily, I've never been here when he's had to alert everyone.

It won't be long before she returns. She'll find it locked and bang and bang away. If I haven't done this damn thing by then, I will have lost my nerve.

The hammer is slowing me down.

The wall will work better.

I step to the side of the mirror. The faded yellow wallpaper is worn down enough that I find a tear where I can line up the hammer at a twenty-degree angle. Or if I hit the flat end of the icepick against the edge of the plastic cover to the wall socket that the television is plugged into, I have a chance.

It won't be precise, but it will work. Might work.

Please work.

My hand runs along the standard plastic wall socket cover that you see in every room in every house in America. Aim there. It will all end if I headbutt forward. I can then heal up. I can save everyone. I just have to move my head forward.

One quick thrust, and I'm functional.

Do it. Just do it.

My head angles backwards. The tip of the icepick is still activating the tear duct, making a steady stream drip down my cheek.

It's time.

Sweat drips down my face. It's already on my hands, oiling up the icepick.

Just do it.

I breathe deep and even my feet out. The bed is close enough behind me to catch my falling body after this is done.

Then, from outside the door, I don't hear a knock. I don't hear Rusty.

Instead, I hear R.V.'s bike bell ring.

And that one sound changes everything.

Chapter Forty-Five

Two-Dollar Bill

Years Ago

It was a blazing summer in the Treme section of New Orleans, Louisiana. As hot as the jazz music that comes from that neighborhood. Mrs. Lin had saved my ass from getting killed three months ago, then she offered me an internship.

I told her not to waste time on a broken person like me.

She merely laughed and countered, "That's okay. I like to fix things."

The internship gave me a decent bed and three meals a day. While it didn't get me much spending money, because she only paid me for any nerd work, *as she called it, it sure as hell beat robbing people in the streets.*

Mrs. Lin had me working four different non-paying jobs. I really didn't mind the dishwasher, janitor, and Orkin Man ones. Dishes need cleaning. Toilets need scrubbing. Bugs need killing. The one job I hated was taking care of the chicken coop that Mrs. Lin kept in the fenced area between our building and the one next to us.

It's not that the chickens are high maintenance. You mainly just keep them comfortable, protected, well-watered, and well fed. The rest is up to nature.

Somehow though, I never got used to the smell of chicken shit. It's not like dog poop or even human poop. Their excrement is more like if you took the smell from of an early morning New Orleans' party central area of Bourbon Street and mixed it with the paste that kindergarteners try to eat.

Every morning at 5 a.m., I was out of bed before the sun crawled over the horizon. I started the coffeepot and grabbed a bucket. I added two squeezes of dish soap and cut on the water. While the bucket filled, I rubbed Mentholated petroleum jelly under each nostril to defend against the upcoming assault of bird poop on my senses. It never really worked 100 percent, but any percentage removed is a wise investment. Then I put on my gear: rubber gloves, rubber knee-high boots, and a bandana over my face. Finally, I would gather the filled bucket, a sponge, and my wits before heading outside to clean up the fallout from the chicken-oc-alypse.

Most mornings, the only other person up was Ole Man J.R. going through the trashcans. He had once owned a lot of farmland that had been in his family for generations. The lack of paperwork was problematic to the family, but opportunistic for the government. The State of Louisiana didn't have it recorded properly, so they used this land to bury toxic waste on the far end of it where the soil was untillable. By the time Old Man J.R.'s family realized what was going on, the poison had ruined their crops. Then the Environmental Protection Agency declared the entire region unsafe and gave the family a hundred dollars an acre in compensation. The rumor is that he still owns it because no one would ever buy radioactive soil.

His beard often caught scraps of gunk from his deep dives in the trash. The frayed, fingerless gloves would catch on scraps of metal, which he would snatch out and recycle for change. He always mumbled to himself the same conversation.

"Damn EPA, taking my land, Waterford, ha, Waterford is crystal, not land, nope, taking my land, damn EPA..."

I would make an extra cup of coffee for him, but he never took it, scurrying away from me rather than making eye contact.

Once I would get in the coop, I would feed the chickens at the opposite side from their pens, away from their poop, ensuring they ate heartily. As the flock ate, I scrubbed. I scrubbed shit off the most random of places: the sides of the pens, the fences, and even their own nests. One time I scrubbed shit from the ceiling of one of these mesh pens that were big enough to walk into without crouching. I remember thinking either how talented or sick the perpetrator was for blasting so impressively high.

Sometimes the chickens would peck me to keep away from their eggs. That's why the boots were knee high. I'd learned the mistake of not wearing them on day two. Mrs. Lin had a good laugh at that one, calling me Chicken Boy *for a week.*

Once I finished this chore, I'd go back into the house, pour Mrs. Lin a cup of liquid black gold, and place it in the same spot every day: by the window, with it raised exactly one inch to cool the black tea, but not wide enough to cause it to get cold.

After those chores, Mrs. Lin and I worked on the things that actually made us money. Mrs. Lin, a jeweler with nimble fingers, called herself a clocksmith, and she specialized in all things that go tick. I was supposed to fix the electronics. I called myself a techie, *but she still just called me* fanboy. *From VCRs to desktop computers, if it had gears and parts that Mrs. Lin didn't want to touch, it was mine to play with.*

No matter the workload, we would promptly stop at one-thirty for lunch, after most people had stopped in on their standard lunch break to bring in or pick up their goods. We put on The Show then.

Let's say that someone had brought in their grandfather's gold pocket watch for repairs last week. When they showed up the next week to get it, Mrs. Lin would bring the client into the Show Room. It was actually the short hallway between the living room-slash-front office and the kitchen-slash-storeroom. In the middle of the hallway was a table about the size and height of a mini-refrigerator. Red velvet curtains were on all sides. The client would find their prized possession resting in a mahogany wooden box the size of a musician's keyboard. For an added touch, Mrs. Lin would spray the box with a potpourri smell before the client got there. She never opened the box herself. That joy was always the customer's, because it was like they were rediscovering one of their favorite treasures.

It was all presentation, mostly smoke and mirrors. Nevertheless, this bit of applied psychology brought in more repeat customers and referrals than any rented billboard could ever do.

I tried to tell Mrs. Lin that presenting a repaired VCR to someone in the same manner was patronizing, but she blew me off.

"Fanboy," I think she said, "if it has any value to the client, then we can either add to that perception, or take away from it. There is no in-between."

I wanted to tell her I thought it was the comedian George Carlin who had the same idea with something like you call your shit stuff, and you call their stuff shit, *but she probably would tell me to go mop something.*

I loved our lunches together, and not because of the food. There's nothing fancy about a bologna on white bread sandwich, even if you put it in a mahogany box. What I loved about them was that Mrs. Lin would read to me.

My own mother never did that. Reading to a child took away from her TV time.

Mrs. Lin would read Bushido stories to me. Some were short ones, like The Three Bonsai, The Duel on the Gojo Bridge, and others. Some tales were long and continuous stories, like Elji Yoshikawa's Musashi. *These serialized stories about the deeds of legendary swordsman Miyamoto Musashi, a warrior who protected people using two weapons, a long sword and a shorter one, instead of the traditional lone Katana, started in newspapers. He also fought his enemies' cruelty and ruthlessness with kindness and selflessness. While others focused on mastering swordsmanship, Musashi focused as much on his inner power as his outer.*

Musashi also said to not pursue the taste of good food, *but since I ate the same basic lunch over and over again, the swordsman and I would just have to differ on this mantra.*

We were into the fourth translated work of the seven-part series, Yoshikawa's The Bushido Code, *the tense, early part where the Ronin arrived and poor Akemi was being shamed, even though she was the one sexually assaulted, when a knock on the door stopped Mrs. Lin's reading.*

It wasn't a traditional knock, one where the visitor raps his or her knuckles once or twice. It was the playful knock, five taps. The old diddy Shave and a Hair Cut. *This was the one where either the visitor or the host knocks back twice, which is the answer,* two bits. *I think it goes back to the 1920s when people were entering speakeasies to buy bootlegged alcohol.*

Only one guest of our *business knocked like that though. And of course, he rang that little damn bell on his bike's handle like he was a prize you just won.*

The vulturous Jedediah McIntosh was at our door.

"Don't answer it," I whispered.

Mrs. Lin responded with a humph *and walked toward the door. She'd dealt with tougher foes than a preppie kid who rode around on a bike with a little bell. Mrs. Lin had lived through World War II as a Japanese-American citizen. She'd dealt with prejudice and doubt. She'd dealt with class segregation and bigotry and all sorts of bullshit my white ass could never imagine. Mrs. Lin had played by the rules and prospered.*

But the problem was that Jedediah McIntosh was rich.

When the enemy is rich, all the rules tend to shift in his favor.

Mrs. Lin took a breath and cracked open the door.

"Mrs. Lin, what a wonderful strike of fortune that you are home."

Mrs. Lin kept the door's chain lock secure at the top of the frame, thus answering the door but not welcoming Jedediah in.

"I was wondering if you and I could have a chat about your...future."

"Hmm..." With pursed lips, Mrs. Lin's eyes never broke the dude's falsely kind stare. "I didn't know you were a part-time fortune teller, Mr. McIntosh."

"Well, fortune favors the bold, and you're nothing if not that." His salesman's smile beamed from his very punchable face. "May I come in?"

"These are lunch hours, Mr. McIntosh." Mrs. Lin sipped her unflavored black tea from a blue and white porcelain coffee cup as she held the matching saucer underneath it to catch any potential drips. "When the office reopens, you are welcome to return."

Jedediah moved out of my view and back, away from our front door.

"Your sign says that your hours in the afternoon are from 2:30 until 6:30."

"That is correct."

"My watch says it is 2:27."

"You seem to own an accurate wrist piece."

Jedediah returned to the door and ran his finger along the rusted faux-gold chain that kept him from opening the door further.

"Is there any way you could open the door now?"

"Unfortunately, no." Mrs. Lin sipped her tea again. "I follow the sign."

"I thought you made the rules?" he asked, trying to get a rise out of her.

"I did. I made them so that I would honor them, Mr. McIntosh."

Mrs. Lin put down her tea and placed both hands on the door. With a heave, she shoved the door shut.

Maybe I imagined it, but I swore I heard Jedediah call Mrs. Lin a foul word under his breath. A large part of me wanted to smack the shit out of him, even though he was at least a hundred and sixty pounds of muscle to my hundred-pound ass.

A folded piece of paper slid under the door.

"Something for you to consider...in two minutes, that is."

With that, Jedediah McIntosh yelled at the mailman, complaining about how hot it was, which was something white people do to pretend to be nice to each other, I guess.

And, of course, Jedediah rang his little bell as he pedaled away.

Before Mrs. Lin could pick up the letter, I snagged it.

"Give it to me, fanboy."

"He's not to be trusted, Mrs. Lin."

"Trust and learning are not mutually exclusive."

With her palm up, she flicked her fingers to instruct me to pass her the note. I lowered my head and handed it to her.

Mrs. Lin unfolded the letter. Her eyes completed one sweep of its contents, and then she refolded it and handed it to me.

As I read the offer to not only buy out her lease but also her store, my stomach tightened. The amount was not insultingly low, but it wasn't fair, either. At the rate we were working, and with Mrs. Lin selling the chickens' eggs on the side for decent money, we would make this amount of money in eight, maybe nine months.

"Do you think he expects you to negotiate?" I asked.

"No," she said, sipping her tea. "Men like that expect me to cower."

The next day, that little bell rang while I was on my hands and knees fighting a weed that clearly had wrapped its roots around the earth's core.

"Hey, kid, do you know where your mom is?"

"I do," I said, "but if you want to speak with her, you're gonna need to use a shovel to dig her up."

'Smartass' was not the right approach, but I didn't care. Jedediah's finely black polished leather shoe lowered his bike's kickstand as the dude looked around for prying eyes. The menace with the perfect fraternity brother swoop of brown hair reached into his back pocket, pulled out a wallet hooked to his belt with a silver chain, and handed me a crisp two-dollar bill.

"Kid, make sure no one screws with my bike, and there's a fiver in my wallet that's got your name on it."

Apparently, this asshole thinks my name is Abraham Lincoln.

As Jedediah walked toward the front door, Mrs. Lin met him before he even could knock. I moved toward Mrs. Lin, but she waved me away.

"Fanboy, you have other chores to complete. Go."

With slumped shoulders, I returned to the weed from hell.

The summer sun was just enough overhead to cast weird shadows through passing clouds. As Jedediah McIntosh stepped back and squared his shoulders, an extra-thick cloud blanketed us in a light shadow.

"Mrs. Lin, it is great to speak with you and I hope that you have come to a smart decision."

"I have. The answer is no, Mr. McIntosh."

The cloud covered even more of the sun's rays. Daylight trickled through our monstrous cover.

"I certainly understand that initial reaction, but I wanted to let you know it is a great time to move." From his khaki pants' front pocket,

Jedediah retrieved a rental property catalog. "There are lots of other places that will work for your business and home. I've even highlighted some properties that I have a close connection with."

"No." Mrs. Lin pointed at her front door. "This, this is my home, Mr. McIntosh."

"Incorrect." Jedediah pointed to the small sign on the corner of the building that read Apartments Available for Lease. *"This is a rental property, and those are always for sale. Everyone else in the building I've spoken to is willing to close out their leases without any...consequences."*

Then Mrs. Lin did something completely uncharacteristic.

She laughed.

She laughed, much like she did when I met her and claimed I was a Bushido warrior. Maybe stupid white boys doing stupid things made her laugh.

Jedediah clenched his fists. I swear steam shot from his ears. Without thinking, I disobeyed Mrs. Lin's order to stay away. I ran to her side. Maybe she, too, sensed that things were about to get ugly, because she put her right hand in my left. Part of me wondered if she did it just to ease my worried mind, but another part of me remembered something that I read a long time ago. It was a framed saying on the wall at one of the rehab facilities a court forced my mother to check into:

Your battle is my battle.

A different smile, not the salesman's one, crept across Jedediah McIntosh's face. This one was wide and trembled as if it were full of mischief, but his eyes were narrow. Beady.

Determined.

Jedediah turned and walked towards the chicken coop. He placed his hand on the latch to the entrance and opened the door wide.

"Don't!" I ran full force toward him. Jedediah still held the latch as my hand covered his and attempted to shut the door.

"Did you just grab my hand, you little shit?" asked Jedediah as he shoved me against our brick wall. "That's assault."

At this point, I also remembered something my paranoid grandfather told me after he fired his antique shotgun in the air when he caught neighborhood kids covering our house in toilet paper one Halloween night.

If they already think I'm an asshole, well then, I'm gonna act like one.

That's when I took my torn, thrift-shop Asics tennis shoe and planted it into Jedediah's nuts with all of my weight behind the kick. The prick slumped over and cursed as I shooed two of our chickens back into the pen.

Jedediah lunged for me, but Mrs. Lin got between us.

"Enough, boys, enough!"

"Oh, you haven't seen anything yet." Jedediah coughed as he adjusted his privates as if he'd just gotten unhooked from a rollercoaster's safety harness. He walked to where he left his bike. As the asshole mounted it, Jedediah noticed that all the air somehow had been let out of his tires.

"Sorry." I reached into my pocket, balled up the two-dollar bill, and threw it at him. "Rough neighborhood."

It was a petty victory, but it was mine.

Jedediah caught the bill and pocketed it. He chewed on the inside of his cheek, glaring at me with the rage of a thousand suns. As he walked his bike away, Jedidiah McIntosh stopped by our mailbox, opened it, and grabbed our mail.

"Mr. McIntosh, that's a crime."

There was an extra level of concern in Mrs. Lin's voice. She'd stayed so level, so focused, throughout the entire ordeal. Now Jedediah was acting out and raging. I guess she knew that this unpredictability made him extra dangerous.

"Oh, don't worry, Mrs. Lin." He held up an envelope that I knew all too well. It had a large purple stamp on the back of it. It was from the company that we paid our mortgage to.

"As a good gesture, this month's mortgage is on me."

As he pedaled away, Jedediah angled toward Ole Man J.R., sending him diving into the grass.

"Damn EPA!"

Once Jedediah was out of sight, a sense of calm hit me. Maybe he was really going to pay our rent. I'd stood up to a bully, and sometimes that was all it took to get them to turn toward the light.

Unfortunately, the way Mrs. Lin grabbed my right earlobe and dragged me back into the apartment, made me realize she saw the situation completely differently.

"Ow!" I yelped as she shut the door behind us. "What the hell did I do?"

"Oh, fanboy, you've disturbed a hibernating dragon."

She walked up and down the room as she chewed her nails. I'd always known Mrs. Lin as a kind yet stoic figure. For her to fret, something was eating through her brain like maggots through trash.

"You, you, you keep wanting, even declaring, that you are a warrior, a Bushi, but what you just did there, that was pure anger. A warrior never acts when full of rage."

"But Mrs. Lin-"

"Shh..." She chewed her perfectly manicured fingernails before she spoke again. "You just went and attacked a stronger warrior head on. He saw you coming. You never had a chance. His money, power, his sword, his Katana, is sharper than yours. Bigger. Mightier. And you just provoked him by swinging at his head. He could've destroyed you if I was not there. And he still may."

"But Mrs. Lin, he's going to pay this month's mortgage."

My voice squeaked on the word mortgage. *Why, I did not know.*

"Oh, yes, I expect that will be the only warmth out of the coming inferno." Her gaze met mine and she coughed. "I also expect much more of a...retaliation...from Mr. McIntosh."

At sixteen, I was too young to know what revenge really was. I'd seen retaliations of various kinds, such as when a bully punched me, and I punched back. Those types of horseplay responses were common.

The next day, I got my first real taste of calculated vengeance.

I awoke at 5 a.m. to the smell of smoke and something else. It was familiar, yet somehow foreign, like how a lit candle that is supposed to smell like summer rain is close, but not quite there. I ran to the kitchen. Pure instinct fueled me as I filled the bucket usually used to scrub chicken shit with cold water.

Mrs. Lin was already outside, standing in her nightgown. Even though I could only see her profile, it was enough to spot the deadness in her flat eyes.

That's when it hit me.

The smoke did not come from inside our home.

Something tightened in my gut. It wasn't just a burning scent, but also a cooking one, the kind that sifts in burning meat and charred flesh into the smoke. A smell that would haunt me from that point forward.

Mrs. Lin was still in her bathrobe when I joined her. I'd left the bucket inside. It was no use to me. I was too late.

Together, we stared as the chicken coop burned. A slight tinge of gasoline tickled my nostrils. I want to say that the fumes were why I started crying, but I'd be lying.

"I, I, didn't, didn't." I couldn't get the words I didn't even hear their screams *out of my throat as an invisible hand clamped down on my trachea and squeezed it shut. All the air was trapped in my lungs, drowning me as another hand squeezed my heart.*

"He's coming for our home with the rage of a thunderous herd, Fanboy." Mrs. Lin's arm was on my shoulder. "And we're going to have to find a way to fight...differently."

There, on the concrete, laid perfectly flat, was a two-dollar bill.

Chapter Forty-Six

Atone

Mrs. Lin's words from that horrible night echoed in my brain. Back in the motel room, seconds away from slamming a pointy piece of stainless steel straight through my eye and into my brain, it hit me that I am pursuing this all wrong.

Fight differently.

The driver of the Gogglemen van, Dendro, who attempted to kidnap me, said as much when we first met about how I could interpret conversations.

'That's different...most can't even handle hearing any spoken words when they are only six weeks out. You're a lot more than that out. Weird.'

Weird is what I have going for me. Something, whether it was my escape or my genetic makeup, allowed me to benefit from medication and understand what people said to me. It gives me an advantage. And that means I don't have to shove this damn icepick into my damn brain.

At least, not yet.

Seconds before Rusty rattled the doorknob, I put away the lobotomy kit. She opens the door to find me reading the Gideon Bible that

I grabbed from the center drawer of the end table next to the bed. The book, covered in dust so thick that bits of it floated in the air, had creaked when I opened it. I'd flipped to the middle-ish section to pretend that I wasn't just doing something crazy, like attempting to lobotomize myself.

"Well, R.V.'s a hard sell, but I got that dancing candy that you've been needing."

Rusty walks to the bathroom and fills a glass of water for me, then hands me a wad of tinfoil with the glass. Tinfoil is a smuggler's favorite because it keeps the capsules or tablets from rattling against the plastic of pill bottles. Anything to minimize police attention.

Rusty plops down on the bed next to me. The bed's springs scream, begging for either oil or to be put out of their misery.

"Didn't take you for the religious type, but then again, no atheists in foxholes, I guess," she says, snatching it from me before I can close it. "Ezekiel Thirty Seven, huh? Isn't that where God raised a graveyard of skeletons and then just sent all the *Return of the Living Dead* back to Israel? Weird story."

My whore is an overflowing fountain of knowledge.

Maybe I'm a weird zombie, back from the dead.

"And what's this little girl doing here?"

I'd forgotten all about the little hula figurine. I don't even remember taking it out of my pocket. Maybe I did it when I was preparing to do the unthinkable to myself.

As Rusty rotates the little dancer, I spot the lone word that my closest friend, AldenSong, scratched in.

Moved. It says *moved*. Not *endangered*, though it also does not say *safe*.

And now this zombie knows where to take his next stumbling steps.

Right now, *moved* to me translates into *hold.* As long as Cyfib and his company do not have a functional capture software like Gakunodo in their possession, they need hackvicts like Aldy and crew to capture others.

That's when it dawns on me: anyone could make another Gakunodo. I'm no one special. With forty other Hackers' Havens out there, there could be forty Gakunodo-type pieces of software too.

I do wish that *moved* meant *safe,* but that is a goal I am working toward.

It is time to atone for my sins.

Chapter Forty-Seven

Painful

Instead of stalking my dead friend Quidlee's sister's apartment from the shadows, I do it as openly as possible.

Over the next three days, I staple fliers for a fake lost dog every day and take them down every night. This way, it looks like I am just replacing the ones that were stolen, even though I stole them.

On the third day, the girl from the photograph in my back pocket, the one that I'd only ever seen that lone still image of, walks toward her front door. She's wearing a torn gray T-shirt, pink shorts, and shin-high black combat boots. Over her shoulder is an overflowing, reusable, nylon grocery bag.

Ten feet behind her, and gaining ground fast, are three thugs with matching tattoos of the green-and-gray fish from *The Creature from the Black Lagoon* on the sides of their necks.

Memphibians!

The thug with the shaved head and spiderweb tattoo on his face places his arm on her shoulder, just as I approach. I slam into the smallest one, a white guy with a dyed-purple ponytail and enough piercings to earn the nickname *pincushion*, worried that the first thug has already hurt Penny. Then a sound like a piece of celery snapping precedes a man's yell.

Spiderweb's right arm is dangling at the elbow.

Penny shoves the man's head against the nearest brick wall and plants the toe of her combat boot into his left temple. A thump as if someone kicked a watermelon resonates. Spiderweb crumples to the ground in a heap, like someone removed all the bones from his body.

Meanwhile, Pincushion knees me in the stomach so hard I taste what I ate for breakfast three days ago. This knocks the wind from my lungs. With his other fist, he aims for my face. I lean into Pincushion's incoming punch with my forehead and his knuckles pop, breaking against my hard head.

My head doesn't feel much better, but I haven't broken anything.

Yet.

The last thug, the African American with a barbed-wire tattoo dangling from his eyebrows, pulls a switchblade from his pocket, pops the blade, and charges Penny.

I step forward, but Pincushion yanks me to the ground by my hoodie. I crash into the concrete, and a broken beer bottle propped against the brick wall catches my eye. I grab the stem and jam it into Pincushion's left calf muscle.

As he screams, I twist the bottle.

It'll take stitches to close that kind of wound.

Pincushion screams and falls to the ground. Using his long ponytail as an impromptu handle, I slam his head against the concrete, knocking him out.

I turn to find Barbed Wire standing with his back to me, blocking my view of Penny. My heart sinks.

I rush toward him and discover Penny staring him down, her sea-green eyes locked on his.

That's when I spot the knife already in Barbed Wire's chest. The brown handle and part of the silver blade sticks out just above his heart.

"I might be wrong, but that's about a three-inch blade you came at me with," she said flatly, with her breathing steady. "My guess is that there's an inch, maybe an inch and a half sticking into your chest just north of the Superior Vena Cava. To put that in layman's terms, that happens to be one of the largest veins in your entire body. It is very, very important. Hence *superior.*"

Tears roll down Barbed Wire's face as he moves his right hand toward the knife.

"Ah ah ah." Penny wags her finger. "I wouldn't touch it if I were you. It's in a very...precarious...position right now. I'd wait for the paramedics. Of course, that also means police, so if you do choose to leave before they show up, I'd take my steps very...deliberately."

Penny gathers her scattered groceries, her attackers now an afterthought. As my hand reaches for a can of tiny corn near my feet, Penny snatches my left wrist and yanks it backward. I scream as a thousand invisible needles stab my arm.

"And just who the hell are you, you dumb little bastard?" She holds fast on my pressure point as her gaze narrows on her prey.

Lightning travels from my wrist into my shoulder. I move my right hand toward my back pocket.

"Slowly, slowly."

I'm sure she is expecting me to pull out a wallet or some type of identification. Instead, I show her a small photo of herself.

"Oh, now you've got to be..."

This photo of Penny on her bike, the one Quidlee snuck into prison, has been with me a long time.

Penny's eyes soften. Her fingers relieve me of the picture with the grace of chopsticks and she lets go of my wrist. I instinctively bend my sprained wrist back as the pain lessens.

"How do you have this?" Penny holds the picture at its frayed edges. "I gave this to my brother the day before his arrest. Do you know my brother?"

I nod.

"Is he okay?"

I look down, breaking eye contact. I cannot fully give her the answer she deserves with a simple shake of my head. There is so much I have to, I must, I can't tell her.

Police sirens build the distance. I point at the two unconscious men and our bleeding statue.

"Come with me." She grabs me by the hand, and we run off to have the most painful conversation of my life.

Chapter Forty-Eight

A Friend

Penny sprints down an alley. For someone in combat boots, the lady can sure haul ass. We get four blocks northwest before she strolls up to a cafe called *The Beat*.

The restaurant has outside seating, four tables under umbrellas. There's something about this country's southern states where, even when it is blazing hot, people want to sit outside. Penny takes a seat at the table away from a family of four, but close enough to the cafe's front window that customers on the other side of the glass can see her.

I take the seat opposite of her as she smiles at the waitress who fills our empty water glasses and hands us each a menu.

"We can talk as we look at the menu."

That makes one of us, Penny.

I reach into my front pocket for my small pad and pen but find only pocket lint.

Shit. It must've fallen out during the fight.

"Hi there!" The waitress, a brunette with hair past the midpoint of her back and wearing a name tag that read *Chloe,* flicks open her pen and holds out her ordering pad. "Have you had time to look over the menu?"

I shake my head and motion for the pad and pen.

"Um...okay..." With a raised eyebrow, Chloe hands me the set.

Fighting a seizure, I scroll one word on the pad.

Deaf.

A tremor that leaves my brain and hits my feet courses through my body as I shimmy. To the outside world, it looks like I just got a case of the *chills.* Inside my train wreck of a body, I take this as my one and only warning sign not to try direct contact like that today.

"Oh!" Chloe leans down and shouts. "Okay! I will give you more time!"

As Chloe leaves us alone, Penny rotates the pad to read the lone word.

"Well, I know that is a lie."

I nod and start writing. After each filled card, I take a beat. I want to protect Penny from the pain of knowing what happened to her brother, but I owe her honesty. There's no way to sugar this poison. It takes ten small index-card-sized sheets of paper to tell Penny who I am and to put the horrors that Quidlee went through into a readable form. His imprisonment in a hidden facility. Quidlee's physical and psychological torture by our warden Cyfib. The plan to help him escape. And, finally, his ultimate death at the wish of the monster of an inmate known as Barca.

Even with the foot traffic growing and the sounds of cars honking and passing by, each crinkle of paper under Penny's death grip echoes in my head. Her green eyes are turning gray as they swell with tears, and she sniffs every few seconds, attempting to hold back not just mucus, but also pain.

Waitress Chloe returns to us, but smartly assesses the situation and tiptoes back into the restaurant without speaking to us.

Penny drops the stack of papers on her menu and wipes a single finger across her nose as she sniffs.

"How do I know you are telling me the truth?"

She has a fair point.

It is not like I have a *Best Friend Forever* locket of him I could just whip out or anything. She needs to know I know her brother in a way only a genuine friend would.

Even though I only heard this once, I transcribe it into a newsletter. This was when we were sitting on the rooftop of Hackers' Haven and watching other hackvicts play basketball. Not only do I talk about how he and his friends heckled this cheating player at a junior college basketball game, but I take it further. I write about how Quidlee told the story, and how his body reacted to sharing that memory with me. The way his smile widened at certain parts. How he played with his hair when he was thinking about what to say next. How he sped through the parts he found boring so that he could slow his cadence to draw out the good parts. And how his actual body moved back when he talked about the part where the player charged them in the stands, and everyone ran for their lives.

Just as before, Penny read these pieces of paper multiple times before she spoke.

"I am glad he had a friend in that hell," she says at long last.

A friend? The thought is strange and painful. *I was the one who captured him.*

I attempt to write about that, but my trembling hands won't allow it.

As Penny places her hand over mine and squeezes, I turn my head up to meet her eyes.

"You want to get out of here?"

Chapter Forty-Nine

Fries

As we walk back to Penny's apartment, I keep my head on a swivel. We each tote one of her grocery bags. Its cotton strap burns into my shoulder. Even though her bag is bursting at the seams, she carries it like a feather.

We take a different route this time, angling south and east, away from the direct route. We can see her apartment building's front door from the alley. The goons who attempted to jump her are long gone, either carried away by police or other goons. Maybe Memphis' sanitation department just gathered them up in a dump truck during a trash sweep.

Penny walks up to the keypad on the door. I look away as she enters four digits.

"Oh, you can know this code all you want."

I raise my eyebrow at that.

A small buzz emits from the keypad and Penny turns the knob, entering the building. A dimly lit hallway, and a flickering forty-watt bulb with a layer of dust so thick it casts small cloudy shadows on the torn-wallpapered walls greets us. Green and white floor tile squares the size of quarters squeak under our shoes. Someone either recently mopped them or there's a thick layer of grime on them.

Instead of going up the stained carpeted staircase to our right, Penny heads straight toward the back door marked *Exit.*

"I live two buildings over." She smiles as she turns her head and sends me a wink. "This way, if anyone follows me or breaks in, they won't find my actual home."

Damn. I wish I'd thought like that a decade ago. It might've kept me from getting caught.

We enter an alley repurposed into a community hangout. Astro-Turf covers the entire alley and white wicker couches and chairs are peppered throughout. There's a grill in each corner, two gas and two charcoal, and a bunch of umbrellas are stacked against a brick wall, just waiting for people to come hang.

Penny flicks her head toward the grill farthest from us. "That's my favorite grill because it has a side burner that you can crank down to the simmer setting. Great for warming baked beans from a can."

We scoot all the way to the end of the alley to a plain wooden pallet about a foot taller and wider than me. Penny places her bag on the ground, and, grabbing from the middle of the pallet, lifts it to reveal a door. She unlocks the door and waves me inside.

"Go on, I've got to reset the cover."

Part of me wants to offer to help, but she appears to have a routine, so I nod and enter.

The apartment looks nothing like any place I've ever visited. I enter through a laundry room. Two top-tier, stainless steel washers and dryers are to my left, looking like something you'd find in a futuristic movie with their blue digital displays. An ironing board and steam iron are to my right.

Straight ahead, through an open doorway, is a hallway with a long thirty-foot rug with swirly patterns.

Looks expensive.

This hallway is the mirror opposite of the one in the other building. A twelve-bulb chandelier, the kind I've only seen in movies, hangs near the far door. That must be the front door. The calming yellow bulbs sparkle from the chandelier's shiny silver frame. The walls of the hallway are dark mahogany wood with actual framed art hung on them. One is of a blue dog riding a surfboard. I'm certain there's a story there. Without asking or even thinking, I touch the art. The ridges of dried paint on its canvas slide under my fingertip.

"Hey, you break it, you buy it." Penny snatches the grocery bag from my shoulder. "And that one is anything but cheap."

As I watch Penny enter her kitchen, something pulls at my left thumb.

"Hi."

Shit! I yank my hand away and discover a child with glasses as big as its head. Stumbling back, I stagger into the kitchen and bump into Penny.

"Hey, watch where you're..." Discovering why I lost my balance, Penny's eyes go wide. "What the hell are you doing here? It's a school day!"

"Incorrect, it's a Teacher Work Day," the boy responds as if it answers everything.

"I should hope so. That's why I pay taxes." Penny stops talking as a stampede of small footsteps comes from overhead. A female child dashes down the stairs. "Why are you and your sister home?"

"Teachers do other work than teaching, Mom," the girl, about six inches taller than her brother, says, somehow simultaneously matter-of-fact and sarcastic. "It's a never-ending and thankless job."

"Look, I know both of you are smart enough to know that I know you're not giving me a useful answer."

Penny crosses her arms and waits. The girl does the same, while the boy adjusts his glasses with one hand and swings a McDonald's Happy Meal box with the other.

Small humans are a tricky area for me. They are impossible to predict and grow into slightly larger children called teenagers that are like the wheels on a shopping cart: they can go wonky and crash you at any given moment.

The girl appears to be about eight or ten years old. The boy, well, with his button-down shirt and khakis, he's six going on sixty.

The girl points at a calendar on the fridge at today's date. In black ink are the words *Kids Home Today.* As a spectator to this parent and child conflict, I give the children one point.

"Well, my bad." Penny turns back to the groceries and puts some eggs in the fridge. "Did y'all eat?"

"Ter did." The boy holds up his box of fast food.

"He calls her the back end of the word *sister,*" Penny says with closed eyes.

"It's like how the comedian Norman McDonald says that the abbreviation *ID* is unfair because the *I* is for *I* and the *D* is for *Dentification,"* says the small banker. "Why shouldn't the end of a word get equal representation?"

Okay, I now like one small human.

"I'm Hazel." The girl sticks out her tiny hand and I shake it.

"Who am I kidding? I'm a hugger!" Before I can stop her, the child has a full grip around my waist. I reluctantly pat her on the head, hoping she will stop.

"You've never been a hugger." With her head inside the fridge, Penny also yells out, "Give Mr. Tanto his wallet back, Hazel!"

I pat my pockets as Hazel drops my Velcro wallet on the counter and heads back upstairs. "Homeless Joey has more money in his wallet than this guy."

I still only like one small human.

"My sister calls me *Lat*, as in *Collateral.*" The boy stares at the ground and shuffles his tiny white tennis shoes. "I prefer Liam."

"I prefer it, too." Penny has moved on to the cabinets as she places some microwaveable pastas on a well-stocked shelf. "He was *suddenly adopted*. Liam's dad owed me money. One day, he dropped Liam off and said he was *collateral* until his next payment. The deadbeat never came back, so we went through the official process, and he's officially part of my fam. Honestly, he's quirky, but he's a blessing, never a burden."

Penny musses the kid's short brown hair. His oversized glasses cover up his Hispanic features. I'd just figured the kids must have had different fathers.

Even if I could speak, the words would fail me. There are no ways to apologize for the cruelties of strangers. There is definitely no way to explain why some fathers attach their sin anchors to their kid's boats.

I want to tell Liam about my mother. About her addiction. About her abuse and neglect that found its primary outlet in me. My chest burns with the desire to tell him about Hinge House, the house I lived in with my mother of which she took all the interior doors off the hinges so that I could never have privacy. There was no escaping her wrath. I want to tell him how much I admire this beautiful home he lives in and how it radiates goodness.

Instead, I take a seat at the white marble kitchen counter. The kid follows suit. He turns the food box on its side. Even though the meal is surely cold, a hint of grease assaults my nostrils. Liam pops open the edges of the box with surgical care. Then he slides out the wrapped burger, gathers the fries, puts the bendy straw in a juice box, and leaves some plastic toy in the box. Liam reseals the box and puts it to the side.

He studies his food before glancing my way and surreptitiously sliding the fries an inch toward me.

"The number of fries I get per box varies between nineteen and twenty-four, depending on the day and if I know the fry cook. I only eat between 88 and 90 percent of my fries. So, if it would make you happy, you can have three fries. I would share my burger, but I tend to eat the whole thing."

They are the best fries of my life.

As he eats, the kid reads a beat-up old leather book, *The Old Man and the Sea.* The main thing I know about this author is that he drank a lot, screwed around a lot, and was broke a lot. If my faulty memory serves me right, this story follows a captain that ostracizes everyone, including his young ward, all the while pursuing one marlin. Kind of a lone wolf *Moby Dick*. I remember that the old man's quest ultimately leads to a school, or maybe sharks surrounding his boat.

I wonder if the Old Man survived his own pride of going after his quest alone?

Will I survive mine?

I feel a tap on my shoulder. "Walk with me," Penny says and I follow her into the living room.

It's comfortably full with nice leather couches, another fancy rug, and a basketball-sized globe of the world on a wooden coffee table. Penny spins the globe before she takes a seat on the couch opposite of me. I follow suit.

"Do you need a pen and pad?"

I nod and withdraw mine from my pocket.

"Okay then." Penny leans forward, her hair floating before her cautious eyes like a guillotine ready to slash my head off. "Tell me everything."

Chapter Fifty

Kill You

For a few minutes, Penny talks. I write my newsletter-style questions. She answers. It is the most *conversation* I have had in months. She leads the chat with the details about how she has this home and why the Memphibians are after her.

Excuse me, *were* after her.

The Eighth Street Bealers hired Quidlee in a need-to-know situation when he hacked the Memphibian servers two years ago. Since then, the Bealers changed leadership.

I'm currently *conversing* with its new leader.

It never occurred to me to ask my fellow imprisoned hackvict Quidlee what his sister did for a living. Penny tells me she runs a nonprofit that focuses on helping vulnerable women find housing and jobs in other cities.

That's the paycheck that Uncle Sam knows about.

"So, when my brother shut down the Memphibians' servers on which they used to peddle their snuff porn, or kiddie, whatever disgusting shit they sold, he pissed off some powerful people. After his arrest, the gang came after what he cared about. His family."

Penny sips some green smoothie that she grabbed from a clear bottle in her fridge. It reminds me of the probiotic crap I was forced to drink in the Double-H. Every time she takes a sip, I think I might throw up a little in my mouth.

"You good, Tanto?" she asks. "You just got whiter than normal."

I send her a thumbs-up.

"Anyway, our parents are dead, so unless that gang had a Ouija board, ma and pa were safe from their wrath. And, because we are half-siblings—dad dipped his pen in multiple ink wells—it took them time to find me."

The faint ringing of prerecorded bells rises from outside the living room window.

"They were dumb enough to send just two guys the first time, which meant I had two different...sources...from which to gather intel." Penny shifts in her seat and clears her throat. "From them, I found out that someone in their gang impersonated me and reached out to my brother. They thought he was in WITSEC, and he would come running if he thought I was in trouble."

While the Memphibians were wrong about the location, they were dead-on right with the result. While Hackers' Haven was about as far from Witness Protection as Hell is from Heaven, it was those posts that hurried our plan to break Quidlee out of the Double-H.

"The Memphibians were going to come for me whether or not I was in police protective custody, so I had to be five steps ahead of them." Her manicured fingernails scratch invisible itches on the top of her hands. "I couldn't come at them directly. I had to work smarter. Different. In a way they would never see me coming."

This is how hackers like me think, so I bet *Penny would make a talented hacker.* A coolness in my gut tells me she probably already is, even if it is the mental hacking of an opposing individual.

I know my people.

“Plus, you shouldn’t jump into a criminal swimming pool if you only know how to doggy paddle. Whether it is domestic or international, it helps to know both sides of the law and how to exploit each. Yes, I technically lead a bunch of social workers, but we know that sometimes the laws work against us. To protect people, well, that requires...finesse." Penny sips her liquid lawn smoothie and runs her long, slender finger across her chin. "The Bealers needed a legitimate reason to operate, a way to make money and to grow their territory. I met with the then-leader, Sanchez, a tough guy who'd made it through life coasting on his size. It took some convincing, but, ultimately, I gave the Eighth Street Bealers something that they were sorely missing: the ability to operate out in the open. They became an official rental security agency, offering their services to the community. It allowed them to grow their membership and force the Memphibians out. Ultimately, most of our rivals now work for us. Those three that attacked me were the last of their leadership."

I can only imagine the headache it was to get a bunch of notorious gang members fake identities so that they would pass a background check. It turns out Quidlee knew nothing about his sister after all.

A part of me, the *Chu,* the *duty* part of the Bushido Code, powers down. I am not her protector. I'm more of a liability than a savior. Hell, Penny needs about as much saving and protecting as Superman does when he's sitting on the sun.

A roar of footsteps overhead precedes Hazel's mad dash down the stairs. By the time she and her brother are at their mother's side, Penny lifts a twenty-dollar bill over her head. Hazel never slows down as she pivots and dashes out the front door.

"Get a Rocky Road for me, kiddos," Penny asks in a flat voice.

"Dairy free or regular?" asks Liam and he looks my way. "I can only have dairy free!"

"Regular," Penny counters. "If it's good enough for the cow, it's good enough for me."

"Mr. Tanto, would you like some ice cream?"

I shake my head. I can't think about consuming congealed, frozen cow piss at a time like this because I'm close to telling Penny about what I did to her brother.

"I'm getting an almond milk pralines and cream. It's the one Mr. Sanders, the Ice Cream Man, says sells the least in his whole truck. I would hate for him to have to throw it out when it goes bad."

This kid's sweetness is giving me diabetes.

Liam closes the door behind him, leaving me about five minutes to tell the rest of my tale. I'd already started this newsletter on several pieces of paper.

When I hand her the pages and pieces in a stacked order, she chuckles at the mess.

This will be the last time she laughs with me. Further, from the moment she protected herself from those attackers, I knew she didn't need me. Even if I hadn't killed her brother, she's more than self-sufficient; she's flourishing. In my gut, I always knew I was romanticizing this damsel-in-distress idea. If anyone is stuck in an ivory tower in need of rescuing, it's the white boy with an Asian name.

The newsletter starts from the beginning, retelling some of what she already knows. From the stack of paper, I share about Hackers' Haven, our purposeful prison, and how it entrapped other hackers in a vicious pyramid scheme of crime. Penny learns how her brother was tortured, both mentally and physically, by both the warden Cyfib and the bully Barca. No amount of watering down this story could turn this piss into lemonade. I owe her the truth, in all its ugliness.

I wrote about how close we were to helping Quidlee escape, and about how much he wanted to help her. How sorry Quidlee was. About Barca and her brother's death.

The tears pool in the corners of her eyes and shimmer in the low light, waiting for one more crack in the dam.

I extend to her one last sheet of paper, trembling like we are facing hurricane-level winds. As I lean her way, a smell of cinnamon and lilies hits my nostrils. I don't know where it comes from and I'm too scared to think of it further.

It is a simple newsletter before her, yet every word stung me when I wrote it.

Memphis, Tennessee

Almost two years ago, a hacker named Tanto led the assault that ultimately entrapped another hacker codenamed Quidlee, a source says. When asked for further comment, the predator said he would answer any and all questions asked. This ends our segment on Hackers' Haven.

I wrote that newsletter without the desire to defend myself. My actions, whether or not I was forced into them, resulted in the capture and death of Penny's brother. I almost wrote the words *I had no choice*, but that is a lie. You always have a choice. I bought myself time by stealing it from someone else. No excuse is strong enough to stitch this wound. For this, and countless other sins, I am beyond absolution.

And, to put it bluntly, this bit of information does not go over well with Penny.

Penny's lips tighten into a fine line. Her shoulders go from slumped to military attention. Instead of the tear-dam breaking, all those tears suck back into her face. Fire shoots from her eyes, and apparently, I'm wearing kerosine cologne.

"You dirty, cheating asshole..." As the fireball of rage formerly known as Penny casts down insult after insult, threat after threat, her body trembles. Most words she yells are English, though sometimes they're merely primal. For every step she takes toward me, she shuffles two back. Penny tosses one, two, then all the plates that are stacked in the center of the table. I don't even flinch as shards of them pelt me. She pulls back her hair in thought-filled rage, revealing a missing earlobe on her left side.

It was there in the photograph. Maybe an earring got yanked during that first attack by the Memphibians.

"Are you even listening to me?!" Penny shouts the question more than asks it. I nod just as the kids reenter.

Hazel walks into the living room, a small pint of ice cream in each hand, and immediately clocks the tension. Reading it as not her problem, she puts her mother's Rocky Road on a coaster on the coffee table and lays a plastic spoon on the top of the carton like it is a landmine that could explode.

"I'm gonna...go..."

As Hazel dashes upstairs, an ice cream cone appears under my face. From behind me, Liam says, "Mr. Sanders said I got a two-for-one deal because no one else bought that flavor today." Liam takes a lick from the top and applies a napkin to the far side of his cone to prevent a drip. I take the cone as the boy, too, runs upstairs.

The sticky sides of the cone fasten it to my hand. I stare at the lone scoop, a brownish-yellow orb. I place my other hand under the end of the cone, cup it, and catch the melted slush before it hits the carpet.

Like a ticking clock, the time passes not in seconds, but melted moments.

Drip.

Drip.

Drip.

"Get out of my home. If I see you again, I will kill you myself."

Chapter Fifty-One

Ronin

As I walk the streets of Memphis, the sun melts the ice cream cone in my hand. I don't yet have the courage to throw away the gooey treat. My body and mind are in an all-consuming battle, so I bump into people, stairs' railings, and even scrape my shoulder against a brick wall as I walk.

I knew this would happen, but I hoped in my soul it wouldn't. Even so, I should only be shaken, not broken.

I walk for minutes or hours. Both are plausible, and neither matter. I am a Ronin without a master, a Chukanbushi without someone to protect.

A small African-American kid taps me on the shoulder. He points at my elbow and finally I look down to see I am dripping blood.

It makes me think about the dripping ice cream and how, once it melted, it, too, had no purpose.

"Hey, man, you should go the hospital."

Was it George R. R. Martin, or maybe Jesus Christ, who said, "Wisdom often comes from the mouth of babes?"

Both have beards, and both are right.

To the hospital I would go, just not in the normal fashion.

Chapter Fifty-Two

Be Still

In the Bushido story *The Tiger of Kai and the Dragon of Echigo,* two brother-enemies used thousands of soldiers in their personal war. During their battle, one stayed true to his attack plan. The other changed his overnight to use the environment as a tool.

It doesn't take a genius to figure out who won.

I, too, must use my surroundings—if not fix myself, slow my progression.

Before I met with Penny, I'd already decided that when, not if, she rejected me, I would focus on my health and possibly wealth. Part of that included checking into a Hostel in Memphis called St. Patricia's Hostel Home. St. Patricia was the protector of mentally unwell people or maybe lost causes. That checks both boxes for me.

At the Hostel, there's a young twenty-something woman with dreads past her shoulders named Danielle, who likes dogs. When Danielle saw Funk Monster and me enter the hostel yesterday, her eyes lit up with questions. Seemingly mundane but problematic-for-me questions, like *what's its name,* and *how old*. As her questions rolled in, the tremors hit me so hard that a pre-med student doing volunteer work in the same building had to calm me down.

Back at the hostel now, I find Funky and Dani cuddled up on Dani's cot, with Funk Monster taking up most of the space. I leave them to their dreams.

I would love to know that peace. Even glancing at the two, I think about how the first thing I did was give Dani instructions on how to contact me in case of an emergency, rather than tell her anything good about me. She countered by showing me her EpiPen and said this was her *in case of emergency aka in case of shellfish.*

Someone bumps into me in the hallway. As they apologize, a small seizure runs up my right arm. Luckily, it disappears somewhere between my neck and my brain. These damn seizures and their frequency are getting worse. Every time someone burns toast in this place, I brace myself. I need medication yesterday. Literally. My pill bottle is completely useless and one day empty.

I grab some things from my rented locker and head to Rusty's haunting grounds. On my way, a particular building catches my eye: MetroMed. From the outside, it looks like a small clinic, maybe twenty rooms, if I had to guess. As for Rusty, unfortunately, I can't find her, so I'm on my own. All I need is a little benzodiazepine here, some myorelaxant there, and I'll be less likely to shake like an earthquake.

When I get back to my computer, I scratch that itch in my brain and investigate MetroMed. From what I can find on the web, this small and private hospital near Memphis' downtown is perfect. It has minimal government funding, which means minimal government oversight. And that means there's a significant chance they use silo software, aka software that doesn't link to an offsite database.

Silo software is surprisingly rampant in the medical community. That's why, when you are a patient at one clinic, you fill out duplicate forms, even in the same hospital. Every department has their own software and hell will freeze over before they combine.

Those are the kinds of situations where hackers like me soak up useful data like a sponge.

It takes two days, and half my remaining cash, to get a plan together.

I have less than two grand, but I know where to start: MetroMed's pharmacy. Once I get into the hospital and snag some pills, only then can I assess the hospital's vulnerabilities.

Like any good crook, I prepare for getting caught. I leave all but two hundred dollars in Funk Monster's new kennel, believing Danielle will take care of her if everything goes sideways.

I get my gear together, feed Funk Monster, pass Danielle a newsletter about the pup's care, and head out. It's nearly 10 p.m. and I'm not even six blocks from the hostel when a migraine hits me. These, too, are increasing in frequency. I press my right thumb into the soft space between my left thumb and index finger with all the force I have. Abusing this pressure point is only a quick fix. I'm on the clock here, and time ain't my friend.

Several of the hostel guests had mentioned Halloween being in a few weeks. I'd forgotten about dates and times in general. When you're on the lam, the only thing to celebrate is another day of temporary freedom.

Those college kids talking about the bastardized Pagan holiday gave me an idea. It'd been years since I played dress-up for hacks. A fake ID and semiprofessional uniform will get you through more doors than any online hack. Since I am only going to be at the hospital for a few hours, I decide on the blending of a common and outrageous disguise.

I snatch a black baseball hat with some sporty-sport team on it and wear it backwards like a tool. Then I grab the largest pair of Buddy

Holly glasses with non-prescription lenses at the thrift shop I can find. Finally, with some Halloween makeup, I adhere a long, thin scar across my face, starting above my left eyebrow, creeping down my nose, and ending at my right cheek. The glue itches like fleas are dancing on my face, but this getup is for one night only.

A quick change-up of my posture from upright to a full-on slouch, and I can hide in plain sight.

In the pit of my stomach, out of nowhere, a wave of guilt engulfs me like I am encased in a life-sucking Jello. The truth hits my gut like a one-two punch: if I can't fix myself, I'm not only letting Cyfib get away with torture, but he's also still got my friends under his vengeful thumb.

Be still.

Those words that AldenSong spoke to me after I found Quidlee's body echo in my brain. Those two words saved my life at that time, and they bring me an odd kind of comfort now.

With newfound energy, I march toward the only hope I have.

Chapter Fifty-Three

Never Bodes Well

MetroMed, a two-story medical center close enough to the Mississippi River that you can almost feel its currents whip your face, hustles and bustles with workers marching like colonial ants during the day. Now, just past eleven at night, only a trickle of employees enter and exit the building. This graveyard shift comprises mostly of cleaning crews and some delivery services.

After watching for the past hour, I've finally picked my mark.

The guy would stand over six feet tall if someone knocked some invisible weight off his shoulders. He is out of shape, though not much—his physique looks solid, and he probably just has an unhealthy diet that pumps all calories straight into his spare tire.

With a short afro and long arms, this man is so zoned out that he doesn't even notice when I approach him near the *Employees' Only* entrance. His RFID badge proclaims *Hygiene Director* in large, black letters. A janitor is still a janitor, no matter how fancy the title is.

Yesterday, at a mom-and-pop photography studio, I used their self-help station to make my ID. Starting with a quick photo I took of a different MetroMed badge from a doctor napping under a tree at

Mud Island a block over and adding the right Photoshop tools, I now have a non-functioning forgery of an ID and a fake work order. A lot of luck and these two items might get me through those doors.

My body is still depleted of necessary anti-seizure medication. As a piss-poor substitute, I took a handful of Dramamine, a motion sickness medication, and a couple of gulps of over-the-counter cough medicine. I'm pretty sure all this did is dull my senses, but if it slows my tremors one iota, I'll count it as a win.

Besides, a hack isn't about *talking*; it is about *taking*.

Still, as I approach the man, nervousness hits me about this choice of action.

He gazes at the ground, radiating exhaustion like odor off a hippie.

When I am ten feet from him, his head shoots up and his eyes go wide.

"Holy Moly, you just scared the fire out of me, boy!" His accent stretches the word *boy* into three syllables. "You can't sneak up on people."

For several seconds, the man scans me up and down like I am a ghost. Maybe something in my stance gives me away. Maybe I'm already caught. Maybe I should flee or knock him out and take his badge.

Breathe.

The Bushido Code considers unnecessary attacks an act against the Virtue of Jin, or compassion. I cannot break my code. Right now, it is all that I know that makes me, well, me.

Then it hits me: I've forgotten to show him my fake work order and badge.

Get it together, Tanto.

I extend my counterfeit MetroMed badge, complete with a shattered cover. That part took a few minutes of grinding it between my heel and some rough concrete.

"Huh. Don't worry, I ran mine over my first day too, man." Then he extends his hand. "Judson. You are?"

A tremor starts in my big toe on my right foot and runs to that leg's knee. I turn my back and grab the damaged-by-the water-from-my-near-drowning business card that Dr. Line gave me that explains my lack of communication. After I hand it to Judson, I then yank out a newsletter. The man reads my card, then I put my newsletter in Judson's extended hand.

His eyes narrow. "Some people just shake, but, well, okay..."

The newsletter explains I do not possess the ability to speak or respond in more than shakes and nods. It also has my fake name and explains that I am here to work on updating the software on all the various departments' computers.

"Eric Vice..." Judson's eyes roll up, then right, and finally go straight forward as he stares straight through me. "Like *Miami Vice*?"

I've never nodded with such enthusiasm.

His words seem positive but jumble in my head because a marble of pain smashes between my ears and shatters my glasslike brain. I grit my teeth as my stare fastens to the ground.

"You good, man?"

The shock passes. I gather myself and journey forward. No matter the long-term damage to my body, I must get to this hospital's pharmacy.

As we approach the *Employees' Only* double-doored back entrance to MetroMed, located between the dumpsters and the Mississippi River, Judson runs his RFID badge over the scanner. On the back of my lunchbox, a Hopalong Cassidy relic from the '50s that reminds me of my goal in the hospital tonight, I'd taped a handheld RFID trapper I found in a pawnshop. Hopefully, this device will catch the signal from Mr. Janitor's badge in case I cannot complete my mission tonight and need to try again.

Sure enough, after it grants Judson access, I switch my RFID trapper from *COPY* mode to *SEND*. The door's sensor beeps, and we enter the building together.

I gained my access to this building with ease and politeness. I bet my childhood idol, Mr. Lon, the Gentleman Bandit, would smile in his prison cell for how I handled gaining access to the hospital without the slightest bit of violence. For the first time in what seems like years, things are working like clockwork.

I should've known that never bodes well.

Chapter Fifty-Four

Life More Difficult

We are not ten feet into the building when Judson's voice hits my ears like someone is ramping his volume up and down. The waves of sound smash into my ears. My equilibrium fails me, and I stumble, only catching myself on the nearest wall.

I need meds soon.

A change from the warm, humid air outside to the controlled and heavily purified air conditioning inside makes my fake scar itch like someone is tickling my nose with a damn feather. Judson notices me scratch it. I turn away quickly and hold my hand on my nose. If the police ask him about me tomorrow, it is the first thing he will tell the sketch artist.

"We all got scars," he says, not asking me where it came from and gazing straight ahead, his mind clearly elsewhere. "You're just lucky yours are on the outside."

Before I can think of anything to write, a greeting comes from a storage closet on the other side of the hall.

"There's mah bitch!"

A twenty-something custodian in a blue jumper emerges from the closet. This white boy has cornrows planted evenly across his skull. His cocked head and smooth slitted eyes say he's either arrogant, high, or both. Then one of his braids catches on the pull string of the closet's light and halts his stroll. He tugs at it, laughs it off, and sends us a flash of a three-gold-toothed smile.

So, probably high.

"Dammit! 'Ey, Judson. Who dis?"

This boy is straight out of 90s parody. Like Vanilla Ice in the not-so-classic movie *Cool as Ice*, where he completely appropriates a culture that isn't his. Granted, people in glass houses and all that, but at least I don't visually assault people like this.

You say tomato, I say appropriation, Tanto.

With spotless shoes and enough gold rings to fill Fort Knox, this guy is not the standard janitor. He's rich and either slumming it to build up some street cred, or he's gotten enough prior convictions that the only way he got a job was his dad or daddy's golfing buddy on the hospital's Board of Directors.

"Hey, Larry, this guy's name is Vice, and I guess he works here now. Vice, Larry."

As the white boy runs his eyes over my body, something in my gut turns. Larry is a solid *unknown* variable, the potential downfall of my plan. Tonight is all about using the worst-paid, most-overlooked employee, the custodian, to get my way. Larry throws my carefully packed barrel of monkeys a wrench.

He is more dangerous than useful. Something in his dark brown eyes gleams. It is like he knows something I don't. It reminds me unpleasantly of Cyfib.

I shake the thought away. He's only in my life for a few hours. I don't need to borrow worry about a guy like Larry. In a long-con, he'd be trouble, but hopefully that won't matter today.

"Wait, Vice?" Larry's heavy Memphian accent sounds like a cross between a drunken slur and stoic chop. "Like Don Johnson and motorboats and big hair and shit? Boy, yo mama love her some silver fox Dee Jay?"

Larry's last words echo down the empty hallway like he just screamed out the punchline at a comedy club.

This moron is eating up my limited window like a kid at a candy buffet.

I nod and stretch my neck with my hands on my temples, scanning for cameras while doing what I can to obscure my face.

I snag a forged work order to upgrade software for each computer in the hospital. From a contact on the dark web, I got a vast collection of PDFs and customizable internal work documents for this hospital. It is different from the intro newsletter I showed Judson. While I doubt Mr. Janitor will give me any grief over this or call his superior on the phone, you never know what will set someone off.

"Man, this is...interesting." Judson chuckles at my work order, taking more time this pass through. My heart races and my mind flashes through everything that could have gone wrong.

The work order format has changed.

The fake signature at the bottom is from someone that got fired today.

I brought the completely wrong set of forms.

Judson pats me on the back. "Walk with me."

Shit. Shitty shit-shit. Shit.

My every instinct is to run, or head to the bathroom that we just passed and see if there is a window through which I can escape.

Instead, I walk alongside Judson. We leave Custodian Jerkface, who picks his nose and flicks a booger Judson's way as we depart.

As we stride toward a sign on a door that reads *Administrative Offices,* a chill runs down my spine at the sight of a security guard walking our way.

I'm screwed. My shoes fill with concrete as each footstep toward the security guard goes against my mind, body, and soul. The mountain of a man nods at Judson as his eyes fix on me. Judson hands him my paperwork. The guard, who seems to be ten feet tall and made of granite, takes my ID tag, compares it to the work order, and grumbles.

"I've never seen this before." The security guard unfastens his handcuffs and dangles them in front of my face. "Why do you want to make my life harder?"

Chapter Fifty-Five

Click

Time has equally stopped and is racing. Some grand force is yanking on my heart, and I'm sweating more than an alcoholic when they spot an open bar. Out of all the ways for me to screw the hell up, this is how I get caught.

Not the escape from prison.

Not the escape from the hospital.

Not even the escape from Cyfib's bounty.

It is by two employees that get paid shit and work a shit shift. So much of my life has been about escaping and outrunning things instead of facing them head-on. Now I finally am doing something proactive, and it is blowing up in my face.

The security guard takes one handcuff and clicks the latch as he studies my form.

Click.

Click.

Click.

If Daimyō Ieyasu could remain patient and pacify Japan when he was getting questioned by an entire country, I can keep quiet while this big guy pokes holes in my story.

I am no more caught thirty seconds from now than I am at this very moment.

Be still, Tanto.

The guard keeps his eyes on the form as he strolls behind me.

Click.

Click.

Click.

In front of me are the double doors to the *Administrative Offices.* The keypad to the right is hackable; I know the model. Still, I doubt I can break through in the three seconds before the security guard tazes me.

Maybe if I peed on it. I heard a story about a guy that peed on a breathalyzer in the police station, and it short-circuited, so they couldn't record his blood alcohol content.

The dude did go from a driving-under-the-influence charge to destruction of public property, public urination, and a few other charges though, so maybe that isn't the way to go.

Click.

Click.

Click.

"So, you are Mr. Vice." The guard's flat voice gives nothing away.

A coolness hits my brow as I accept my arrest. Okay, I'm caught. Maybe getting shipped off to Guantanamo Bay won't be that bad.

And maybe a cayenne pepper enema is a pleasant experience.

The man taps my shoulder. "What does this mean?"

I open my eyes, not realizing I had closed them. Before me is the form. A sausage-sized index finger points at one word.

Pentest.

Curse me for overthinking my work order. I spelled out in too much detail that my job is to update the software on all the computers and test the firewalls to make sure that they are secure from penetration, also known as pentesting.

This is what happens when you use a ten-dollar word when a ten-cent one works better, Tanto.

"Dude don't speak, Moscow," Judson says, leaning over to look at the form. "Oh, yeah, that's that new website where people put up photos and shit and other people click on them and share recipes and photos of dinner and stuff. My wife loves it."

Having spent the last decade in either prison or on the run, I have zero way to confirm or deny any of this.

"Why does he have to do it?"

"Hell if I know, man. But people love it. Like that's their life kinda love, man."

I stand in silence as Judson and Moscow discuss the merits of a website called Pinterest that I've never even heard of. I so badly want them to shut up. I am so close to getting the drugs I need that my mouth waters.

Click.

Click.

Click.

I glance at the handcuffs in Moscow's hands.

"Sorry." He frowns and puts them back on his belt. "I do it whenever I want a smoke, which is always."

Moscow hands me back the form. "What do you want me to do?"

Give me access, you buffoon.

"He needs to get to the computers. Any higher-ups working?"

"No."

Moscow looks at my RFID badge. "Yeah, you broke the chip, Human Resources can get you a new one.

Then Moscow screws me over. "Since your card's broke, you can shadow J'son."

"Hold on, man."

Apparently, I'm not the only one who doesn't want to partner up.

"I've got rounds," Judson says.

"You've got garbage to pick up and floors to mop," Moscow retorts, reminding Judson of his place in the pecking order. "I'm not following him everywhere to unlock every damn door."

My dislike for Moscow grows like a weed.

"Fine." Judson reluctantly shakes off the insult and puts a hand on my back. "Vice, let's roll."

As we walk away from the *Administrative Offices* and toward the *Waiting Room*, my stomach sinks and my right hand twitches like lightning runs through it.

It starts as a smell. Corn nuts and piss. Then I feel that hot stinky breath on my neck.

Barca's not here, but my lack of meds aren't keeping his ghost away.

I'm out of time.

Chapter Fifty-Six

Gin Gin

When I started planning this caper, all I needed from the janitor was to get into the building and to be left alone in the Pharmacy. Unfortunately, you only get half of what you want in life, and you make the best out of the rest.

I shadow Judson as the ghost of Barca screws with me and makes me jump at shadows. From the occasional grumble of "Princess...," to his engulfing shadow, Barca is as here as Judson is.

Even with the devil on my shoulder, I move forward. Judson's routine focuses first on cleaning the empty *Waiting Room*, then the empty ICU rooms, and so on. This goes all the way through the empty patient care rooms and nowhere near the Pharmacy, impeding my progress like a piece of lint gums up a zipper.

For hours, we enter room after room. I play my role of stereotypical IT Guy: find any electronics in the room, hook up my external keyboard and CPU that I have in my worn thrift-store Jansport backpack, cut on the hospital's gear, look for anything useful, and then actually update their software.

Just because I am a thief doesn't mean I will not help; whoever is really supposed to be doing this IT maintenance is phoning it in. For a newer hospital, most of this software is really outdated.

Maybe they got scammed.

The Intranet has a few systems connecting to each other. This many standalone systems screams inefficiency because they're not tested and proven like Internet systems. And that equals vulnerability, hence opportunity, for hackers like me.

Judson rocks out with some headphones on while he cleans. This makes me semi-invisible. He starts with ceiling fans and works his way to the floor. For much of his work, I am intentionally in his side view, building trust through optics.

Midway through one of our cleaning sessions, a pharmacist barges through the door. My heart jumps from my chest to my throat. I'd figured anyone making over twenty bucks an hour was long gone. For a second, I wonder if he is another figment of imagination. The guy waves at me, more of an acknowledging flick than greeting, and taps Judson on his shoulder. He whispers something to Judson, then hands him two tens.

Maybe it's just that I'm a crook, but the whole thing screams "illegal" and "under the table" to me.

Turns out, it's equal parts lazy *and* illegal. A common crime cocktail among amateurs. MetroMed's relaxed atmosphere extends beyond the loopholes I've exploited to gain entry. It extends all the way to the point of government negligence.

My hacker brain thirsts, because there are so many possibilities if I wanted to make real money here.

Legally, when prescription drugs are taken from a delivery truck, anyone from janitors to CEOs can carry the boxes inside. Only certified personnel, like pharmacists, can "unpack" them. According to the guidelines on their website, the State of Tennessee defines unpacking as the *anthropology of the state.*

So, as long as the pharmacist *studies* or even *looks at* the drugs, they've done their legally required job of unpacking.

When we finally finish putting all the drugs on the shelf and in the moisture-controlled storage room, I stifle a laugh. The night pharmacist who *unpacked* as Larry, Judson, and I unboxed and shelved tens of thousands of dollars' worth of prescriptions, all for ten bucks a laborer, runs his sweeping arm across the row after row of pharmaceuticals. While he never looks up from his cellphone, the man equally meets the required government guideline of *unpacking* and looking like the laziest priest blessing his congregation.

At ten to three, an alarm on Judson's worn Timex chimes.

"Lunch, Vice." Though the exterior of his eyes are red and their sockets dark with exhaustion, he sends me a wink. "Wanna join?"

I can't remember the last time someone asked me to eat with them. Well, I can. It was Penny. And her invite was more out of the necessity of meeting in an open area because she didn't trust me.

And she never will.

My lunchbox opens with a rusty creak. I'll oil the hinges if I ever get the courage to return it to its original owner. I scan my separated Ziplock bags and decide to start with dessert: two Gin Gin candies.

Eating these were the only reward I maintained while I was busy being pimped out by our Federal Government. Hunting mostly ignorant people in Hackers' Haven gave me plenty of indigestion, as did creating Gakunodo.

The little spark of ginger that I thought would be my refuge reminds me that, at any moment, I can be back in captivity. I'd rather die than go to The Bay. Luckily, the Bushido Code focuses on always keeping your death in mind. Be prepared for it, and always prepare like every fight is your final one.

I shake my head, but the tremor continues. It is not just that I am full of too many bullshit thoughts running around my noggin. I need my meds.

Barca's shadow jumps from the corner of the room and comes nose-to-darkness with me, with bloodied eyes and shark's teeth.

"Vice, you good?"

Shit. I forgot I have an audience for my one-man show.

Without thinking, I counter the momentary lapse by handing the other candy to Judson.

"What you got there?" Judson asks as he takes the blue wrapper from my shaky hands. "Oh, fancy!"

He rips it open and flicks it in his mouth. "Got some bite to it, don't it?"

I nod.

We eat in silence. Not the awkward kind, though. I am dining with a kindred spirit. Neither Judson nor I are trying to impress or entertain the other.

If I was here longer, I might look forward to these times.

Stay on target, Tanto.

An alarm goes off on Judson's Timex. "No time to slow down now, Vice." He hangs his head for a second, like he somehow deserves the weight of this thankless job. I understand self-punishment better than most.

"But first, I need to make a deposit at the bank."

When Judson snatches up a copy of Sports Illustrated from the trashcan in a patient's room that we've turned into a dining room, I realize he is about to pump out a brown bullet.

What he doesn't take with him is his RFID badge, which sits next to his barely eaten lunch.

My window to steal the badge, get into the Pharmacy, find the meds I need, hack the system to remove the bottles, get out, and return the badge is here.

And it's limited to less than five minutes.

Fly, Tanto, fly.

Chapter Fifty-Seven

Badge

I'm not five feet outside the ICU door when I bump into Larry. He holds a giant customized smoothie from one of those fancy health shops. It probably cost more than the food Judson packs for the rest of the week.

"Watch it, man," he says, narrowing his eyes. The last word morphs into the Memphis heard slang of *mane*. "I'll bash your face in if you spill my drink."

I duck my head and scoot around him. This isn't the pissing contest I'm willing to get soaked over. Larry snickers, victorious and reveling in his no-prize of false domination. By the time I round the corner, he has pushed his mop and bucket into a room and shut the door behind him. Glancing around for the security guard, I smack Judson's ID card against the electronic pad for the Pharmacy. I would use mine, but I bet my card only copied the front door frequency, not the interior ones.

A green light flashes. The click of the door unlocking salivates my mouth.

Time check: I now have roughly three minutes. I dash to the closest computer. It's already booted up but requires a password. I flip over the keyboard and find a note taped to it:

Dolph, don't forget I changed the password to 1SierraPapa. I've always said the easiest part of hacking is harnessing people's stupidity.

Does everyone in this industry do this?

The Pharmacy's software is fairly user-friendly and easy to navigate. I find where my anti-seizure medications are stored and run to the shelves. After grabbing two bottles of each drug, I return to the computer and delete those from the database.

I check the system for backups.

I find none.

I could have fun here...

Shaking my head, I log off and dart down the hall. Time is running out.

I dart back into the room just before my timer goes off, to find Judson staring down.

Right where I'd taken his RFID badge from.

Chapter Fifty-Eight

Hungry

Shit. I had literally planned the Pharmacy break-in and the badge theft around the time it took me to take a shit.

Judson is so focused on looking under furniture that he hasn't glanced my way. Like a true empath, he's blaming himself for losing the key instead of asking me if I stole it.

I'm breathing hard from the run. I know this, not because my heaving chest tells me, but because the hot air escaping my mouth fogs up my glasses.

"Where the hell is it?"

As I gently fling the badge across the room like I am dealing out cards in a poker game, I time a cough to coincide with its impact on the tile floor. The metal clasp's *ting* and the card's *fwap* go unnoticed.

I tap Judson on the shoulder and raise my arms in the universal motion of *whaaaaat?* He tells me about his missing badge, so for the next few minutes, we look for it. I keep my distance from where I threw it. For this charade to work, Judson must find it on his own.

During this Easter egg hunt, I sneak to the side of the room and dry swallow four of my newly confiscated pills. From experience, they are fast-acting. By the time Judson yells out *Ah-ha!* a smoothness coats the insides of my body.

I have conquered the shakes. For now.

To keep my cover, I finish out my rotation following Judson from room to room like Funk Monster following me into the bathroom, though not as creepy. I even update the systems on every computer. This confirms my hypothesis: these dedicated servers operate behind a proprietary firewall. That means a good hacker with the Godlike access of a root kit can get away with anything without a buttload of work. If I wasn't leaving all this behind, this setup might just work for Deep Web jobs. Most hackers are trying to break *into* the firewalls.

No one would expect a hacker to hide behind one at a hospital.

Leaving one of the last rooms, Larry attempts to trip me with his mop as I enter the hallway. Perhaps this is a little horseplay to signify I am now their noob. Hazing me as one of them. A Bushi is not only graceful but courteous, so I pretend to stumble, if only for his amusement.

"Cut it out, Thugly." Judson stands up for this stranger, which I appreciate, but do not need. I'm almost out of here.

"Man, you know I hate that nickname."

At the end of Judson's shift, he and Thugly battle it out in a game of Rock/Paper/Scissors to decide who hauls the trash out to the dumpster, which Larry wins decisively.

"Yeah, boy!"

He's maybe a little *too* stoked to win.

Judson shakes off the loss. It's probably the least of his problems.

As I hold the *Employees' Entrance* double doors that lead to the dumpster, the sun creeps between the buildings. Slivers of amber float up and over the Mississippi River. The wet-dew smell fills my nostrils as a smattering of crickets sing in the distance. I wander past the dumpster's metal covers and lean against one of the few trees in the area, soaking up the morning view.

Maybe it's the lack of consistent meds in my system. Maybe it's the feeling of victory when things actually go to plan. Whatever the case, everything about this moment is peaceful. Calm. Serene.

"I see what you're doing, and I can't blame you," Judson yawns behind me. "This is one of the few perks about working the graveyard shift."

The sound of glass breaking quiets even the crickets.

"Vice...don't...move."

Then, out of the corner of my eye, the slither on the ground quickens my heart. My jaw, usually worthless and tight, now flops open. I watch in horror as a snake as long as I am tall, so dark brown it borderlines black, angles across my left shoe.

Bushido demands that, no matter how scholarly or pure of thought or eloquently you have lived your life, if you lose your shit at the time of your death, you also lose all of that good work.

At this moment, I embrace the disgrace and scream like a child that just ran headfirst into a spiderweb. In a panicked attempt to backtrack away from the predator, my left foot catches on my right toe. I plummet backwards onto the concrete.

Lightning shoots up my back from the impact. Scrambling to my elbows, I've lost sight of the snake.

The predator has not lost sight of me.

My killer's pale snout slides up my right thigh and weaves under my right arm, and even anti-seizure medication cannot keep the shakes away. I want to recoil my arm as the creature advances toward my head. Frozen, I cannot.

I close my eyes and move my head back. It might just be the fear, but I swear I feel the flick of its forked tongue hit my chin.

I must not fail my training. If I must die, I will die with honor. Even with years of dedication to the Bushido Code, when this moment of death arrives, icy fear replaces my blood as it courses through my veins.

Then, instead of slicing pain, the screech of metal on concrete replaces what I expected to be a hiss followed by a strike.

When I open my eyes, I immediately recoil. The snake's fangs are inches from my face, almost hovering. Then I notice a warmness on my chest that grows as I crab walk backwards. The predator's detached head rolls off my chest, leaving a splattering of blood on my shirt.

Standing over me, my savior: Judson the janitor, standing in the center of the rising sun's rays. In one hand, he holds a fire axe. His other hand is extended, offering to help me up. Not only has this new acquaintance saved my life, but he also spared me from a shameful death by the creature I most fear.

I take his hand, but the adrenaline surge in my legs does most of the work of getting me on my feet. After a pat on the back, Judson strolls away, as if this last minute never occurred.

What kind of fortitude does this stranger have that an action as brazen as this passed through his character like a breeze through the trees?

If some all-powerful cosmic being exists and guides us, would that being have put a burned-out janitor in my path to save my life? Only now, as the janitor yanks a dangling wash rag from his back pocket and cleans the axe, do I even blink.

"You good, Vice?"

Now that I'm coming down from the shock, I nod at the speed of a bobblehead on the dashboard of a car going a hundred miles an hour.

"I'm going to go grab a broom for the broken glass."

A great warrior, hidden in plain sight.

A migraine sets in right between my eyes. Fear wreaks havoc on the blood sugar. Hard as I try, hitting a pressure point near my right thumb does not stop the pain. I turn my gaze back towards Judson, who is now picking up the spilled garbage. How he is focusing on the spread-out waste instead of his heroic action is beyond me.

Since Lance-a-Little's murder, I have no master. I've been a Ronin, a masterless warrior. Even my mission to protect Penny became obsolete.

I've been looking at it all too narrowly, focused on my own struggles. Not until I almost lost my life, did I gain what is necessary in this life.

Drive.

Focus.

Hunger.

The hunger that Akira Kurosawa alluded to in *The Seven Samurai.* In that masterpiece, when the seasoned samurai with a valiant spirit, Kambei, assembled his team, a village elder provided Kambei with the main trait he should find in his warriors.

Find hungry Samurai. The wise man adds *even bears leave the forest when they are hungry.*

I must now leave my forest and journey with this man.

As of this moment, I decide to do more than merely make amends. Many a Bushido Daimyō took a stance behind a more powerful general when it worked to his advantage or when a debt was owed. I never view myself as a Daimyō, a Lord or Leader, even though that rank is still below Shogun or Bushido Master. I will lower myself, as many a great general did, to serve one of a pure heart and courageous spirit.

Words could never express my gratitude, nor convey the oath I now swear to myself, so I tap the shoulder of the sweeping janitor. As he turns, I extend my hand. His kind eyes meet mine, and he lowers his head as he shakes. I refuse to let go until my heart lets me.

I squeeze, not with strength, but intent.

"You can let go, Vice."

I follow this order, and as of this moment, I am more than Mr. Judson's Chukanbushi.

I am his Sentinel. I have a mission. One that I actually can focus on while I am healing.

And this makes me hungry.

Chapter Fifty-Nine

Zombie

A Chukanbushi, while the most common Bushido rank, is multifaceted. Often, the Chukanbushi serve their lords in multiple capacities, such as guarding someone from harm, both internal and external, or as sentinels. The watchmen do more than study the horizon for enemies. We no longer think for ourselves, but for our generals.

I consider myself this rank. Anything higher would require that I demonstrate little-to-no fear. Today proved I have more fear than I can comfortably admit.

Mr. Judson and I finish the rounds. We do not speak. Not about the snake, nor about anything else. As we depart our work, he waves me goodbye. I return the gesture. As he walks away, I keep still, holding under the shadow of a large tree. I let Mr. Judson get a good ways away before I do what any good vassal would do, given the opportunity:

I stalk him.

By keeping to the alleys and hiding among landmarks, Mr. Judson never suspects my shadowing of his entire route home.

His kindness to strangers does not surprise me. Mr. Judson spreads his kindness like the way a bee pollinates every flower it encounters. It occurs when he speaks to a lady pushing her fussy pig-faced baby in a stroller and makes a funny face that turns a cry into a laugh. Or when, instead of ignoring a sleeping homeless man with a dirty gray beard who is splayed out across the warming concrete, he puts his own audio cassette from the graveyard shift in the man's large plastic cup with "God Bless" on it, along with a few bucks.

I'm certain there is a story there.

We pass multiple bus stops. Just like most cities, Memphis has designated routes, so if you want to get home earlier, it pays to hoof it to the correct one in your sequence. Mr. Judson even greets the driver like an old friend. However, instead of getting on, he marches onward.

Maybe he just gave away the money for his buck-fifteen ride. Maybe he is clearing his head to not bring the work home.

Growing up, Mom told me that Dad transitioned from work to home life the same way. That was until the ease of bringing the bottle home overtook him, stopping in for just one or two drinks at a local dive bar. With the money he saved from getting his buzz directly from the liquor store instead of a bar's up-charge, he justified drinking a pint of whiskey a night over a pint of beer. That pint became a fifth. Then a liter.

And at the end, we found two empty pints next to the emptied shotgun that gave him his final reprieve.

As Mr. Judson approaches a building that is equal parts glass windows and boarded-up ones, he speaks to a young black man in a fast-food uniform who darts across the street, high-fives the janitor, and loops his run to coincide with the arrival of a city bus.

I slip over to a community bulletin board with dozens of resumes stapled to it for cover.

Mr. Judson enters the dilapidated building, so I spend the rest of my morning walking the four square blocks around his home. Only during this time do I realize I am a zombie. The stress of the night, mixed with the double dose of new medicine coursing through my veins, leaves me dragging my feet as I walk the perimeter, encountering more desolation of both people and property.

People at the bottom of the barrel aren't oblivious or immune to optimism. It all depends on your outlook. In *The Shawshank Redemption*, lifelong prisoner Red believes that hope is dangerous, while his counterpart Andy believes it is the best of things and is unkillable. Life has beaten most people down so many times that the mere thought of hope hurts more than it helps. When that happens, the only way to understand life is to suffer, to bleed in order to feel anything, and to scrounge for crumbs in the corners. And that's when addiction and escape rear their opportunistic heads.

This part of the city is so bleak that even the gangs avoid it. Why wouldn't they? If an area is run down, on the point of breaking, you might squeeze a few more drops from a neighborhood's lemon. When it is broken, you won't get blood from this stone. The storefronts are all boarded up, even the corner stores. Citizens hang their heads as they pass me. There is no pride in living among the trash. I know that thought all too well.

By the time I reach midmorning of my stroll, four children too young to be in school near an open fire hydrant and play in the spray. It's an oddly hot fall day. Adults roll out folding chairs and bask in the momentary joy, until the fire department shows up and ruins the fun.

These Memphians are certainly likeable. If I am to be grounded somewhere with a mission, I must become someone new: someone unique yet forgettable.

I need to immerse myself in this *Vice* identity. To do that requires roots. I also have to share, not lie. Bushi warriors became friends with others.

While I am unsure what lies ahead for me as Mr. Judson's Chukan-bushi, I prepare room in my heart for my Daimyō. In my mind, I prepare for work. I will customize my life around him. Even if he keeps me at a distance, I will work toward his best interests. My secondary goal is now to use the access I have to MetroMed to find a cure for myself. One that doesn't require an icepick.

Only then can I return to my mission to stop Cyfib, stop Poseidon United, and end my friends' torture in Hackers' Haven.

I chuckle as my shoes slosh through the puddles made by the fire hydrant's shower.

It's just like me to make a simple mistake, like a bit of thievery, and change it into a complex situation.

Chapter Sixty

Opportunity

I spend the next day anchoring myself to this city. At work, Mr. Judson usually keeps his headphones on with a random tape. I catch the treble-heavy audio that comes from cheap wired headphones when he sweeps near me, so I know he prefers something usually Motown or bluesy. At the start of our next shift, I take the initiative and open my heart, as much as I can, in a newsletter that reads:

Memphis, TN – This reports an embarrassing situation, but a certain IT worker can only communicate through newsletters and printed copy. Shared confidence in this situation is "hush-hush." This story continues in the next issue.

I had alluded to Mr. Judson that my muted situation was nuanced. If I am to grow closer to my leader, I must explain more about myself. And how to work against my limitations.

In all my life, I've always prepared myself, steeled my heart and armored my mind against outsiders. It isn't until I wait in silence as Mr. Judson reads the newsletter during our 3 a.m. lunch that a great wave of exposure crashes against a small surge of comfort in my soul.

Mr. Judson folds up the paper, smiles, and pockets it. "I think I can work within these parameters." He takes another bite of his bologna sandwich and drinks directly from his thermos of hot tomato soup.

The silence in which we eat covers my heart in a warm blanket. It reminds me of time spent with AldenSong.

Never could I believe I would find another friend that could hold a candle to my big Samoan. With Mr. Judson, I don't quite find a flame, but I do see a spark.

Outside of IT work, I am fortifying body, mind, and all the things that they benefit. Staying in one spot is the first step to becoming one with the community. That's why I stay at the hostel. However, with that many unfamiliar faces bouncing in and out, I tire of handing out business cards that read *Mute* on them. The fundamental problem with this is that every other person says this:

"Whoa! Really? I've never met anyone who was mute! So, you can't talk at all? Are you reading my lips? Wait...that's deaf. What's being mute like? Oh, wait, you can't talk..."

This is always more annoying than comical. Plus, I really want to keep my physically-strangling-people-to-death scorecard at zero.

Now, as I walk out of the 24-hour gym I just joined, because a Bushi must always remain combat-ready, I settle into the routine. My average day consists of meditation, physical exertion, shadowing Mr. Judson, and, with my fake work orders, *updating* computers at MetroMed. The private servers at work allow footprint-less access to the Deeps, aka The Dark Web. I limit my access to once a week, but even that is risky as hell. Cyfib and what he did to Lance-a-Little and all the Gogglemen still haunts me. As long as I am free, the warden will jump at any digital shadow hoping I'll be the one casting it.

Currently, the news is reporting KronosPay got crushed by federal investigation. That means there is a void in the digital currency marketplace. As Aristotle said, *nature abhors a vacuum.* Someone, somewhere, is going to pick up those pieces and create a digital empire.

This would be a great way to make the money I need to fix myself. It's risky, but possible. I key up a private screen and set a timer on my watch. If I can't find KronosPay's portal in thirty seconds, I'm unplugging this computer. In ten seconds, I discover the payment portal for the system still on the web. At fifteen seconds, it occurs to me to scan the code. And then, at twenty-two seconds, that's when I see it: the page is a non-functioning simulation. In the code of what would appear to be a non-functioning widget are tracer worms that attach to any IP address attempting to log in.

I unplug the computer from the wall. The zip of power leaving the monitor catches Mr. Judson's attention.

"Hey, I thought that unplugging a computer like that is bad."

Even though he is 100 percent correct, I play ignorant and shrug.

It isn't until I lay my head on my pillow—excuse me—Funk Monster's pillow that used to be my pillow and now has a drooling mongrel on it that insists on sleeping with her nose facing mine, that an idea fires a piston in my brain.

Ever since I started using KronosPay, back before my incarceration, I kept an encrypted file from all the payment distribution centers that I encountered. That, coupled with my prototype software that does the same exact thing, brings a great opportunity. Instead of extortion like the Russians did, I could contact some of the local distribution centers through a fake email address on the Deeps from behind MetroMed's proprietary firewall. I could offer better security and anonymity than the Russians, plus I wouldn't have to work with those thugs.

Who better to set up an untraceable service than someone who used to track and trap people?

I'd charge a 15-percent handling fee for all withdrawals, clearly expecting each client to negotiate to ten. Previously, the Russians were collecting over 50 percent for using their withdrawal system.

In three days, I'd made forty-two contacts. Not a single one of them negotiated the fee down. Apparently, being offered a great deal when all you've experienced is bullying made for eager partnerships.

I dance along the Dark Web and set up several pay portals with fluctuating IP addresses. This cuts the risk of government tracking me down to a percent of a percent. Even so, I also set up a few phantom pay portals, each with six bots exchanging small amounts of currency frequently. This way, the Feds can shut something down when—not if—they discover this system. I mean, I'm damn good at smash-and-grab hacking-and-hiding jobs, but I've never set up decoys like this. I'm just planning for the worst and hoping for the best.

A many-headed hydra allows for hackers and their clients to work in much the same way KronosPay did, except with less intimidation and a greater sharing of the wealth. One day, the Russians will return for their business, just like Barca did when we broke into warden Cyfib's office, the Cube of Death. I've stepped on a landmine. At one point, it will go off.

Of course, this is all before my life took an even more complicated turn at Larry's drug-dealing barbeque.

Chapter Sixty-One

Barbeque

Every week, Thugly cooks up *some sweetass bee bee cue* in his townhome association's community courtyard that is the size of a city block. Surrounded by two charcoal grills and one propane, Larry's cornrows flop against his pale neck as he wipes spilled sauce on his *Blow the Cook* apron.

I go to this for two reasons: one, the wide-open space to run would benefit Funk Monster. Even with our early-morning and late-night walks, she needs exposure to more people than just Danielle. And two, Mr. Judson would be in attendance.

Funk Monster and I break my rule against taking public transportation today and risk cameras recording my face. The reason for this is because the bus stop for the barbeque is in clear line of sight of the courtyard. Just like this outing, I need to add short-term exposures to my long-term disguise.

Having Funk Monster with me at the cookout brings out another bonus besides fresh air: people love dogs, and having a dog at a party means people will focus on her and not me. Plus, I recently bought a bunch of film and a pretty decent Polaroid camera at a pawnshop, so I take pictures of other people holding her and hand them out. People love having their photo taken and this *old yet cool* technology blows away some of the little kids, so it keeps me busy avoiding conversations.

Here, I meet Mrs. Cher, the bone-thin yet kind woman that Mr. Judson has chosen to spend his life with. When we first lock eyes, I recognize something in them. It's not the look in them, but around them: her eyebrows, though pencil thin, seem to drag into her sunken skull. Under the pinkish Sclera, the part of the eye that is supposed to shine white, are bags like dishwasher gel packets between her lower lids and cheeks. As someone who knows sleep deprivation and stress, like what Mr. Judson is doing to himself, her face holds something else. There is a sickness that runs the gamut of her body, from her shuffling, twitchy feet to her dead and dying hair.

Even so, she stands straight before me, shoulders back and her head held high. Whatever demon, whether physical, mental, or other that Mrs. Cher is at war with, she refuses to let it infect her soul. While something is ravaging her vessel, there is an aura around her, like her Ki, or life force, burning hotter than her disease.

Besides her natural beauty and kind yet firm demeanor, I instantly glimpse what Mr. Judson sees in her when she speaks.

"Hello. I'm Cher." She extends her skeletal digits my way.

I shake her chilly hand with a loose firmness, slightly fearful of breaking something. Mr. Judson whispers something in her ear. The word *mute* kicks my brain.

Mrs. Cher smirks and kisses her husband's cheek as he strides toward a frantic Larry, fighting back a flare-up on the propane grill.

"My husband just loves to make me repeat myself." A twinkle escapes her bloodshot eyes. "As I was saying, I'm Cher, and I understand you're more of a listener than a talker. I just wanted to let you know I am glad you are with us today and want you to know I thank God for your friendship with my husband."

She puts her arm under mine and steps us toward a vacant area of the courtyard. I normally fight any type of coercion, but her grip is secure yet loose, giving me a reassuring autonomy, as even as she guides me, I can choose at any moment to step away and her grip would drop. Once we hit thirty yards' distance from prying ears, she continues.

"My husband keeps to himself at work."

At first, I think that this is Mrs. Cher's way of telling me to keep away from Mr. Judson, but then I follow her eyes as they lock on Larry.

"I pray for Larry; he is not...a positive influence. He's an obligation, and some obligations only amount to headaches. I'm tattling, but I appreciate you looking out for Judson at work. He could use a friend like you."

It occurs to me that Mr. Judson probably didn't tell her he saved my life. He's not a person who collects debts, nor good deeds.

About this time, Timmy, their son, a tween with a Boy Scouts book about the Engineering Merit Badge in his hands, darts over. Though young, he's only a few inches shorter than me.

"Hey Mister, can you name all six different types of engineers?"

As a tremor hits, I turn my head away. It's rude, but I can't afford to have any seizures in public. The last thing I need is to wind up back in the hospital because I don't get lucky like I did the last time.

Mrs. Cher counters, "Timmy, Daddy's friend Mr. Vice doesn't really talk to people."

"That's weird. Why?"

"It isn't polite to ask. Accept that that's the way God made him."

The boy shrugs, which is all the acceptance I expect from strangers.

Without missing a beat, he asks, "Mom, can I take apart our toaster?"

"That depends." She crosses her arms. "Can you put it back together?"

"Maybe!"

I twist back to the conversation, and Mrs. Cher jerks her head back and a playful laugh pops out. Her shoulders bounce as if to knock off an invisible weight. Though I barely know this woman, I bet we both wished her husband could bask in a moment like this, one without the world on his shoulders. Even if it is for just one deep breath.

"Uh-huh, no." She taps his forehead with a single finger. "You can if you say yes and mean it."

"I'll get there!" precedes Timmy's run to a spot under the shade of a tree in the courtyard's corner.

"He always has a book with him," she says with a smile.

A car horn blaring in the distance shatters the moment. It's deeper than the average horn, almost like it comes from a ship at sea. An unmarked black SUV circles our courtyard, its tinted windows so dark a laser couldn't penetrate them.

Have they found me?

My spine shifts from curved to a tent pole. Funk Monster is fifty yards away, dashing between a handful of kids. To get to her, I must run toward the vehicle.

As I plant my feet, part of me wonders if she would be better off with these children than on the run with me.

The back door of the SUV opens. My heartbeat slows as a white guy covered in enough gold chains to put Mr. T from *The A-Team* to shame emerges. He chugs from a forty in a paper bag.

Even the Feds aren't that deep undercover.

Of course, I've been wrong about that before.

"Timmy's brilliant, yet focused on only one thing, building, so it is a challenge for him to fit in."

With the threat assessed, I turn back to Mrs. Cher. I want to tell her that I know what it means to be both comforted by your individuality and still desire for a sense of community.

"But what am I saying?" Her words dance through the smoke that wafts our way and covers us in a hickory cloud. "You understand what it means to be viewed as different, don't you?"

If I could've nodded harder, I would've.

"You're a good man, Vice." Mrs. Cher pats me on the shoulder. "Don't change."

And that's about the time the guy in gold chains strolls into the barbeque with a gold pistol pointed directly at my head.

Chapter Sixty-Two

Purple Drank

"Who dis punk?" My would-be assassin holds his baggy pants from falling with his free hand and rotates the pistol sideways with the other.

I breathe a sigh of relief. I've spent enough time on the profitable side of the law to know this is posing, not intent. He's not shooting anyone. If this guy wanted me dead, we wouldn't be stopping for a chat.

Still, I can't help but remember gunfire all around me during the DoGoodR case. It almost killed me and my team.

A line of sweat runs along my facial scar. Most of the time, I forget I glued it on. It is as natural as putting on the large glasses I also wear. I move my hands to my pockets to keep it from looking like I am reaching for the weapon and not escalate the situation.

"You get that gun out of here, you piece of shit!" Mr. Judson dashes between me and the firearm, then knocks the pistol away. "Larry, calm your dumbass cousin down before I slap him so hard his grandma feels it."

"Dawg, my grands ain't alive."

The gunman clearly is not a Mensa graduate.

"That's because it's gonna be that hard, Quentin."

Larry slams down the lid on the grill and stomps over to his fellow thug, takes the gun, and looks straight down its barrel like the genius he is.

"Q-Bar, is that a Volkmann?"

"Yeah, boy."

"Aw yeah!"

Larry tosses the gun between his hands and spins the gold piece like a wannabe cowboy.

"Larry!" Both of Mr. Judson's hands fly toward the gun and push its barrel downward. "Don't play with a gun. You could shoot yourself."

"No worries, dawg, the safety is..." Larry yanks the pistol back, glances on the left side of the gun, then clicks a small handle down, "on." Thugly flicks his head back as he glances my way. "Yo, Confused-cus, if you wanna learn how to shoot sometime, you could join me. I know J'son hates guns, so he ain't invited."

Q-Bar takes my lack of eye contact as the intended animalistic victory he desired. He strolls over and punches me in the shoulder, as if he hadn't just put a gun to my head.

My Daimyō, however, defends my honor and puts his finger in the thug's face.

"No! No, Quentin, you don't get to play this one off, you dumb little shit."

"J'son, I'z just playing—"

"No, you weren't. You just brought a gun out in public where my kid is! Where my wife is! Where your damn cousin and others are, just because you thought you could roll up here all *big* and *bad*. We all know why you own a gun, but that doesn't mean you need it here."

"J'son, that's *exactly* why I need it." Q-Bar steps back and throws his hands to the side like he is shaking cobwebs from them. "You never know when someone's gonna come gunning for me, and I gots to be strapped."

"The only thing you *gots* to be is getting out of the drug business, Quentin. Stop selling that crack or whatever you're peddling."

"Naw, you be getting me wrong. Heroin was 90's, and Crack was the aughts, bro. I'm all about them scripts now. Man, that's the money!"

It doesn't take a rocket scientist to figure out that this After School Special reject isn't the brains of this drug operation. Or any operation.

In any case, I don't enjoy having a known dealer in my proximity. The less heat around me, the less likely I'll get burned.

Mr. Judson angles his finger at Larry and Larry avoids eye contact by pretending to rub something out of his right eye with his middle finger.

"A'ight, J'son, this was my bad. My bad."

Almost on cue, Mrs. Cher whispers in my ear, "Judson hates treating Larry like this, pointing at people like they're children, but Larry's more caveman than man. And cavemen only respond to action, not words."

Larry attempts to hug it out with Mr. Judson, but my Daimyō puts a hand up to keep Thugly at arm's length.

Mrs. Cher adds, "The other Eminem wannabe is a dealer for the local drug lord named Kingfish. We play nice because his dad is CEO of MetroMed."

And there it is. The only thing worse than a stupid thug is a stupid, untouchable one.

Looks like I'll be coming to the rest of these BBQs from now on. My Daimyō needs me.

"Ding, ding!" Larry, now back at the grill, chimes out and holds up a paper plate. Like a cattle call, the crowd lines up and he loads up plate after plate with ribs, chicken, and burgers. I get in line behind Mrs. Cher until Mr. Judson heads toward the end of the line. I wave him into the spot behind his wife. He nods, thinking that I merely held it for him. When he turns to talk to his wife, I take his place at the end of the line, and he never even notices until he gets to the plates. As he looks back my way and waves me forward, I shake my head, though I send him a smile.

A good Chukanbushi must assist his Lord without desiring praise or incentive.

Even though I am near the end of our food caboose, when I get to the front, my plate overflows so much I grab a second one for potato salad, baked beans, collard greens, and cornbread. I plop down next to Timmy, and everyone around me has at least two full plates, some four.

At the end of the meal, Larry and Q-Bar disappear to the back of the heavily tinted SUV. They are cocky enough to leave the door open, thinking that since it shields them on three sides, no one would dare see them from the fourth.

Q-Bar pours from a bottle of prescription cough medicine into a jug and then mixes in some soft drink. The thugs emerge from the vehicle and pass the cup around between each other like a joint. Picking at my mountain of food, I keep watch.

By the time they stumble our way, they're all giggles and slurred speech.

"Y'all...wanna some...Dirty Sprite up in here?" Larry holds out a classic brown-and-black clay moonshine jug. A few adults partake, though none of Judson's crew. When Larry dangles the spout under my nose, chemicals with a hint of mint clear my sinuses. I push it away and Larry downs a swig himself, then lets out a sound like air escaping a punctured tire.

"Day-yum that's good!"

I've tended not to drink intoxicating substances lately, especially since anti-seizure medication and alcohol could relax my lungs to the point where they stop functioning. I believe it was Kansuke, a famous Samurai Lord, who drank himself to the point of oblivion while another Daimyō stormed his fortress and took his holdings.

For my sake and the sake of others, I must keep my wits about me.

"Larry, how much that run you?" The question slinks out of Mr. Judson's throat like it would crawl back down at the first sign of judgment.

"Too much." Larry smirks and stares at the jug. "That tiny bottle cost me two hundo."

"A liter?"

For once, Larry and I agree on something: it costs too much. I understand expensive medicine. My daily combo of either lamotrigine and carbamazepine or levetiracetam and phenytoin, whichever the MetroMed pharmacy has extra of, runs me four times more on the street than a pharmacy's price.

"Huh. I wish. This is for, like, a quarter bottle. Got to make it last, so I live large on the cheap."

"I wish I could just get some for Mama."

From our 3 a.m. lunches, I learned all about Mama's weakened immune system. It comes with frequent chest infections, which equals lots of coughing, especially in the dry air of night. She could avoid emergency room bills if she had access to the necessary medicine.

"Damn, man, I knew she could party. J'SON'S MAMA LOVE THE PURPLE DRANK, SON!"

"No. She just can't stop coughing and legal codeine is hard to get with our insurance."

"Well, she best get her ass to work, cause this stuff is goot!"

Several times during this chat, Q-Bar's eyes trace my body. His pursed lips and creased forehead give away his laser stare that hides behind tinted Oakley's. He's reading me like I am a question, probably afraid I am a cop. I run my fingers along my scar because the Southern heat is wreaking havoc on the glue.

"And, J'son, you scrape together two hunneys, I got the hookup for some nectar."

Mr. Judson's heavy eyes focus off into space as his cheeks sink in, as if invisible hooks in the dirt drag him down.

Right now, two hundred spare dollars is the same as two million for Mr. Judson.

This gives me an idea. If this wasn't for my Daimyō, I would never even consider it. If I have to put my freedom at risk to improve my leader's life, then there is no greater honor.

Chapter Sixty-Three

First Fix

Thirty-six hours later, I am back at MetroMed. The day after Mr. Judson saved my life, I started tracking personnel turnover on the HR computers. Setting up and altering personnel history is something I used in my mercenary hacking days because you never know when you'll need info. Everything from social security numbers to home addresses and salaries are available to a hacker who knows how to work the system. This allowed me, a new employee, to weave password-free access into three personnel files and pay schedules so that I could gain access to any system through the *grandfather approach* and not set off any red flags.

For example, my first target, Stephen Darabont, has over ten years of work at MetroMed. He is a Level 2 employee. That means he doesn't have access to Levels 3 and 4. If I change his status to Level 4 starting today, that might cause a digital alert or a red flag. Conversely, if I go back into his file and set his clearance at Level 3 starting six years ago and then give him Level 4 access starting three years ago, no red flags fly.

For this to work, I also increase Stephen's salary, insurance premiums, and retirement compensation. Sure, Mr. Darabont will get a surprisingly larger paycheck at the end of the month, but I doubt he will complain to HR.

I do this for all three targets. This makes these red herrings much more likely to set off a red flag than anything my minimum-wage-making ass will do.

My pre-Hackers' Haven mantra rings true: Don't just break the law. Shatter it.

We enter the Pharmacy, with Mr. Judson intent on his job, and me intent on doing more than just my usual stealing of pills and changing the quantity in the database.

The tools required for this level of felony are minimal. People think hacking is 100 percent about finding a weakness in the system. In all actuality, it is about 40 percent system weakness, 50 percent people weakness, and 10 percent timing. You must total it all up to a hundred for a perfect hack—an untraceable event.

The "good timing" part of this hack is that a pharmacist finally transferred to another job. That is key, because if management fired one, that means a cancellation of his or her access to all systems within an hour of termination.

But when someone takes another job, like "Reagan, Tibbs" announced in her two-weeks-notice letter about accepting a faculty position at the Harvard Medical School, system administrators get lax about ending their access. That person is not a threat, so that work order is about as important as removing lint from a pocket. Thankfully, it has been less than forty-eight hours since Tibb's last day at MetroMed, and I have her credentials. By the time anyone discovers what's happened, they'll chalk it up to a glitch or be unable to trace the theft after the access code gets deleted.

Of course, after all of this planning, when I shuffle over to the system, the workstation's green power light is *On*. I shake the computer's mouse to discover the system not only *On* but unlocked.

Better to over-prepare, I guess.

In the Pharmacy, there are 'cameras' in the loosest sense of the word. The cameras I checked in the corners on my first day breaking in have overdone flashing lights on them powered by nine-volt batteries. They don't have any wires or antennas extending from them.

They are merely decorative.

It makes sense, in a way. According to a document I came across on the H.R. Server, no one in the administration wanted the responsibility of watching any security footage. That's the problem with using real security cameras. It becomes someone's thankless duty of watching the footage for wrongdoing. A *Head of Security* is mainly concerned with keeping people out of the building, not the goings-on of the inside. Granted, currently no one at MetroMed has any idea that one of the top five hackers in the world has accessed each computer and can easily trespass behind flawed yet proprietary firewalls.

Mr. Judson's routine of cleaning from top to bottom with his headphones pumping out some Motown or Blues brings me unobserved safety as I hack the pharmacy's computer. Of course, I keep a window open in the background, so if he does come over, I am only a click from a page of computer code that will baffle the untrained eye.

I scroll through the placed-yet-not-processed orders coming into MetroMed this week. On the list, I spot my test subject: two bottles of MGP promethazine codeine ordered for one Mr. John Jacobson today. It's just a small order to test the process.

My plan requires a clear head, which is more than a minor problem. I'd forgotten to eat this morning, so my meds are wrecking my train of thought like it just ran smack dab into a mountain. With a cotton-ball-filled mouth and head, I grab the sides of my skull and hold tight.

This will pass. This will pass.

I jerk as Mr. Judson's calloused hand squeezes my shoulder. As my head slightly clears, he points at my computer screen. One featuring an order of codeine bottles.

"Vice, man, what the hell are you doing?"

Shocked, I scramble quickly, my meds turning tremors into energy. As a cool sense of calm hits, I do not run from my crime. I embrace it. Within four keystrokes, I duplicate the codeine order. Then I hit *Order* command. Before Mr. Judson can speak, a ping chimes on the computer like a new email hitting an inbox. Two keystrokes later, the entry disappears.

To the naked eye, no order occurred, but that's the joy of hacking. When done correctly, you can make the data say anything you want it to.

"Man, don't scare me like that."

Clearly, he thinks I deleted the order. That ping means confirmation of the order by the warehouse's computer. On my end, the actual order from our pharmacy just got deleted and is about to be digitally filed away on a partition of the server that I set up.

I need some kind of accountability, so having a list of my crimes will have to do.

Mr. Judson crawls back under the blood pressure machine, gum scraper in hand. He grunts something about me being weird yet harmless, but I know these come from frustration with my interrupting his routine. I understand that irritation, but he will soon find out that I lead by my intentions. My benevolence, well, it rides sidecar to my mischievous tendency to kick the beehive, not for just the honey, but because it is there to be kicked.

Since I am a product of addiction, I clearly forget the truest mantra about drug dealing.

It always starts with the first fix, but it never ends there.

Chapter Sixty-Four

Target on My Back

The next several days run the usual routine: up at 4 p.m., walk Funk Monster, eat, meditate, analyze my side effects and paired medicines, shadow Mr. Judson, eat a snack, take Funk Monster to the park for random kids to play with, put her up, and then start my shift.

I learn a lot about MetroMed, but not what the public knows. The world sees articles about the award-winning staff, breakthrough medical procedures, and worldwide acclaim.

I find the dirt.

This hospital, while effective, isn't efficient. From their books, they have numerous unused rooms, like they built an expansion when there is not a single need for that expense. Dancing through some unpublished meeting notes that were kept from the stockholders, I discover that the builder is actually the Chief Financial Officer's brother-in-law. In the notes available online, it names two other companies that bid on the expansion, but a quick finger trip to the Tennessee Secretary of State's office shows me that those builders incorporated about the same time as the bidding.

And, wouldn't you know it, they weren't incorporated by individuals, but by law firms.

Hiding behind lawyers is like loading up a set of scales, with one side being labeled safe and the other suspicious. From reviewing other internal documents, this Board of Directors appears to be filled with so many yes-men, they might as well be trained parrots.

While safe behind the firewalls, I check in on Hydra-Cash, my open-source black-market payout system replacing KronosPay. It seems to work so well that a Beta version knockoff, Bitcoin, emerges on the main Internet. Their version is a little buggy, like how they are setting up mining algorithms that run on a blockchain that runs merely on transaction data when this is clearly a neural net opportunity, but maybe we've both started a revolution.

Even gangster Al Capone's evil empire led to legitimate changes, like expiration dates on milk.

Rumors from the Deep Web trickle my way in forums. A few other crime syndicates have popped up like termites to take over the money laundering rackets.

I was so focused on the Fed that I forgot about the Crooks. It won't be long before someone comes after Hydra-Cash.

Not only do I have to protect my Daimyō, but now I've got vultures circling my cryptocurrency.

Like a slow sunburn, the target on my back grows.

Chapter Sixty-Five

Damned-if-I-Do

The latest shipment of pharmaceuticals arrives early the next day. Mr. Phone-Addict Pharmacist hands Judson two tens without ever looking up from his phone and stumbles back towards the staff lounge, leaving us alone to do his work. Larry and Mr. Judson take turns checking the manifest, with one unpacking and the other matching order numbers.

Not surprisingly, when Larry unpacks two codeine bottles and Mr. Judson fails to spot them on the list, Larry literally jumps for joy.

"It's a Christmas miracle, dawg!"

Shit. Those weren't supposed to arrive until tomorrow.

Of course, Larry pockets one immediately, which angers me, but when he tosses the second to Mr. Judson, I lessen my glare.

"Larry, we can't just take these."

The janitors argue over right and wrong for the next minute. I want to chime in that this is a victimless crime, but I let them fight it out. They need to work through this *gift*.

"No one will notice." Larry whisper-shouts, probably hoping his enthusiasm will win out.

"Yes. Yes, they will."

"It's two bottles, man. What's that matter?" Larry caresses *his* find without a second thought. "I know exactly what I'm doing with this, dawg."

Mr. Judson stares at the bottle. I can only imagine his inner dialogue right now, a game of pinball bouncing all over his brain pan. I hold my breath, hoping I haven't overstepped, and it isn't until he shoves it into his jeans pocket that I breathe a sigh of relief.

They finish unpacking in silence, though Larry's smile shines so brightly that one of his gold teeth catches the overhead light and almost flicks a migraine into my skull. Now I wish I'd thought to order my own meds this way.

I hope the codeine will ease the pain in my Daimyō's family. If not, well, I tried. I'd rather be damned-if-I-do than damned-if-I-don't, because those that refuse to act on the road of life get run over.

As Larry leaves the room, Mr. Judson strolls up to me and taps the bottle in his pocket.

"Thank you, but don't make a habit of this. Do you understand me, Vice?"

I nod, though something turns in my stomach, telling me this is far from over.

Chapter Sixty-Six

Ten Times Harder

Usually, Larry eats his 3 a.m. lunch with Moscow, mainly because they both follow the Memphis Grizzlies basketball team and enjoy equally rooting for and ragging on the same players. So today, when Larry barges in during my quality time with my Daimyō, you can tell from his skip that he has news he is itching to share, like a kid who's just learned a secret and can't wait to spill it.

"Guess what, y'all?" the jackass asks, knowing full well I cannot answer.

Mr. Judson *guesses* with an eyeroll and shrug.

"So I told Q-Bar about that found Purple Drank, and he took it off my hands for four hunneys."

A chill runs through my body like a winter window pops open.

This complicates things.

Complications lead to compromising positions.

And that is how I get caught.

"For the love of God, Larry, please tell me you at least removed the prescription label?"

"Did better than that, dawg. I bought a completely blank bottle from the Dollar Tree and filled that sucka up! He told me that Kingfish is always looking for new suppliers, and we could make some serious bank if we did like one big score."

Larry, you talking chimp, please stop this vehicle of thought before you drive us off a cliff.

"Larry, that's a horrible idea," Mr. Judson says, voicing what I cannot.

Then Larry does something I never thought he would: he steps back and plants his feet. He's ready for this answer.

"Why? It's been, like, three days, and nobody's noticed," Larry says, simultaneously justifying their actions and speaking to Judson's core fear, getting caught. "And you said that ole boy here got the dirty deed done with no paper trail."

Apparently, my Daimyō had discussed my part in this magical medicine appearing.

I could be mad at their private discussions about me, but I chew my non-working lips and shake my head in disappointment. My role of defender requires diligence, so I must wait for any opportunities to protect, not intrude.

Larry lays out the pros and cons for the next two minutes: money, a near limitless supply, and the timeliness of this opportunity. Reason after reason pour forth, like an expert mason building a house, with each layer of brick higher than the last. It wouldn't surprise me if his family came from lawyers, politicians, or some other creatures that would eat their young given the right incentive. Also, if I didn't know better, I'd say that Larry has cracked a negotiation book or two.

I eventually clap and wave, focusing enough on the conversation to get a headache. I make eye contact with Larry and cut my throat with a finger to shoo the idea away. A spasm hits my brain and I bend over in pain.

"See? Vice agrees," Larry says, intentionally misinterpreting me. "So, let's make it a regular thing. I got a guy that can flip 'em."

"Your cousin can't even tie his shoes." Mr. Judson's comment, while cutting, does not match his tone. "That's why he wears Velcro."

Something in Mr. Judson's voice lingers, like he is actually considering this horrible plan.

"Naw. He wears dem because he's retro. Look, Kingfish can handle the distribution."

The throbs in my head echo my thoughts; Larry is now more dangerous than I ever suspected.

Straightened, yet leaning forward slightly, Judson's eyes flash. Like how a man dying of dehydration might look if he spots an oasis within crawling distance.

Larry's arms flail like a windmill. He is in his own little world, full of floating dollar signs.

"This stuff sells for thousands of dollars. *Thousands*. Man, if we get half a grand per thing, split three ways, that's like, I don't know, real money."

With those actual dollar signs peppering the conversation, Larry hooks him like a fish as Mr. Judson's irises expand. And, just like a caught trout, his mouth continues to argue a losing cause.

"I just don't know how this won't blow back on us, Larry."

"Well, it seems you ain't the man with the hookup. Vice, you down?"

Damnation. The only way to save us all is to lead the charge, but let Larry think his idea influences every part of it.

I hang my head.

"I don't want to go down in life as a drug dealer." This is Mr. Judson's real objection. "I've worked too damn hard and I ain't putting that anchor on my family."

"Vice man has the skills." Larry's eyes meet mine, and he harpoons me with his next words. "He will keep us safe."

Curse you, Larry.

Now my job as Sentinel is ten times harder.

Chapter Sixty-Seven

Malorie Lereau

Nothing proves what you can do more than showing someone what you've done. For this con or heist or whatever the hell it is to work, I'll have to fuel my leader's confidence a little more. I know how to steal without a trace from my days in the Deeps. Most of those crimes were one-offs, so the odds of getting caught were slim.

To set up a *business*, however, will take every bit of my knowledge and some outside help. But that comes later.

Every business is subject to the laws of microeconomics. These are the decisions that revolve around limited resources, such as funds and products. The hardest part of drug dealing is not the police; it is the supply. The best suppliers work an unbreakable masterplan because they are essential. That would force the wheels of progress to stop turning. That's why Mexico's kingpin El Chapo reigns supreme in the land below the free country of Texas.

At MetroMed, I've attached us to a goldmine. With most medical departments running their own silo system, these isolated computer networks that hinder internal communication between the divisions, the orders have minimal chance of discovery from a database end.

From the human side, Larry and Mr. Judson already unload all the pharmaceuticals, so we just have to grab the extras before the pharmacist *blesses* the shipment.

What's more, the work orders already placed for the next six months show the scheduled installation of additional silo programs.

This all means that MetroMed has zero plan to integrate its software and keep me out.

And with prescription drugs in high demand, we move beyond the traditional problems of any other startup business in existence: free supply in a volatile market.

For two days, I let Mr. Judson and Larry argue out ideas on how to do this. They need to burn through their bad ideas before they'll open up to good ones from this fun house mime.

After their discussions, Mr. Judson always puts together a newsletter, neatly handwritten, and slips it to me. While this information transfer allows me to catch more meaning of their discussions, I think it also allows Judson to process the information fully. Most times I do not send a response, because my Daimyō is not ready, as Thugly might say, *for dis jelly.*

Naturally, Larry wants to go full throttle into making one big score. His leading the charge would be a disaster, like a chain-smoker running an oil rig: bad in theory and also in practice. Larry's watched too many crime movies where guns and violence are the first option, which always equals problems from all ends.

Mr. Judson wants to start small, like we did with the two bottles, and supplement his income. He is too concerned about jail time and his family. His mindset is good-hearted yet simple, like stealing from the gas station's leave-a-penny-take-a-penny tray.

What he does not realize is that you cannot do something of this magnitude without willingly and decidedly setting up a gain greater than the penalty.

What we were thinking about doing is illegal, so if you're stealing, steal big. Don't worry about getting caught shoplifting at the dollar store, when you could just as easily be worried about getting caught stealing the Hope Diamond: both mean jail time, and both get you fired from your job.

Then Mr. Judson corners me one night when I am on the Deeps in the cath lab and hands me a note.

Memphis, TN – Two janitors walk into a criminal enterprise and they need a pro to keep the end of this sentence from either being jail, death, or the setup to a really bad joke.

I reach into my hoodie's front pocket and whip out the heavily stained and wrinkled paper that has lived in my pocket for the past six days.

Memphis, TN – An anonymous source has provided a tip that a criminal mastermind works in the area. While the exact business of this more handsome "Al Capone" was unclear, he did inform this reporter that it would be wise to background check Malorie Lereau.

"Who the hell is Malorie Lereau?"

Chapter Sixty-Eight

How Far I Will Go

I pull up a non-tracking search window in a private browser. Not that the proprietary firewall isn't secure enough, but to appear safer for Judson. He walks over to the computer, plops down in the chair I just vacated, and finger-pecks out "Malorie Lereau."

Three links pop up. I point at the oldest one. After a click, Judson scans a news article from the *Boston Herald* about this woman under suspicion for murder. Lincoln Jameson Lereau and his wife, Malorie, were at the top of the social rung in Boston. He was a successful surgeon that dedicated his free time repairing children with cleft palates in Africa, and she ran a charity connecting inner-city youth to the arts. Together they had two children, one that committed suicide at an early age, but they'd built their lives around the second one. The Lereau's appeared to be the perfect power-couple.

That illusion, unfortunately, was shattered when the police found Lincoln's body with Malorie's grandmother's silver carving knife in his chest and arrested her two states away. They found his blood in her car. She'd converted all her assets to cash. She appeared as guilty as a cat with canary feathers in its mouth, and the prosecutor pushed for the case to immediately be put on the docket. A *gold digger*, he said, killed one of the city's most philanthropic men.

Interestingly, Widow Lereau's attorney accepted this momentum to try the case, only because he used an intermediary to reach me.

I was living in Seattle. The Widow Lereau's lawyer represented a few of my...associates. He'd gotten them off on technicalities, and he knew things that would sway a jury without him personally leaking details. He worked like a good lawyer should: on the razor's edge, right between criminal and ethical, though leaning to the side with more money on it.

The job was two-fold: one, hack a series of systems and, two, hack them louder later, intentionally tripping the firewalls.

I opened the next link for Mr. Judson. This article details the hack of her attorney's server and the sharing of his personal notes on the case. The woman had been mentally and physically abused by her husband for twelve years. She never pressed charges and only shared these events with her therapist, who also was her husband's older sister.

Like magic, somehow the therapist's notes leaked to the press as well. The abuse started small and was mostly harmless, like asking who she was just talking with on the phone and went to limiting her with a locked cellphone with only his number in it.

The control extended over when she could see their son, exiled to a boarding school, and banning Malorie from ever talking to her parents again. The abuse went from whispers to yells and from firm holds to bruised faces. Nothing was ever prosecuted.

The therapist hid all of this under her weak-ass firewall.

I leaked the right information, as well as strategic information from the prosecutor's and court's computers to the press. It sent the whole local law system into a frenzy.

That information was just enough to tamper a jury. I leaked a few other scandalous things to fill the courts with noise. No one dared convict an abused woman, and the third link's headline read "Lereau – Not Guilty." In the article, it stated the state had indefinitely suspended the double-crossing sister's therapy license.

Judson reads between the lines. He nods a lot during his second pass through the articles. I've always done questionable things for good money, but I upheld a code. Maybe that is how I justify my crimes.

I know that if I am to be the man behind the throne of this operation, I have to let my Daimyō understand I will protect him and his family, no matter the outcome. He has seen what I do for strangers.

Hopefully, this will fuel his imagination to let him have just a taste of how far I will go for a friend.

Chapter Sixty-Nine

Shady

While I never explain to Mr. Judson how I know so many illegal things, he never seems to judge me for my past. That makes setting up this operation fun.

In order for a grift to work, the mark has to believe that the con has always been like this. This, what we are doing, is merely *business as usual.*

I alter the records for the hospital like I've done for my close-to-three-thousand life-insurance capers: before physically taking anything on my end, I create a plausible history of skewed payments and poor inventory control.

In the old days, from there I could create a false payout history. While those early payouts to me never existed, except in my account, I would go back and edit the amount to leave a red herring, making it seem like the life agent was getting a greater cut of the proceeds. In all actuality, those inflated numbers and money never existed, and the agent never made a fuss, since their files and paychecks were correct.

So, when the policy's premiums mysteriously lowered to their correct amount, I was getting a payment that was supposed to be "pure profit" for the company.

I mean, when you get what you're owed, why cause a stink?

I got the idea from *Superman III* and *Office Space*, except with life insurance companies instead of banks. If you're going to copy something, copy something damned near flawless. Then make sure you take as much as you can for as long as possible without causing an alarm.

Finally, always have an exit strategy.

For our new con to work, I create duplicates in the system, then delete them from the past five years. I even add line items for shipping and handling, while using no actual funds.

Since the accounting software doesn't naturally connect with the pharmacy inventory system, I fabricate a history file. This will add the illusion of normalcy.

The current storage space for the unopened boxes of pharmaceuticals won't handle a giant increase of product, so we fill our need for a larger storage area and uninterrupted privacy in one move. It takes some fake paperwork, but we set up a suggestion box outside of the pharmacy for a week. Then we put up posters for a fake contest by an outside consulting company called Zap Murphy. Visitors and employees are asked to submit for the best idea on how to handle the overcrowding of our pharmacy and the winner will get a nice prize. Wouldn't you know it, our graveyard shift pharmacist won for his idea, which we submitted, for using the empty room down the hall?

The man's so thoughtful.

It is mighty convenient that this very room is away from cameras and near an exit. In addition, the night pharmacist received a nice prize: an iPhone and a two-hundred-dollar gift card to its master, the iTunes Store.

With his phone obsession, this gift guarantees that Mr. Judson and Larry will always unpack the scripts in the private room, while our lazy pharmacist stays occupied. From there, we can move our orders out without drawing any prying eyes.

Moscow, the security guard, might be a problem, especially if he sees us taking stuff out. Even though the storage room is now out of his line of sight, we move the product outside only during his breaks.

Most criminals become convicts by making stupid mistakes. Something turning in my gut tells me that Larry lied to us about changing the codeine bottle before he sold it to Q-Bar. We can't do much about that bottle though. Going forward, there is a container store two blocks from Larry's apartment that carries everything from empty eye-drop bottles to plastic containers the size of a fridge.

Larry wants to get unique bottles shaped like a chalice for the *Dirty Sprite*. While I appreciate his layman's understanding of branding, the safe play is the opposite.

Invisibility is our friend.

The plan is to buy small amounts from the container store. We need a transport to get the product from the hospital to the buyer, so we hit up Craigslist and buy a Volvo with over a hundred thousand miles on it. Again, nothing flashy. A common vehicle in the area with serious trunk space and a dependable motor. The last thing we need is a car so beat-up it might break down and leave us stranded-and-red-handed.

Larry buys it for cash and registers it with a fake ID. Larry proves to be a surprisingly careful driver, so he handles the deliveries.

With the rule that no bottles or containers with hospital markings leave the building, we transfer all liquids and pills on site, then dispose of the empty containers. It helps that Mr. Judson and Larry's actual jobs include trash disposal.

So, with everything on our end set, from storage to delivery, but with no idea of how to actually sell drugs, we do what all shady people do:

We go hire a shady lawyer.

Chapter Seventy

"Innocent"

When hiring a shady lawyer, you need to look for confirmed success, not perceived success. Desperate lawyers wear too-expensive-for-their-own-good suits and name their firms with repeating letters in the phone book, like AAA Attorneys. Professor Quinn Atkins, a University of Auburn professor turned white-hat hacker, used to call them the stutterers.

We're not looking for a one-off transaction, and stutterers aren't good for long cons or hacks. Plus, in a post 9/11 world, the more legit you appear, the safer you are from the Feds.

That's why I have Larry looking through a book the size of two stacked loaves of bread called Martindale-Hubbell, while I'm twenty webpages deep in LexisNexis. The enormous book lists the best-rated lawyers according to their peers in several categories: professional excellence, communication skills, legal knowledge, and more. Larry is ripping out pages for the local lawyers who scored decently in those areas I mentioned above but came in last in one particular category.

Ethics.

No one in this hospital room has time for ethics. We need a lawyer that, though known as a shit individual defending equally shit individuals, is also a giant among men. Someone who is so good at the job that the fellow attorneys cannot help but give praise where it is due.

I'm double-checking each page that Thugly hands me against any case history with pure criminal intent: distribution, extortion, bribery, money laundering, and conspiracy.

Only the classics for our venture.

When Thugly hands me the last page, I recognize the name. While I've never used this lawyer, she has defended some of my...associates. Comparing her on the database and on the ripped page, she fits our model like Thugly fits in at a frat party.

I tap the name with my index finger.

Ingrid "Innocent" Vincent, we're about to make you a whole lot of money, unless you turn us over to the Feds.

Chapter Seventy-One

Time to Dance

Something true from the movies and TV shows about cheap, sketchy lawyers: they rent offices in strip malls that have seen better days. Half the storefronts surrounding them are as empty as a canteen in the desert. The other stores leave something to be desired in the excitement department.

Fred's.

Dollar Store.

Generic Accounting Firm.

Random Spanish restaurant, usually with the words *house* or *taco*. It is optional whether those words are in English, Spanish, or a mix.

And a Sketchy Law Firm.

High-end sketchy lawyers, on the other hand, own their own building. They know that appearance is almost as important as success. That's why Mr. Judson, Thugly, and I are standing in front of a building straight out of a movie.

Four round columns over two stories tall in the front of the building welcome us. As we ascend ten white marble steps, two giant metal double-doors intimidate us. I touch the one on my right. The steel door with intricate carvings of the scales of justice on it burns my hand. It's the midday sun heating the huge chunk of metal, but the paranoid part of me wonders if it is a warning.

"Are we still in Memphis?"

Thugly's question has merit, though he fidgets in his suit like a toddler in church.

"I can't say," adds Mr. Judson as he adjusts his tie, one of three he owns. He told me that this morning. Mr. Judson points at the two yellow-brick steps in front of the door. "But, if we open this door and see a scarecrow or a talking lion, I'm out of here."

I hold my breath as I touch the wooden handle that looks like a giant uses it. Then I push open the door.

The moment we enter the room, cold air rushes over our bodies. A warming glow of recessed lighting welcomes us. The smells of honeysuckle and mint flood my nostrils. To the right of the door is a bubbling fountain the size of a coffee table with water so clear that I want to drink it up.

To the left is a row of chairs. They aren't the basic metal folding kind, or the standard wooden ones that come when you buy a table. They are spacious massage chairs like you would find in the middle of a shopping mall. Next to them are some plain wooden chairs.

"Sweet!" Before I can stop him, Larry plops down into the brown leather massage chair closest to him and grabs the massage remote from the side of it. "Now where is the shiatsu setting?"

I reach out to grab his arm, but Mr. Judson pulls me back.

"Do you think he's more helpful here, or opening his mouth up there?"

I follow Mr. Judson's finger as he points at the reception desk.

I wish we'd left him, but it must be all of us.

Mr. Judson and I walk across the beautiful handmade carpet that reminds me of the rug in Penny's hallway. At the end of the rug is a receptionist desk, complete with the most chipper person I've seen since the florist during the DoGoodR case.

"Welcome to Vincent and Associates. How may I help you fine gentlemen?"

His shimmering silver suit, white starched shirt, and purple bowtie cost more than our Volvo. His dark brown eyes, light tan skin without a single line or wrinkle in it, and a wide smile that covers his entire face make him look like a friendly human Pac-Man with perfect teeth.

"We have an appointment with Ms. Vincent." Mr. Judson's voice cracks as he speaks.

"And this is regarding?"

Mr. Judson and I turn toward each other.

"Supply chain...management." Mr. Judson's voice raises an octave on *management*, which makes his answering a question sound more like a question itself.

"No worries here." Sensing our nervousness, the well-dressed dude stands up, revealing a height at around five feet even. He puts his hands on our shoulders. "I'm Dave, but most people call me Spinee."

"Because you spin records and shit?" asks Larry, his voice wobbly from the massage.

A slow, pitying smile crosses the receptionist's face. "I am here to make everything all better."

Spinee hands us each a clipboard, then narrows his gaze at Thugly as he moans loudly in the massage chair.

"Can that one read?"

I can tell that Spinee and I are soulmates.

"Oddly enough, he has a Master's in urban planning." Mr. Judson takes the extra clipboard. "Now, whether that means a hill of beans regarding his literacy, who knows?"

"Please take a seat and, when you finish the forms, we can get right down to it!" Spinee's smile slinks back for a second. "Also, I am required to let you know that Ms. Vincent does not accept many clients and is very selective."

This is a two-way interview, and she's already vetting us.

Mr. Judson and I sit in the wooden seats. Larry attempts to fill out the form while his chair vibrates. Finally, he switches off the upper body part and scribbles in his answers.

I am midway through the form when a beautiful woman with porcelain skin emerges from a large mahogany door next to the reception desk. Her blond hair sweeps past her shoulders and her devil-red lipstick pops against her game-show-host, white teeth.

She could be anywhere from 30 to 60, but with her ramrod posture and impeccable physique, there's no way to really know. Hell, I know some twenty-year-olds who look older than her.

She marches our way. The thumps of stiletto heels on the carpet stop as she lowers her librarian-level glasses and studies us.

"These two are fine," she says, pointing at Mr. Judson and me. Then she points at Larry. "Great Value's Jesse Pinkman has to go."

"Ms. Vincent, they all came in together."

"Well, shit." The lady clicks her tongue against her teeth as she takes off her glasses. "Two outta three ain't bad. Come on, y'all."

Larry stutters, "Ma-Miss, er, I'm not done with the paperwork..."

"Is your name on it?" she asks.

"Yes."

"Will you kindly sign it?"

We all do. Then she snatches the boards with one hand, takes my pen, and signs her name on the line: *Potential Representation.*

"If the rest of the interview goes well, you can fill out important parts." She turns her back and heads to the large door. As she turns her head back, her hair flicks across her face.

"Alright, kiddos, I hope you've got your tap shoes on, because it's time to dance."

Chapter Seventy-Two

Tacos

"Usually, the massage-chair interview is clear cut, but then y'all had to screw that up by bringing three people and being mostly smart." Ms. Vincent's voice, a whiskey-smokey voice straight out of a 1-900 commercial, is low yet commanding.

It also confirms what I'd surmised: the chairs were a test. If you take the serious chairs, aka not the massage ones, you're a serious client. That makes sense; she only has a three-star average on LawyersSuckHard.com because the happy clients and rejected clients are so polarizing in their reviews.

Hate her or love her. There's no middle ground when dealing with Ms. Vincent.

Our team walks down a long hallway full of awards and plaques fastened to the side walls. Some awards are for community service or pro bono work. Included among the acclaim are photos with famous people, from President Bush to Clinton, and even one with Clint Eastwood.

Ms. Vincent opens another door and we enter her office. It is bigger than three MetroMed hospital rooms put together. On the far wall is an inlaid floor-to-ceiling bookshelf full of brown and black law books. In front of the collection is an oak desk the length of our Volvo. And, in front of the desk, are four comfortable leather chairs with straight backs.

"Please, grab a seat."

Larry takes the middle seat, flanked by Mr. Judson and me. If he says something out of line, one of us can hit him.

Ms. Vincent puts on her red reading glasses, looks over our forms, and glances at a piece of paper that Receptionist Dave handed her when we all left the lobby.

"Oh, first things and all that." Larry, being Larry, reaches into his pocket and puts a dollar on the table. "You know, to make it official."

I hang my head and silently scream in my skull.

I can't say that time stands still because lightning shoots up my spine and makes me squirm every micro-second that dollar is there.

Ms. Vincent glances at the dollar, then the three of us. She drops the clipboards, takes off her reading glasses, and chews on the glasses' temple tips as she glares at the dollar.

"Money is a funny, often abused, concept." She adjusts and leans forward in her large leather chair as her eyes study Larry, then Mr. Judson, and then finally me. "Our country started using paper currency before the 1700s, with the best of intentions. But really, that's when everything went downhill."

Ms. Vincent pushes the dollar bill around and around with her glasses as she talks to us. "While it had a pure initial goal, to fund military expeditions, that idea instantly led to illegal counterfeiting.

It was close to fifty years of that until Ole Bennie Franklin created a paper with raised patterns. You know, you can really tell the difference in the feel of real and fake...money, that is." She taps her temple as her eyes trace the ceiling.

The way Ms. Vincent says *feel* and chews on her inner lip shows me she's *feeling* this situation.

"So, if you think putting a dollar, a concept of trust, down like a made-for-tv movie tells you to do is a smart move, I understand you have one role in this business," she says, pointing at Larry. "Driver."

"Wait, I do more than that."

"Shh..." Ms. Vincent puts her finger to her lips. "Drivers don't talk. As for you two, please remember that I am an upstanding citizen and have no desire to be associated with criminal activity."

"Well, that's, well..." Larry shifts in his seat and reaches into his torn leather briefcase, a recent three-dollar find from a thrift store. "We were wondering if you could help us set up a corporation so that we can funnel—"

"Funnels are for oil changes and shooting beer." She wags her finger as if Larry got caught talking in class. "You want to free up cash flow from *Accounts Receivables*."

Ms. Vincent motions for Mr. Judson to hand her our paperwork.

She glances through our spreadsheets and other documents, before saying, "You distribute tacos, am I correct?"

"We don't do—"

I toss an elbow into Larry's ribs, which works well enough to catch Mr. Judson's attention as well.

"Yes. Tacos."

Codewords are mother's milk to hackers like me.

"Of course, you're in the taco business." She leans back and puts her fingertips together like a CEO in a movie about Wall Street. "You've got to worry about taco overhead, taco supply, taco—"

"We have an endless supply."

Mr. Judson's response raises a perfectly detailed dirty-blond eyebrow.

"Well, all hail the gravy train, then. So, you've set the supply, but you've got to worry about taxes, insurance, paperwork, yada yada yada. The things that keep a businesswoman awake."

Ms. Vincent points at me.

"Why doesn't he speak?"

"Can't," responds Mr. Judson.

"Deaf, mute, what?"

"Oh, Vice can hear, but can only answer questions phrased in yes's or no's with head movements and communicates through third-person newsletters."

I don't like Mr. Judson standing up for me like I'm an infant, but this interview is far from over.

"And him?" She points at Larry.

"Oh, girl, I'm all—"

Ms. Vincent grabs a letter opener from a jar next to her notepad and stabs the blade deep into her notepad. "If you ever call me *girl* again, I will turn you into one."

Larry adjusts himself, nodding.

Ms. Vincent leans back, far enough to get a full look at our motley crew.

Damn, I like this woman's confidence.

"Fine, everybody who can shut up, shut up."

Ms. Vincent spins in her seat as she studies our information. The intermittent flow of air conditioning makes me acutely aware of how much I am sweating.

Ms. Vincent leans over and hits a button on the intercom.

"Lil Al, get in here." A scrawny kid around twenty-three with jet black hair and black Buddy Holly glasses, not unlike mine, dashes in holding a yellow notepad and fumbling for one of the four pens in his front shirt pocket.

"Yes, Ms. Vincent."

"Please start the paperwork to incorporate a limited liability out of Delaware called..." Ms. Vincent's eyes go from us to rolling up and to the right in her head. "Smith & Sons."

"Now hold on, we're not not—"

Ms. Vincent holds up her hand and silences Mr. Judson.

"It's a name. I know they're not your kids. Hell, you'd have had to be like five when you bumped uglies to make that horseface."

Somehow, Larry takes this as a compliment and aims an invisible hat tip at Ms. Vincent.

"But," she goes on, "people love a business that reads *& Sons*. That family dynamic and all that horseshit. Lil Al, we're going to need the...white glove treatment on this one."

"Um, I don't know what that means, ma'am," he says, clearly nervous, but never breaking eye contact with his boss.

Ms. Vincent sighs and hits her intercom button. "This is what employee turnover will do to you, Davey? Give Lil Al some white-glove reading material and get me a reservation at Rendezvous."

"I love that place!" Larry sits up in his chair like the teacher just called on him. "Dry rub, no rub, ribs baby!"

"A reservation for one." She lets off the button and waves Lil Al away. "Lil Al will set you up because most of it is online and I don't use a computer." Ms. Vincent says this line with a layer of pride. "That's why I have law clerks."

It also allows her a layer of plausible deniability.

"Why Delaware?" asks Mr. Judson. A good question that I already know the answer to. *Delaware not only has the best tax benefits in the country; it also has the strictest privacy laws.*

"Because I said so." Ms. Vincent shoos her assistant away.

As Lil Al leaves, she reaches to the side of the bookcase and grabs a Crystal decanter and four etched glasses.

She pours four small bourbons and says, "Shit, forgot. Anyone Mormon, AA, any other reason you can't drink some Pappy's to impregnate this puppy?"

I almost nod, but then realize whatever reaction my meds have to this drink will be worth it to seal this deal.

As we all raise our glasses, a smirk crosses her face.

"To tacos," she says. As we clink our glasses, my guts tighten because this was the easy part.

Chapter Seventy-Three

Tell Him

Before we leave, Lil Al gets the paperwork for our corporation filed. Mr. Judson heads off to get ready for work. Larry has a meeting with Q-Bar. I'm just glad I got a break from all this mental exhaustion. I pop twice as many phenytoin pills as I normally take, dry swallowing them and hoping they work faster that way.

I get back to the hostel, walk Funk Monster, then take a shower. At least, I think I do all this, because I'm still damp and the pup is asleep on my bunk. It's like my mind is cloudy with an 80 percent chance of forgetfulness.

I know a Bushi must always keep his wits about him, but my meds are messing with my brain. I can't remember which part of the Code Duty aligns with. Maybe the Chu. Or Gi.

Chu-Gi sounds like a Pokémon. Heh.

Snap out of it, Tanto. I think this as I'm apparently walking Funk Monster again. I don't even remember putting on my shoes. I check my watch and decide to take another couple of phenytoin pills.

Maybe the effects of a megadose will sober me like a dart between the eyes. Instead, they cover my body slowly, yet completely, like the blob did in that movie. I think it was called *The Blob.*

The next thing I know I'm behind a computer at MetroMed, installing software updates. Time has jumped again somehow. Part of me loves this feeling. The way the marrow in your bones gets replaced with cotton candy. How your muscles go from taut to Gumby-like. How your top eyelid and bottom one kiss each other a lot and want to hug constantly.

At times, I catch outlines of Mr. Judson as he moves around us like he is attached to a series of mirrors, making smaller versions of himself that mimic his every move. I think at one point Mr. Judson wrote me a newsletter, but I have no idea what I read.

Another living shadow joins us: Moscow. The man, whose size is a cross between a freight train and a split-unit fridge/freezer, smiles as he picks me up. I think I am talking to him, but he keeps putting a notepad in front of me.

Since my handwriting is more atrocious than normal, Moscow plops me down in front of an active computer terminal yet leans his mountain-man body over mine and types.

Why cannot you talk?

I answer his question in newsletter form. I explain about my body shutting down and my inability to verbally respond. I write out that my body needs a steady supply of phenytoin, which causes vertigo, and lamotrigine, known to smack your skull with a blurry double vision. I don't know why I gave him the side-effects, but then Moscow glances over his shoulder. I, too, look, because of the other medical toxins coursing through my body, thus fueling my greater sense of paranoia.

When we spot no spying eyes, Moscow types more.

Were you born this way?

I shake my head.

Did someone do this to you?

That question sobers me up for a split second. Moscow knows nothing about me, much less any of our illegal activities.

That's one problem with drugs: they can lower barriers you should always keep up.

So, I do something completely counter to my fake name, fake disguise-wearing self.

I think I tell him everything.

Chapter Seventy-Four

Painful

When I wake up a few hours later, the flavors of an entire vacuum-cleaner bag fill my mouth. *These meds and their side effects are worse than my disease!* My head feels like a mallet-swinging Mario from Donkey Kong has crushed my brain barrels.

My brain is mush. All time and yet no time passes. The next thing I know, someone drenches my body in cold water. I scurry from my spot on the floor to standing like my mom just walked into my room and caught me jerking off. Mr. Judson drops the plastic bucket, and hands me a cup of coffee in a Styrofoam cup.

"Good morning, jackass."

As I shiver, I take the cup. Its warming outer edges squeak as I try to suck all the warmth from the cup.

Mr. Judson drapes a towel over my soaked shoulder. Meeting his stern yet disappointed eyes, my stomach sinks as if I just got grounded. It doesn't help that Larry is standing next to him, laughing his ass off.

"Man, you were wasted last night!"

While that is completely true, it bothers me that Larry is as clear as river water.

The clock on the wall says 6:26 a.m. I must've passed out, but I don't feel rested at all.

I handwrite a newsletter asking Mr. Judson how long I was asleep, but he pushes it away. Tough love from my Daimyō today. When Larry snatches the piece of paper, his smile stretches from ear to ear.

"Dawg, you didn't sleep that long because you only stopped chilling with Moscow like an hour ago."

A haze covers my brain, almost like it is preventing me from remembering what Moscow and I talked about on purpose.

"You two were so chummy I thought y'all were gonna form a traveling band."

I dig into my half-shaken Etch-a-Sketch brain, catching bits and pieces of memories, like a translucent jigsaw puzzle that only shows me part of the night.

Since his shift ended an hour ago, I won't be able to ask Moscow anything until tonight. After drying off, I grab my lunchbox to leave with Mr. Judson and Larry. As I open it, a folded piece of paper lies on top of my uneaten plastic-wrapped sandwich.

My bloodshot and throbbing eyes focus on the one word on it that jabs a knife into my brain.

We should talk, Tanto.

"You ready, dawg?"

I slam the metal lunchbox shut in reply to Larry's question, hoping he didn't see the note. Clearly, Larry didn't write it; his handwriting is so illegible that it looks more like a line chart from a polygraph than anything resembling the English language.

Moscow. Shit. How much did I tell him?

I suck in my gut and exit MetroMed with the crew. We stroll down the street to Woo's Diner, a 24-hour Asian cuisine place with a dash of soul food on the menu. I've heard this type of cuisine called Seoul Food. We've hit it a few times since I started working. It is amazing how much a little soy sauce adds magic to Memphis BBQ. Their brisket-and-kimchi dish with okra is fusion at its perfection. Also, they make an amazing pizza that my hangover craves like a vampire craves neck juice.

At this time of the morning, no one greets us at the door when the bell sounds. I make eye contact with Larry as he burps loud enough to stop traffic.

Glad to see he has at least some side effects from last night.

"Morning. Y'all hungry?" says Mr. Chan, a pleasant man with a perfectly shaved head.

Mr. Judson orders for all of us. He clearly is not in the mood to deal with Larry and me more than he has to. Larry withdraws a pint-sized bottle of Angry Mutt from his coat pocket. This generic malt liquor has a smell that is a cross between stale bread and power-steering fluid. He gulps a swig and holds it near me. I almost vomit on him as the gag reflex hits me. Mr. Chan slaps Larry's head and snatches the bottle.

"You got issues, boy." Mr. Chan tosses the bottle hard enough into the closest metal trash can that the sound of breaking glass cuts my brain.

I reach into my hoodie pockets. My heart stops, then goes full throttle as I realize I am touching another piece of paper.

Oh, no.

As I lean back and slide it out of my pocket, I read it under the table.

Tanto, I'll be in touch.

As Mr. Chan places three coffees on the table, I hold mine instead of drinking.

"Yeah, son." Larry reaches into his pockets and slides our payments over to each of us. "Man, you shoulda seen me. I was wheeling and dealing like there was no tomorrow. Got the big man eating out of my hand. Mister Quiet was pretty good as well, but since I speak, I'll be doing the meetups from now on."

I have no clue when Larry met with Kingfish. If I'd stayed sober, maybe I could confirm what Larry said. Instead, I'm a burglar working with a conman.

Just like a school bus speeding toward a ramp, that idea won't fly with me and definitely won't land with Mr. Judson. Larry's too unpredictable to be left on his own. His eyes are twinkling too much to my liking. I can't tell if it is the hangover causing me to sweat all over the paper placemat, but something feels wrong about taking this money.

Mr. Judson, on the other hand, stares at the money. That is why my next protective action for my Daimyō will be even more painful.

Chapter Seventy-Five

Crafty Little Fool

Outside the restaurant, I wave at Larry as he pimp-walks away, off to spend his money.

I pull Mr. Judson to the side and hand him a typed and personalized newsletter. I wrote it days ago, but just now have the courage to hand it to my Daimyō.

Memphis, TN – It is with great regret that this reporter must inform his editor and all staff members that none of them can currently spend any earnings from their newfound relationship with Smith & Sons.

"You've got to be shitting me."

I've just told a man dying of thirst who had just found a full canteen that he can't take a sip.

I point to the next paragraph on the newsletter.

This reporter has spent many years working in a different industry outside of journalism. This skillset allows the reporter to know the cracks in a system that are not just computer-related. An individual must report any financial windfall to the government.

"Oh, this keeps getting worse," mutters Mr. Judson as he scratches his chin and continues reading.

For example, the public believes that the gangster Al Capone ordered the execution or actions that caused the loss of life for over one hundred people, extorted hundreds more, and committed many crimes that would've put him behind bars. However, none of these actions did him in.

"I saw *The Untouchables*, Vice. I know his income got him in trouble."

Predicting this, I tap the paper.

People who saw the movie The Untouchables *believe Capone's $100 million annual income from illegal operations threw up a red flag for Federal Agent Elliot Ness to put Capone behind bars. That is incorrect. Elliot Ness only focused on the prohibition enforcement, which was unsuccessful. The two things that resulted in Al Capone's downfall were pride and spending.*

The Feds subpoenaed Al Capone to be a witness in a case about prohibition. He refused to show up, stating he was sick. That day, locals saw him at a boxing match. They arrested Capone for contempt of court. Pride started his downfall. It opened the door for more arrests.

It was his spending, not his income, that put him behind bars for good. He lived a lavish lifestyle, and his reported income did not match those perks.

Pride and stupidity got most mobsters. Most were shot. Even Lucky Luciano went away for prostitution.

People rarely talk about the smartest criminals. Like Carlo Gambino. Modern literature rarely discusses him because he was secretive and low-key in his actions, yet he was integral in almost all criminal activity in US history. He never spent time in jail and cooperated with police questioning, probably because he respected the system. He died at home at 74, though the success of his criminal organization continues today.

The reporter would like to make a note that, in order to be safe, we must be legitimate regarding income. Finally, the reporter would like to make a note that he is not any type of animal, which includes a Judas goat, and will not lead his editor to slaughter.

The Money Section *of this newsletter will outline the correct practice for dealing with additional income.*

"So, we're taking all the risks and getting none of the reward?"

Then I hand Mr. Judson the Money Section. As he reads, a smile crosses his face. The weight from my shoulders drops as he scans the plan a second, then a third time.

"Vice, you crafty little fool."

Chapter Seventy-Six

Fix Me

Laundering money is a lot like cooking barbeque; to make it perfect, it takes the right tools and continuous patience. Too many crooks get money and then spend it like it's on fire.

Drug money is not that different from hacker money: it starts dirty, so you must baptize it. With KronosPay, I got slightly less dirty money for my dirty deeds. With Hydra-Cash, we are filtering the money through online banks that are not FDIC-insured, paying a wire transfer fee, and then paying a distribution fee to our outlets, which are former Russian-extorted businesses.

The most challenging part is the bookkeeping, because we are doing something counterintuitive: overexposing our books by showing that we are using a shell company to pay us with money that we already have online. It's a dizzying concept, but the trick is that the IRS have Gap Men, experts that look for hidden information. A Gap Man's key priority is to make sure a person's paid his fair share of taxes. These experts drill down on the gaps between your spending and your income, not at the mounds of data about payments you made to the government. If they were ever to run an audit on a person who overpaid, it would mean that, before prosecuting someone for receiving and laundering money for illegal activities, the US government would first have to write a check back to the criminal.

And that's a headline that would not only kill several jobs in the IRS; it could call for a complete overhaul of the entire tax system.

To break the income down simply, for every dollar that I as a hacker made, I made sure that 50 percent of that illegal money got wired off in a payment to the good ole USA tax-collecting bucket. Sure, that only left 29 percent for yours truly, but when you get over ten-thousand-plus bucks a hack, you'll settle for three grand for two hours' work. Plus, in my experience, greed means insecurity.

The result also meant that I'd wind up with money so clean you could perform surgery with it.

That's roughly what my newsletter article to Mr. Judson says. Bushido states that if I give advice, I must always speak truthfully to the one to whom I am offering that advice, because I am becoming his confidant.

I am Mr. Judson's watchman and advisor, and an advisor full of false truths is a self-serving and worthless one.

My usual process will not work for Kingfish's payments because he is giving us cash. And, despite what the movies say, cash *can* lead to traceable actions by the IRS. Let's say you buy a sports car with that cash. Well, eventually you'll have to pay for the insurance through a bank account draw.

No one pays insurance for something they don't own.

We have turned paper money into income for my Daimyō and Larry. I don't know what to do with my share. My every fiber screams against it, because just looking at a pill reminds me of my overdosed mother. So, instead of selling my share of the haul to Kingfish, I will store my medicine in a low-cost storage unit in a seedy part of town until my gut says otherwise.

Maybe I could find the Bushido section that closest advises about *stealing drugs from a multi-billion-dollar company and then selling them for money to people it might kill.*

Too bad the Bushido Code doesn't have an appendix.

Once the newsletter explains the rough process, Judson extends the cash from the payout earlier to me. I know these bills will not be our downfall, but I honor the gesture and I put it with my money in the Hopalong Cassidy lunchbox.

"Maybe we could use the money to fix your voice."

Sweet Mr. Judson. Just because I am broken doesn't mean it is your job to fix me.

Chapter Seventy-Seven

Flu Season

Thugly, on the other hand, doesn't take the no-spending as well as Mr. Judson.

"Are you guys on crack? Am I being punk'd? Dawgs, we're getting paper. You spend paper. Now you're saying we can't spend it?"

"No, Larry, that's not it." Mr. Judson puts his hand on Larry's shoulder like a parent telling a kid the dog died. "We just have to be careful *how* we spend it."

"Oh, right. That's smart. 'Oh, hey, Mister Government, I want to report that I now make four times my weekly salary and I don't want to tell you how I do it, but here's your cut.' Does that sound stupid to anyone else?"

Mr. Judson raises his eyebrows and meets my gaze. I hate that Larry's rebuttal sounds solid, but I shoo Mr. Judson into continuing the discussion.

"J'son, man, you can't go telling me an extra thousand a month wouldn't help right now."

"Larry, it would be the biggest blessing I've ever known, but we can't."

"Why? Because Confucius over there says it ain't blessed?"

Confucius said that *life is really simple, but we insist on making it complicated*, so another point to Larry.

"No, Larry. Because he knows a thing or two about illegal activities that include more than loitering, trespassing, and vandalism."

"Man, why you gots to call me out on that? That sucker was embarrassing to go to court over."

"Your dad bought the building you got arrested in anyway. But that's not the issue. Remember Vice wants us to succeed, and he's got a plan. Granted, it's a slow one, but aren't you the one who likes to 'slow his roll'?"

Larry tugs at his hair and mutters, "Ain't the same thing."

"Look, we knew this might be a hard pill to swallow, but if you need to spend, please wait a month and Vice'll set up the paperwork to make it look like a family member died, leaving you money."

Larry licks his lips before he asks, "How much money?"

"Dammit, Larry, I don't know. Just... could you hold off on spending any damn money?"

Larry kicks his head back and shouts like a kid forced to eat his broccoli. "Fine!"

In my gut, I know this issue with Larry will be the rash that keeps coming back. Right now, I have bigger game to hunt.

Like ordering our first big supply.

Thank goodness we started this business at the beginning of flu season.

Chapter Seventy-Eight

Fork in the Wall Socket

The next day, I enter the MetroMed building and hand Larry an envelope. He rips it open and, since only Mr. Judson and I are around, he reads it aloud.

Memphis, TN – Obituaries:

Janice Arbuckle Walker of Knoxville, Tennessee, passed away suddenly on December 7, 2008. Everyone who knew her said she exuded dignity, class, grace, distinction, and love in her life and shared all with her family and friends.

Janice was born on April 22, 1938, in Middleton, TN, and grew up in Knoxville just like generations of her family. She grew up in a home filled with laughter and love. She graduated from Knoxville High School and served as a piano teacher until her passing.

Janice preferred the company of a few rather than many. While she never married, she was close with her nephew, Larry Jonathan Vanlandingham. She did not want to list all her family she left behind, because her friends were as close as family.

Instead of flowers or a service, mourners can donate to St. Jude's Children's Research Hospital in honor of someone you love and care about.

"Um, who dis?" Larry asks this as he pulls out the envelope's other contents. A notarized Will. A draft of the obituary that will run in Memphis' major paper, the Commercial Appeal. And a letter from the lawyer handling the estate: Ms. Ingrid "Innocent" Vincent.

To get Thugly some hush money, all it took was for me to hack the coroner's office database, invent a false yet completed work order, and then submit the right paperwork to the newspaper.

Since we are not counting on Uncle Sam's social security checks or any type of insurance policy payout, I didn't even need a body. I just needed an Internet connection. And one of Ms. Vincent's escrow accounts and the accompanying paperwork.

For her standard fee, of course.

"That's your rich relative you never knew you had, Larry." Judson places his hands on his hips like he is Paul Bunyan surveying the hills. "And I bet that is all the paperwork you need to spend that cash in your hand."

"Oh, hell yeah, Vice! Got me a dead aunt and everything! Yo, this is some *Breaking Bad* shit!"

Having zero idea what that means, I'll take Thugly's word for it.

This is not foolproof, but it's enough to keep Larry occupied. Idle hands are the Devil's workshop; mischievous ones shove a fork in the wall socket.

Chapter Seventy-Nine

Worried About You

It turns out that when twice as many boxes as usual arrive at our pharmacy, the attending staff groan instead of asking questions. The delivery guy shoves them in the newly allocated storage room, sweat dripping from under his cap. Our predictable graveyard shift pharmacist, with his head so focused on his new phone that his chin might as well be sewn to his chest, gives Larry some cash for the grunt work of unboxing. Mr. Judson and I *help*. When my watch alarm beeps, signaling the security guard's break, Judson, Larry, and I gather trash to haul everything to the dumpster. Along the way, we fail to spot the dancing fly in our ointment.

Moscow.

The man leans against the wall near the exit. We make eye contact. He waves me over. My stomach knots up, but my feet decide for me.

The next thing I know, I'm handing him back the note he left for me in my lunchbox.

Even though all it said was we needed to talk, my gut bets we've already had one hell of a discussion.

"Judson, I need Vice's help in the server room."

"Sure," Mr. Judson says, more annoyed that there will be one less set of arms and legs to carry scripts.

Larry grunts as he picks up a box with his back instead of legs.

The duo shuffles past us as a hand the size of a personal pizza pushes me through a different doorway. We enter the computer-filled room.

Maybe it is the natural electrical static of the machines making the hair on my arms stand up, but I seriously doubt it.

Moscow takes one of the two metal chairs next to the small wooden desk. He chews on a pen as I sit in the other chair, hands clasped, unsure of what is happening.

"I know you can't talk, but you can listen."

Moscow reaches into his back pocket and pulls out a notepad. He flips it open to the first page, then the second, and so on. I so badly want to snatch the pad from him, halt this tension, and jump to the ending. Unfortunately, it would shift more power to Moscow.

After he reads several pages, he closes the pad. Then smiles.

Shit.

"So, Tanto, escaped hacker from a secret prison, you seem much more clearheaded since we last...spoke."

My stomach jumps up through my chest and punches my throat.

"You showed me what you could do. Impressive. Also, I now know why you are dealing drugs out of my hospital. It is admirable that you want to help Judson. So, I want two things from you."

Double shit.

Since I'm not in any position to argue, I reach for my pen and pad. After I click the pen, Moscow puts his hand on mine.

"No need." The way he pats me is more sarcastic than consoling. "I'll remind you." Moscow leans back in the chair as it squeaks in protest. "One, I get 30 percent of your take. And, two, anything you learn about your Hackers' Haven, you share with me."

The first part I expect. I mean, I would be more alarmed if he *didn't* ask for money. The second part is what gets to me.

What did I tell him that made him want to know more about the prison?

I know it appears that I am considering the offer as I chew on the inside of my cheek. In reality, I have no choice, so I nod. Moscow extends his acre of hand to me.

"Now we get to screw it to your government like they did it to you." He slaps my shoulder as he shakes my other hand like a dog with a new chew toy. "Ah, I love your government. If you use them right, you can accomplish anything. My brother is a driver, way up in it. Good benefits, better connections. That's what your country is about, no?"

Why do I feel that I've made a deal with a new devil?

"Don't worry, comrade," he says, seeming to read my thoughts. "Remember, not all Russians are bad."

I'm not worried about all Russians; I'm worried about you.

Chapter Eighty

What Are We Becoming?

I enter the storage room and have no time to explain what happened. Larry and Mr. Judson look like kids caught with their hands in the cookie jar as Moscow sends a pageant wave their way.

"Shit, he knows."

I never expected Larry to speak first.

"No worries or hurries, comrades. We are all on the same team."

Mr. Judson drops his box and gets in my face. "What did you tell him?"

Moscow slides between the two of us. "Enough to know you need my help."

"And what help is that?"

Moscow holds up one finger and pulls out his smartphone. As he taps on the screen, Mr. Judson glares at me from under Moscow's massive right arm. I slither further behind Moscow's back, just out of view of those stabbing eye-daggers.

Moscow speaks to someone in Russian. My Russian is non-existent except for toasting or ordering vodka. I can tell from the tone that Moscow is not asking for anything.

He is demanding.

Once he hangs up, Moscow puts his phone away and steps away from Mr. Judson and heads toward a whiteboard on the wall. It has a series of names, probably nurses and patient pairs, lined on it in different colors. Moscow erases it and grabs the black Sharpie dangling from a rope next to it.

"You have supply, and you have distribution, and your distribution has buyers." He draws three bubbles next to each and connects them with arrows. "These are essentials in business. If business were pure, then this would be all one needs. This is not the case."

He erases the arrows, then re-draws them going down at a forty-five-degree angle. Next to the tips of the arrows, he puts empty bubbles. From those bubbles, he draws arrows from them up to the original words.

This leaves us with a diagram that reads Supply to blank to Distribution to blank to buyers.

"Moscow, I'm in no mood for guessing games," Mr. Judson says, his white-hot anger shifting back to simmering.

"These types of...ventures...are not without normal business risks. Between your supply and distribution, you need logistics."

"Dawg, we got that with the—"

"Good logistics always has a layer or two of...security."

And there it is. Muscle. Goons. Whatever you want to call it, Moscow is offering guys built like him that no one would jump to steal the goods.

As much as I hate to admit it, that is a Grand Canyon-sized hole in our plan. One or two robberies and Kingfish would have our heads on his cane.

Moscow writes the word *logistics* and then taps the marker on the empty bubble.

"Anyone?"

He points at me and laughs, knowing I can't respond.

I respond with The Finger and a tremor.

"Market factors include competitors moving in on territory, political pressures of police and policy regulators, and so on."

"So, breaking legs and bribery?" Mr. Judson sighs and holds his head.

A simple plan gets dirtier by the day.

Moscow places the top back on the marker. Its click echoes in the hallway. "It is best to not concern yourself with the details."

"And you want what, Moscow?" Larry's question comes out directly, his gaze even with Moscow's stare.

"Thirty percent."

"Shit." Larry kicks his Nike against the wall.

"Twenty." Mr. Judson stares at the ground as he speaks but not because he is afraid to meet Moscow's eyes.

He is ashamed.

"Twenty-eight."

"A quarter it is." He extends his hand to Moscow. As they shake, Mr. Judson closes his eyes and swallows hard and says exactly what I am thinking. "What are we becoming?"

Chapter Eighty-One

For All Our Sakes

I don't allow myself to think about what happened. We're pieces of shit drug dealers right now. That may change, but I can't bring judgment on what we're doing.

Not now.

Since Moscow is now officially on Team ShitBirds, he grabs empty boxes and breaks them down with us near the dumpster. After we finish, he spits his gum out and reaches into his back pocket. He withdraws an unopened pack of cigarettes and holds it like it is a breakable antique.

"They said once you open a pack, despite your best efforts, you finish them all."

Mr. Judson lets the silence linger as Moscow stares at it. "How many days?"

"Days?" asks Larry as he wipes sweat from his eyes.

Moscow closes his eyes. "Seventeen."

"You've made it into the solid double digits." Mr. Judson extends his open palm to Moscow. "Can I hold them?"

Moscow places, not drops, the pack in my Daimyō's hand. Mr. Judson turns the rectangular box of cancer sticks slowly before he thumps them twice on his other hand.

"Didn't know you smoked, Judson."

"Don't." He holds the pack up to his nose, closes his eyes, and takes a big whiff. "Not since my wife got me to quit."

"How long?"

"Oh, who knows?" Mr. Judson checks his watch. "It's not like it's been six years, four months, two weeks, one day and an hour and thirty-two minutes since I had a puff or anything."

"Do you want to do the honors?"

"I do, I really do." Mr. Judson hands the pack back to Moscow. "I'd better give this to you."

"If I open it, will you light up?"

The look in Mr. Judson's eyes is like a lighthouse to his soul. He wants that puff as badly as a starving man wants a steak.

"It won't fix anything or make anything better."

"I didn't ask that, did I?" Moscow wraps his thumb and index finger around the pack's tear-away cellophane tab. He pulls it a quarter of an inch before Mr. Judson shakes his head.

"Do you want me to lie and say it gets easier?" he asks.

"Lie." Moscow takes a big inhale of the pack. "Please lie."

"It gets easier."

Moscow chuckles and pockets the pack.

We scoot past the dumpsters and toward our Volvo as Larry comes out with our generic boxes. He loads a portion in the trunk, while Mr. Judson cracks open a box. He splits the alprazolam, promethazine with codeine, and hydrocodone, along with my anti-convulsants, into a plastic grocery bag and hands it to me.

"What the hell are you doing?" asks Moscow.

"Vice wants the meds, not the cash," he responds and seals the bag before putting it in the front basket of my recently pawnshop-purchased Huffy bike.

"Hold." Moscow grabs the bag and opens it to look inside. "How do we know he will not sell it on the side?"

"Moscow, what in the world screams *street drug dealer* about Vice? He just wants it for his own personal use, or whatever."

The giant studies me from head to toe, and I cover one nostril and pretend to do a line of cocaine off my arm.

At this, Moscow laughs. "I get 30 percent of that value."

"You get 25 percent, even of that till." Mr. Judson's flat response shows me that all that goodwill he just spent on keeping Moscow from breaking his smokeless streak just bought a flea's fart of additional trust.

"Also, when you want to invest in other...ventures, let me know. My family, we like to...acquire distressed assets, fix them up."

That's a bed I will not be jumping into anytime soon.

Larry cranks up the Volvo to head off to meet with Q-Bar. Right before he pulls out, I catch something in his face that tightens my back. Some mischievous flash in his eye that scares me.

He could sell the drugs in that car for much more than a few thousand to Kingfish.

I can't tell if he is going to take the drugs, or the money, or both, but I recognize that glint from many a hacker biting off more than he can chew. There's a high in that thrill of risk. I already know about his drug use, so maybe he is a scheming junky as well.

That's why I am glad I put a global positioning tracker on the Volvo.

As he heads out, I hop on my Huffy.

"Vice, where are you going?"

I ignore my Daimyō's query, because I have to watch Thugly. For all our sakes.

Then I find out that Larry's moral compass is magnetized by money, so he crosses a line so easily it might as well have been made of dust.

Chapter Eighty-Two

The Only Way

Being right all the damn time is one of my least favorite skills.

I pedal like my life depends on it. My legs ache as I arrive at a parking lot in one of the many abandoned strip malls discarded in Memphis. Larry is talking with Q-Bar, which is supposed to happen for this transaction.

Just before Larry exits the Volvo, he snags a bottle of codeine out of the box, as well as two bottles of pills, and hides them all under the driver's seat.

Three total bottles aren't a big deal in a one-off situation. However, that's the thing about doing the wrong thing: the first time is tough, then it gets loads easier with each subsequent violation.

Consider this probation, Thugly.

The wannabe gangsters hug and exchange a bulging envelope for boxes. Neither checks the other's contents. Then they both depart, though Larry heads to the Burger Baron on the corner to grab our breakfasts.

I bike over to the side of a closed bank with just enough room to view Larry as he counts the money. If he skims before we even get the wheels of this caper spinning, we'll have to shut it down. Hard.

Instead, after he sniffs the money a few times, even rubs it on his face, he shoves it all back in the envelope.

At least there is a drop of honor in him.

As he enters the restaurant, I pedal back to MetroMed as fast as my hungover ass will let me, sweating out toxins, chemicals, and malt liquor. I probably smell like a C-list actor on Spring Break. I still feel like I could puke a river. I make it to the hospital's parking lot thirty seconds before the Volvo arrives.

I throw up in someone's half-assed attempt at a flower bed and stroll up to the lowered car window. Larry tosses a breakfast sandwich into my chest.

"Why you out of breath, dawg?"

Mr. Judson reaches into the vehicle, grabs his own sandwich, and replies on my behalf. "He had a mean poop."

"Ah. Been there. Beer shits're the worst."

"How'd it go?"

"Man, awesome. Kingfish was there and told me we're killing it. He wants as much as we could handle. Full throttle."

I let Larry live in his lie. Anything to keep the wheels of progress turning.

Then, out of nowhere, Larry bear hugs me, knocking the wind from my chest.

"You're the man with the plan, Vice. You're my homie." He holds me by the shoulders and says, "Homie don't rat, homie don't break, homie don't run."

I've traded the Hackers' Haven mantra *Burn Bright, Burn Fast,* and *Burn Down* for one that starts with the word *Homie.*

Out-freaking-standing.

Just thinking of the Double-H's mantra clears my nostrils. I guess it is easy to miss your prisons. Larry hands me the stack of cash. I try to wave it away, but he says, "You're the man with the plan, Vice. You hold on to the cash."

I open my lunchbox and Larry drops the envelope in. I take this as a sense of trust. Maybe Larry might not trust himself with the money.

Warriors always must strive to do right, but the Code knows you cannot keep from doing wrong. The world of black and white does not exist, only gray.

Chapter Eighty-Three

A Reminder

In addition to our burgeoning drug empire, our team must do our actual hospital jobs. That's how crooks get caught; they slack off from doing their cover. That's why it was a good time to do my IT upgrades.

As I sit at a terminal in ICU, an alert goes off on a dummy email account I have set up through an outdated search engine provider. My stomach drops, because that is no *You've Got Mail* alert: it is one set up to alert me on anything with Hackers' Haven or Hydra-Cash.

My personal tracking board flashes, an hour and a half before my next medical reminder. When I open a private window to examine the alarm, the entire screen is so lit up that it pulses like a disco ball.

My pulse races as one of my darkest fears comes true.

News article after news article fills my inbox. In Philly, those bastards burned four of our Hydra-Cash fronts to the ground.

I log into the Deeps and dive into our Hydra-Cash forum. It's been days, no, a week since I looked at this. *Curse my ass.* My focus on drug damn dealing has left this venture exposed. Had I paid actual attention, I would've prepared for what the Russians found: a pattern in our security guards' rotation that they used against us.

Shit. They discovered a twenty-minute downtime between shift changes that I thought had been covered already. That might've been in a different city. These slipped through some of our many cracks. Other notes show that two fronts in San Antonio and one in Phoenix had everything from broken storefront windows to broken store owner limbs. I am now equally pissed about the failure in scheduling around-the-clock protection and the hurt inflicted on the people we promised to protect.

My code requires Chu, a focus on duty and honor.

And I have been betraying both.

I follow a hollowness in my gut and check up on our number of stores through the same forum. We've lost over half of our stores. Four fronts have closed shop. Maybe threats or perceived violence took them out of the game. Two stores are unaccounted for, possibly hiding until this storm blows over.

And sixteen Hydra-Cash fronts have converted back to KronosPay, even with the government watching that money laundering ring.

Part of me is worried that the store owners might want to plea bargain with the Feds for working with known criminals and get out of the money laundering game all together. The benefit of Hydra-Cash is that we have no single head. We share power, so there is no one to rat out and trade for immunity. Still, going to the Feds would mean admitting illegal activity.

And only an idiot trusts the Feds with a plea deal because a plea deal is like being asked which perfectly good limb you'd like to have amputated.

For the Russian Mob on the other hand, taking this back is all about pride. Pride fuels them more than homegrown vodka, and they love their freaking vodka. They are scaring people and using blitzkrieg tactics, which is only a short-term gain.

I, too, have failed to think long term. The Russian Mob is thinking about their next move in this contest, probably which stores to smash next. I need to flip the board and make sure they are removed from this game for good.

The simplest solution is to hack them, but I can't risk that type of exposure right now.

So that leaves only one option: put my faith in someone who wants my head.

Chapter Eighty-Four

Deal

Despite running a gang, Penny is just like the rest of us: she has her patterns.

I wait in the same chair at the cafe where Penny and I first chatted. I could've taken a shorter route to getting a meeting with her by going to her home. But that not only would betray what little trust she had bestowed to me, it would also give her the opportunity to drag my ass inside and shoot me, claiming I was an intruder.

The coffee should taste excellent—a fair-trade Guatemalan blend—but my nervousness is filling my throat with bile, and the citrus and chocolaty undertones of the brew are lost on me.

After two hours of pissing off the waitress by refusing to order more than this delicious cup of bean soup, I spot her in the distance. She's across the street, hands on hips and a resting beast face.

She stomps my way, straight into traffic. Car horns blare. Tires screech.

And Penny has no shits to give about it.

By the time she towers over me, I'm staring so hard into my cup of black coffee that I might as well be summoning a spell in a witch's cauldron.

"You've got a lot of nerve." The sentence comes through teeth gritted so hard they could crack a diamond.

Her body trembles with rage and eyes water as she rocks side-to-side. A cobra ready to strike.

I extend to her a piece of paper. She yanks it out of my hand, balls it up, and tosses it into traffic. I'd worried about that, so I pull out a duplicate from my lunchbox.

I actually have five of the same thing. If she destroys them all, I'll take the less-than-subtle hint and bail.

"I told you I would kill you if I saw you again." Penny's mouth is looser, so I hear the complete sentence, but the anger still coats her words. "Give me one good reason I don't do it right here and now."

Lady, the reason is in your hand.

If I didn't have my medical issues, I'd say it.

Then I would be two or three teeth lighter.

Instead, the silence between us does its job, letting her rage simmer into something less murder-y. Penny flips open the newsletter in disgust, profanity-laced grumbles preceding it. She takes a seat after she reads the first paragraph.

"Ma'am, what can I get you?" The waitress had bad timing.

"Piss off." Penny turns to the second page, the waitress a buzzing fly in her focused ear.

"Excuse me?"

"Piss off and get some hearing aids while you're at it."

I extend a twenty-dollar bill to the waitress. She pockets it and leaves as she, too, grumbles some profanities.

"So, why me?"

A fair, if not obvious, question.

"You could go to any gang. There are even offshoots of the Russian gangs that hate the corruption in the Motherland enough to war against their own people."

Not all Russians are bad. Moscow's voice rings in my head.

I don't know why I do it, but I do. I reach into my left pocket and pull out a single, folded piece of paper.

"Again, with these damn class notes." She is more sarcastic than angry. "Fine, give it here."

As she unfolds it, the lone picture I have of her falls out. I have no need for it anymore.

Memphis, TN – The reporter wants to inform his readership that there is a certain online money laundering business that needs the protection and wisdom of someone who understands how criminals work. Further, once the reporter's former prison has been exposed, he will turn himself in to the authorities and disappear from his readership's lives.

"You're lying."

I shake my head. To both statements, there are no lies. If Penny demands a sacrifice for my sins, I will do so. That is what the Bushido Code is all about.

Our eyes meet for the briefest of moments before Penny commandeers my coffee for herself. She takes a huge gulp, almost draining the entire cup, before those previously fierce eyes morph into calm, accepting ones.

"Deal."

Chapter Eighty-Five

The Death Frog

We walk the Memphis streets toward Penny's home. The entire way she talks to me about cities where she has grunts stationed. She discusses her contacts, and in which cities she has yet to gain a foothold. She is talking more for herself, kicking thoughts around her head. She even smiles when discussing an old foot soldier that went legit in Phoenix who may have contacts. Unfortunately, just as quickly as her eyes hit mine, Penny drops the smile and keeps walking.

From the four-page newsletter, Penny understands she will do more than provide better protection for our money-laundering fronts. She will become one of Hydra-Cash's many online heads. Her gang will take over my profit participation portion. This kills my income, because I still don't want to take any drug money, but I have no choice. I cannot do this alone, but I cannot split my focus anymore.

That's when on our walk we approach the Yield sign that means much more to me than the average driver. My blood runs cold as I spot an alert as simple as a white chalk mark that rings in my head like a Klaxon alarm in a diving submarine.

Three x's. Dani at the hostel's mark for emergency.

Shit! Why didn't I walk by here earlier?

I jot down as fast as possible a newsletter telling Penny that I have to go, but that I will be in touch soon. I turn to run, and she grabs my hand, spinning me around so we're nose-to-nose. Her hair smells of cardamom and her breath smells of fruit and wine-layered coffee. She takes almost two seconds to step back. I don't know how to read it, but she still holds my hand.

"Be careful...I still need to learn more before you dip out of this business."

I nod. My sprint doesn't stop for six blocks north and three east until I wind up at the hostel. Winded and my body aching like a truck hit me, I enter the building.

Once inside, I cannot find Dani in her room. There aren't personal items on her bed. She's not here.

After I dart to the front desk to ask the clerk where she is, I never even look at the person working. I just start jotting down my newsletter until a well-manicured hand taps on the glass.

"Hey there, stranger."

Without looking up, my body relaxes. It's Dani. Part of me wants to reach through the small hole in the glass and hug her. Instead, I embrace the calming moment and write out a newsletter, asking what the emergency is.

After I hand it to her, her head kicks back like she just tasted something sour. "I never made that mark."

Well, she's the only one who could've...wait...

I turn my attention upward. The last time I was here, there were no corner security cameras. There was only the one directly behind Dani, one that I know only uses an old VHS tape that is recorded over every twenty-four hours.

I step back and scan the rest of the entryway. No other security measures, such as better locks or keycard entry, exist.

Only new cameras.

"Oh, you got some mail while you were gone."

And there it is. This is about me.

Dani opens a few drawers on her desk until she finds a simple, sealed envelope. She pushes it through the glass hole. It teeters, then thumps to the lip of the desk in front of me.

I have three choices right now.

One, run. Fast and furiously away.

Two, stay here and wait. Do nothing right now. See if I can figure out who knows I'm here and left this package.

Or three, open the letter.

The least safe, yet quickest, thing is opening the letter. Which is why I do it.

I tear open the manila padded envelope with the words *To T., My Hero,* on it. Inside are two pieces of paper.

They appear to be stuck together with glue, and it sticks to my hand. I wipe the gunk on my jeans, instantly regretting ruining them, but that's a problem for a Tide Stick, not me.

As I unfold the first piece, my brain thumps against my thick skull. It's a prisoner transfer order, a 427-B like I had on my back when I escaped the Epilepsy unit.

Except this one is from Hackers' Haven.

To Guantanamo Bay.

For AldenSong.

My ass hits the tile floor. The world spins. I smell something burning, probably from the adjacent communal kitchen. My throat dries like it's in a microwave. Dani dashes to me, but I swat her away.

Cyfib and his damned corporation have hit me where I'm most vulnerable. By failing to protect my friend, I condemned him for my sins. Like Lance-a-Little. Like Quidlee before him. Like a reverse Midas, everything and everyone I touch turns to shit.

Instinctively, my trembling hand opens the second note.

Just because you dragged me from the river doesn't mean I'm not dragging you back home. Love, Dendro.

The only other thing on the paper is more of that glue.

Is it semen? That's so childish if it...if it...

That's when it hits me. I'm not in mental shock. It's physical. There's nothing burning.

It's poison. Just like on the note in the Internet café that put me in my first hospital stay.

As a spasm runs up my spine, I remember what Dendro's full handle stands for.

Dendrobatidae.

The death frog.

Chapter Eighty-Six

They Are Not Invincible

Somehow, I am simultaneously suffering from hypothermia and burning from the inside out. My pulsing eyes want to jump out of my skull and flee the spike someone just shoved into my brain. I clench my teeth and taste my tears in my mouth instead of much-needed air.

I think Dani is touching my arm, trying to hold me upright. My leg muscles snap like a too-far-stretched rubber band as the cramping crumbles me into a ball of pain on the floor. My vision goes in and out as I spot the poisonous pieces of paper near Dani's Nikes. With everything I have, I reach out and snatch up the paper and slide it into the nearby air vent.

I can't let anyone else touch this gooey death.

No one else will suffer for my sins.

My heartbeat drops from thunderous lightspeed to a near stop like it just saw a ghost. Everything sounds underwater. My throat increases four sizes, attempting to rip through my skin while also strangling me.

I have failed. I always do. No one will stop what is happening. Hackers' Haven, The Poseidon group, Mercator Agency, all my enemies have won.

Black and white dots flash before my closed eyes. That's my brain losing oxygen.

I brace for a seizure. That will come next. In my line of work, you hear enough stories about poisons and toxins from criminals who got revenge on their victims.

I just never thought I'd become one of those victims.

The world spins until it stops. Everything hits a quiet level. There is no ambient noise. No air conditioners or lightbulbs humming. No sound of my heartbeat or the whoosh of air leaving my lungs. I taste nothing. I smell nothing.

There is only peace.

A sharp pain assaults my left thigh. Maybe this poison isn't done with me. Maybe it is slowing my muscles the way it slowed my heart.

As my mind fills with regret, my heart does something completely different.

It beats on. No, it speeds up, like I got struck with a bolt of lightning.

I sit up and scream through a throat that would rather suck in air than let it out. The world pulses back into view.

First, I see Dani sitting catcher position, eye level. Around us are other residents of the hostel, some sipping coffee, others recording me with their smartphones.

Finally, I glance down at my leg and see my savior: a yellow-and-orange miracle worker that is the same size as a Home Depot glue stick.

Dani's EpiPen.

This lone device shouldn't be enough to save my life. It is merely designed to help breathing and muscle cramping, and supply additional adrenaline to jump start the heart.

The seizures still should have occurred after I touched the poison. My anti-seizure medicines have done more than just their job protecting me from translating conversations. They must have built up a resistance in my body to whatever is in that sticky poison.

By working on myself, I hacked my own body.

That means Cyfib, Dendro, and the rest of Hackers' Haven and Poseidon United do not know everything about me. They are not invincible. They are only desperate.

And that is the key to taking them down.

Chapter Eighty-Seven

Drown the Assholes

I'm on my feet sooner than is healthy. Dani is attempting to get me in a chair, but I push her away. I'm a shark, in that if I don't keep moving forward, I will surely die.

The pain in my leg reminds me I have a freaking hypodermic needle in it. I yank it out of my jeans and toss it in the nearby metal trash can with a loud clang.

I point at the can and then back at Dani. Though her eyes are still as wide as Frisbees, she smiles.

She's saved my life. *Damn, who hasn't?* If I wasn't already amid fulfilling one life-debt, I'd have hers to contend with.

One thing at a time, Tanto. You cannot serve two masters at once.

I lunge forward to give Dani a hug. She embraces me the way a mother does a child, full-bodied yet loose, and whispers in my ear, "Go."

I step back, shake my head, and point at the cameras.

"Oh, the owner said that those are to lower our insurance deductible."

If that's the case, I have the Queen's jewels in the front of my pants.

I grab the closest chair, slide it under a camera, and hop up to view behind it. Sure enough, there is a transmitter. Thankfully, it is one I am familiar with. It's low-grade and only transmits for about a hundred-yard radius.

That means there is a receiver nearby.

Where there is smoke...

I glance over my locker for any booby traps. Finding none, I grab my gear out of it and dash out of the hostel. Whoever put the cameras here, Dendro, Cyfib, or any other crony, would want the receiver somewhere hidden yet obvious.

After a full lap around the building, I realize my body is on the verge of collapse as it shifts from feeling super strong to made of Jell-O. I will crash in a matter of minutes. With my hands on my knees and my head dangling, that's when I see it. A simple box with simple words.

Warning - Alarm Will Sound When Opened - Thrud Securities.

In Hackers' Haven we used Alviss, a piece of software named for the mighty dwarf that was to marry Thor's daughter.

Thor's daughter's name? Thrud.

Spotting no cameras or heavily tinted windows on the nearby parked cars, I pop open the case. Inside, I find the simple hardware of a receiver and a detachable USB flash chip—the thin rectangular chip standard in all flash drives. Luckily, I always carry a blank USB flash drive in my bag. I reach in, break the plastic cover off mine, and trade them out.

This probably won't work, but at least it offers a chance that Poseidon won't be able to use Dani against me.

I'm running on borrowed time. They've shipped off AldenSong to The Bay. They just tried to either kill or, more likely, incapacitate me so that I wind up back in a hospital. That would get me back under Cyfib's thumb.

I've been treading water way too long.

Now it's time to turn the tide and drown the assholes.

Chapter Eighty-Eight

Be Bad

When our shift at MetroMed starts, I pull Mr. Judson, Larry, and Moscow into the conference room. Even though I have a laptop hooked to a projector, I hand each a copy of the same newsletter. In it, I tell them what is about to happen: I'm about to go away, so it is time for them to learn how to handle this business without me.

Even as it pains me to step back, I can tell it pains them as well. Moscow, who knows me the least, merely changes his posture throughout the reading. Larry, probably not knowing his own subtle actions, sighs a lot.

It is Mr. Judson who keeps raising his questioning eyes as I shift my gaze from his.

Unfortunately, coaching them about ordering meds, hiding the paper trail, and laundering our money is like teaching a hungry panda how to perform heart surgery, except probably less fun.

Even though it is a multiple-page newsletter that explains almost everything, their questions require me to write out response after response on the laptop/projector combination. For example, if you utilized federal documents right, then filing public records becomes your friend. They allow the illusion of legal business activities because they only skim the surface for necessary details for legitimacy: a name, address, tax ID, and bank account that all link to each other. That is a legalized knot with no beginning or end. They could not undo it without a lot more effort than the Feds care to muster.

First, I show them how Ms. "Innocent" Vincent and her associate, Lil Al, set up a series of limited liability companies through the state's website. Each of these links to real brick-and-mortar bank accounts with a hundred dollars in each.

Speaking of money, despite what TV shows tell the audience, there is still nothing illegal about having a shit-ton of cash. However, once you try to spend it or deposit it, that's when it pays to use more than just a lawyer.

You need an accountant.

For his part, Moscow's team would continue to bring a backpack full of cash to Ms. Vincent's firm. There, she would transfer it to an accountant of our choosing.

Just like every criminal enterprise needs a crooked lawyer, it similarly needs a legitimate accountant. Most rookies screw this part up. Your books need to be so sterile that surgery can be performed on them, so I'd asked Penny who she uses. Being the smarty that she is, her guy's resume includes twelve years at the same firm. He also does the taxes for six rock-and-rollers, two athletes, and five elected officials.

I spread the file on one Leonard Frey, CPA out on the mahogany conference table. I'd met with him earlier this morning. At five-foot-one and three hundred pounds, Leonard Frey's combover pales compared to his mustache that connects to Wolverine-level sideburns. If someone ever needed a spot-on lookalike for the year 1976 for a movie extra, Leonard is your man. When we met in his office near the Oak Court Mall, he stated that he preferred that I could not speak. He hates conversations, but said he loves puzzles. No other context, just that.

He's perfect.

From there, Leonard will continue to count, sort, deposit, and send checks for the taxes to the government. We will get serious money from our venture, but not today. Maybe not even this week or month. But it will take time for perceived legitimacy to produce monetary returns.

The rest of the meeting is the boring stuff: a reminder of how to order then delete medical orders. Keeping the night pharmacist occupied. And so on.

As I head toward the door, an arm grabs me. To my surprise, it's Moscow.

"Vice, when you need us, you must contact me." The normal flat look on his face is now replaced with soft eyes. "Remember, not all Russians are bad."

I nod. In the background, Mr. Judson and Larry are in heated discussion. Part of me wants to dart over there and referee the whole thing.

But that time has passed.

As I grab my gear and head out the door, I chuckle.

But what about when I need Russians to be bad?

Chapter Eighty-Nine

Bullseye

My first few nights at MetroMed, while the computers I updated and secured ran through their checkups, I'd done my best to beat this curse, this disease that Cyfib, Dr. Fel, and Poseidon United put in me. I'd read so many medical journals that I probably qualify for a damned doctorate. I scoured the United States for a cure. A private hospital in Palo Alto, California, has some stem-cell trials that are promising, but without immediate results. Boston Med in Massachusetts has started light therapy and has results, but nothing that wouldn't require nine months of multicolored blasting by a high-tech kaleidoscope.

I've since changed my search parameters. I'm not looking for a slow fix. I needed something, if not permanent, then drastic.

Like the ice-pick lobotomy, but hopefully with better side effects.

Who could have guessed that my best bet would come in the form of a small clinic six miles away from MetroMed, in the heart of West Memphis, Arkansas?

This city, separated from its sister city of Memphis, Tennessee by the mighty Mississippi River, has two surgeons, four doctors, and ten nurses. Its website does a fine job of breaking down what they do into one sentence:

We help those who cannot speak regain their voice.

Granted, a lot of what those surgeries include are putting electronic voice boxes in lifelong smokers. I found two medical journal articles about this place. In one, they helped a child who got migraines when people spoke to him. Now he is able to handle conversations without medications. In the other, they helped a woman who was having epileptic seizures every time someone said her name.

That is why, weeks ago, I started this plan. For everything to come together, it took every bit of manipulation I had in my hacker- and conman-arsenal. Now that all the pieces are put into this puzzle, I put this plan into action by hitting the *Send* button.

The false memo in the attachment *originates* from the MetroMed Intranet and looks like a patient referral form from MetroMed's own Dr. Richard Octon. From there, it *appears* that his head nurse, Mrs. Barbara Flash, requested that a certain surgeon at the Butterfield Partners Clinic see his client, one *Eric Vice.*

This surgeon's expertise is in epilepsy. But getting *him* on board is just part of the game. For this to work, I need his whole medical team to play ball.

That's why everything took so long. Even though I've worked out so many details, the odds of this succeeding are still like winning the lottery without buying a ticket.

Today, I stand at the doorway to Butterfield's conference room. The surgeon, his staff, and the nurse in charge of scheduling are on the other side of the fogged-out glass. They think they are there for continuing education. And, while I hope for the best, I also spot the closest fire exit in case this all goes ass-up.

I can't remember a time I sweated this hard in a suit. Liquid fear pushes through my pores like an alcoholic in the Phoenix summer heat. Wearing a suit works two ways: one, people usually calm down or clam up when they see someone approach in a suit. Plus, it lowers the likelihood of anyone calling the police. Secondly, if they call the police, at least I have a suit to wear to jail.

Unless they ship me back to the Double-H.

Upon entering the white-walled room featuring several windows with views of the lush green trees, the lunchbox in my possession clangs against the long oak table, which I nervously stumble into.

With my other hand, I put down and attempt to open my oversized briefcase too quickly. After fumbling with the gold latches, I yank it open. The polished wooden surface creates a frictionless environment and the sealed brown envelopes spill across the table. I scramble to snatch them up and completely fail. One envelope slides in front of a lady I recognize from her online profile: Nurse Stinger. She snatches up the envelope that reads *Gilmore, T.* and then glares at me.

As she stares at it, I swear my heart is beating so loudly that everyone in the room probably hears its drum solo.

She runs her long fingers through her short brown hair, looks at me, and squints at me through small, librarian-style reading glasses.

"Well, shit." She drops the envelope on the table and leans back in her chair and throws her arms wide. "It's another damn audit, or someone's suing us. Dammit, dammit, double dammit shit." Then she points at me so hard it is as if she wants to stab my soul. "Who? Who's suing us, you little shit?"

Since I can tell immediately that this is a woman I do not want to cross, I just start sliding the folders to their future owners.

"Crap, not another one." Dr. Brent puts his head in his hands. "I'm so tired of meeting with lawyers."

"That's why we gots 'em, Doc." Having read her gardening blog, I know that Assignment Nurse Cody is the eternal optimist of the group. "I'll start working on days and times to work around."

"Fine." Dr. Brent grabs his folder and sighs. "Let's get this over with."

For the next few minutes, I am merely a fly on the wall. A symphony of gasps, sighs, muttered questions, and confused grunts and random words, sometimes directed at me, other times at nothing or God Almighty, floats through the room. I cannot blame them for each and every outburst; each person in that room, at the same time, just discovered that, for the last month, I'd been silently improving their lives.

Each envelope has a newsletter that is tailored to that individual. While all have had little deeds done for them, such as better credit reports and parking tickets removed, each also has unique *blessings*, as Mrs. Cher calls them.

For Nurses Stringer and Ronaldo, they discover why their financial situations went from bleak to prosperous. Scheduling Nurse Cody now understands why his getting power of attorney over his unhinged stepbrother arrived in the mail and how that power was given, not earned. Finally, Nurse Gilmore cries as she realizes who helped her daughter do something no one in her family has ever done: get into an Ivy League school that pretty much guarantees her any job she wants upon graduation.

Everyone's envelope explains all the work I've done, except for Dr. Brent's. His packet has a newsletter and a photo. His was the hardest, yet the most satisfying to write.

Memphis, TN – This exclusive report follows the quest for an item long considered lost.

Dr. Robert Brent is one of the top epilepsy surgeons in the United States. He grew up in the small town of Newton, Mississippi, where he married his high school sweetheart, Karen Green. Unfortunately, during his residency in Little Rock, Arkansas, the two lovebirds separated and ultimately filed for divorce. The divorce proceedings lasted for nineteen months, during which Dr. Brent moved out of the family home and into an apartment on the south side of town. It was during this time that Karen sold most of his belongings at a yard sale in a moment of what the court documents described as "accidental rage."

Over the years, Dr. Brent has scoured offline stores and markets and online resources, such as eBay and Craigslist, for one item sold during that "accidental rage."

Despite his best efforts, no such luck prevailed, and Dr. Brent continued his search until today.

When I slide the Hopalong Cassidy lunchbox across the table to Dr. Brent, it is like I am watching a man enter his own surreal world. For a good thirty, forty seconds, Dr. Brent does nothing. He merely stares at it like it is not there. Then, like the box will mysteriously float away, he locks his hands around it. He flips it over, end over end, and studies it like it contains an antidote that he's searched for his whole life.

I've carried this same lunchbox with me through my work at MetroMed. I found it in a junktique under a pile of stinky, faded Care Bears. It was the first step in this long-shot plan that I never thought I'd have to take.

The red color on the lunchbox has faded over time. Dr. Brent swallows hard as his thumb picks at an area on the lunchbox that makes it the real McCoy: the gray metal dents the size of pebbles in the cowboy hat.

"My father..." The words catch in his throat like fishhooks, pulling them back into his chest. He clears his throat, but never takes his eyes from the container. "My father said he used this lunchbox as a shield when the neighborhood kids played BB gun wars with their Red Riders. He told me Rogers Davis caught him dead-to-rights one time. If he hadn't pulled this up as a shield and let ole Hopalong take the shot for him, he'd have lost an eye."

The latch, rusted too, pops loudly when Dr. Brent opens it, and a creak fills the room.

"The first troops into Vietnam came out of Fort Campbell, Kentucky. 101st Airborne. Dad's division. This was before the mandatory draft. Dad...volunteered...because it paid more. He wanted to make sure my sister and I had plenty of food to eat, that Mom had a pretty dress to wear on Sundays to church. Before he shipped out, he gave me this lunchbox to take to school. He said that, in case bullies ever bothered me, well, I had a shield. I had my protection."

He smells the interior, which I know has no odor, but memory is a funny thing. There's no telling what is going through his mind.

"It didn't even happen during the first skirmish." Those fishhooks return and snare the words. No one in the room speaks.

"Ahem, excuse me. Or the second assault. No, it happened one random night, and it wasn't even the enemy. A sleep-deprived, scared kid trying to protect his country jumped at a shadow. He did what was he was trained to do: kill. He forgot to ask or give a code word or whatever. He freaked out and shot at a man returning from the latrine."

I know this story as well as my own. I've read interview after interview about how Dr. Brent supports this military family here or leads this veterans' fundraiser there. It doesn't make the tears on my cheek sting any less.

"As my father bled out in the arms of his killer, he said that he forgave his friend for this mistake, that he loved Jesus, and the only thing he'd miss was seeing his kids grow up and his wife grow more beautiful every single day."

Tears flow down Dr. Brent's face as well, and on the faces of the nurses. There is something about this moment, agony coupled with love, that words cannot convey or even prepare me for.

"After Mom's house burned, this lunchbox, the name he gave me, and an etching of his name on the sixth panel, fourth row of the Vietnam Memorial, were all I had of him."

With a sniff and snort, Dr. Brent wipes away the tears. "Stranger, you certainly know how to make an entrance." He sends me a half-smile as his bloodshot eyes twinkle beneath the joyful pain. "How can we help you?"

That's when I reach into the briefcase and grab the last envelope and slide it across the table to Dr. Brent. My soul sends something out to the universe. I don't know if it is a wish, a prayer, or something more.

I've tossed my Hail Mary. I've fired my lone shot. Now to see if it hits the bullseye, because anything less will screw me.

Chapter Ninety

Gladiator

I know Dr. Brent might ask for a family medical history to start his work with, but I don't know much. We have no file folder of detailed medical traumas. We're just a bunch of white trash that floated in from various oceans.

In the folder I passed to Dr. Brent are all my medical files from my brief stint in the epilepsy hospital and every bit of information I'd stored away about any medical procedures available to fix me. Some are from medical journals, but most are from other resources.

"You went on WebMD.com, didn't you?" he asks, with a massive sigh dripping in. It reminds me of my mother asking me if I ate the last piece of cheese in the fridge while staring at the empty cellophane wrapper in my hand. "Everyone on the internet thinks themselves a medical expert."

Each thump of his hand as Dr. Brent slams down each page on the wood table tightens my sphincter.

"Are you kidding me?"

I don't have to guess which page he is on.

"A temporal lobotomy is archaic, inhumane, and downright bizarre for these symptoms. You don't fit the parameters that even consider this procedure. This, at best, has a 10, maybe 12 percent chance of stopping the seizures and, at worst, could reduce you to a vegetable."

I want to grab his Mont Blanc pen from his shirt pocket and jot out why I included that idea: *I want this to stop. I need this to end.* Part of me doesn't even care if I have to end *who I am* to become *functional* because a little of me is getting stripped away every freaking day because of this disease.

"Dr. Brent, we're not seriously considering this course of action, are we?"

The first doubter has spoken up: Nurse Gilmore. I'd almost forgotten that everyone else is still in the room.

Even though she's created a crack in my plan's dam, she used plurality when she spoke.

We're not, not *you're not.*

"I'm merely evaluating." Another thump of paper kicks me in the teeth. "Talking is not action."

"A judge might consider this conspiracy." Scheduling Nurse Cody tosses that grenade, though I am not sure if that's how *conspiracy* charges work.

"Which law school did you attend?" Nurse Stinger comes to my aid.

Fixing her credit score was the best twenty minutes of work I've spent.

"You know what I'm saying." Cody's tone is flatter than snarky, so maybe that explosion was a dud.

"Uh huh."

"Look, I think if we discuss this as a case study, then it is not against hospital regulations."

Nurse Gilmore's comment hangs like a falling leaf in the autumn wind, dancing through everyone's minds.

After a few seconds of quiet, the room erupts. Stinger grabs a giant whiteboard on a cart from the back wall. Gilmore hooks the laptop to a USB cable that extends from an overhead projector that is flush against the ceiling. Ronaldo dims the lights. Cody pushes a button on the wall and a screen lowers to catch the projector's beam.

Without being prompted, the team jumps into high gear. I'm invisible, which is exactly how I like it.

Dr. Brent rarely pulls his head up from his notepad as he asks questions. His team narrows down possible answers. They pore through medical databases, private forums for medical personnel, and online portals. They bat medications back and forth, but the team dismisses most of them. Everything from light therapy to chemotherapy to unpronounceable words ping pong around the room.

The well-oiled machine of a brain trust repeats this process over and over for an hour. I try to follow but I'm too lay and too exhausted to stay in it fully. At one point, I rest my head on the wood table, and before I know it, my eyelids fill with concrete.

My mind floats joyfully over the idea of getting my life back. Yet I picture Lance-a-Little's Gogglemen, all lobotomized yet functional, standing around me in a circle. Judging me for not following the path they paved for me.

"Hello, princess."

Awoken in a pool of my drool, I shoot up. Nurse Cody slides a box of tissues my way. I do a half-assed job of cleaning myself up, wipe my eyes, and shake the pixie dust from my brain.

"We've decided." Dr. Brent closes his notebook and removes his reading glasses as he meets my gaze.

My stomach drops into my shoes. Unless I just slept for several hours, they've decided way too quickly for a *yes*.

Just when I thought I had found my gladiator, he's realized this isn't his fight.

"I won't do this surgery."

Part of me understands. A total stranger is not worth the risk.

Then the silver-haired man rises from the table, strolls over to me, and, of all things, blasts a gleaming white smile my way.

"Stranger, have you ever read *Dilbert*?"

Chapter Ninety-One

All or Nothing

I've dealt with a lot of odd and even confounding things in my life. I've grown up in the shadows of society and survived through an ancient Code created by men in dresses. I've broken into more banks and financial institutions than all the Mafia combined. I've even lived as an indentured servant slash lab rat in a covert prison.

None of that could have prepared me for the eventuality that, in a world surrounded by science and medicine, the key to my salvation would come in the form of a cartoon character lacking pupils?

With the Hopalong Cassidy lunchbox under his arm, Dr. Brent escorts me to his office. He waves his staff off.

On his back wall are rows of medical journal paperbacks in front of a large, dark oak desk. Dr. Brent turns his back to me to study the medical cases listed on the spine of the brown books.

Is this a stalling technique, or is he really looking?

Hesitation is powerful. Many hacks rely on inaction as much as action. One time I needed to get into an apartment building for a client. She needed to get her *adult hugging* tape from her ex-boyfriend's hard drive because he was threatening to send it to all her friends. I couldn't get to it online because the bastard changed computers, cursed Black Friday sales.

So, I ordered the stinkiest pizza from the most authentically Italian restaurant I could, complete with anchovies, extra garlic, and roasted radishes. Then I kept it in the sun for a whole day. When I took that steaming pile of rotten donkey droppings to the key-carded and security-guarded building, all I had to do was wait in sniffing distance of the pregnant door lady.

Yes, it was a low blow, but after she almost threw up, she let me in to deliver the stinkfest. Once inside, all I had to do was pick the lock, snatch-and-grab the old PC, and make my getaway. I snuck it out in my pizza-warming bag. And before I left, I hid the pizza in the guy's sofa cushions as a *F U Matthew* from the client.

On my way out, I slipped the guard a twenty, saying the customer tipped me *too much*.

Back in reality, Dr. Brent pulls down three books. He flips through one and puts it in a large stack off to the side. Apparently, that's his *To Be Filed* stack.

"Nope, that's not where I read it," he says, then sucks his teeth for a good minute, leaning over his keyboard and typing away. The reflection of the screen in his glasses shows me some database that I've never had access to, but now want. I shift in the leather chair, trying to not make that pooting sound that cotton does on dead cow, until finally, the doctor's bushy black eyebrows raise. "Hold on—I've got it. Look here." Dr. Brent rotates the monitor toward me and slides the computer's mouse over to me. "You peruse that site."

As I lean forward, Dr. Brent yanks two medical journals off the shelf.

"I'll be jotting down some notes of my own."

As I read the article, it makes me think about my time under Dr. Line's care. My grandfather used to tell me that when you only have a hammer, every problem looks like a nail. Dr. Line was the epilepsy hammer and, since my symptoms fit those of auditory epilepsy, he treated me the only way he could.

Neither of us would've thought I had more than one disease running loose in this blood-sack vessel.

The article Dr. Brent put before me features an interview with Scott Adams, the creator of the cartoon character Dilbert.

In a separate web browser window, I open some comic strips so that I could figure out who the hell this character is. From what I piece together, Dilbert is a cubicle drone. He owns or, more accurately, is owned by a talking dog. Also, Dilbert apparently works for the devil because his boss has horned hair. So far, the comic is a lot of witty banter about nothing meaningful. Maybe I am just jaded. Granted, Dilbert probably hasn't been shackled to the government and forced to hunt others like him seven days a week.

As for what I discover about Scott Adams, are rants that may originate from his disease. Anger and hostility fill a lot of his posts. As someone who follows a code that focuses on sincerity, honor, integrity, and more, his posts leave me anything but comfortable.

I don't have to like the man to learn from his affliction.

Mr. CartoonMan lost the ability to have conversations. His body shut down. He got around it by pinching his nose and speaking in rhyme.

Stranger things have happened.

For two hours, Dr. Brent and I work in silence, with the only sound being paper shuffling between us with notes and the occasional clearing of throats. His desk phone never rings, though sounds of the staff holding off appointments and drop-bys float through the door.

From Mr. CartoonMan's interviews to dozens of websites and medical journal articles, the two of us follow a trail of disease-ridden breadcrumbs to this conclusion: I am one screwed-up genetic casserole.

It's like when you take your car to the mechanic because the service engine light is on and the air conditioning won't work. You think it's one thing. And it is that thing, but it's also the transmission. Plus, the belts are bad, and so on and so on. Yes, I have auditory epilepsy, but my old doctor, Dr. Line, focused only on the problems Cyfib and Poseidon United implanted in me. He ignored another culprit.

My father's suicide.

Mama always told me that Dad just stopped talking. She never considered he couldn't respond. That something trapped him in his own body. My father was a prisoner, much like all my friends in Hackers' Haven. My mother just focused on her own self-doubt. And I'm sure the pills she was taking did not help.

From what I read, Mr. CartoonMan is one of the less-than-ten-thousand American men that suffer from spasmodic/voice dysphonia or SD. If I have this disease, not only am I the youngest, I am also possibly one of the most severe cases, mainly because I also have this auditory epilepsy smacking my brain around from my time in the prison.

Oddly, finding out I have another disease is actually a relief, sending a sense of calm across my temples. That's a good thing, because high anxiety can cause flare-ups in my symptoms.

That might explain why this really escalated when I escaped Hackers' Haven and had to hide. According to this website I shouldn't have had any symptoms, let alone *all* the symptoms, until I am middle-aged. I'm not even thirty yet.

Eighty percent of people with this disease only stutter. I noticed that in Hackers' Haven, but I thought it was nerves and stress. Unfortunately, I am the extreme case that freaks out in a conversation like I am a vampire that spots the sun rising on the horizon.

"'Scuse me." Dr. Brent leans across me, picks up his desk phone, and presses the quick key for *Pharmacy*.

"Yeah, hey Carrie, it's Bob. Can you get me two units of OnabotulinumtoxinA? Thanks, please give Chris a hug for me. Bye." He hangs up and gets back to his reading.

Two minutes later, a knock on the door sounds. "Come in." Nurse Cody hands Dr. Brent a white sealed bag. "Thank you." As he leaves, Dr. Brent tears it open in the middle and pulls out one of two syringe boxes.

"Don't worry, it's just Botox."

From what I've read, that still is a poison, but beggars can't be choosers.

"This has had a positive impact on 99 percent of patients, so I think we can start here. Please hold still."

After he pricks it into the left side of my throat, he mumbles, "Now, I'm going to have to make this disappear into the paperwork, because we have a very strict inventory control system."

Thinking of MetroMed, I am tempted to laugh. However, the shot must've worked because I do not tremble at all.

"I'm not expecting this to solve anything, but it will buy some time." Dr. Brent puts the cap on the syringe and tosses it into the red medical waste receptacle next to his garbage can. "I won't do this surgery because, A, I'm not risking my staff's careers and, B, that's not my level of expertise."

The rock in my stomach instantly gains five pounds after that sentence.

"You weren't totally off-base by finding me. In all seriousness, you missed your target by only a few genetic markers: my half-sister shadowed the creator of a particular surgical technique that could rewire your muscles. Also, don't tell her I said this, but she's the best surgeon I've ever seen south of the Mason-Dixon line. A thing of beauty."

Dr. Brent paces the room, gathering his thoughts.

"I can't guarantee *she* will do the surgery, but she does a lot of work around this disease, charitable and otherwise, so I'll beg. But my gut says she'll perform the operation."

As he strokes his hair back, he takes a seat on the corner of his desk. "For other patients, the surgery is relatively quick and easy. I'll assist my sister in the operating room." Dr. Brent rubs his chin and hesitates. My gut tells me why. "In basic terms, we're going to cut a chord in your jaw and attach it to a new nerve cluster. On other patients, those with only minor SD, it has stopped the patients' tremors completely and allowed for a sense of normality in their daily communication. No one has attempted treatment on someone with your level of...severity."

He leans forward, yet his eyes shoot over me as he reads some kind of invisible chart.

"Any surgery has risks." Dr. Brent's eyes then meet mine. "I cannot find where anyone has even attempted this surgery on someone with your extreme reactions to communication. This surgery could cause the opposite effect. It may amplify the seizures. We'll have to run some scans, but your nerve cluster may be so worn that it may be what is minimizing the vibrations from the auditory epilepsy. Again, I'm only speculating at this point. Any change could kill you. It could ramp up the seizures. This could be like replacing a nine-volt battery in a remote-controlled car with a nuclear reactor."

I nod. I will sign any waiver. Death is better than this.

Dr. Brent reaches into his pocket, pulls out his Mont Blanc pen, and puts it and a small notepad down on the desk.

"There's a reason I've never asked your name, until now." I swallow a brick as I break his gaze. "My gut tells me you're not here on a...me dical referral...like the message said for one Eric Vice, because my gut tells me you aren't some missing kid from Nebraska."

Shit. I didn't calculate that he'd look up my cover name.

"I don't care about why you are using a fake name or who you were, but I need to know who you were . . . medically. Anything you can share with me, I'll keep just between us. If you give me your real name, I may be able to find some medical information about your family history."

Even a *search* for my real name could trigger a hit for Cyfib and Poseidon United.

How much do I risk?

Is now a time for all-or-nothing?

Dr. Brent places a firm, yet kind, grip on my shoulder. "Also, I needed to know who I'm risking my neck for."

For the first time in over a decade, I jot down my past. My mother's past. My father's past, and so on. Including the name I shook off back in that trailer in Texas.

Chapter Ninety-Two

Armor Up

I spend the next two days looking over my shoulder. Two of Moscow's associates stay near the West Memphis clinic to monitor things. Not just to make sure the staff are safe, but also to make sure that no one is watching them. Dr. Brent's online search of my birth name may have triggered nothing in the Hackers' Haven or Poseidon United alerts, but we must act like they may know that I am one of his patients.

And, even though it will take Dr. Brent that long to get back to me, I don't spend that time resting on my laurels, whatever the hell laurels are.

I get on a bus heading west and return to the scene of the crime: Houston, Texas.

The remains of Hackers' Haven.

With a bag full of gear and a limited window, I know that there is no point in going into the abandoned funeral parlor. The Poseidon United, the Gogglemen, or both, cleaned the place out. But I have one advantage they do not.

I know where I threw the Administrative key from Hackers' Haven after I escaped. If I can just find it.

Luckily, I work best when someone stacks the odds against me.

Just within a stone's throw of the leveled lot of Hackers' Haven is one particular storm drain. The one that Barca chucked the basketball into from the roof of our prison. The same one that I flicked the flash drive into so that Barca would not get it in the event of my death.

The cover looks like a mouth with flat eyes and a scowl. My body tightens as a faint bit of copper hits my nostrils. Each body blow by that giant still resonates, especially in my joints on chilly mornings. My jaw pops with the memory of Barca's giant fists slamming over and over into my head. I rub the empty area in the back of my jaw on the right side, the tooth that Barca knocked loose, and I spat in his face as a last bit of defiance.

Even with all that remembered pain, I whistle as I put down my duffel bag of gear, more hopeful than careful. Sure, I am being watched. Luckily, I know that the shadow approaching me is just a figment of my imagination.

"You had to complicate everything, didn't you?" The anger of a dead man's voice hovers between my ears.

I've gotten used to this ghost of my mistakes haunting me. I don't know if Barca is part of my guilt or disease. In any case, I smile.

"What's so funny, Princess?"

Without turning around, I flip the poltergeist the finger.

From the duffel, I withdraw my tools: a flashlight, a metal detector, and a metallic net. I lay flat on the wet, dirty ground and blast a flashlight's beam into the grate. Mainly, it reveals globs of junk congealed in the corners of the drain. I take a dual-action extendable baton slash metal detector and shove it into the gunk. I turn the knob to the right. As I move the round tip of the rod into the closest gunk ball, it beeps.

I remove the metal detector and extend my metallic net on a baton to the gunk. I cover the nastiness and drag it my way.

In the first ball, all I find are a few bottle caps, two candy wrappers, and a used condom.

Similar results come from the other balls of bullshit.

It never is easy.

Next, I find the closest manhole cover and enter the sewer. For the next several hours, I go through enough nastiness to truly believe that humans are indeed killing the environment with our junk.

And, while I fail to find a bunch of turtle ninjas led by a giant rat, I find something better.

There, stuck in a hardened ball of what might've been the remains of someone's fast food wrapper for close to a year, is the Administrative flash drive.

After a five-hour sleep and quick shower at the closest truck stop to the Greyhound station, I'm on the bus back to Memphis. I get a text on the burner phone in my duffel. Only Dr. Brent knows the number. It reads:

Memphis, Tennessee - The staff at Butterfield's are preparing a patient for outpatient surgery tomorrow. Continue stoppage of all medicine until further notice. Said patient is required to be at the facility by 5 a.m. to begin the prep work. The story continues with the next issue.

I guess Dr. Brent's sister said yes, especially because it is *off the books*. How he got her to agree, I'll never know.

The arrival time on my ticket says six-thirty in the evening. I have a lot to do in under twelve hours.

I might die either on the operating table or in recovery, but I've prepared for that. My Daimyō and Thugly know how to cover up the orders. Penny has Hydra-Cash set. I even dropped off Funk Monster with Dani before I left. They are all in good hands if I don't make it back. Hell, even Ms. Ingrid "Innocent" Vincent and Lil Al have their marching orders.

I need only one final player to armor up. Armoring was crucial for a Bushi. This was not just a time of preparation, but also reflection and meditation. This man will dislike me if I live, and especially hate me if I die.

And he is as unpredictable as a squirrel on crack cocaine.

Chapter Ninety-Three

In Like Flint

Kilroy is none too pleased to meet with me, especially when it is on such short notice. Just like in the Internet Café, he looks like a paranoid hippie, his long hair whipping around as he keeps checking his six. He might shift to pure anger when he finds out what I want—no, need—him to do. I used a Ham Radio and Morse Code to communicate with him using a damned demo model at a pawnshop. The headset's rusted buttons and faulty wiring were the least of that relic's problems. The Botox in my system counters my lack of meds, due to doctor's orders. Thankfully, it must've done the trick because I only shook like I was standing under a vent's draft through most of the message. By the end of my transmission, I am glad I got the message out before I had to grunt through the migraine.

I guess the Botox isn't a cure-all.

We meet at midnight at one of the area's abandoned landmarks: the Firestone Tire and Rubber factory. This faded smokestack surrounded by the remains of demolished buildings in northern Memphis used to employ thousands of people. It produced over a hundred million tires, and even made gas masks, life rafts, and more during World War II.

Now all it produces is dust and despair.

And, with the amount of Environmental Protection Agency warning signs in the area talking about possible pollutants in the soil, it's no wonder that the site is as empty as a homeless man's belly.

"You know, the only reason the EPA exists is because Nixon was getting blowback from military contracts and donors after he announced the US was *honorably* leaving Vietnam."

Even though I've arrived at the site thirty minutes early, Kilroy is already here, complete with a backpack slung over his shoulder and skepticism leaking through his pores. He's probably been here since agreeing to this meetup. If time had allowed, I would've been.

The long-haired hippie kicks a clump of rubble in the shape of Iowa off into the weeds. "Yeah, Nixon was determined that the corporations weren't going to run his presidency anymore, so he kicked off the new year in 1970 by creating the EPA, the Mammal Marine Protection Act, and the Clean Air and Clean Water Acts. When the donors met with him on January 2, the rumor is that Tricky Dick had them all meet in the smallest conference room in the White House, cramming millionaire after millionaire elbow-to-elbow. He let them grumble, moan, and complain for an hour before he uttered a word. Then the president told them that the bidding for contracts to *address* the cleanup and regulations started at ten million dollars."

"Someone in the room figured out *addressing* the cleanup was a lot like cancer research." Kilroy yanks a giant cobweb from his hair and hangs it against the closest piece of exposed steel rebar, then wipes his hands on his gray jeans. "Like cancer, there's no money in the cure, but a whole helluva lot of it is available in pretending to look for one."

I reach into my back pocket too quickly for Kilroy's tastes because he fast-draws a nine-millimeter from his back belt loop. Thankfully, he doesn't aim it my way, though I take the hint. I turn around, showing him that there are only two folded pieces of paper in my back pockets. When I complete my orbit of the sun, he holsters the pistol.

I take both letters, lay them on the closest rock, and step back. The number *One* on the top reflects in the moonlight.

Instead of approaching, Kilroy opens his backpack. I know what's happening next. As one paranoid to another, I know my peeps. I spread my arms before Kilroy even gets to me. He runs his handheld bug detector over my body.

"So, they haven't bagged-and-tagged you to go home yet, huh?"

I shake my head.

After I pass the sniff test, Kilroy snags the letters and steps back. He places his back to the smokestack.

A hair from my ear, I let the monster stew in his own dead rage and ignore Ghost Barca. Even though he stinks of Corn Nuts and angry sweat.

"Damn."

He's reading the first one. That's the one that tells him what to do if everything goes dong-up if I die in the next forty-eight hours. He'll know by my lack of posts on Woot.com. I'll do one before surgery, then one after. I figured I'd take one last page out of Lance-a-Little's hacking book, especially since I might wind up worm food like my mentor.

"This is screwed up. Trust me, I know screwed up."

Then he opens the second letter, the more complicated one.

"Shit. Shit. Shit-no. No."

This is the one that tells him what to do if I live.

"Even if such a thing exists, that level of exposure, I would need a Faraday room with triple encryption...also a way to isolate the servers' operating systems at a root level..."

That's when I reach into my pocket and toss him the Administrative Key to the databases for Hackers' Havens. I plugged the device into a demo laptop at the pawnshop to make sure the environment hadn't corrupted it. That old computer didn't even have WiFi capabilities, so there was no risk of exposure...unless Cyfib or one of his cronies was right behind me when I did it.

I tried to make a copy of the drive. In true clandestine bullshit fashion, the formatting on it is a cross between FAT32 formatting and something I've never seen, so it is impossible for me to replicate.

A lump leaves my throat and splashes down into my stomach as I release the drive. The flash also has the LODIS files, our advanced targeting system, on it and Gakunodo, my world-ending software. The drive has everything that mercenary Barca was sent to steal and more. The USB has all the parts of their code, from digits to databases. It has every file.

Kilroy only needs one.

He paces, kicking the remains of a long-dead business as he internally debates the pros and cons. Kilroy goes over the risks. He uses his always-moving index finger to outline the amount of detail it will take to do this right.

He never has a conversation with me, only himself.

When he does finally utter something, it has the smallest trace of optimism.

"This is so risky, damn near impossible."

I smile. He said *near* impossible.

I check my watch under the full moon. I've got to be at surgery in under four hours.

No rest for this wicked one tonight.

When I glance up, Kilroy stands in front of me, his fingertips touching like a James Bond villain. I let my smile meet his, though his looks to be one worthy of Batman's Joker as it matches his flaming eyes.

"I'm in like Flint."

Having never seen the actual 1960s movie, In Like Flint, *I'm gonna guess that's a yes.*

This shuffles the Wild Card into my deck. The final game begins post-surgery. I still don't fully know how I'm going to do everything. I have one shot to do this right.

As I walk away, I would love to take my victories where I can. Now all I've got to do is survive a miracle surgery.

Chapter Ninety-Four

Trucker

As the sun rises, everything blurs at the clinic. Blood tests, MRIs, CAT scan, measurement after measurement fill the day. The staff keeps calling me *Mr. Vice*, which I should be used to. A sense of shame covers my body as I remember I borrowed the name and social security number of a long missing kid.

Maybe it's the fear of death during surgery that's causing my brain to bring up my sins.

Dr. Brent's sister, who looks a little like him around the eyes and carries the same kind yet authoritative voice, runs through the procedure with me. The next thing I know, I'm staring at a surgical light that carries the same wattage as the sun and inhaling from a urinal-shaped gasmask.

As the beeping of my heart monitor fades in my ears, my mind floats down through the operating table. My essence spins, then sinks into the floor.

I'm in a white room like the operating room. Wait. It is not a room, but a vast landscape of white. All I can see is nothing.

Except for a long wooden bench with a lone occupant on it.

Lance-a-Little.

He looks just like I remember him, yet completely different. He's of the same firm stature, but somehow stronger. Healthier. His previously silver eyebrows now are the same dark brown as his kind eyes. He's wearing a white suit, a triple-breasted one that you would see on a mobster in the 1920s. I can't see his hair because he is wearing a baseball cap that has a mesh back and a front logo on it that keeps changing from one Asian symbol to another. The first letter looks like a stick figure with a bow and arrow standing on a table, then the second looks like a circle with part of a fence. I think it is Japanese, no, Korean. Maybe.

"Why are you wearing a trucker cap?"

The sigh that oozes out of Lance's throat echoes in the void. "If that's your main question to a dead man, then you're still doing everything wrongly, T."

He motions for me to join him on the bench. I do. His hat now has a symbol O and L and H.

"So, I screwed up and I'm dead?" Even if I'm not dead and just dreaming, I'm failing. "I make things too complicated. I should've-"

"I didn't say wrong." His hand is on my shoulder, squeezing. "I said *wrongly*. Sure, my grammar ain't up to snuff, but I'm pretty sure that word works. Sorta. You're trying to fix everything by yourself, like you always do."

"It's my responsibility, Lance. It is my job to protect them. No one can fix this but me."

"Who the hell told you that?" Lance swats me across the back with his trucker cap. "I'll tell you who: you."

He puts the hat back on his head and straightens the bill, evening it with his nose.

"You're the most prideful, stubborn, and self-pitying sonovabitch I know. And that includes me, myself. Sure, you're the first to take the blame, but did you ever think that your ideas, your grand plans, could use some outside perspectives? You're always seventy, maybe 80 percent of the way to a workable plan. What if you got some help from your team instead of spouting off orders that you sugarcoat as your damned newsletters?"

"Oh, so the guy who tried to get me to shove an ice pick through my brain is lecturing me about taking feedback?"

"Exactly!" Lance-a-Little pops up from the bench and raises his arms skyward. "Hallelujah, the boy's almost got it!"

As Lance turns toward me and puts both of his hands on my shoulders, he looks me in the eye. "You were drawn to me because I am as bullheaded as you. And look where that got me."

"I'm..." is all I get out before I stop talking. Then, like a shot of vodka kicking in five minutes after taking it, this warming sense of revelation flows through my body.

I don't have all the answers.

Lance steps backward. His trucker cap's logo ends with a C and part of a fence. I know I won't remember these symbols, but somehow, they give me peace.

Of course, that's all before I wake up screaming.

Chapter Ninety-Five

Shitty PG Player

The cold sweat covering my body and the throbbing sensation in my head solidifies; I am very much alive as I scream myself awake.

"Whoa now!" Dr. Brent pushes me back into the bed. "I guess that answers the question about if you can speak post-op."

As auras of light pound my eyes in the recovery room and garbled voices turn to words, a flu-like whole-body pain creeps through me. I know it is the anesthesia fading away from my body, but I still feel like a piñata after a five-year-old's birthday party.

"Can you talk?"

I reach for the pen in the doctor's pocket, but he swats my hand away.

"We know you can make noise, so let's see if we can say one word. Any word."

My speech has been gone so long, I am clueless as to what to say.

"Oh," comes the voice of one sassy angel, "I bet once that little bastard starts speaking, he'll never shut up."

"P-P-Penny?" I tilt my granite-filled head over and spot her propped against the window.

The lone word must fight its way up to my lips, but I still get it out. Its journey feels like my disease covered the word in hot barbed wire because my throat burns and itches at the same time.

"That'll work." Dr. Brent hits a button on the railing to my bed to raise me to a sitting position. "I had to call the contact you had listed under spouse so that she can drive you home. And while this young lady may or may not be your wife, as you had listed her, she's loudly said your relationship is...complicated."

I didn't even notice that I did that. Maybe I thought that was the Emergency Contact slot? *Why did I choose her?* Now there's a fifty-fifty chance Penny will kill me for it when we reach the parking lot.

"Mrs. Vice, can you—"

"Penny," she interrupts, her blue eyes flashing my way as she mouths the phrase about what I could do to myself if I practiced yoga. "I'm not one for labels."

Make that eighty-twenty, in favor of my death by a small Korean lady.

"Mrs.—er—Penny, here are your husb—you know, just here is this person's effects." Dr. Brent holds out a plastic bag to Penny.

She snatches it away.

"Um, I'll get you a wheelchair."

I send a pitiful look to Dr. Brent. *Please don't leave me alone with her.*

He breaks eye contact while pretending to take a phone call from his smartphone.

"Oh, and the little humans send their love or whatever to you and hope you get better soon." Penny hands me a drawing with two stick figures with ice cream that has the words *Ice Cream Soon.* I flip it over. On the back are the words *Don't Die.* It doesn't take a genius to figure out which kid sent each message.

Penny dumps the bag of my junk in the closest chair. As my clothes and knickknacks splay out, so do two pieces of paper.

In there is the picture I have of Penny from Quidlee. I think she will grab it. Instead, she picks up the second piece of paper.

The last letter I have from Lance-a-Little.

As she unfolds it, it crinkles. Penny holds it to the lights. She's reading the code that Lance hid there that the water from my near-death dive off that bridge unveiled. I'd completely forgotten about it.

Those numbers must've meant something, but just like most things, I failed at figuring them out.

"Huh, seven numbers per line."

That is the first thing I noticed. Seven across, nine down. I've tried every type of code breaking I know. I even put them through code-breaking software called A-Tur, named after the famous code-breaker and visionary of the Internet Allen Turing.

Nothing worked.

"You're a weird one, T."

I have the urge to award her the title of Captain Obvious, but I gave that to AldenSong on my second day in prison. Maybe she's Sergeant Sarcasm.

"You didn't write this, did you?"

I shake my head.

"Well, just because I hate you don't mean I won't help you...hm m...well, maybe...there's a chance that this code writer might be a PG player, and a shitty one at that."

My lack of poker face clearly fails me as I dart up from my bed and scurry my bare feet along the cold tile floor. When I reach Penny, we both look at the paper under the light. She runs her fingers along the numbers.

"You know, Pai Gow Poker is like Chinese dominoes, but done with double hands for poker. Five cards in your best hand on the left, two cards in your worst hand. That's what this is, right?"

This explains why I couldn't crack the code. I was focused on individual numbers and singular or parallel patterns. Just like most codes, these numbers needed the right key.

One of the last things Lance-a-Little said to me before his murder flashes before my eyes.

Life is not like a box of chocolates; it's like a game of chance. It's poker, and the deck is as stacked as a swimsuit model.

The code *is* poker, just not white-boy poker.

The scent of lilac and rosemary hits my nose. Penny's perfume. I sniff my shoulder. Even post-surgery, I still smell like a custodian: stale sweat and antiseptic.

My body works faster than my mind. I dive into Penny's purse, looking for a pen. Instead, I find a gold-and-black tube of lipstick. I snatch it, pop open the top, and dart to the mirror with the piece of paper.

Just before I write the first pair of numbers, Penny clears her throat.

"You ruin that lipstick, I'm gonna ruin your lipstick."

I catch her meaning and as I turn to put the lipstick back, she holds out a Bic pen. On a piece of scratch paper from the trash, I write the pairs.

"I mean, I can see why most of the hands are set up this way, but some of these moves are rookie mistakes." Penny holds up the original code to the light. "Like, why wouldn't you set up four of a kind here when you had the chance?"

Because those last numbers are what matter.

Then, for the first time in a long while, I uncomplicate things: I add the pairs together and get a nine-digit code.

If I knew Lance-A-Little one iota, this is how I get into Hackers' Haven, maybe even Poseidon United's, database.

As we stare at it, even Penny understands what we've got.

"That's a hell of a way to hide an IP address."

Chapter Ninety-Six

Slams

Penny wheels my able-to-walk ass out of the recovery room in the west wing of Butterfield's Partners Clinic. We've got an IP Address and, if we guess correctly, the password to get in: 1000110. That last part came from wins and losses of hands. Penny based this on a common Jacks-or-Better ruling that I'd never heard of.

The hallway is lined with evenly spaced framed articles lining the walls. Most are generic accolades, or at least awards I know jack squat about. One article catches my eye: *Mother of Two's Voice Returned Because of Local Clinic.*

What would my life have been like if my father could have had his voice returned?

The optimist in me thinks about the talks we would've had, the ease that could've been.

The realist in me knows that this thought is pure bullshit. That was the world through a child's eyes. Whatever relationship my parents had was much more complicated than a lack of words.

As Penny and I approach the exit, Dr. Brent hands me a filled prescription for oxy. I shake my head and hand it back.

"The pain will come in waves." He pushes the pill bottle into my chest, so I reluctantly pocket it. "You're better than you were, but you need rest. I'm talking forty-eight hours of straight bed rest, minimum."

Dream on, good doctor.

"We won't know the extent of your improvement for days, maybe weeks." Dr. Brent strokes his chin as he curates his next words. "This surgery should help with communication, but I do not expect it to fix the voices you said you hear. Those are a...different beast all together."

In the back of my mind, I don't just hear Barca's chuckle. I feel it in my damn bones.

"Mrs. Vi...hold on...what did you say I should call you?"

"You can call me *Leaving*."

I swear I hear the old western gunfight whistle in the background as these two square off.

"O...kay...do you think you can watch over Mr. Vice for the next seventy-two hours?"

"I doubt he'll sit still for seventy-two minutes." Her gaze meets mine. Her blue orbs draw me in, even though her squint is that of a disciplinary parent. "Are you going to rest like the doc orders?"

My dull eyes answer that stupid question.

"Yeah, I figured as much." Penny moves from behind my wheelchair and extends her hand Dr. Brent. "It's been real."

He shakes her hand, then grumbles all the way to his office.

Penny rolls me just outside the clinic's doors, then basically dumps me on my feet. We walk over to her car. I stare at her purple Hyundai, lost in my own train of thought.

She taps the hood.

"Are you going to be one of those people that thinks a car can't be purple?"

Then I point at the handicapped sign in front of her four-door sedan.

"Oh, shut up." She double-clicks her key fob, and the doors unlock. "Isn't every patient in a hospital sort of handicapped?"

As Penny drives me back to her house, we cross the bridge that connects Arkansas and Tennessee. As I lean out the open window, enjoying the cold air on my face and tickling my ears, a sense of calm hits me.

Until a large van slams into the back of our car.

Chapter Ninety-Seven

Game On

"What the he—" is all Penny gets out before a second hit rocks our vehicle.

The impact knocks my head into the headrest. The rear window shatters into cereal-sized bites and pelts us. Tires skid and scream as Penny corrects our path just as our vehicle glances against the railing. Sparks fly as metal assaults metal.

In the van's driver's seat is Dendro_Crusher. Even with the tape across his broken nose, his smile and beady eyes blast his intentions into my soul.

There's a chance Dr. Brent's online search for either my real name or fake one triggered something back in Hackers' Haven or with Poseidon United's search alerts. I can't think about that now. All I can do is figure out how to get him from ramming us off this damn bridge.

"Let me guess, you know this a-hole?" Penny's comment drips with enough sarcasm to be called a mother-in-law. You know you're in trouble when the head of a criminal gang can use that tone about your associations.

The van slows down, preparing knock us again. With no other cars on the road, Dendro has no witnesses to worry about.

Barca's voice tickles my ear.

"The only way to stop me is to put me in the ground for good."

But Barca is wrong. I just have to stop the van, not kill the driver.

Looking around the vehicle and finding nothing of use in the floorboard, I pop open the glove compartment. Inside is what I expect to find: insurance papers, chapstick, lipstick, migraine medicine, a map of Tennessee, and other odds and ends. I toss most of it backward. Some of it lands in the backseat, but most just bounces out the window.

Then I see it: a window-smashing tool.

This hammer-sized vehicle necessity is designed to not only smash a side window in the event of a crash, but also it has a razor in the handle to cut the seat belt.

"Oh, what're you going to do, throw that at him like a 1940s Superman?"

Good reference, if not especially helpful. I grab the map and lean back, holding it wide.

Dendro is close enough that I see him lick his lips as he slams his tank into us.

My neck snaps back with the impact and I bite my tongue. Copper floods my mouth. I toss the map. It fails to cover our attacker's windshield. Dendro reaches out his driver's side window and yanks it away. That brief distraction gives me the chance to toss our miracle at the passenger side's front tire.

The hammer somersaults as it hits the concrete and bounces under the exact tire it is intended for. All that happens is I hear the crack of the casing, and a slight pop as the truck raises as it plows over it.

Shit. That was our only option.

Then a louder pop fills the air like a balloon exploding. Though the diamond hammer missed the front tire, a piece of it must've punctured the back tire.

With damage to the rear-wheel-drive tires, the van turns right, and then left. Dendro frantically turns the wheel trying to even out. His eyes are full of panic as the momentum of the turns overtakes the van's inertia. The van rolls. It completes a full rotation crashing onto the remains of our trunk.

With the added weight, our speed drops from ninety to forty like we just saw a cop with a radar gun. Even hanging upside down and clearly injured, Dendro reaches into his pocket and grabs a pistol.

Penny, now calm and collected, actually chuckles. "No time for stowaways, Dr. Jones."

She hits the Pop Trunk button near the bottom of the driver's door. The lid releases from our vehicle. The van's grip ends as our anchor breaks free and we speed off.

For the next five minutes, neither of us speaks. I'm just focused on remembering how to breathe. Penny takes every side street and alley she can.

We can't assume that Dendro was the only one following us.

Once we get to a stoplight in Midtown, I find my bag crammed under the passenger seat. After opening the door, Penny's hand touches my arm. When our eyes meet, everything that needs to be said passes between us.

"I've got to get the kids somewhere safe."

Penny's priorities are spot on. I nod. As the light turns from red to green, a car horn from behind us blares. Penny flips the driver off, which is the Memphis sign-language equivalent of *go around me.*

"You need me, you call me, you dumb little bastard."

I can't tell you why, but I blow her a kiss. She catches it and tosses it out the other side of her car.

Although, after the toss, she does send me a wink as she drives off.

I check my watch.

5:45 p.m.

I reach into my bag and pull out Lance-a-Little's decoded sheet. I know where I can get a laptop and a fresh burner phone in the next fifteen minutes.

Now all I have to do is get to my planned gig site, prepare the hack, and get ready for all hell to break loose.

I must finish this. Now.

Game on.

Chapter Ninety-Eight

In Disguise

As I set up my gear, a sense of relief instead of worry floods over me. I'm as close to my final destination as possible. Even if this entire plan goes to hell, that's where I'll wind up, anyway.

The room I've rented in this hourly motel smells like the fallout of a porn shoot. Oddly, they have solid WiFi.

The sun set about two hours ago. In front of me is what I should call FrankenTop. I had to buy three different machines from three different pawnshops to assemble the computing power I need. I've strewn together cable after cable on a bed covered in enough stains to be considered modern art. The old Dell had the best processors. The Compaq had the best graphics card. Finally, the Palo Alto computer had the best memory. In the past, I would have taken them apart and soldered the parts I needed into a supercomputer, but I'm tired. I'm healing. And I no longer give a shit what this looks like. I only need it to work. Just once.

Two burner phones are on a table, fresh as newborn babies. I pick up the first one, a plain black generic sucker made by a fake company trying to play off a famous name: MaterRola. It's the cheapest phone. Everything about it feels fake. Hell, it is so light and flimsy that I think it would do a better job of dispensing chiclets of gum than making calls. I make one call. I let the phone ring six times. Then I hang up, snap the phone's backing open, and swallow the SIM card. Snapping it or stomping it could still leave salvageable info on it. Of all the stupid things I am about to do, someone finding this would screw up my plan the most.

The second phone is sturdy, like those old Nokias that you could throw at an attacker or use to jack up a car. I power it up. The welcome screen chimes a familiar tune that finds me reminiscing on another hack that all came down to the wire.

The phone's warmup sound is that of a little bell, tinny as it comes out of the speakers.

It makes me think of Mrs. Lin. And the power of planning for other people's bullheadedness.

Chapter Ninety-Nine

Little Dagger

Years Ago

The morning after the chicken coop massacre, I didn't even bother with any chores. Even with concrete in my legs and eyelids filled with lead, I got up. Mrs. Lin was already up when I stumbled outside. I'd slept maybe thirty minutes max after the fire. I doubt her head even hit a pillow.

As usual, near the curb, was Old Man J.R. going through the closest trashcan with his usual rambling. Today though, when I looked his way, he kept my gaze. When he saw the burned coop, his posture straightened. The half-filled black garbage bag on his shoulder clanged to the ground when he dropped it and walked toward the ashes.

Standing with him side-by-side, I didn't even care that he smelled of rotten eggs and piss.

Especially when he placed his fingerless-gloved hand on my shoulder and squeezed.

"Damn EPA."

I choked down a sob. "Damn EPA indeed, J.R."

Old Man J.R. leaned down and picked up something. He presented me with the two-dollar bill Jedediah had left as his calling card. I shook my head, so Old Man J.R. pocketed it and wandered back to the street.

I was about to clean up the refuse when I heard it.

That damn bell.

The young punk saddled with an ancient name rang his bell like he was trying to get the world's attention as he dismounted his bike and lowered his kickstand.

"Y'all cooking?" Jedidah McIntosh's flashlight-bright smile flickered in the daylight. "Because something smells good."

Like electricity, I shot at him, but somehow Mrs. Lin stood between me and this asshole. My body must've told my brain to take a hike because I didn't even notice that I had balled up my fists and sped at the bastard until I felt Mrs. Lin's kind yet firm palm with the perfect nails against my chest.

"How can we help you, Mr. McIntosh?"

Jedediah reached into his jacket pocket and pulled out a folded piece of paper. The sun was behind us as its rays angled through Mrs. Lin's thick glasses. It sent an amplified beam into Jedediah's chest. More than a small part of me wanted that laser to cook the asshole like an ant under a magnifying glass.

"I regret to inform you that this entire apartment complex is now part of Orleans Parish's Auction this coming Friday."

Jedediah must have a loose definition of the word regret. *The auction house takes 10 percent of the final bid, 20 percent to the parish, and 70 percent to the owner. He hands her the paper, but never misses a beat.*

"It is all part of their blind bidding process for properties. You see, the supervisors will divide up the properties that they have deemed...in

need of revitalization...but they put them in unnamed portfolios so that whoever wins them will not know in advance which properties they won."

"If it is now part of a blind bidding process, how do you know it is part of a certain package?"

With the way Jedediah's head kicked back, you'd have sworn Mrs. Lin had just told him the funniest joke.

"I'm just...speculating..."

Mrs. Lin flipped open the paper and skimmed it. She refolded it and narrowed her eyes. "We will fight you over this."

"Not in the four days you have, you won't."

"We will find a lawyer and keep this from moving forward."

"That only works if you own the property." Jedediah whispered the last two words in Mrs. Lin's ear loud enough that Old Man J.R. could probably hear them. "You rent."

"What if someone outbids you?" I don't know what prompted my question, but the look on his face wasn't anger. Nor was it one of fear.

It was one of doubt.

Jedediah tipped an invisible hat, first toward Mrs. Lin, and then to me. As he mounted his bike, he rode at Ole Man J.R. so aggressively that the homeless man dove into the nearest trash bags.

"Damn EPA!"

And that's all it took for my own bell to ring. I only had a hunch and the few pieces of the puzzle that Jedediah McIntosh let slip about the upcoming auction to power 10, maybe 12 percent of a plan.

But it was something.

Mrs. Lin stared at me looking like she was seeing a burnt dinner and accepting that all of it was going in the trash. "Fanboy, we better get to packing. I will see what boxes I can get from the liquor store, you see what newspaper scraps you can find from—"

"Mrs. Lin, I need to do something."

She must've heard the mischief in my voice, because she grabbed my shoulders and righted me to face her eye-to-coke-bottle-lenses.

"No, fanboy, you do not get to go and do something stupid."

It was a solid effort, but when you are about to do something that could get you arrested and plan to do it anyway, there are no words that will derail your stupidity train.

Taking my silence as an acknowledgment of upcoming shenanigans, Mrs. Lin slapped me across the face.

"You cannot fight him. Whatever you are planning will not be mighty enough to topple him. He has too much power, money, influence. He will crush you."

A car horn in the distance blared as we squared off. I had only one chance to convince her that my hair-brained, grain-of-rice sized plan was worth pursuing.

I took a deep breath, unclenched my jaw, closed my eyes, and took a breath.

"He flinched, Mrs. Lin."

Then I held her gaze before continuing.

"'In battle," *I said, quoting the Miyamoto Musashi she'd read to me so many times before,* "if you make your opponent flinch, you have already won.'"

She didn't say anything, not a word, but her eyes betrayed her. Instead of looking glazed over, she stared off in the distance. It brought to mind another Musashi quote:

In strategy, it is important to see distant things as if they were close and to take a distanced view of close things.

Mrs. Lin started a laugh, but her throat caught it, and shoved it back down into her gut so hard she coughed. Something in my eyes, or maybe in what I said, must've told her I was serious.

Mrs. Lin looked over at the exterior of her apartment. She chewed her pinkish bottom lip for a full minute before speaking.

"Okay, fanboy, what do you need from me?"

"Please don't slap me again, because I need your age."

***

I told Mrs. Lin about my plan. She shot pizza-sized holes through it. After each shot though, she added a way of handling each problem. When it was all mapped out, we had a plan that was twice as good as my original one, if three times as complicated.

We spent the next two days bouncing between public office after public office. Land grants. Public works. Bankruptcy. Public housing. You name it; we went there. I needed Mrs. Lin's valid ID, credit history, and a paid utility bill to get access to the files we needed.

Clerk after clerk met every single request for documents with the standard response of it will arrive in five to ten business days. *We countered that bullshit and got the paperwork immediately the way you should counter most excuses: with a twenty-dollar bill.*

It is amazing how much more work someone will do when you give them a green rectangular piece of paper with Andrew Jackson on it.

Once we had all the ammo, I only needed one more thing from Mrs. Lin: a distraction at the closest library.

That's why Mrs. Lin pretended to not understand English when she spoke to the librarian as I snuck in and hid during closing hours.

Sure, what we did was both racist and ageist, but no one will ever call me a saint.

After the last employee left, I emerged and logged into a computer in the main office. It was easier to hack than the door I had to pick to get in.

Once in, I downloaded a basic VPN masker, an IP address duplicator, and a cryptography cracker, along with some odds and ends.

I wish I could say that I got everything done in no time. In reality, I worked all night and finished my task and uninstallation of my software, plus the wiping of the Internet history, with a mere ten minutes to spare before the first worker came in at 6:45 a.m. I returned to my hiding spot until Mrs. Lin arrived when the doors opened at 7:30 a.m.

Then we walked out of that public building like I hadn't just committed five felonies and sixteen misdemeanors.

Quite literally running on no sleep, we dashed toward the folding chairs near the courthouse steps. The buses were running late, and we'd arrived five minutes into the auction.

Thankfully, though, the auction started with minor items taken from drug busts and built its way up. They auctioned off the impounded automobiles after the clothing and jewelry. Finally, it came time for the land auctions.

The call sheet contained three lots. Two were real. One was fake. Well, not exactly fake, but a late addition to the roster. My stomach was in a knot as the auctioneer, a fast-talking guy with a plastic cowboy hat, pointed at something on his sheet as he showed it to some city official. This balding gentleman looked like a Greater Value generic Benjamin Franklin in his bifocals and three-piece suit.

Doubt crept in, and I chewed my lips. I thought I'd played it safe in the naming of the new group. The trick was making the fake lot sound authentic enough.

The three lots were:

New Orleans Land and Seizure (NOLS) 13-A

Trident Liquidation Capital (TLC) 17-B

Waterford Exquisite Property and Acquisitions (WEPA) 12-C

As the official patted the auctioneer on the back, I unclenched my fists. Over my shoulder, Jedediah McIntosh stood in the back, bidding paddle in hand. He sent me a wink. I sent him the finger.

The first lot, New Orleans Land and Seizure 13-A, started at a bidding of ten thousand dollars. After several rounds of paddles dancing through the air, this auction ended up at $275 thousand. I knew the contents of the auction despite it being "blind". Abandoned farmland. Worth ten times that amount to the right bidder. The gentleman with a sun-scorched face and overalls was going to do well by it.

The second auction was for the Trident Liquidation Capital 17-B lot. Ten thousand was the starting price. The first paddle up was Jedediah's.

What caught him off-guard was that the second paddle came from Mrs. Lin. I hadn't hacked anything to get her in on the bidding. All that took was a quick credit check and a letter from the bank for a line of credit.

Then a third party got in on the bidding: a gentleman in a suit with a cellphone up to his ear. Clearly, he was representing someone else in the bidding process.

When the amount of the bids reached a hundred thousand, Mrs. Lin put down her paddle, kicked back her head, and let out a sigh.

For the next two minutes, the bidding war between CellPhoneMan and DickHole was neck-and-neck. Once the numbers got into the seven-figure mark, however, it was only a matter of time before Jedediah won.

"Sold, at $2.25 million to Bidder Thirty."

People clap. Jedediah nods and waves. I break eye contact with him.

Then the last auction goes live:

"Bidding for WEPA starts at ten thousand dollars. Do I have an opening bid?"

A paddle goes up. Its owner doesn't raise it like a mighty sword, more like a kid who is raising his hand to ask if she can go to the bathroom.

"Ten thousand. Do I have fifteen?"

Silence. Mrs. Lin checks her watch. After three seconds, the auctioneer points at the current bid leader: a man whose wife just punched him in the arm as he lowers his paddle.

"Fifteen. Do I have twenty?"

Mrs. Lin's watch ticks five seconds before the auctioneer repeats the question.

Mrs. Lin raises her paddle. "Eighteen thousand."

"Ma'am, the bid is for twenty thousand."

"And no one is bidding it, so I bid eighteen thousand."

There is a rumble, which is exactly what we'd counted on. There is nothing in the Orleans County Auction rulebook that says there must be a standard increase in bidding amounts. By bidding just under the next bid, it undercuts the value of the package. At least, that's what it said on the auction strategy tips I read on Yahoo! Forum last night.

"Okay, eighteen thousand going once, going twice..."

I'd have crossed my fingers if Mrs. Lin didn't have a death grip on my hand.

"And sold for eighteen thousand dollars to Bidder Forty-Two."

I screamed and hugged Mrs. Lin as people politely golf-clap. We dart over to the folding table with the sign Pay Here. *Mrs. Lin pulls out her checkbook.*

As we wait, the most annoying voice in the world chimes in.

"You bid on the wrong one. Now you're stuck with whatever crap you just got in that package".

Jedediah practically covers me in spit enunciating the P *in* package.

He hits me over the back of the head with his sealed manila folder. "All. Sales. Final."

I keep quiet. Until we have a Paid in Full *receipt in hand, anything I say or do could screw this up.*

The paper slides against paper as Jedediah opens the envelope.

"Now, let's see what goodies are in this pic-a-nic basket." Jedediah's impersonation of Yogi the Bear sounds more like Ray Romano with a head cold.

Quickly, I bump into him with everything I have. Papers spill out onto the slick, dewy grass below. I loudly apologize, plant one foot on the paper, and do my best Three-Stooges-stepping-on-a-banana-peel fall, complete with a scream and crash down. My hands crumble and slide the papers everywhere. Mrs. Lin glances my way. I send her a wink and nod at her checkbook.

Jedediah picks me up by my belt and snatches the papers, cursing the whole time.

"I don't know what your game is," putting his finger to my nose, "but if you aren't moved out by Monday, I'm showing up there with the police to throw you out."

Mrs. Lin swats his hand away with her own sealed manila envelope. "Mr. McIntosh, we will see you Monday."

***

I think it was Jimmy Buffet who sang Come Monday, it'll be alright. *For Mrs. Lin and myself, he was right.*

For Jedediah McIntosh, Mr. Buffet missed the mark.

As Mrs. Lin and I sat in folding chairs in the parking of our apartment building at 7 a.m., we sipped coffee in the cool, dewy air.

The police showed up five minutes before Jedediah did. Even though I was 60, maybe 70 percent certain they weren't here to arrest us, I was still sweating. When Jedediah showed up, ringing that little bell, he dismounted his bike and walked toward us.

"Time to go, people," he said, clapping to emphasize his douchebaggery. "Move-move-move."

"Why, Mr. McIntosh, erm, whatever could you mean?" Mrs. Lin said with the flatness of a southern lady who was tired of someone bothering her during her nap. She probably cleared her throat just to seem more hoity toity.

"I own this property, so it is time for you to go."

"Really?" Mrs. Lin lowered her sunglasses and raised an eyebrow. "Since when?"

"Since Friday."

"Then what is this?"

Mrs. Lin is clearly having more fun than she should with this, but who am I to refuse a victory lap?

She stood and handed a lone piece of paper to the closest police officer, an African American guy with a Burt Reynolds mustache. Scanning the paper, he rubbed his chin before handing it back to Mrs. Lin.

"Pack it up, boys. We're headed home." The man nods at me, then Mrs. Lin. "Sorry for the inconvenience, y'all."

"Wait, hold up, give me that—" Jedediah yanked the paper—the deed for the building—from Mrs. Lin. Nowhere in that deed did he find his name, only Mrs. Lin's. "This can't be right..."

He delivered this last line with all the self-awareness of Wile E. Coyote realizing he'd run off the cliff.

From his satchel, Jedediah withdrew his crumpled papers. As he flattened them out, his eyes flashed.

"What the hell? Three thousand acres in Dionna? The Waterford Exquisite Property and Acquisitions?"

"Waterford, Waterford," I mused as if Mrs. Lin and I hadn't rehearsed this a dozen times. "Wait, isn't that the land that the EPA accidentally dumped something on?"

Mrs. Lin lowered her sunglasses for dramatic effect. "That's right, I think it was part of the blind auction."

"By jove, I think you're right." This was the only time I'd ever used the expression by jove. *"But who owned the land before Mr. McIntosh here?"*

"A good query, my friend." Mrs. Lin tilts her head and looks past Jedediah. "Oh, hi, J.R., how're you?"

"Damn EPA!"

During my night in the library, I created two shell companies. The first one contained only a quitclaim deed for Old Man J.R.'s damaged and toxic lands. These three thousand acres were the same family land that the government paid him a hundred bucks an acre in compensation. The only solid the gov't did for Old Man J.R. was that they ruled that you never have to pay taxes on land that was damaged.

I guess there's a silver lining for Jedediah after all.

"This is clearly a mistake."

That sentence nourished my soul.

"I'm going to get them to overturn this and rectify this immediately and-"

"Mr. McIntosh, wasn't this a blind auction?"

"Shut your mouth."

Mrs. Lin zips her lips and pockets the key.

I get up from my chair and stroll over to him. I point at three words on the final bill of sale. Then I repeat those words, his words at the auction, back to Jedediah, as slowly as possible.

"All. Sales. Final."

Violence often follows confusion. Actually, I counted on Jedediah McIntosh's anger because, as Musashi said, the important thing in strategy is not to suppress the enemy's useful actions, but to use them against your enemy. *That was why I did this while the officers were still in their patrol cars, radioing back to HQ. Jedediah lifted me off the ground. As Jedediah pinned me against the wall, I let out a Jamie Lee Curtis level of scream, thrashing about as much as I could to draw attention.*

Before he knew it, they'd pulled Jedediah away from me. In a rage, he swung out wildly, his fist meeting the face of the closest officer.

There were two hard, fast, and golden rules I knew about dealing with New Orleans police. One, never go against them in any capacity.

And two, never give them a reason to beat the ever-loving shit out of you. Because they will.

I want to say that the ambulance that took Jedediah away was overkill. He'd lost some teeth from a baton's blow. His nose broke from the impact of the concrete after they slammed him down. I'd even say those broken ribs from boot kicks left him in walkable condition.

In any case, I wouldn't have to press charges because assaulting an officer was its own fresh hell for Jedediah to deal with. He probably would get off with probation, but it would be a costly time-suck, which would have to be enough.

And as an added bonus, all the tenants who watched his ass-beating from their windows that morning would know how seriously to take him from now on. Not at all.

As Mrs. Lin and I sat in the chairs in silence, the police long gone, she let out a yawn loud enough for people in Shreveport to hear.

"I'm thinking we take the day off today."

"Sure. I could use a nap."

"Tomorrow we can hire a lawyer to deliver J.R. payment for his sold land."

"My schedule's flexible that day, too."

"Two days off is all we need. This is not, as you kids say, a vacay.*" She chuckles and cleans her sunglasses with the hem of her green flowery dress. "And then we can move the deed of this building into that company you created."*

Mrs. Lin meant the second shell company I created. Once we moved the apartment complex into it, we could set it up as a business that generates income.

Even when we lowered the rent to actually make this affordable housing.

Even with no one mowing, the air smelled of freshly cut grass.

"Fanboy, we need to talk."

Nothing easy ever starts with we need to talk.

"Yes, Ma'am?"

"Stand up."

Mrs. Lin dragged me to the middle of the parking lot. She took my hands in hers, then turned her head to cough.

"Are you okay, Mrs. Lin?" I asked.

"Just, tired, erm..." She cleared her throat, then shoved her shoulders back. "When I met you, you were a little shit of a person..."

"These compliments are making me blush."

"Silence." She lowered her head and then met my gaze. "I took you in because I saw potential in you. These past few days, you've shown that your actual potential is even greater than what I saw. You first told me you were a Bushi, a Bushido warrior, when we met. Do you remember?"

I nod.

"But you aren't just any Bushi. Most trained and fought with only one weapon, the katana. They were mountains of men, so they used weapons that fit them. You are not strong enough, rich enough, or even connected enough, to fight like that. Jedediah McIntosh would cut you in

half if you met him on his battlefield. But not only did you change the field, you changed your weapon."

Mrs. Lin stepped back and withdrew an invisible sword from an invisible sheath on her dress.

"You showed your false weapon, your katana, but didn't dare use it in attack. Instead..." She lowered the sword, sidestepped me, grabbed at her waist, and jammed her empty fist into my gut. It was for show, but the impact brought a couple of coughs.

"You learned it is not always wise to come at someone with a sword. A sword can be bulky. Unsteady at times. No, you came at this man stealthily. Deadly. You are not a sword, fanboy. No, you are a dagger. Small yet precise. Calculating."

As she placed her small yet strong hands on my shoulders, an accepting smile, a blessing smile, one with loose lips and only a few teeth, crossed her face. Her rosemary perfume slightly watered my eyes.

"From here on out, I will no longer call you fanboy. You are a little dagger. You will conquer many a giant, and they will never see it coming."

As she touched my forehead to hers, her upcoming words branded me so permanently that it would've had less of an effect if she'd stuck a hot poker to my skin.

"You are Tanto."

Chapter One Hundred

Trace

Back in reality, I down an entire energy drink in ten seconds. It tastes like antifreeze, piss, and lime, in that order.

My knuckles cracking sound as if I'm popping popcorn. When I stretch my neck, it sounds like Styrofoam breaking.

Subgoal: get in the database.

Main goal: turn the tide.

I check the readings on FrankenTop: VPN is running. IP scrambler is on. I enter an FTP screen and enter the IP address that Lance-a-Little's Pai Gow code provided.

My screen flickers. *They're attempting a trace.* It's a standard webpage filler. This one is a white screen with the words "Unavailable at this time."

I've dealt with many a decoy homepage. They're easy to spot. First, hit Ctrl-A to view all the details on the page. A decoy will have a blank section of the screen that stands out from the selection.

And wouldn't you know, there in the bottom right corner: a rectangle with the words *Subnet now visible.*

I click it. A startling buzz erupts from the laptop.

"Please say your password. You have ten seconds."

There is no blank spot, no flashing cursor, telling me where to enter the code. The code is only seven digits. And they linked it to an executable command of VoIP: Voice over Internet Protocol.

That is why I had to have my voice fixed. Sure, I could've asked Penny, Rusty, or some stranger to do this. The problem with that is I'm on a suicide mission for one, and I've already hurt too many people to endanger someone more.

An audio recording wouldn't have worked because recorded audio adds a coded layer to a file. It's like how you add preservatives to food so that it will last longer. VoIP looks for this coded layer and instantly rejects it.

"Please say your password. You have ten seconds."

I clear my throat, lean into the microphone, and spout off as slowly and deliberately, even robotically, the password. Those seven digits that Penny and I figured had to be the code: *1000110.*

The screen goes blank, then comes right back to the same screen.

"Please say your password. You have five seconds."

Shit. What did I miss?

This is another test. I remembered those numbers perfectly. I'm great with memorization.

What if my meds are messing with my memory? It's happened before.

"Please enter your password. You have three seconds."

I lean toward the mic again, but my gut grabs my throat and closes it. I hear AldenSong's mantra from our days in Hackers' Haven float through my ears.

Be still.

The screen goes blank. No flashing cursor. No perceived entry.

Then it happens: the Intranet layout of Hackers' Haven's database is laid bare before me.

I scream for joy, which is short-lived as a red light flashes in the corner of my toolbar.

Damn. Someone's almost past my firewall.

They're attempting to get a lock on me, figure out why I'm in the database, and then lock me out. Other places only want to kick out intruders. Hackers' Haven wants to know everything about them before they swoop in and haul them in for slave labor.

I hit the kill command on the firewall. Boom. They have a lock on me. Well, my VPN, which is my intention. It'll do what I need it to do.

I dive into folder after folder, gathering files. I can't decipher any of it because they have more medical terms than a dictionary, but I can't stop yet.

I see it: Dr. Fel's personal files. I drag and drop it onto the folder on my desktop entitled "Open Upon Death."

As it downloads, alarm after alarm goes off. I'm fine. I need these alerts.

My cockiness gets a moment to shine. I hit a command that I know opens up Alviss, the chat window all hackvicts use. I type six words every hackvict knows by heart.

Burn bright. Burn fast. Burn down.

Just reading those words gives me an extra adrenaline boost. This is the first step to freeing my tribe.

Then the sound of an application crashing, the *du-dump* noise, blasts from my speakers.

My VPN drops, as does my stomach.

They have a trace on my location.

They're coming.

Chapter One Hundred One

Easy Part

I have two, maybe three minutes. Tops.

I grab my burner phone but pause. I need the call to last the right amount of time for a trace, but nothing too soon to mess up the most important part of this plan: turning the tide.

I insert a clean USB flash drive into FrankenTop and drag the folder "Open Upon Death." Once the folder transfers, I shut down the laptop, flip it over, and snap out the cables, dropping FrankenTop through my shaky, sweaty hands. I pick it up and keep going. Using a screwdriver, I remove the hard drive and smash it with a ball peen hammer.

A car door slams. It could be a coincidence.

The click of a door lock popping open flairs my nostrils. At least the chair I have placed under the doorknob prevents lockpick-level entry. The impact of a foot on a door shocks me. The last time someone kicked my door in, they hauled my ass off to Hackers' Haven.

I grab the burner phone, dial, and drop the phone when it gets answered.

Another bash and wood on my side of the door sprays splinters. My trembling hands fumble with cracking open the flash drive. I only need the storage part of the drive, not the casing. I'd planned on inserting it rectally, but fear has my ass tighter than a chastity belt.

Metal screeches against metal. A ping hits the air, followed by the sound of metal on concrete. Someone's prying the hinges off the door using leverage.

The flash drive's hard plastic cover holds tight.

Another popping sound. Another hinge lost. Only one left.

Screw it. I shove two fingers down my throat, instantly compelling my body to recoil. I gag but hold fast. With the other hand, I shove the thumb-sized electronic into my throat.

Then my fingers slip and my throat closes. Around the flash drive.

All airflow ceases. My eyes swell as I've just successfully sealed my windpipe. My body fights my mind. My esophagus wants the foreign intruder out. I want the USB to go lower.

I caress my throat as the last hinge falls. As does the front door.

There, with crowbar in hand, is the asshole who is either going to kill me or help me change everything. Dendro grunts through his heavily bandaged face. He shoots daggers from his eyes as he lunges at me.

The flash drive almost slides down my throat, but then Dendro picks me up and slams me into the hotel's boxy TV. Glass shards enter my back. My body instinctively tries to scream, but all the air is stuck in my lungs.

"I told you I'd be the one to bring you home." He sits on me and slams his bear-sized fist into my chest. The impact is almost CPR-worthy, in that it forced some air from my lungs, turning the USB in my throat.

I need to provoke Dendro to get this damn thing into my stomach. So, I hit him dead in the face.

My hand throbs and a good two seconds pass as we both realize that my glorious act of retaliation was more of a soap opera slap, all flat and more loud than painful.

"Oh, it's on, little man."

Dendro slams blow after blow into my face and chest. The fourth one brings the blood. The sixth somehow opens my throat. The seventh propels the blood-covered flash drive down my throat and opens my airways.

I scramble out from under Dendro. He grabs my right ankle. With one heave, he whips me around the room. I crash into my electronics pile.

Dendro puts me in a headlock. "Go to sleep, little man."

If I fall asleep, everything falls apart. I'll lose any chance I have of this plan succeeding.

Fight, dammit, fight.

I reach out with trembling fingers for anything and everything. My thumb connects with FrankenTop's shattered computer screen.

The world goes bright red, and then darkness floats in the corners.

My fingernail catches the glass, but it only wobbles instead of breaking cleanly free.

The dark clouds overtake all my peripheral vision.

I reach again, but this time Dendro notices and pulls me back.

"Ah ah ah..."

The darkness is now almost complete. The bumping bass beat of my heart fades.

I have one last-ditch dirty trick I can try. I slip my hands behind my back and grab Dendro's balls, taking a full turn like I'm winding a grandfather clock.

"AHHHHH SHIT!"

Dendro and I fall on the floor in different piles. I cough and sputter as I crawl onto the bed. Dendro erupts out of his fetal position and pulls out a knife from his boot.

"Screw this, you're dead."

Outside, car doors slam. I fear they are too late.

Dendro raises the knife with two hands over his head. I blindly stick my hands out, but he's strong. Strong enough that he might just stab through them and plant that knife in my throat. As Dendro slices downward, the voice of an armored angel fills the room.

"Freeze! Drop the weapon!"

Blood splatters across my face from the exit wounds. Two center-mass shots from a standard issue 9mm, probably hollow points, took the light out of Dendro's eyes.

One officer checks for a pulse as another calls for backup and an ambulance. Meanwhile I steel myself.

Because this was the easy part.

Chapter One Hundred Two

Mudslide

Dendro's death was not something I predicted. Honestly, I needed him alive for the police to link him to Hackers' Haven or Poseidon United. His death screws up my plan more than a fork does a microwave.

I refuse the ambulance and get into the closest squad car. For this to work, I need to get to the police station ASAP. By my estimate, I have under ten minutes until the Feds come in and take over. Without Dendro, I'm counting on half a plan to do a whole job. I needed him fingerprinted and booked and into the system to give me a sliver of hope.

That is why I called 911 when Dendro started attacking my door. I needed everything to stay local.

When we get to the police station, my lawyer, Ms. Ingrid "Innocent" Vincent is there waiting. She was the phone call I made from the other burner phone, the one whose SIM card is in my stomach.

Along with a full-sized flash drive.

This upcoming bowel movement is gonna suck.

I don't talk to anyone, which is why I have a lawyer. Even though we are sitting in the hallway of this police precinct, which is two-tenths of a mile from my hotel, something in the stale air bothers me.

"Mr. Vice, please come with me." A detective who looks like the tall man from the Phantasm horror movies motions us into a room that I know all too well.

Interrogation.

"Now hold on one second." Ms. Vincent is in his face before I can blink. "My client was attacked, and you want him to go into I-8 for questioning, Tom? You do realize that he has no reason to go in there, and they will throw anything he says out of court because my client—just—got—assaulted, right?"

Detective Tom leans around Ms. Vincent. "You need to come with me."

"Is he being charged with a crime or is he free to go?"

"Ingrid, don't do this."

"Charged or free, pick one, go!"

The bald cop rubs his head and takes a breath. "Charged."

"Well, that's some rookie bullshit, Tom." Ms. Vincent grabs her purse and my hand. "With what?"

"A federal branch thinks Mr. Vice is not who he says he is."

Well, the water of my plan just got hit with a mudslide.

Chapter One Hundred Three

Hello, Tanto

As far as interrogation rooms go, this one's not too shabby. I'm not exactly an expert, but I sure am not a rookie, so I give this one a C, C+ score. It has the standard metal table I'm cuffed to. The two-way mirror glass has smudged fingerprints across it, but no cracks. The metal chair I'm in actually has four even legs. Plus, the air conditioning isn't freezing or blazing hot.

This is better than my last motel.

Ms. Vincent checks her gold Rolex watch. Some officer had tried to take her purse, but she told him where he could go, by what means, and what he could do to himself once he got there.

Hence, she still has her purse.

For twenty minutes, we've sat alone. She's already told me three times to keep my mouth shut and let her do the talking. It's probably something she says to all of her clients. Plus, considering she doesn't realize I now possess the ability to speak, she probably thought that was a done deal.

A bass beat reverberates in the room. No, it's in the entire building. It builds and builds until the building itself seems to buckle.

Unfortunately, I know that sound: that's a military helicopter landing.

Ms. Vincent grumbles and says, "Well, I'm glad I put on my waders, because shit's about to get deep."

I am unsure what division is coming through that door. The FBI or CIA, probably. Each will want the first crack at me. That I can handle, even from the CIA. I'm with a lawyer on American soil. Those two branches must follow protocol.

And that means they can't ship me off to Hackers' Haven.

But you know what they say about controlling events in your own life:

How do you make God laugh?

You tell him your plans.

The door flings open. I think it is part of an upcoming Good Cop / Bad Cop routine.

Instead, I instantly know that all the plans I've come up with for this day just got thrown out the window, rounded up, and shot, then shot again.

She doesn't have the purple frames she wore the first day we met over ten years ago. Her red pixie cut is now replaced with flat brown hair in a ponytail. Hell, someone probably even made those freckles on her face way back then with a Sharpie pen or something.

There's even a 1 percent chance she doesn't recognize me. She's probably arrested a hundred, maybe even a thousand other criminals since then.

Then all that false hope melts away when her green eyes narrow in on me and fire shoots from the damn things.

"Hello, Tanto," says Agent Michelle of the Mercator Agency, the woman who got me thrown into Hackers' Haven to begin with.

Chapter One Hundred Four

The Empty Chair

"You must be in the wrong interrogation room." Ms. Vincent stands and extends her hand. "This is Eric Vice, and I am his council, Ingrid Vincent."

"Eric Vice, right..." Agent Michelle puts her leather briefcase on the metal table and opens it so that only she can see inside. "A runaway boy from almost twenty years ago."

Technically, I did run away from home, so I'm not a complete phony.

Agent Michelle takes my driver's license from a sealed evidence bag. I guess the chain of command of evidence doesn't mean shit here.

She reaches into her briefcase and slides two photos across the table. One is of the real Eric Vice, or at least an older version of him. The other is the old photo the family used in the runaway flyers.

"So, you aged up this photo." Ms. Vincent snags it and snickers as she pulls out a photo of herself and slides it back across. "Here's me, aged up from my junior high photo. I have

better hair and no extra chins compared to this digital trainwreck. Made me look like I got squished by a steamroller, if I may say so myself, so excuse me if I don't fall to my knees and worship Adobe, the God of Photoshop."

"Your client is not Eric Vice."

"I have close to ten years of filed tax returns that say my client has been an upstanding citizen. Now, one of us is wasting time here."

That's a lie. We have seven years. Enough to handle an IRS audit. Still, I appreciate Ms. Vincent's hardened bluff.

Agent Michelle drops a folder on the table. Its contents splay across, a move she's probably practiced a million times.

My lawyer picks up the file and glances at the contents. I don't even need to look her way to know that this file is my file, Tanto's file, from Hackers' Haven.

I try not to look at the mugshot, the one with my sunken eyes and busted lips. The photo was of a young kid who thought he was broken but had zero idea of the pain he was about to endure at Hackers' Haven.

"Well, it certainly looks like you have a nice file on a total stranger."

"Cut the shit, lady. I know who you have there." Agent Michelle points her green fingernail at me. "That's Tanto."

"Who? No, wait, hold up—" Ms. Vincent's eyes grow wide. "Are you trying to say my client is not who he says he is, that he is this other white guy named Tonto or something?"

"That's correct."

"That's not only wrong, it's profiling, and a little racist."

"We're all white in this room."

"I said what I said. No, what you have is a file that says one Eric Vice, a white boy who not only looks like my client, but is him, ran away from home at age sixteen, is that correct?"

"Yes, but—"

"Butts are for sitting, not discussions," interrupts Ms. Vincent. "My client ran away from home, which is not a crime. Had he spoken to me back then, I'd have helped him gain emancipation status due to his unfortunate home life."

"Horseshit."

"Correction, pigshit." Ms. Vincent twirls her finger in the air. "You're in a cop house, it's pigshit. Don't bring horses into a pig fight. Agent, do you have anything to disprove that my client is one Eric Vice?"

Agent Michelle reaches toward her briefcase but stops. She checks her watch. My lawyer and I exchange a glance.

Then, without looking at it, Ms. Vincent points at the empty chair. "Who are we waiting for?"

"Excuse me?"

"Damn, I know you must've gotten lost in my beautiful southern accent and not heard what I was saying. It's okay. It happens a lot more than you imagine. I'm asking, who are we waiting for?"

A knock sounds on the door.

"Enter."

And then my plan got more screwed when one of my former clients opens the door. Smiling like he is the damn Joker. And wearing a name tag for the Mercator Agency.

"'Sup, Tanto, remember me?"

How could I ever forget Epic_Chaos?

Chapter One Hundred Five

Per Legem Directam

Agent Michelle is from the DoGoodR case. Epic_Chaos is from Hell. He was one of my first clients, a case I did with my fellow hacker, Mane-Eac. It was a successful hack until we all got drunk and he forced Mane-Eac into a bathroom.

Unlike Agent Michelle, Epic_Chaos looks exactly like he did over a decade ago. Same bleached blond hair that swoops across his brow. He has the same ripped build.

Except, because of Mane-Eac, he's missing part of his dick.

Now Epic_Chaos has a name tag that reads Agent Prestane.

Of course, this asshole has the most preppy, asshole name I've ever heard.

Both people hired me at one point in time. Both got hurt because of me. And both are now part of the organization that put me, and hundreds of others, away.

Agent Michelle's eyes remain beady and focused. She's still salty over my helping DoGoodR, just some kid who was trying to find his place in the world. Back then, the government needed someone to make an example of, and he was just the easiest target in town. They were going to give the kid life.

That wouldn't happen on my watch.

Now they are here, and my plan is hanging by a thread. I glance at Ms. Vincent's watch.

Nine minutes until my digitized bombs start going off.

Epic_Chaos waves at someone outside.

"We will be with you soon." He closes the door and takes the empty chair.

On the table, he lays out picture after picture of my computer and all its components from the hotel.

"There was a recent intrusion into a government database." Epic_Chaos puts the photo of the smashed laptop in front of me. He hopes I'll flinch.

I will not.

"We found shattered electronics in your hotel room."

Ms. Vincent snorts. "Your theory is so loose and dangly you might as well call it my daddy's ball sack. Oh dear, are you also going to charge him with the nine robberies or eighteen assaults that have occurred in Memphis today alone because he has access to butter knives in his motel room kitchen?"

My motel ain't that fancy, Ms. Vincent. I'm just lucky it has a toilet seat.

Agent Michelle taps her fingers on the desk like she is typing her idea out.

"Ms. Vincent, your client is a liar."

"All of my clients are liars!" She sweeps her arms skyward, as if she's welcoming everyone to church. "That does not make them guilty of a crime, unless we are talking about lying on the stand or under oath and those actions I do not condone." She wags her finger for extra emphasis.

"Ms. Vincent," Epic_Chaos says opening the door, "would you be a dear and wait in the hall?"

The only thing worse that this moron could've said would have been telling Ms. Vincent to *Calm Down*.

"Oh, I will not." She's on her feet like there's a spring in her ass. "In fact, I'm taking my client out of here unless you show us one bit, one speck, one grain of damn rice, that you have any evidence on my client."

"Digital forensics will take a few days to examine the computer's contents."

By which time, I'll have either thrown up or pooped out that file-filled flash drive that is bouncing around my empty stomach.

"Then you can get a warrant and come get him at my office. Mr. Vice, let's go."

It isn't that Epic_Chaos grabs Ms. Vincent's arm that bothers me. It is that I notice both he and Agent Michelle still have their sidearms on them.

That is against every interrogation protocol I know of.

"Do not touch me." Ms. Vincent snatches her arm from Epic_Chaos's grip. "One more move like that and I will report you to your supervisors."

At this Agent Michelle laughs.

"Oh, did I say something funny?"

"Have you ever heard of the Latin phrase *Per Legem Directam,* Ms. Vincent?"

"Well, I'm willing to bet my pink panties you're gonna tell me what it is, whether I want to hear it or not."

"It is the mantra our agency, Mercator, has run under for over a hundred years. It means *by Law direct,* and it is drawn from Article I, Section 2 of the US Constitution. By legal interpretation, that means our entire division has unlimited power until Congress takes it away."

"Which division is this, Agent Michelle? FBI? CIA? The damn Girl Scouts?"

"The Census Bureau."

A large part of me wants to laugh, that a subdivision of the Census Bureau is the group that hunted down me and other hackers. The people who knock on your door and demand you tell all the secrets you and your roommates have once every ten years have a division set up to grab hackers.

Then the damned logical part of my brain kicks in. If what Agent Michelle said is true and the US Constitution does have a *by Law direct* empowerment clause, then it makes perfect sense that the Census Bureau is the umbrella for the Mercator Agency.

What better group to chase down people who use false identities every single day online?

Epic_Chaos snickers. "You're just lucky we're agents. If you dealt with one of our Enumerators, you might not leave this room alive."

"Oh, is it time for a pissing contest?" Ms. Vincent pops her knuckles and leans forward to rest on them. "I have not yet begun to piss on your case with my fourteen-inch, anaconda-sized dick." She stands and makes a zipper noise. "I mean, I'm gonna slap you, her, everybody at whatever the Mercator Agency is, with it until I either get bored or get off." She zips back up and sits down. "Legally speaking, that is."

"There's no need for crass language, Ms. Vincent."

"It there ever was a time for it, it's now." Ms. Vincent's emphasis on the word *ever* shakes the room. "We're getting out of here."

"Mr. Vice." Agent Michelle ignores my lawyer's comment and hits me with a verbal knockout as she locks eyes with me.

"Where's Barca?"

Chapter One Hundred Six

Sank Like a Stone

Barca.

My face shifts between frozen and on fire. I stare at the ground, but my eyes dance along it like I'm following a scurrying rat. Of all the damnable questions Laurel and Hardy could throw at me, why did it have to deal with a man I helped kill?

"Mr. Vice, where is Barca?"

"Do not answer anything, Mr. Vice." Ms. Vincent tries the doorknob.

Locked.

She bangs on the door. "Hey! Hey! Come let us out!"

"Mr. Vice, we can let you and your lawyer out of this room, if you lead us to where Jabez Arnold is."

It takes a second to realize that Agent Michelle just casually told me Barca's real name. Maybe she's trying to humanize that bastard.

It won't work.

I stay quiet, even though I can honestly answer that I have no idea. The last time I saw Barca's body, he was in Mr. Longfellow's trunk. Whatever he did with the corpse is between Mr. Longfellow and God.

"We know you escaped with him. We know that he stole proprietary software, administrative codes, and sensitive information. We need him and what he stole. When was the last time you saw him?"

After my hack, I know why they're worried.

"Don't answer anything." Ms. Vincent bangs on the door harder. "Officer! Officer! I know you can hear me out there!"

"Look, here..." Agent Michelle withdraws from her briefcase a piece of paper with a giant seal of a map in a circle: Mercator Agency. "This right here is the golden ticket, Tan, er, Mr. Vice."

Even Epic_Chaos is now conveniently supportive. "Read."

"Are you telling me that my client and I cannot leave this room, even though you have not officially charged him, or me, with anything?"

"Official is such a...rigid word, Ms. Vincent."

"So is *cocksucker*, but neither of those words are opening that damned door."

I look over the form. I hate Epic_Chaos for his correct assessment of *golden ticket.* It's a blanket pardon, formal. It is for all my crimes, both known and unknown, committed up to my incarceration.

And the President of the United States himself already signed it.

This one-page document clears my name and frees me of my jail sentence. It is boilerplate, in that anyone could fill it in and gain immunity. All it needs is my birth name and signature, and it is official.

"As a token of goodwill, we have removed Cyfib Inic of command. In a manner of speaking."

I don't know what gets to me more: that Poseidon and Mercator have *removed* my old warden so quickly for this screw-up, or that his actual name is Cyfib Inic and not a handle.

After a breath, I slide the paper back across the desk.

When there's this much honey, hungry bears are nearby.

For a good minute, no one speaks. Agent Michelle nods at Epic_Chaos. He opens the door and yells, "Get in here!"

Part of me had briefly wondered who they had in the hallway since Epic_Chaos entered the room.

We'll be with you in a moment, he'd said.

Larry, or Mr. Judson, maybe? I wouldn't blame either of them if they turned on me. Maybe they have Penny out there. If my imprisonment brought her one ounce of peace over the hand I had in her brother's death, it is worth it.

When they brought him in, my heart equally jumped for joy and then sank like a stone.

He looked raggedy. For all the time I knew him, he was always clean. It was part of his upbringing, I think. Cleanliness is next to Godliness and all that. His sunken eyes, as if sleep jumped ship, sparkle under his pain. He's even lost weight, but I can tell it is the type from stress and suffering, not diet and lack of exercise.

As he sits down in Epic_Chaos' chair, our eyes meet for the first time in what feels like a lifetime.

"Well, I like what you've done with your hair."

Even from the depths of hell, AldenSong could put a smile on everybody's faces.

Chapter One Hundred Seven

One Minute Left

For eight of my ten years stuck in Hackers' Haven, the two-tons-of-fun Samoan sitting across from me was the beam of light that kept me going on the darkest of days. He helped me survive, and ultimately escape, that hellhole.

Now I have to pretend that I don't know my best friend, or risk giving the Mercator Agency more ammo to their already loaded firing squad.

I push back from the table and look at Ms. Vincent's watch.

Four minutes until checkmate.

"If you give us Barca and the software, the deal on the table goes for both of you."

Those dirty bastards know how to get to me. Throwing me the chance for Aldy to gain not parole, but freedom, takes the wind from my sails.

Could I find Mr. Longfellow and where he put Barca's body?

Probably.

Could I track down Kilroy and get the flash drive?

Doubtful.

But all they are showing me is gold, the carrot.

What kind of stick are they going to use if I turn them down?

I push the paper aside and shake my head.

"Okay, we're done here." Ms. Vincent grabs my shoulder and squeezes. As she heads toward the locked door, Epic_Chaos blocks her way.

"Sit down."

"You'd better move, son, or you're going to find out that this lady doesn't need to call for help."

Ms. Vincent grabs the handle. Epic_Chaos raises his flat black dress shoe. He puts his full weight into the stomp that crushes her wrist. Ms. Vincent screams and clutches her broken hand close to her chest.

I stand, but Agent Michelle fingers her sidearm in response. "Give me an excuse."

I sit back down as Ms. Vincent does the same. Epic_Chaos opens the door. Agent Michelle walks past him.

"You've got one minute left," she says, "to make the right choice."

Chapter One Hundred Eight

On Our Own

A lot can happen in a minute. A car you're driving can crash and change your life. A team can win or lose a sporty-sport in that time.

Yet when Agent Michelle and Epic_Chaos reenter the interrogation room, they clearly think nothing has occurred in that minute. Without making eye contact, I hand them the signed yet folded piece of paper. I'd already torn off the carbon paper copy it made. Ms. Vincent has it in her purse.

"Well, that was easy." Epic_Chaos cannot keep his smile from shining through. "Tanto, by the power vested in me by the United States Government, I'm placing you under arrest."

"On what charges?" asks my lawyer. I'm just lucky that Ms. Vincent is a better poker player than Epic here.

"Your client has admitted to identity theft, in that he never was Eric Vice."

"Oh, if that's what you're after, you're still missing the target like a moron misses the point." She flicks her wrist at the paper in Epic's hand. "Read, children, read."

Epic_Chaos and Jedidiah McIntosh have something in common: they take everything for granted.

Also, they're entitled dicks, so two things.

I'm not a betting man, but the sensation of winning against all odds must feel like this. As Agent Michelle and Epic_Chaos look over the form, they find one name on the document, and it sure ain't mine.

"Who is Ne'igalomeatiga Pese?"

The only thing worse than the way Epic butchers this pronunciation is that his ignorance shows me he hasn't done dick for homework.

"And how did you get this notarized?"

"Why, tis I, good lad and lady!" AldenSong's Shakespearean accent is a B, B+ at best. "As for the Notary, this young lady had it on her."

"A lot of lawyers are Notaries." She crimps invisible documents with her palm-sized seal using her good hand. "I always carry it with me." Her other, the broken one, lays limp in her lap, except for the occasional spasm. "So, everyone in this room is leaving right now."

"Like hell you are." A chambered round and a muzzle tip to AldenSong's skull later, Epic_Chaos takes the upper hand.

"We're getting a confession out of you, or your friend here reached for my gun. Isn't that right, Agent Michelle?"

"I must apologize, because I was too busy dealing with the head wound Mr. Vice gave me."

"Whoa, what head—" AldenSong's question is immediately answered when Agent Michelle slams her head against the metal table. She screams as a trickle of blood starts at her eyebrow.

Ms. Vincent's watch scares me as much as any handgun.

My Hail Mary was supposed to come through two minutes ago.

We're on our own.

Chapter One Hundred Nine

Running on Broken Bones

The sweat that drips from my temples is now touching my lips. I wipe it away, but still taste my salty fear.

"You really think you've got everything figured out, don't you, Tanto?" Agent Michelle rubs her bruised, bleeding head and winks at me through the pain. "You think you can just steal an asset from us, like AldenSong here, or even Barca?"

And that's when I screw up: the first laugh erupts out of my gut. For months, the worry that I had helped kill a federal agent, a monster named Barca, the guilt of it weighed me down. As it turns out, I'd helped a man, Mr. Longfellow, take vengeance on a criminal just like myself. Barca was just a piece of federal property like me: a tool to be used and discarded.

More laughs and a few tears pool up.

The Feds are just mad they've lost one of their playthings.

Ms. Vincent's peppermint breath hits my right ear as she speaks through gritted teeth. "Mr. Vice, kindly stop that shit."

As I shake it off, a miracle happens.

It starts on Epic_Chaos' phone. Then on Agent Michelle's. The sound is almost like an error sound on a Windows machine: jarring, and full of bass.

Epic snatches his phone from his belt and hits a button while he keeps his gun on AldenSong.

"Agent Michelle and I are leaving with you or..."

A second buzzing. This one gets Agent Michelle's attention. She leans over her phone.

"What, how is it two Amber Alerts back to back?" asks Epic.

"It's not." Agent Michelle's words are tiny and full of weight. "It's through that system, but it is not children."

"Then what is it?"

It takes everything I've got to keep the smile from my face. This was supposed to happen during Dendro's interrogation. Now that he's dead, at least I get to see the chaos.

This moment also makes me think of Mrs. Lin.

The agent flips to the first message as a third arrives. She studies it and grits her teeth so hard I hear her jaw pop from across the table.

"It is a name and capture information for Danny Alwin." She flips to the next. "Then Tony Anderson. Then Stephanie Antlica."

Capture information. That confirms two suspicions of mine: one, that I didn't erase all the data file from Gakunodo when I escaped and, two, these people may have been captured because of my software. It makes sense; I did have a ticking clock in one hand and a homicidal maniac in the other at the time I attempted to erase the software while also escaping Hackers' Haven.

Her phone vibrates again. And again.

Mrs. Lin's words dance through my brain. *Jedediah McIntosh would cut you in half if you met him on his battlefield. But not only did you change the field, you changed your weapon.*

Agent Michelle's laser stare is so full of hate that I can't help but smile.

Our miracle came through.

A sword can be bulky. Unsteady at times. No, you came at this man stealthily. Deadly. You are not a sword, fanboy. No, you are a dagger. Small yet precise. Calculating.

"And every single one of these damned things mentions the Poseidon Group and Mercator." The words emit like puffs of smoke from Epic's face chimney.

You are a little dagger. You will conquer many a giant, and they will never see it coming.

"What the hell did you do?" asks Agent Michelle.

Instead of answering her, I leave my chair. Epic_Chaos' gun is already at his side, all the steam taken from his locomotive. I turn my back to everyone and face the door.

"Open it." My voice does not croak or shake when I say the words. For once, I am not faking my confidence.

"Hold up, we are not done here."

Two more buzzes come through. I keep my eyes on the prize.

"Look, just make this stop, and we can get back to discussions." Her octave shifts as fear laces Agent Michelle's voice. She's worried about her job now.

Everyone in her agency should be.

Three more buzzes fill the silence as I refuse to answer.

I stretch my neck and pick at a scab under my nose.

"What do you want?" she asks, panic rising in her voice.

I do not turn. "Open. The. Door."

Our captors talk among themselves. Two buzzes later, Epic radios for someone to open the door. As it swings wide, I grab Ms. Vincent by the shoulder, careful not to jostle her injured hand more. AldenSong steps in as I rub my bruised ribs.

"I've got her."

I nod and walk.

I stroll through the police station. Every officer looks my way. Someone told them I was a threat or something amazing, a high priority target. The same buzzing from the interrogation room comes from their phones. Most of the eyes are on us.

Kilroy came through. He started a little later than I'd asked, but, by now, he's already sent out to the public the details of a dozen or so people, like me, that are considered *missing*. I pass by one officer's desk, pick up his coffee cup, and take a swig before I put it back down.

I walk through the main doors and am greeted with an old familiar friend: laser sites on my chest. From behind Humvees to rooftops, red dots dance on my chest.

Agent Michelle and Epic_Chaos arrive behind me.

Two phone buzzes go off.

The cool air hits my face. I keep my hands by my side as I count the number of gunmen.

Twenty-six.

"If you think you are leaving here, you are insane."

She's wrong on the first part but hitting the bullseye dead center on the second.

I turn and face these two agents. One of whose career I ruined when saving DoGoodR, a kid who made a bad choice. The other got part of his dick cut off for attempted rape. To be honest, I'm not sure who is more damaged from having met me.

I spread my arms wide and with my back to the gunmen, I flip these two assholes *the bird.* I kick my head back. Then, I keep my fingers up as I spin. Again and again. Red dots dance across my body. All it will take is one pissed-off cop to end me.

And no one can risk it.

The game has shifted.

It is time for everyone to know it.

Buzz after buzz fills the air. I am vulnerable and invincible at the same time. Nothing can stop me, yet one ounce of lead from any of the snipers can end me.

For the first time in over a decade, I am no longer a victim.

I am an apex predator.

A warrior.

A Bushi.

I only stop spinning when Agent Michelle speaks into her radio.

"Stand down."

Agent Michelle's order carries the weight of *we surrender.* One by one, the dots disappear. I wipe their phantom crumbs from my shirt.

"Make the alerts stop." Epic_Chaos' eyes are full of fear, a change for once.

"Not yet."

I don't dare tell him that Kilroy is sending everybody from the A's through C's whether or not they kill me here.

"If the general public knows about what we've been doing, there's no telling how bad it will get. Protests. Riots. Innocent lives could be lost."

That boils my kettle right over, and I spit through gritted teeth.

"Since when did you care about anyone innocent? I'm done. The last time we went toe-to-toe, I got by with a bluff. I'm done bluffing. I'm so done playing by your made-up, bullshit rules. No, from now on, I'm not fleeing. Not anymore. I'm bringing the fight to you. To Mercator. To Poseidon. You've never dealt with me head on. You've only dealt with me when you've had the upper hand. That's long gone. I'm coming for all of you. It is time you understand that, because I am done running on broken bones."

And I leave, AldenSong and Ms. Vincent flanking me as we stroll through the center of the SWAT officers.

We get to the closest cab, and I open the door for Ms. Vincent.

She slides in and yells to the driver, "Hospital! Now!"

After I shut it, AldenSong opens the front passenger door for me.

"Aldy, I think I'm going to walk."

"Are you sure, T.?" He glances over at the crowd. "They're going to follow you."

"I wouldn't have it any other way."

We hug, and I depart.

I walk the streets of Memphis with my police tail. A breeze tickles my nose. It's one that you normally don't get in this town. I used to think my nose itching was a bad thing. Now, I'm pretty sure that this is what they mean when someone says the winds are changing.

Kilroy will probably run out of the A-through-C selection of hack-victs in the next few minutes. I don't care. If someone wanted me dead, I wouldn't even hear the bullet that snuffed me out.

This is the first time in a while that I've trusted others to win. I trusted Kilroy to get the names out on the Amber Alert frequency. I trusted Ms. Vincent to represent me and keep me from saying or doing something stupid. I even trusted AldenSong to take that risk and sign that paper.

With people like them, we can do more than stop Poseidon United and Mercator Agency.

We can change the world.

As the police cars abandon their pursuit, I skip down an empty Memphis street. I have hope.

The truth is, what I have done in the past didn't work. I cannot shut down Hackers' Haven without risking everyone getting erased. I have to shine a light on it so bright that even the devil himself sees it from Hell.

To do so, I need a team. The likes of which no one has ever seen. There's no telling how much I can do when I put a crew together to take down Hackers' Haven, Poseidon United, and even Cyfib, if he's still a threat. I cannot trust Agent Michelle's statement of his removal from command. And, even if it is true, and he knows I did this, he's coming for me.

And he's more unhinged than the entire Mercator Agency combined.

As I pick up a penny that I find heads up in the street, all this means one thing to me: I've been burning fast. Now it is time to burn it all down.

To Be Concluded in Burn It All Down - A Tanto Thriller. To learn more, please go here: https://tinyurl.com/tantoseries

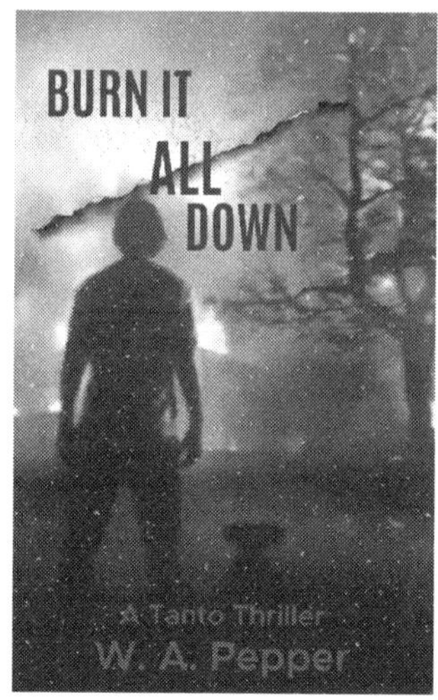

(Temporary Cover)

To read the first chapter, please continue to the next page.

BURN IT ALL DOWN: Chapter One

New, Old Friend.

Unlike my first abduction, this time there is no ringing of stun grenades in my ears when someone slips the bag over my head. Also, I'm fully dressed and not in my underwear. Instead of getting shoved face down into my stinky sheets, they shove me into the trunk of a car. As the slamming of the trunk echoes through my brain, one overlapping feeling exists from my first time being captured:

No one can save me.

AldenSong and my lawyer, Ms. Ingrid "Innocent" Vincent, are at the hospital. Penny does not know my location. Even Mr. Judson and Larry are at work, cleaning the floors of MetroMed, while also smuggling prescription drugs out of the building.

My hands fumble in the darkness as I yank off the hood. Each bump on the road tosses me against the spare tire. I grasp for a latch to pop the trunk, or snag a weapon, anything.

The empty trunk provides me with nothing useful.

When I had heard the movement behind me, I was three blocks from the police station. I should've known that my outright cockiness at exposing the Mercator Agency, Poseidon United, and even my old covert prison Hackers' Haven would bring the wrath of God down on me.

I didn't care. I'd made a giant bleed. That win was supposed to fuel my crusade to stop the government from entrapping hackers and forcing us to capture our own.

Now I'm headed to who-knows-where. Maybe back to Hackers' Haven.

It's unclear how much time passes before the vehicle stops. Two car doors open, then slam shut. Footsteps crunch gravel. A key enters the trunk's lock. I brace myself for an attack.

As the trunk pops open, a garage's work lamp shines from overhead. It blinds me to the point that I put my hand up to block it out. Someone grabs my wrist. I ball up my other fist and swing. A hand deflects it, and something stops me from swinging again.

It's not the person's touch, but the smell. Like minty soap, a hint of lemon, and rage.

Only one person I know smells like that.

"Well, are you going to sit there like an escroto or get out?" asks the Portuguese-American hacker that saved my ass on way too many hacks to count.

"Mane-Eac!" Before I know it, I'm on my feet and I've engulfed her in the kind of hug that practically breaks the recipient's back by bending them in half. "Holy shit, you're not in prison!"

"Nope...also...can't...breathe..." I loosen my grip but keep the pint-sized powerhouse in my grasp as I hold her like she's a figment of my imagination. "Ah, better. The day the Feds catch me is the day I die."

"Why the hell did you kidnap me?"

"One, you're an adult, so it's called an abduction." She brushes her short brown hair as I look into my friend's eyes. "And two, we had to get you off the street quickly because you're really screwing with what we've been working on."

"Who's we?"

Mane-Eac points her purply painted fingernail behind me. I turn and face the other figure. The guy is probably my age, but he's about fifty pounds heavier than me and three inches taller. He's smacking a CPU that's got a strange *whirr* to it and muttering, "You hold together, you hear me?"

There's something in his eyes that is foreign, yet familiar. Somehow, I know him. It is like when you recognize a celebrity, but can't quite place what movie he was in.

"I've been wanting to meet you for a long time, Tanto." My old, new friend with a shaved head and full black beard extends his hand to me. "I never thought I would work with the man that saved my life."

As we shake, it happens. I un-age the man with the scruffy beard by a decade. My mind shaves him and puts him in a long black leather trench coat with mirrored sunglasses.

"DJ?" I ask, more in shock than in question.

He responds, "We've got a lot of catching up to do." A smirk crosses his face as he adds, "Also, since you still go by your handle, you can just call me DoGoodR."

BURN IT ALL DOWN: COMING IN 2025

To learn more, please go here: https://tinyurl.com/tantoseries

Book Club Section

Hustle Valley Press, LLC Presents

A Group Discussion Guide to *Running on Broken Bones* by W. A. Pepper

Introduction and a Brief recap

After escaping the convert prison Hackers' Haven, Tanto loses the ability to process conversations. After a brief hospitalization, he escapes and sets up a criminal empire. Once Tanto survives a risky surgery, he exposes the agency that put him behind bars and prepares for the inevitable upcoming war.

(Starter questions for your book club begin on the next page).

Book Club Questions

Possible Topics and Questions for Discussion

1. Would you have given the book a different title? If yes, what would your title be?

2. Are there any books that you would compare this book to?

3. Did your opinion of this book change as you read it? How?

4. Did you have a favorite character? If so, why? Would you be friends with that character in real life? If so, what would you two do for an activity together?

5. Which character or moment prompted the strongest emotional reaction for you? Why?

6. Were there times you disagreed with a character's actions? What would you have done differently?

7. Foreshadowing often helps the reader gain an *Ah Ha* sense in

the book. That said, did you predict anything in the novel? Did you see the ending coming?

8. How did you feel about the ending? Would you change it? How?

9. What do you think is happening with the Mercator Agency now that Tanto has exposed them?

10. Finally, one of the readers suggested that Tanto would have been better off if he'd have lobotomized himself. Do you agree?

Acknowledgments

Too many of us, when we accomplish what we set out to do, exclaim, 'See what I have done!' instead of saying, 'See where I have been led.' – Henry Ford

First and foremost, I must thank God for blessing me with the opportunity to not only write, but to share my writing. For a large portion of my life, I was told I was not and never would be a writer. Somehow, a Higher Power kept that desire to write, an ember, burning in me. The positive influences in my life stoked that fire and helped me produce the novel you have before you.

Secondly, I would like to thank my wife Taddy. She's equally my biggest supporter, top cheerleader, and biggest stickler. She is the reason that any book of mine is every published and of quality. Without Taddy, not only would there not be any stories, there would be no *Tanto* (and what a shame that would be). Thank you, Babe. You are my everything and you are the leader our company needs.

In addition, I would like to thank the following people who contributed to this work currently in your hands:

Our developmental editor Meaghan Wagner encouraged me to stay on target with this book and make some tough cuts (that made the story better). Our cover artist Damon Freeman and his team made this cover feel like a true thriller. Finally, David Sandretto's excellent eye for details caught many a mistake as our proofreader. Thank you to this amazing team.

Our team of Beta Readers pointed out details and insights I never would've caught on my own. A big thank you to Cathy T., Josi D., Kenneth M., Margery T., Michael I.-C., Richard D., and Tabitha H. Your contributions to this and all of Tanto's world make this book go from good to great (in my biased opinion).

Below is a much-too-short list of people (and influencers) that I would like to thank. I tried to list everyone, but at the time of writing this, I have certainly left names off. For this, I apologize in advance and appreciate your contribution to my life and writing.

Authors I would like to thank include (in alphabetical order): Tara Alemany, Lee Child, Chuck Dixon, Meg Gardiner, Stephen King, Mark Leslie Lefebvre, Riley Sager, Jeremy N. Smith (and his friend, a hacker named "Alien"), Andrew Van Wey, and Ruth Ware.

Others I would like to thank include (in alphabetical order): Dan Alexander, Pam Burleson, Frank Darabont, Sam Esmail, Ricardo Fayet, Tom Fontana, Bryan Fuller, Jorge Garcia, Zach Gilford, Larry Gordon, Jim Jarmusch, Akira Kurosawa, Rami Malek, Jason Momoa, Lon Perry, Jimmi Simpson, Forest Whitaker, Matt Willig, and Beau Willimon.

And to all our of readers. Thank you for letting me share Tanto with you.

About the Author

W. A. Pepper puts lies on paper. His wife puts them in books that people can buy, borrow, or steal. He is a multi-awarding-winning *USA Today*, *Wall Street Journal*, and *Amazon* Bestselling Author for his contribution to the business anthology *Habits of Success*. Under different names (and his real one of Will Pepper), he has published in multiple academic journals, interactive e-books, anthologies, and online. During the COVID-19 pandemic, he and his wife Taddy (plus their dog Danger) started the publishing house Hustle Valley Press, LLC. Through it, they published four e-books that have amassed over one hundred five-star reviews. Further, the husband-and-wife team donated the first six months of revenue from the sale of each of those books to charity; this resulted in thousands of dollars raised for the reader-selected charities that support racial equality, COVID-19 relief, veteran affairs, and St. Jude Children's Hospital. He has a PhD in Management Information Systems or, as he calls it, Business Computing, from The University of Mississippi. Finally, he, his wife Taddy, and their dog Danger split their time between Colorado and Mississippi.

CONTACT INFORMATION

- will@hustlevalleypress.com
- Instagram:@wapepperwrites
- Facebook.com/wapepperwrites
- Tiktok.com/@wapepperwrites

Made in the USA
Columbia, SC
20 October 2024